WHO WOULD HURT OWL?

Calista sank down in her chair. "Charley . . . "

"What?" The sleepiness had vanished instantly from her son's eyes.

"Something happened last night. I found Owl in the garden." She opened the plastic bag and took out the disfigured stuffed animal. A shocked gray look crept across Charley's face. He swallowed hard.

"I don't want you to get too frightened, Charley. I think people who do stuff like this, well, it's kind of like obscene telephone calls. They don't act out any further. It's just sort of a perverse pleasure in scaring."

"But they have acted out further. They've murdered Norman Petrakis . . . "

Look for Kathryn Lasky Knight's
Trace Elements
Featuring Calista Jacobs
Available from Pocket Books

"The characters are ⌐xquisitely drawn, and the mystery moves right along . . . "
—United Press International

Books by Kathryn Lasky Knight

Mortal Words
Trace Elements

Published by POCKET BOOKS

MORTAL WORDS

KATHRYN LASKY KNIGHT

POCKET BOOKS

New York   London   Toronto   Sydney   Tokyo   Singapore

POCKET BOOKS, a division of Simon & Schuster Inc.
1230 Avenue of the Americas, New York, NY 10020

ISBN: 0-671-68449-3

First Pocket Books printing July 1991

10 9 8 7 6 5 4 3 2 1

POCKET and colophon are registered trademarks of
Simon & Schuster Inc.

Cover art by James Conrad; design by
Lance Anderson

Printed in the U.S.A.

FOR ERIC SWENSON

I am indebted to Simon Garfinkle for his knowledge of computers, hackers, and crackers, and for his patience in explaining so much to me.
—K.L.K.

MORTAL WORDS

1

"So how are the dragon-fanged tulips?"
Calista asked the small elderly woman sitting next to her
in the car as they swung out onto Mount Auburn Street.
They were headed toward the Larz Anderson Bridge,
which crossed the Charles River to Boston from Cambridge.

"Blagghh!!" The sound gurgled up like scalding
phlegm, and Margaret McGowan made a face to match
it. She kept her eyes fastened on the wings of the light-up
fairy that was the hood ornament on Calista's Volkswag-
en. "You've got to treat them like annuals, Calista. Even
the dragons. Very wimpy." Although she had lived in the
States for over three decades, Margaret still had a trace of
Scottish brogue that was a wonderful condiment to her
speech when she spoke like this.

Calista laughed. She liked Margaret a lot. Margaret
was an author of children's books. Calista was an illustrator. They were both on their way to a children's
literature conference in downtown Boston where they
were to speak on their art. Margaret did not illustrate at
all but was an eloquent spinner of high-fantasy novels for
young children, high fantasy being that genre of fiction
that pulled heavily on Arthurian legend and the general
arsenal of Celtic and Nordic mythic elements. Thus, her
well-crafted stories were laced with quests, magical forests, and wizards. Calista was the more well known of the
two. She was in fact renowned in the field of children's
literature. She illustrated fairy tales, folktales, and small
stories of her own. Her reputation had been built over
the last twenty years, and her books were consistently

1

best-sellers. She had twice won the Caldecott Medal for Best Children's Picture Book of the Year. The second medal had been announced just months before for her version of *Puss in Boots*. She would be the drawing card at today's event.

"Don't tell me you have to treat tulips as annuals, I just planted hundreds last fall. I got some of those dragon-fanged ones, too, because they looked so good in your garden."

"Not dragon-fanged, my dear. Dragon Flames. That's how they are listed in the catalog."

"Well, whatever, they look great."

"Not this year. Although I can't really tell yet. It's still too early. I mean, my grape hyacinths are just starting."

"You get more sun than I do on your side of Cambridge." They lived on opposites sides of Harvard Square, Calista in a very old neighborhood with the largest trees in Cambridge and where such luminaries as William James and George Santayana once lived and where it had been said that when those two old lugubrious souls got together, "even the dogs howled." Margaret lived on a small street off Brattle where the sidewalks were still brick but the trees were not as big and the flowers could be flashier because of more sun.

"Stop moaning about my tulips. Tell me who else is on this panel with us," Margaret said.

"Norman Petrakis. You know, the nonfiction writer for children."

"Oh, yes, of course. I met him at an American Library Association meeting a couple of years ago. Charming, handsome."

"I know," Calista said.

"So?" A delicately curved eyebrow shot up and hovered in the suspension of fine wrinkles of her brow. "He's closer to your age than mine, my dear."

"Well," Calista said noncommittally, and shrugged her shoulders.

They were driving east on Storrow Drive, now hugging the Charles River. Some of the crew teams were out on the river.

"Well, what? Is he married?"

"No."

"Is he gay?"

"No. Nothing's wrong at all."

The only thing that was wrong was that Calista hated these conversations. Norman was enormously attractive both physically and intellectually. She should be so lucky. But that was the problem. Luck had not been in the cards since she had been widowed over three years ago. Colossal bad luck with men—well, just two, really. Her husband, who had been murdered, and then a man whose name fought to remain unspoken even in silence. Gun-shy, was she? You bet. But there was no denying it: Norman Petrakis was attractive. And she could do worse, and her luck could be better.

The auditorium was packed to capacity. It was a typical mixture for a children's literature conference—ninety percent librarians, the rest students of children's literature and library science, teachers, and parents. It was a panel discussion on directions in children's literature. It was being held at the Hynes Auditorium in downtown Boston.

Calista had made few appearances since her husband's murder three years before. After cracking that peculiar case with the help of her son, Charley, she had become a full-fledged celebrity. Her books, which had always sold well, now sold extraordinarily well. She had called her most recent Caldecott Medal her *Butterfield 8* award, likening it to the time Liz Taylor won an Oscar for a less-than-great performance simply because she had nearly died of pneumonia. When one's husband gets murdered and son nearly killed in trying to solve the crime, it seemed to provide more than adequate grounds for universal sympathy. The world had felt sorry for her; hence, the award. That was how she interpreted it, although everyone else had told her it wasn't so.

She peeked out now from behind the curtain. Norman Petrakis had already taken his seat and was chatting, while the mikes were off, with David Cummings, the moderator of the panel and an editor of children's books himself. In the audience she spotted her editor, Janet Weiss, who had flown up from New York and just made it in time, as her plane was late. She'd dashed backstage to give Calista a quick kiss before finding a seat. Calista wished that Janet could be right there next to her on the panel. She was so comforting. But where the hell was Margaret? Calista was having a bad case of butterflies and didn't want to have to walk out there alone.

"Ready?" She spun around. Margaret looked more frail here in the wings of the stage than she had in the tight confines of Calista's VW. Frail but still spirited. She had a gnomelike quality and could have stepped out from one of her own books. Her thin gray hair seemed to hover rather than actually grow from her head. She had been wearing a knit hat in the car, and now that she was without it Calista noticed that Margaret's hair was much thinner than she had remembered. She could see some of her scalp. It seemed rather like a patchy fog blowing off a headland.

"Oh, Margaret! I'm feeling very jittery. I don't want to have to walk out there alone."

"Me too!" She grasped Calista's hand and grimaced, her pale blue eyes flickering softly. "Let's go." Calista felt a gentle tug, and they walked onstage holding hands like two little kindergartners on the first day of school. A ripple of applause began and then rolled into a crushing sound like a breaking wave.

"That's for you, my dear!" Margaret whispered.

"But it's not for my work."

"Don't be silly!"

They took their seats as the moderator introduced them and briefly explained the format and procedure of the panel. Each of the three participants would give a brief talk, ten minutes, on their work, and then the session would be thrown open for questions. First Margaret, then Norman, and then Calista. Calista was in the hot spot. Margaret was an easy one to follow. Unlike her books, she was not particularly organized as a speaker. Her talk tended to ramble. She interrupted herself repeatedly. Norman, on the other hand, was brief, witty, and to the point. He had wonderful anecdotes about his previous career as a high school science teacher. He was very attractive in a donnish sort of way. His black hair was flecked with some gray. He had a slightly beaked nose and deep green eyes that peered out from behind black wire-rimmed glasses. And there was a dimple in his left cheek that was not really flirtatious but very engaging. Most attractive, Calista thought as she observed him speaking. There might be other places she would prefer to be following him to than the speaker's podium.

"And now my time is up," Norman was saying. "And I think that we all want to hear from our third speaker."

How gallant! Calista thought. She wished that all these other writers wouldn't be so self-effacing just because she had won the damn medal. She was not going to talk about *Puss in Boots* anyhow. She had to save that for her acceptance speech in Dallas. She would talk about her animal characters Owl and Hedge and "the buddy theme" in literature, or something like that.

She finished her talk in under ten minutes, and now the floor was open for questions. There were several for Calista, and then the audience began to ask Norman about the differences between writing for children and his twice monthly science column for *The New York Times*. The questions were fairly predictable. A hand went up in the back of the room, and a rather wan-looking man in his early thirties stood up. "My question," he began, "is really for all of you because, although all of your work appears quite different . . ."

It was the word *appears* that made something deep within Calista flinch. "It seems to be part of an increasing trend . . ." With the word *trend* Calista knew they were heading for trouble. "A trend toward secular humanism." An audible groan rolled through the auditorium.

"Oh, shit!" Norman muttered.

"Mr. Petrakis," the man continued. Something turned in Calista's stomach. She could feel Norman tense beside her at the table. "In a book of yours in which you write about human evolution for children, are you not supporting a particular religious belief?" There was a stunned silence, and then a single hiss scrawled across the still air of the auditorium.

"Sir, are you finished with your question?" David Cummings spoke in an icy voice.

"No, not yet. I would really ask the same question of Miss McGowan. In her portrayal of medieval kings and the like, is she not really portraying and suggesting our Lord Jesus Christ as a mythic figure?" There was a roar of boos now.

Margaret McGowan looked absolutely white. From the corner of her eye Calista could see her rather thin hand with its bulging veins begin to tremble.

"Get him out of here!" someone yelled.

Norman coughed, hunched forward a bit, and picked up his mike. "No. I'll take this," he said emphatically. "My views on human evolution have absolutely nothing to do with my own private religious beliefs." He emphasized the word *private*.

"But for a Christian nation . . ." the man continued.

That always pissed Calista off royally. She started to speak, but by the time she realized that her mike was not turned on the man was full steam into his diatribe. "We find that it is intolerable to foist on our children a so-called evolutionary theory that is inimical to religion and morality."

"I do not understand first of all why you refer to this as a so-called theory and then—"

Calista opened her eyes wide and looked at Norman. He was actually going to try to address this buffoon and continue a dialogue. The man interrupted him, however. "It is a philosophy that, along with books like Miss McGowan's, fosters godlessness, promiscuity."

"Well, I never!" gasped Margaret. The audience was beginning to hiss loudly.

"Now hold it right there, sir," Petrakis barked. "It is not a philosophy. It is a testable theory, a theory that says species do not remain fixed and immutable. It has been proven in countless lab experiments using thousands of millions of fruit flies, not to mention the evidence of the fossil record. Recent biochemical evidence establishes a molecular time clock that indicates precisely when the apes separated from early humans. I would ask you now what proof you have that this theory causes godlessness and promiscuity?"

"It is well known, Mr. Petrakis, that it has crept into all forms of modern thought—Marx, Freud, Nitzi . . ."

"Nitzi?" Calista wondered aloud. Nietzsche, she guessed. But the pitch of the man's voice was becoming higher. The air seemed shrill with the rasp of a blind paranoia, demagoguery. It was as if a poison gas had begun to fill the room.

"This is frightening," whispered Margaret. It was then that Calista became furious. What right had this man to disrupt and frighten, to come in here wielding his ignorance like an M-16?

"Order! Order." David switched off his mike and looked at Norman weakly. "Jeez, I didn't think to bring a gavel."

Calista switched on her mike and leaned forward. "What about me!" Her voice was just a scratch in the angry tumult. There was a slight quieting as people realized she was trying to say something. "What about me?" she repeated. "I feel left out." People began to laugh.

"Well, you, Mrs. Jacobs." There was a hush now as the man began to speak. "Your Owl and Hedge books, which you call a celebration of friendship, and also in your book *Nick in the Night,* where you have portrayed a small boy in the nude, are supporting homosexuality, and as a known heterosexual fornicator . . ."

The crowd went crazy. Some people collared the fellow and began moving him out. David Cummings was down off the podium yelling for security.

Calista's head swam. She felt Norman's hand on her arm and Margaret's birdlike grasp of her wrist. "Don't worry! Don't worry!" she felt compelled to reassure them.

David Cummings was now leaning across the table toward her. "He's just one of the nuts planted by those fundamentalist groups. They've been going around doing this lately. They broke up an International Reading Association meeting and a New York Library Conference. Just incredibly offensive, into book burning, the whole works."

"Don't worry about me. This is nothing." Calista felt compulsive about reassuring these people. How could they ever realize that after having your husband murdered, then to be seduced by a CIA agent while trying to solve the crime, and nearly losing your child, all of which subsequently became front-page news, to be called a "fornicator" at a children's literature conference was hardly grounds for a mental crack-up. "I'm fine," she kept saying. What she meant was, "I'm tough."

Janet Weiss came bustling up. "Are you all right, Cal?"

"I'm fine, what about you?" Calista replied.

Janet, usually as neat as a bandbox, looked totally disheveled. A hairpin was hanging absurdly over one ear, her blouse was untucked, and one leg of her panty hose was torn from her knee to her ankle. She was also missing one shoe.

"What happened to you?" Calista gasped as she took in the full impact of her editor's physical state.

"I tackled the bastard."

"You?!" Calista was stunned.

"Yeah, me and these two rather wimpy-looking, but very effective, graduate students who 'escorted' him out. Come on," Janet said, "I'm taking this whole crew for dinner and a good stiff drink first." She nodded at Margaret and Norman and Calista.

"With one shoe?" Calista asked.

"No, it's back there somewhere where I was sitting."

The crowd had cleared out, and Janet had found her shoe, minus one heel.

"Did you hit him with it and with luck left it spiked in

his groin?" Calista said as Janet limped into the Genji, a Japanese restaurant on Newbury Street.

"I can't really remember." She then turned to Norman. "This was an inspired notion of yours, Norman, coming to a Japanese restaurant. I suppose I could even check my shoes with my coat." But she took them off and carried them to the table.

"Perfect atmosphere after that fracas," Margaret said, patting her forehead with the warm damp cloth that the kimono-clad waitress had just given her. They passed up the hot tea and the sake for vodka martinis. All except for Norman, who asked for bourbon on the rocks.

"Bourbon!" said Margaret dreamily. "How charming. I haven't heard of anyone ordering bourbon in years. Are you from the South, Norman, originally?"

"Originally? No, from Athens originally."

"Oh, of course, dear."

Margaret McGowan, Calista thought, in a certain sense was just the way children's book authors were supposed to be—full of wonder and bewilderment, ready to walk through looking glasses into magical realms. But then she might say something totally off-the-wall, as she was about to do right now. Calista felt it coming. Raising her glass, Margaret smiled sweetly. "To Calista, one of the nicest fornicators I know!" She blushed furiously. "I mean, of course, not that I actually know." But the table was already laughing.

"We know what you mean, Margaret," Norman said, giving her a clap on the back.

"Well," Margaret said, furrowing her brow, "this attack was no laughing matter."

"Hardly." Janet Weiss shook her head. "I don't know. I think we're really sliding backwards."

"How do you mean?" Calista asked.

"We get more letters now. It's scarier in a way. The letters aren't so specific. It's not just like the ones we got over *Nick in the Night,* where people were upset about the nudity, or complaints of miscegenation when we have a book illustrating a white rabbit and a black rabbit playing together."

"Rabbit miscegenation?" Norman asked.

"Oh, yes, my dear. When I worked at Harper and Row—this was years ago—we did a book called *The Rabbits' Wedding,* and boy, did we take flak. And then there was *Sylvester and the Magic Pebble."*

"Who could object to that book?" Margaret asked. "The one about the donkey, right?"

"Yes. It was fine that Sylvester was a donkey, but not so fine that the policeman was a pig."

"Oh, God!" Norman sipped his bourbon. Calista noticed his dimple again as he looked across the rim of his glass at her. It was definitely not a flirtatious dimple. It was simply a part of the grammar of his face. She liked the face and the intelligence behind the eyes.

"Oh, yes. William Steig, that sweet man, was accused of ridiculing law and order," Janet continued.

"So what's worse now?" Calista asked.

"It tends to be more general, which is scarier as far as I'm concerned. We get complaints from groups about books that are 'overly imaginative.' Paranoia about books that lead children into 'imaginative forays' that will encourage everything from defying authority to masturbation. It used to be that people who were into censorship simply took paragraphs or words out of context. They didn't read. Well, they still don't read, but now they don't take even a word out of context. They just have their minds made up: imagination's no good. Everything must be fact. And some facts are ungodly, as we heard today. It's scary."

"It sure is." Norman nodded. "The Arkansas creationist law was challenged and overridden . . . what? five or six years ago? But those creationist groups just formed up again and seem to have come back stronger."

"And I am loath to say"—Janet picked up her drink and swirled it—"that our publishing brethren in the textbook divisions of certain companies listen to these groups."

"They do." Calista nodded. "You should see Charley's science textbook. It devotes all of two pages to evolution and two sentences to Charles Darwin. Of course, the teachers in Charley's school don't rely all that much on the textbooks anyway and bring in other stuff to supplement. Thank God. But that textbook is a joke when it comes to evolution."

"That's for Texas," Norman said.

"Why Texas?" asked Margaret.

"Because Texas buys more textbooks than any other state. And if it is adopted, as they say, by the Texas Board of Education for use in the school system, it means millions of dollars for the company. I've got an article coming out about all this in the *Times* next month."

"After the one on designer genes?" Calista asked. "I just love that title."

"What?" exclaimed Margaret. "I take it it's not about Calvin what's-his-name."

"No." Norman laughed. "It's all sorts of things—cloning, cancer research, a lot with twins research and that whole project up at the University of Minnesota, and then the human gene project."

"What's that?" Margaret asked.

"It's a plan to decipher all the human genes, the entire set."

"And then there's all that stuff, isn't there, with DNA profiling and its use in solving crimes," Janet said.

"Oh, yes. That's become the most important breakthrough since fingerprinting, and there is the molecular time clock stuff which gets back to evolution again."

"Molecular what?" asked Janet.

"Molecular time clock. It's a particular kind of genetic research where they look very closely at the blood proteins. You can compare them between species. The more closely related two species are, the more similar their blood proteins are expected to be. The greater the difference between the blood proteins, the longer ago these two species forked apart, or diverged. The DNA tells the tale within the blood proteins. Zebras from horses, for example, diverged relatively recently."

"And more to the point, remembering our friend in the audience . . ." Calista paused. "What about apes and humans?"

"Aha!" Norman's eyes sparkled warmly across his drink at Calista in a way that caused a little flutter within her. Her question was obviously appreciated. That excited her. He was attractive, and he was smart.

"You mean the Texas school board isn't going to like the answer," she said, laughing.

"Not at all! Humans and apes diverged within the last five or six million years."

"No kidding!" Janet gasped. "I didn't realize it was that recent."

"Truly kissing cousins, then," Margaret added.

"More than that, my dear," Norman said. "If you look at the DNA, you will find that there is less than a fraction of one percent difference between our chromosomes and those of a chimpanzee. Chimps and humans diverged within a very narrow range of time. Say within the last four million years, we shared an ancestor with chimps. In fact, there is more genetic similarity between humans and chimpanzees than between chimps and gorillas."

"Amazing!" Janet said. "So that's what they do in these high-tech gene labs."

"No, just a very little of that, actually. Most of the genetic work is related to cancer research. That's how they get into all this cloning business and the transgenic mice, which is basically transplanting human genes into mice so they can study growth of tumors. They do a lot of that right here in Boston, or rather Cambridge, at the Martin Institute."

"Charley is supposed to have some sort of student internship there through his school," Calista added.

"Do you think there could ever possibly be a nonfiction book in that for children?" Margaret asked.

"I don't know. It's technically very complicated. DNA, RNA, and now all this new stuff with the mitochondrial DNA."

"What about cloning? If you just limited the book to a

very simplified explanation of what cloning is, what they've done so far. Kids, you know, are fascinated by that. They all know about cloning in a vague sort of way."

"Yes, Charley knows about it," Calista offered.

"Well, Charley!" Janet exclaimed. "We can hardly go by Charley as a measure for the average kid."

Calista blushed slightly. She had walked right into that one. She did have a very bright thirteen-year-old. He was, in the parlance, "gifted." The gift, in Calista's mind, came from his late father, Tom Jacobs, one of the world's foremost astrophysicists. But gifts had funny ways of turning into terrible burdens. Calista had assiduously avoided sending him to fancy private schools. She had done her homework in this area and found the programs not to be that special, but dreadfully elitist. He could get the so-called enrichment by virtue of living in Cambridge and through their own Harvard connections. But by going to a normal public school, she felt, he received the gift of learning how to get along in a world that was made of diverse people with diverse IQs. She and Tom had both agreed on this. A good public school had more to offer than the most high-powered prep school.

The conversation shifted now to trout fishing. Norman was quite interested, and he knew that Calista was an experienced trout fisherman.

"Fisherman, fisherwoman?" He laughed. "What does one say?"

"Fisherman is fine," Calista said.

"For God's sake, don't neuter it!" Margaret exclaimed. "Calista, did you see the sign in the window of that little restaurant on Brattle Street advertising for a 'waitron'?"

"Oh, God!"

"Where do you go fishing?" Norman asked.

"Vermont, mostly. I have a vacation home there. When I get a chance I like to go out to Montana. It's the best. The Yellowstone, the Madison, the Gallatin rivers. You can't beat them."

They talked streams and flies, and Calista promised

that if there were time after tomorrow morning's session at the conference, she would personally escort Norman to her favorite rod and tackle shop.

"You are all, of course, welcome any time to come to my summer place in Scotland. You know I'm in the Mecca for trout fishermen and women," Margaret said.

"Oh, I've always wanted to go to Scotland." Janet sighed.

"Well, you and that lovely husband of yours should come."

There was an uncomfortable pause. "I'm afraid, Margaret, that Jack and I have separated."

"Oh, dear, I'm so sorry."

"Well, it was a long time coming, but it's a good thing to be on the other side of now."

"Yes, yes. I know how it feels. You know I was divorced years ago. It was awful when we were going through it, but gradually I began to reclaim a part of my life that I had nearly forgotten about. At first, however, before I really sorted things out, I had this inexorable urge toward chintz."

"Chintz?" they all said at once.

"Yes, chintz. You know, men don't like chintz that much, and so women always have to keep it under control in home decor. I just chintzed everything up . . . And then there is the other urge, of course." She paused briefly. "I slept around a bit. But everybody does that after a divorce."

"Margaret, you are something else!" Norman said.

After dinner they put Margaret in a cab to go home. Norman was staying at the Sheraton only a few blocks away. The evening was mild for early April, so Calista and Janet had decided to walk all the way down to the Ritz where Janet was staying. Now, however, as they walked with Norman, Calista felt it to be slightly awkward. One of them should be with this attractive man, not both of them, and it should be Janet. She needed it more than Calista after that rotten drunk of a husband who only sobered up long enough to have an affair with Janet's old boss! She wished now she had just driven Margaret home.

"It's so clear tonight," Norman said. He paused and looked up. "I don't believe it!"

"Believe what?" Calista and Janet both said at once.

"Look, ladies! Over the Hancock Building. You can see part of Auriga, my favorite constellation—the Charioteer!" The soft wonder of his voice melted into the darkness. "Look, even the tracers," he said, pointing with his finger toward some trailing stars.

Oh, dear, Calista thought. One of us should be alone with this lovely man.

2

She had just finished taking a shower after sending Charley off to school the next morning. When she turned off the water she heard the phone ringing furiously. She grabbed a towel, raced out of her bathroom, and did a dive across the bed to reach the phone on the other side.

"Yes!" she nearly barked. "Or rather, yes," she said in a gentler, less rasping voice.

"Calista!" Janet's voice seemed breathy and trembling on the other end.

"What is it!" A black fear began to fill her.

"Norman. He's dead."

"What!" Calista gasped.

"Murdered."

"No!"

A limo was sent from the Boston office of J. T. Thayer

and Sons, Calista's publisher, to pick up Calista, and soon she arrived. Ethan Thayer, the patriarch of the firm, walked through the door, having flown up from their main office in New York.

"I know this is terrible for you, Calista. Too much violence in a young lifetime." He patted her hair and took her by the arm.

They went to a conference room down the corridor, where Margaret McGowan sat with two Boston policemen. Ethan seemed to know more about the procedures and what to expect than Calista.

"They just want to ask you and Janet and Margaret a few questions since you were the last ones to see him. David Cummings is coming over with Norman's editor from Sundial. He's meeting him at the airport now, I think."

He looked up as two men arrived. Calista recognized them. They were lawyers for the publishing house. But she couldn't remember their names.

"Calista, you met our counsels here in Boston, Fred Begelman and John Kieffer."

"Yes, of course."

Margaret was practically a basket case until Ethan got the bright idea of getting her a little shot of good rye whiskey that was kept in a cabinet in his office. Calista declined. They had tried to answer as best they could all of the lieutenant's and the other man's questions. But it was hard for Calista to concentrate, and she had so many questions of her own. She felt vague and distracted, but Janet seemed equally so.

"So you can't think of any enemies Mr. Petrakis might have had?"

"Enemies?" Calista whispered.

"We told you about the obnoxious man at the conference," Janet said.

"He hated us all!" Calista said, and saw Margaret's pale blue eyes widen in horror at this sudden realization.

"Yes, we'll run an MCIC on all the fundamentalist

groups, and we're checking through Sundial to see if Mr. Petrakis had received any kind of threatening mail recently over the publication of his book on human evolution. The conference people are checking all of their registrations." Lieutenant McCafferty paused. "Mrs. Jacobs, have you ever received any threatening mail or calls?"

"Why, certainly," Calista said crisply. "You know, of course, of my little run-in with the CIA a few years ago." Her voice was drenched in sarcasm. "That was very threatening, to say the least. It nearly resulted in the—"

Ethan Thayer grimaced. "Calista, they're talking about offensive mail in regard to your books."

"Oh, well, yes," she continued. "All the time, from all sorts of groups. The born-agains, the Moral Majority."

Ethan Thayer coughed and began to speak. "Calista's talking about a picture book of hers called *Nick in the Night*. It's about a little four- or five-year-old boy who dreams he can fly and takes a magical flight through the night. Very innocent, but sometimes his nightshirt gets caught in a gust of wind and you can see his . . . er . . . er, anatomy."

"Here!" Calista jumped up. There were shelves full of books published by J. T. Thayer and Sons just behind where the cops were sitting. Jeez, she thought, sometimes Ethan's genteel ways were cumbersome. She plucked a book off the shelf. Flipping through it quickly, she found the pictures in question and showed them to the two policemen. "See, there's a penis. They don't like them." She felt Ethan wince.

"It was the first time that there had ever been that sort of nudity in a children's book," Ethan began to explain. "It was all very tastefully done, mind you. But some people objected."

"Huh." The lieutenant was impassive. It was clear to Calista that Ethan's overweening delicacy was ridiculous.

"And then, of course, there were those radical feminist groups, and remember SCUM?"

"SCUM," said the plainclothesman, the one without a name tag.

"Society for Cutting Up Men," Calista said. "Remember them? One of them shot Andy Warhol."

"Yeah," said the plainclothesman. "They don't like you, either?"

"They don't like my princesses."

"Your princesses?" McCafferty looked up and tapped a gold-edged front tooth with his pen.

"Oh, yes!" Ethan's face brightened. He clearly preferred keeping his authors away from discussions of anatomy in favor of the more nuts and bolts aspects of fairy tales. "Calista does the most extraordinary princesses. You should see."

Oh, God! Calista thought. She dearly loved Ethan. He was the most devoted, supportive man in the world, but he could be wearisome, she thought. These guys did not want to hear how beautiful her princesses were. They wanted to know about how SCUM had written her those scummy letters.

"Yeah." She broke in on Ethan's eulogy for her princesses. "You know. I do stuff like *Sleeping Beauty, The Twelve Dancing Princesses.* You know, your basic fairy-tale princess stuff, and I like drawing boobs, and I like drawing hair, and these radical feminists can never get beyond that; you know, they're so doctrinaire. They see that and they immediately think wimpy female. My princesses are distinctly unmagical. They rely on brains more than potions. They are wily, you know, more in the mold of a Ulysses."

"Yes." Janet nodded, although she was uncertain as to how much Boston's finest was really absorbing of this brief foray into the genre of children's literature.

"And what about you, Miss McGowan?"

"Yes?" Margaret looked up from her glass of rye.

"Do you ever receive any offensive mail about your work?"

"Well, now." She spoke slowly. "It depends on what you call offensive. Just last week I received a letter from a little boy. It was one of twenty letters from a class out in Elgin, Illinois. The teacher, if you can believe this, made the entire class write me a letter after they had read one of my books, *The Twilight of Kyre*. It's the first in the Knights of Kyre chronicles. It's bad enough thinking of a roomful of children being forced to read one of my books, let alone having to write me. So this little boy writes, 'You are a complete bore. I hated your book. I'm being forced to write this and I hope you drop dead so I won't ever have to read another one of your darn books.' Now that is offensive. But I can hardly say I blame him."

Both cops nodded.

"But," she continued, "if you're talking penises . . ."

Ethan Thayer visibly blanched. He had not been expecting this from Margaret's quarter. He reached inside his pocket for his nitroglycerin tablets. For Ethan Thayer, scion of one of the oldest publishing families and chairman of the board of one of the few remaining houses that had not been swallowed and conglomeratized, this had obviously become an angina-producing situation.

"Well," Margaret continued, "I don't have them in my books because, you know, there's so much armor and all. It would be very awkward. There are not that many illustrations in my novels anyhow, and, well, somehow I can't imagine showing a troll in the buff. There are lots of trolls in my books. It could get a little revolting. But as we were saying, that goon at the conference seems to think I've done something to his Lord Jesus Christ. I really loathe this proprietary manner in which people speak of God. The possessive pronoun, when used with God, is rather like lemon in milk—it curdles."

Calista wanted to get back to the murder. "You say it was a very professional job." No one so far had asked many details of the death. "What do you mean?"

"It was quick and quiet," the plainclothesman said.

"As opposed to noisy and messy?" Margaret asked.

The cops exchanged uneasy looks. Janet and Calista looked at one another.

"What aren't you telling us?" Calista demanded suddenly.

"Uh . . ." David Cummings, who had just arrived with the editor from Sundial, shifted on his chair and began to speak for the first time. "Calista, there were some very . . ." He paused and compressed his lips into a bloodless line, "Some messy details that I think you'd rather not know about."

Calista looked straight at him. She was a beautiful woman in her early forties with a luxuriant tumble of prematurely silver-gray hair. It was her trademark, but suddenly she looked older than Margaret McGowan. Her dark hooded eyes, normally warm, twinkling, and slightly mysterious, had turned lifeless and opaque. "David," she said in a low, dusty voice, "death is a mess." And she didn't need to tell him that she knew that better than most. She turned sharply toward the two cops. "Now what happened?"

Janet Weiss was thinking that if these two dudes didn't know about Calista's princesses before, they did now.

"Well, ma'am," McCafferty began, "there was a lot of blood, considering the MO."

"MO?" Calista's mind was going in slow motion. These guys always talked in letters, initials. What was the MO? The method? Hadn't they said something before about strangulation?

"Garroting."

"Isn't that something the Mafia does?" Janet asked.

The plainclothesman shifted in his seat. "Yes, they've been known to. They don't have an exclusive, though."

"There wouldn't be much blood from that," Calista said. "Where did it all come from?"

"That's what we'd like to know. Some from him."

"Some?" Calista was bewildered. "What do you mean, some?" McCafferty fiddled with his ball-point pen and looked over toward his partner.

"Not enough," the plainclothesman said almost abruptly.

"Not enough?" Calista asked. "Enough for what?"

"For the writing on the wall."

"Who wrote on the wall?" Margaret McGowan's voice sounded like sandpaper in the still room.

"The murderer, presumably," McCafferty replied.

"What did he write?" Calista leaned forward. Neither man answered. "Tell us, what did the murderer write?" She clenched her fist and hammered it on the table.

"Monkey's Uncle." The plainclothes detective said the words in a low voice.

Calista settled back in her chair and primly folded her hands in her lap. She felt her eyes fill up, but she knew she would not cry. She was the most disciplined person on earth. It was both her blessing and her curse. She had needed to know these loathsome details so she could get beyond them. But now she knew precisely what her duty was. She must remember Norman Petrakis, this gentle man, as she had last seen him. The man who had found the Charioteer over the Hancock Building in the black velvet of a Boston night. She would look for the Charioteer every night through its ascendant spring, as it made its transit across the skies until it slid out of sight in midsummer. Then she would wait for it again in the cool nights of autumn.

3

There was never any hiding of anything from Charley. Luckily Charley would not be coming home directly after school, so she would not have to tell him immediately. It was the night of the big performance of his school at the Loeb Drama Center, and he would be participating in it. It was called *City Step* and was a collaborative program between Harvard undergraduates and Cambridge Public School kids. It was a dance program that was somewhere in tempo and energy between aerobics and jazz. Each spring they gave a performance at the Loeb, home of the American Repertory Theater on Brattle Street. Charley would be upset about Petrakis. Although he did not know him personally, he had a shelf full of Petrakis's books, especially those that were devoted to model airplanes, flight, and aeronautical engineering.

There was no way Calista would miss Charley's performance or spoil it with this news. There was time for a drink, another shower, and a bite to eat before the performance. She put on a nice sedate pair of trousers and an elegantly cut Armani jacket. It was a man's jacket, and she had found it in Filene's basement. Out of habit she still went to the men's section even though she didn't have a man to buy for anymore. The deals she had picked up for Tom! Every once in a while she found something in what she called their Napoleonic Division that would fit her. This jacket was one. She liked to look nice for Charley especially when a lot of his buddies were around. Although he wore the most repulsive and outlandish clothes, and on occasion she had to censor his T-shirts for their suggestive inscriptions, he had very rigid and conservative sartorial guidelines for his mother. He wanted her to look "normal." Sometimes she apparently looked abnormal, like the time she had worn a Celtics jersey—number 33 no less, Larry Bird's number—with a pair of white silk trousers to some event. Charley was mortified. "I know you like Larry Bird. I like Larry Bird, but you shouldn't wear that in public. It's not like a normal mother."

She managed to get to the theater in ample time and send a message backstage to Charley that she was there. It was a wonderful performance. The kids were so high, so beautiful, so pleased and proud of their marvelous dancing and of their marvelous bodies. It had actually been easy for Calista to forget the horror of the last few hours. Nothing could attest more to life than the one hundred kids from the public schools in all shades and sizes, plus the twenty from Harvard who had worked so lovingly with them, as they lit up the stage with their energy, their rhythm, and their faith in themselves. The energy was absolutely contagious. The audience had gone wild and demanded encore after encore. The *Harvard Crimson* and the *Boston Globe* and the *Cambridge Chronicle* all hailed it as one of Harvard's finest hours—those hours when the kids of Cambridge came together to dance. Yes, it had been easy for those two hours to forget what had happened, to drive out the images that were somehow etched on her brain—images of strangulations and of words scrawled in blood on hotel room walls.

After the performance Calista and Charley and his friend Matthew McPhail and his mother and father had gone to the Border Cafe on Church Street, a favorite Mexican restaurant of the kids. Charley and Matthew were still high on the performance and high on the fact that the teachers had suspended any real homework for this week due to the performance.

"Too bad we can't do this all year long. Just think, no homework, no book reports."

"Oh, book reports!" Charley exclaimed. "I hate book reports. They are so stupid. Why do we have to do book reports? There is absolutely no good reason."

"If you want to be a book review critic," offered Joan McPhail.

"Never!" Charley said. "Critics are a dirty word in our house."

"Charley!" Calista blushed furiously. "That's not true."

"You hate 'em. You said so."

"Why?" Fred McPhail asked. "They always give your mother wonderful reviews."

"Most always," Calista said. "So it's only the ones who don't that I hate. And I don't really hate them. I just think they're stupid. I never said that I hated them, Charley."

"Well, you said that one was stupid."

"Yes, but it's not the same thing. And anyhow I don't think book reports are a bad thing."

"Yeah," said Charley, "but it's so much more fun doing stuff like *City Step.*"

"Or Project Look Ahead," Matthew said.

"Oh, yes. When does that start?" Joan asked.

"Next week," Charley said, referring to another program in the Cambridge Public Schools which teamed junior high and high school students with professionals in the area.

"And you're both going to be at the Martin Institute, right?" Fred asked.

"Yes," Matthew said. "We just don't know which labs yet."

"Yeah," said Charley. "If we could only dance in *City Step* and then do this real-life stuff—that should be what school is. You should never have to sit down and write book reports or take spelling or math tests. You should just do it in real-life situations."

Calista smiled at her son. "You mean no practice, no drills, no skill stuff?"

"I mean nothing boring, is what I mean. Working in labs isn't boring, building stuff isn't boring, but being tested is boring and being programmed is, too. Hands-on, like Dad used to say—real experience!" Charley smiled a sweet-sad look to his mom.

That look of Charley's always got her. But she wouldn't trade it for the world. He would remember his dad even though he had shared barely a decade with him. She had shared nearly two decades. A sliver of time, it seemed. But when she looked at Charley's face and that expression, she knew it had added up to much more.

Calista took a sip of her beer now. The din of the restaurant had become like a white noise to her. It was easy to fall into private silences and remember. Calista had met Tom in her junior year in college. After gradua-

24

tion and when she was starting her career as a children's book illustrator, she divided her week between New York and Princeton, where Tom was still working. Gradually she moved most of her stuff down to Princeton. Easier for an illustrator to move a drawing board to Princeton than for a particle physicist to move an accelerator to New York. Tom called Calista's New York place her "morality apartment." Although by the end of three years when they got married Calista was fairly certain her parents knew that she was virtually and unvirtuously living in Princeton. They got married and then went to Cal Tech and then to Harvard.

Joan McPhail was looking out of the corner of her eye at Calista. Calista sensed that she was worried that this talk of Tom was disturbing her. It wasn't the talk of Tom, really. It was the creeping red-tinged shadows of the violence, of the bizarre bloody images of Norman Petrakis's murder, that were stealing back into her now. The wild energy and joy of the children's dancing was beginning to dissolve.

They stepped out onto the curb of Church Street. A wet chill air smacked them in the face.

"This doesn't feel like April weather," Joan said.

"And what does April weather in New England feel like?" Fred asked.

"Probably this," Joan said. "I can't seem to remember that Boston doesn't have a spring. Lived here ten years and can't remember. Virginia had such lovely springs."

"Indiana, too," Calista added.

"I keep forgetting that you come originally from Indiana, Calista," Fred said.

"The springs were very nice," she replied almost tersely, as if to suggest that there were few other charms. She was watching the boys. They were running ahead with their skateboards under their arms. Charley and Matthew and their friends rarely went anyplace without their skateboards. The gates on the far side of Harvard Yard would be closed at this hour. The boys had crossed

Mass. Ave. As soon as they reached the other side and the sidewalk that led around the west side of the yard, they put down their boards and took off skimming by Harvard and Hollis halls and Holden Chapel. Calista smiled to herself as she watched the lithe youngsters whiz by those plain homely brick buildings behind the iron gates of the yard. Built in the Colonial period, they were among the oldest buildings of the college. Charley sliced through a cone of light from a street lamp that illuminated for a brief instant his fierce red hair. He wore it long, and now it flared in the apparent wind of his movement, flared in an aureole of flames, a ring of fire, actually, more than a halo. Siva, the cosmic dancer! The Hindu god! Siva, the Creator and the Destroyer, the deity who moved in a ring of fire while balancing the forces of creation and destruction. Charley wheeled on through the night, rounding the corner by Philip Brooks House onto one of the paths that crisscrossed the space between the Science Center and the north side of Harvard Yard.

"The springs—that's it for Indiana?" Fred said.

Calista had not meant to get so lost in her thoughts and visions of Charley.

"Oh!" She laughed. "Well, the dogwoods are beautiful, and the redbud. There are just miles and miles of redbud. You go down into southern Indiana in May and you've never seen such stretches of pink and red. And there are cornfields."

"And that's about it," Joan said. Calista was not sure if it was a statement or a question.

"Well, that used to be it. But in Indianapolis, where I come from, the cornfields have been eaten up."

"By what?" Fred asked.

"Shopping malls." Calista sighed, thinking of her last trip to the Midwest. "Indiana has been malled—malled to death." She paused. They turned the corner, following their boys. She supposed that the space that the boys were now whizzing through could be considered a kind of shopless mall. A long wide rectangle crisscrossed by paths culminating in Memorial Hall. Some had described Memorial Hall as a cathedral mated with a railroad terminal. Calista, however, thought of the Victorian edifice as the Matterhorn of Harvard in its somber, inescapable thereness.

On the left side of the shopless mall was the Science Center. Built from poured concrete and steel, it was by reputation exemplary of the New Brutalism in architecture, but to Calista the building seemed more funky than brutal with its clear expression of mechanical and structural elements. Generators, air-conditioning, and heat stacks erupted through the roof—the building's guts encased in massive concrete cubes. Suspension trusses rose over the roof, forming low-slung triangles from which the two major auditorium ceilings were hung. The effect on this night of gathering mist was that of a cubistic jumble of concrete blocks hovering just above the ground.

The boys were having a great time. Pedestrian traffic was light. A few students walked from the Science Library toward the Holworthy Gate, which apparently was still open into the yard, and Charley and Matthew, showing no fatigue from their nighttime dance performance, were beginning yet another performance.

"Is that what you call an Ollie?" Joan asked as she saw first her own son and then Charley go airborne on a stretch of path.

"I think so," said Calista. "What I don't understand is what is a power slide?"

"Me neither," said Fred. "Hey, Charley," he called. "Demonstrate a power slide for us."

Charley crouched down on the board and grabbed the edge. One side of the board lifted, and it was now traveling on only its outer wheels. He shaved the edge of the path leaning backward and, picking up speed, headed toward a grouping of rocks from the base of which rose a very fine spray of water.

"Why would they have that fountain on now?" Fred

asked. "On a night like this? There's enough humidity around already."

"Who knows. But Charley's going to get wet. Charley!" she called, but it was useless. He was already slaloming through the maze of rocks.

"What did you call those, Calista—meadow muffins?"

"Yeah. The fountain's a nice idea, but the rocks look like piles of cow manure. I've never seen uglier rocks. They're so rounded and even, and the way they've got them lined up, so rigid and predictable."

"I see what you mean," Joan said. "The rocks you have in that Japanese garden of yours are much more interesting."

"I mean it's a nice idea, the spray and everything. But round turdlike rocks set in asphalt would give a Japanese gardener pause, if not cardiac arrest, I would think," Calista said thoughtfully.

Charley emerged from the spray of the rock fountain beaded with a fine dew.

At the corner of Oxford and Kirkland the two families parted ways. The McPhails headed up Oxford to the house they had recently purchased on Gorham, less than a half mile from their old house, and Calista and Charley headed straight up Kirkland to their house on James Place tucked behind the Harvard museums and the law and the divinity schools of the university. They had lived there for almost fifteen years—Calista as an almost new bride, then young mother, and almost now, well, yes, middle-aged mother and widow.

4

The sky appeared marbled with clouds, and the trees with just a stain of green in their bare dark branches seemed more frail than ever. Calista resisted making a comment about the weather, however. She had just told Charley about the murder of Norman Petrakis. Weather talk was after all the conversational counterpart to hamburger filler, and she had been tempted in order to break the tension, or perhaps simply to try to move the conversation, the mood, into more neutral territory. But she knew this was not right or good. Charley needed to digest this piece of news. Even though Charley did not personally know Petrakis, and he was not a friend, still a reader had lost a favorite author. And this carried with it its own kind of sadness. He was particularly fond of the series Petrakis had done on the making of model airplanes.

Charley now dragged his fork in a light tracery over the surface of the yolk of his fried egg. Then he jabbed at it in one swift motion. "Did he have children?" he asked.

"No," Calista replied.

"Well, I guess that's someone less to miss him."

For a dreadful and seemingly unending minute they were drawn back to that awful time three years before when Tom Jacobs had died. At the time, of course, they did not realize he had been murdered. And when they had found out a year later, it had been like experiencing those awful days all over again. Tom Jacobs had been an outspoken opponent to nuclear arms. Three years before, he had died a peculiar death in the desert that at first had appeared to be natural—as natural as a rattlesnake bite could ever appear, Calista thought bitterly. It had been Charley and Calista who had ultimately proved that indeed it had not been a snake with malice aforethought, but a human, and that although the CIA had not been directly implicated, they were not precisely heartbroken to see Tom Jacobs out of this administration's hair. Tom Jacobs, when not contemplating the mysteries of the origins of the universe and building theoretical models, liked to build little machines. One of these little machines was called the Time Slicer. It could not only do very refined dating based on magnetic variations in certain rocks and minerals, but it could also detect underground nuclear testing.

Jacobs had been in the desert with the Time Slicer at the specific request of Archie Baldwin, a Smithsonian archaeologist. Baldwin had suspected that a Paleo-Indian site was being seeded, that the artifacts were phonies and had been brought in from other locations. At that time he had no way of knowing that Peter Gardiner, the archaeologist, was crossing over into a deep paranoia, and that in fact the mission he was sending Jacobs on would end in tragedy. It was because of the information that this machine could yield that Tom Jacobs had died, that a child had become orphaned and a woman widowed. Right after Tom's death Calista had been plenty upset with Baldwin, although she had never met him. But a year later Charley himself had very nearly gotten killed in the process of trying to solve the murder. And this time it had been Baldwin who had saved Charley's life. Calista was eternally grateful.

Although Norman Petrakis's death had none of the same intensity for Calista and Charley, the fact that it was a murder brought with it a chilling resonance. Charley ate silently for a while. Calista looked out the window and watched clouds build. They were high and thin, and they stretched like snaggly fingers clawing the sky. She had drawn witches with fingers like that—in *Hansel and Gretel* and the ogress in *Rapunzel*—those dreadful fingers clutching the scissors in one hand and wrenching the girl's head back with the other.

"Why?" Charley finally said. "Why would anybody do that? A children's book author?" Calista winced quietly to herself. "Why? How did it happen?"

Calista told the story, starting with the obnoxious man in the audience and finishing with the peculiar words scrawled in blood. Charley bit his lip as he concentrated on the story. It was a habit that he shared with his mother. Calista marveled that either one of them had a lip left to bite.

"It doesn't fit," he said at last.

"What doesn't fit?"

"I'm not sure," Charley said vaguely. "But it's something about the blood on the wall, the words *Monkey's Uncle,* and this dude at the conference."

"Well, I told you what the police said—that it was too much blood to have come from a person murdered that way."

"Yeah, yeah. I know you said that. But it's more than that that doesn't fit."

"What?"

"I'm not sure." His expression was blank. The dull eyes and the nearly motionless face would signal to most people that something less than scintillating was occurring in the cranium, but Calista knew it was just the opposite. She had seen that same expression on Tom's face and was convinced that it had been encoded in the DNA as precisely as the red hair and the pale gray eyes and all the other hereditary baggage. It was the expression that went with contemplating uncertainty, with the endless fascination and astonishment at the unpredictable nature of things. Tom and now Charley were particularly agile at dealing with uncertainty on an intellectual level. They found an odd kind of comfort in pondering the breaks in patterns. Tom had been the world's foremost theoretician of black holes, those quirks in the cosmos where all the known rules of gravity and physics break down. And something had now broken down in the pattern of the story of Norman Petrakis's murder that intrigued Charley, that made his face grow stony in its contemplation and his pale gray eyes become as opaque as the cloud-marbled sky.

The news story of Norman Petrakis's murder was buried on a back page of the *Boston Globe*. Calista showed it to Charley, and he read it quickly while he zipped his parka. The news account did not even mention the scrawl of blood on the hotel wall.

"It doesn't fit, that's for sure," Charley said, clamping his lips into a firm line. He slung his backpack over his shoulders and, grabbing his skateboard, went out the door to catch the school bus at the end of the block.

Calista had aimed to kiss his cheek but wound up with his earlobe instead. "Take care," she called.

Her drawing board was set up. The text for *Marian's Tale* was finally edited, the dummy approved, and now the galleys of the text had come back from the typesetter, all the drawings pencil-sketched in, and she was ready to begin finished artwork; to blow up the dummy into the dazzling experience—a children's picture book. There were two times that were most exciting in the process of creating a picture book. The first point occurred after the story had been written and it was time to plan the layout and make the dummy. The dummy was a miniature of the book. And Calista's dummies were even more miniature than most, often measuring only two and one-half inches by three for a book that in its final form would have a trim size of eleven by fourteen. But these tiny dummies in their intensity and exquisite detail possessed a shimmering brilliance. In a retrospective of Calista's work the previous year at the Morgan Library in New York, one critic had likened them to Fabergé Easter eggs. "Looks like you laid an egg," Charley had commented when he heard of the critics' praise.

The second exciting moment in creating a picture book came when it was time to blow up the dummy into the finished art. She was at that point now. She had spent two and a half months working on small pencil sketches, and now she was ready to start with pen and ink and paint. She should have been tremendously excited. Her drawing board was ready, the galleys chopped up into the proper blocks of text, and on her Plexiglas cookbook holder to the left of the drawing board in her study was a two-hundred-dollar book of the *Très Riches Heures du Duc de Berry*—the most exquisite reproduction to date of the *Book of Hours* that was in the Musée Condé in Chantilly.

It was the medieval pictorial conventions of the books of hours that would play a dominant role in the graphic style of *Marian's Tale*. Calista liked the gilt of these books of hours, but she liked the skies even more. The Limburg brothers, the early illustrators of the duke's first books, had an extraordinary feeling for both the country-side and the luxury of the court. Together the brothers were probably the most brilliant illustrators of architecture in history. Between that book and her frequent trips to Harvard's Houghton Library, where there was a treasure trove of other books of hours, she was set to work on a splendid tale—Robin Hood as told from Maid Marian's point of view. But now she balked. It was hard to get into the gilt and the splendor of the books of hours or the lush verdancy of Sherwood Forest with those other images, the ones of the bloody scrawl, so fresh in her mind. She would procrastinate just a bit.

She went out her back door. It was time for a turn through her garden. She was a great and eager monitor of the earliest vernal stirrings. By this third week in April the crocuses were past history. But she nearly shrieked as she spied the sudden start of red in the bed by her brick terrace. Spurting from the earth like blood, the small tulips grew low and scarlet near the ground. She had forgotten about the new exotic mixture of early blooming tulips that she had put in last fall, and she certainly had not remembered that these were such a violent shade of red. She believed that they were called Little Red Riding

Hoods. The catalog had not done them justice. But then again, since the murder of Norman Petrakis her imagination had been working overtime.

Calista held a spectrum of color in her brain that was constantly shimmering even in the dark. She hardly had need of waves of light striking her retina to get excited about a color. It was as if her optic nerve could do it alone without retinal stimulus. Now it was getting a little out of hand, particularly in terms of the hues of red. She tried to convince herself that the gush of red tulips from the black wet earth did not look like a major artery bursting open. They had delicate little cup-shaped blossoms that the catalog had promised would look just like Little Red Riding Hood's hood. That had done it for her. She had ordered thirty-six bulbs. Calista had been a Red Riding Hood freak as a child. Always wore a red cape and hood. Even had one now that she had made up for herself from bright red wool.

She continued walking around the garden. Under a mountain laurel that she had pruned back violently last year, the earth was stippled with a jeweled potpourri of miniature bulbs just springing forth. There were dwarf irises, snowdrops, something called Dasystemon that exploded from the earth like yellow shooting stars. She must come out and sketch them before they went by. They reminded her of some of the borders in the books of hours, particularly the plates of the biblical passages. She squinted at the ground, and the blues and golds merged. The *Fall of the Rebel Angels*? One of the Limburgs' best with the extraordinary cascade of angels from the sky. Yes, the snowdrops still dewy could be the silver helmets at the heavenly host's feet. And the blue dwarf irises would be the tunics of the falling rebel angels. Those dashes of color were enough to send her back into the house and her studio.

5

I shall make you love books more than your mother.
— from *The Instruction of Dua Khety,*
Egyptian text of the Middle Kingdom

The inscription had been beautifully transcribed with a calligraphic pen onto handcrafted marbled paper. It hung just to the right of the heavy walnut sliding door to Calista's studio on a paneled wall, directly above a cast-iron grill. Another calligraphic inscription below it read, *"Hey, there's ladies here!"* The second one was attributable to Mel Brooks, a quote from the 2,000-year-old man alluding to the discovery of women on the planet.

In the studio there were, of course, the tools of an artist. The ink pots, the sable brushes in gradations of size purchased dearly in Chinatown, a stack of Wattnum board, one of her favorite surfaces for drawing, paints, acrylics, oils, watercolors. All of the walls except for one were dark walnut and shelved with books, mostly reference books—bestiaries, costume design books, hundreds of horticulture books. For her work she needed to know not just how a plant or an animal or a dress looked then as well as now, but also how people's imaginations worked then. She had a deep and passionate interest in the evolutionary pressures that had been exerted not merely on the human form that turned hominid to human in terms of opposable thumbs and upright posture, but most particularly in those transformations of

35

the brain. Calista was interested in what throughout the ages had frightened people. What made them laugh? What did they find intolerable? How did they perceive children, and how did children perceive them?

No one perceived children more peculiarly in Calista's mind than the Victorians. She had a valuable collection of nineteenth-century first-edition children's books and drawings that included Beatrix Potter, Randolph Caldecott, Arthur Rackham, and others. There were also in this collection numerous arcane cookbooks. One was a book of Elizabethan cookery, and she periodically threatened Charley with hedgehog *en dorée*. Charley was a dedicated McDonald's fan and the only child in Cambridge who still ate white bread as far as Calista could ascertain.

So the room seemed more of a study than a studio, a Victorian study at that, with its love seat upholstered in red-and-white velvet candy cane stripes flanked on either end by small Tiffany lamps. Tasseled ivory curtains hung in the three windows of the bay. The floor had been painted a lacquer green and was mostly covered by a worn but still elegant ancient Oriental rug that sparkled like old rubies in the evening light of the room.

On her drawing table were numerous small toys. Calista liked to fiddle when she got stuck. Her favorite "toys," though, were her trout flies that she tied herself. She even had clamped to the table an Anderson Model C flytier's vise. On a small stand now rested her most recent efforts. She had retied the entire life cycle of the mayfly from nymph to dun and on through to its maturity and spent stages.

Opposite her desk was an eighteenth-century wing chair. Elegant and quiet, it contrasted nicely with the striped love seat. Charley often sat on it talking with his mom as she worked. Now, however, it was occupied by one of Calista's stuffed animals, one of the good buddies of the Hedge and Owl series. The two characters had been made into stuffed animals and sold at F.A.O. Schwarz and department stores. They had become hot items. All those yuppies were starting to reproduce, and

Hedge and Owl dolls were as indispensable to them as the cappuccino machines.

She sighed, opened a bottle of ink, and reached for her favorite thin-nibbed pen and what she called her eyelash brush. The trim size of this book was ten and one-half by eight and one-half inches. This was her world now. It must be for the next seven hours. She could not allow anything intrusive to disturb her. There could be no thoughts of bloody scrawls, only very deliberate strokes of this number-three pen. It was safe, it was confined, and she controlled everything that happened here on this small field of white.

The frontispiece of the book faced her. The design spilled over onto the title page. It looked simple. It looked spare. But it was not. The blank space that occupied nearly 75 percent of the page was important. In spite of the borders, which were a fairly direct borrowing from the elaborate ones of the *Book of Hours of the Duc de Berry,* the illustrations on these two pages had to have a movement and tension. They had to leap beyond the decorative frame and lead into the story. Illustration was an interpretive art: it added to the text. It illuminated meaning, shed light, and even sometimes created mystery simultaneously, but it never translated directly. If it did, the magic of the book stopped. The pictures became oddly opaque. The text must flow ceaselessly, and the images of the pictures should intertwine subtly. It must all appear seamless, effortless—a knock-off. This was what picture book illustration was about.

Calista was a person who lived inside of books, particularly picture books. And although there were values embedded in her stories, she never preached. She was a storyteller first and last, which meant that her imagination was important, but her reader's imagination was more important. It felt good now to be entering this forum with its eight-by-ten dimensions, to be inside her books where she could control the characters, where the world was predictable. Nottingham, after all, was a simple place. You knew who the bad guys were, and the crimes were not high crimes of murder. And most of the time only the bad guys died for good.

The illustration sketched in pencil showed an arrow being shot from a narrow slot in a stone wall and sailing over a cultivated garden into the blankness of the facing page. From the extreme edge of the facing page, as if growing from the paper's edge, were the inky greens of the forest's foliage with a sliver of a tree trunk showing. The gulf of white separated the lush verdant forest from the stone convent. And always through the book there would be this tantalizing juxtaposition of the world of stone and built form against that of the wildness and green freedom of the forest. This was the torsion of the book. *Marian's Tale* began in a convent. For that was where in Calista's retelling Maid Marian had fled to escape the amorous attentions of the foul-breathed, pockmarked greedy Prince John. Research had shown that Marian had not entered the cycle of the Robin Hood tales until well into the sixteenth century. She did so as Matilda Fitzwalter, the historical wife of Robin Hood. She had been toyed with ever since in retellings.

Three years before, Ethan Thayer had bought the rights to the novel-length Paul Creswick version, and Calista had done the first paintings since N. C. Wyeth's for the book. She had had to stick to the text, but this other idea of a tale told from Marian's point of view began to simmer on some back burner of her brain. Now it was her turn, Calista's version of the tale. It was to be Marian's tale, and everything would be different. No more matinee idols for Robin, and Marian would be different, too.

She had found an almost suitable face on the subway one day. There was a guy who had gotten on at Kenmore Square and off at Charles Street. Luckily, when the train comes between those two stops it rides into daylight for a short stretch on the Longfellow Bridge over the Charles River. The man's face was not really a handsome one at all in the classical sense. It was too rough. Great bone structure, but hacked, or perhaps rough-hewn, rather than chiseled. This had resulted in startling collisions of the facial planes. It was a face, she had suspected, that was slightly too old in its structure for the person. He would have to grow into it. And as the train rushed into the light of day, he looked up directly at Calista. The incongruity of the rather puerile mud brown eyes confirmed her suspicions. Some faces could sustain such oxymoronic quirks. Others could not. The latter was the case with this face. She would have to think about the eyes, but she'd take the bone structure.

For Marian she had the eyes worked out. They would be slightly vampy, a touch of Louise Brooks and Anita Loos. As she worked on the frontispiece she began to softly whistle "Diamonds Are a Girl's Best Friend." She loved that song. She had loved the movie. There was a baby in one of her early books that had Marilyn Monroe eyes. She was listening to Morning Pro Musica, but Robert J. Lurtsenia was sighing deeply over the news at that moment as she sketched out the stones of the tower. She caught herself subconsciously waiting for Robert J to mention something on the news about Petrakis. But there was no reference. She forced herself back to the business at hand—crosshatching the stonework.

By eleven forty-five she had the tower inked in and had begun the dense crosshatching that would give volume and shadow to the stones. A Hanson Romantic concerto was swirling through the air. She felt a twinge of hunger but decided on a coffee break instead. She walked to the kitchen and poured herself a cup of coffee from the electric pot she kept going. Back at her desk she reached into a tin box that was the shape of the Albert Hall in London for a *biscotti*. She was thinking about that color of green, the one of the books of hours and the one of Sherwood Forest, and how she would make it flow from one page to the other in the border motifs and then into the forest.

She tapped her feet lightly as she bit into the cookie. Robert J was sighing again. She couldn't bear any more grim reports about a devastating earthquake in Peru. She resumed tapping her feet gently on the floor. Gads! She just remembered her tap-dancing class was tonight. She never missed her tap class. Charley was mortally embarrassed to have a mother who took tap dancing. Why couldn't she take aerobics like other mothers? He had sworn her to secrecy about this vice of hers and made her promise she would never perform anywhere at all ever in his lifetime in this galaxy.

"Do lobsters ever get rabies?" he had asked once when he had caught her practicing.

"I don't think so. Why?" she had answered.

"Well, if they did and walked upright, they would look like you tap-dancing."

This did not deter her. She enjoyed the exercise and looked forward to her class that evening.

She worked through the afternoon. By four o'clock she had finished the pen-and-ink work on the frontispiece and title page. She would have to think seriously about color now. She knew it was time to quit. She had to think about that transition of green in the borders, and at the end of a long day she was not up for it. But she wasn't up for thoughts of murder, either. And it seemed as soon as she stopped working that was what she thought of— Norman Petrakis. Why hadn't the police ever called her back? They had said that they would keep in touch and tell her if they had any leads. But she had heard nothing, and it had barely been mentioned in the newspaper. She supposed there would be no harm in calling up the Boston Police Department. She could ask to talk to one of the detectives. She ransacked her brain for the cops' names. McCafferty, she was almost positive that was one. She dialed the number and asked for Lieutenant McCafferty. He wasn't in. How about his partner? What partner? The one that had been on the Petrakis murder case? Petrakis murder? Oh, yeah, it seemed to ring a distant bell, but she had better call back in the morning when someone who knew more about it would be on duty. "Doesn't anybody know anything about this?" Calista asked with a slight desperation in her voice.

"Don't worry," the officer on duty said.

"Don't worry?!" she screamed.

"Honey . . . ,"

Oh, yuck, Calista thought. How far could you get with a cop who calls you honey? He was going on now about a series of drug-related murders in the Mattapan section of Boston. Innocent people getting cut down by stray bullets and how this was using most of the homicide detectives. In short, the death of Norman Petrakis had failed to become a top priority. It did not fit into a pattern of violence that was threatening the city; therefore Norman had become just a statistic to be swallowed up in the morass of other forgotten souls whose demises failed to pique the interest of the department because of the circumstances. If Norman had been ensnared somehow into the web of drugs, either as an operative or an innocent bystander and died within that ring of fire, then someone would have been working on it. But dying alone in a hotel room with a bloody scrawl on the wall, well, that fit into no patterns and was so bizarre as to not be considered a threat in at least an endemic sense. There was something ineffably sad about it all.

6

Charley had soccer practice after school. Calista left a message with the school secretary that he should take the Mount Auburn Street bus out to Watertown Square and meet her at Stellina's, their favorite Italian restaurant, for dinner after her tap class. She went upstairs and grabbed her tap-dancing gear along with her swimming suit. She always stopped in at the Mount Auburn Club to swim off the tap sweat and take a sauna and steam after class. People at the Mount Auburn Club were not into tap dancing. They were into aerobics with a vengeance, squash, tennis, networking parties where business cards were traded while eating sushi and sipping burgundy, a combination of food that appalled Calista almost as much as the meadow muffin rocks set in asphalt. But indeed there had been a notice on the club board for a sushi-and-burgundy–tasting party.

Mindy Berkhauer was over sixty years old and the tap teacher. She had briefly been a Rockette, and she talked just like Dr. Ruth while she tap-danced. She didn't talk about sex, though. She talked about listening for the correct sounds of the taps. She talked about "feathering" a brush stroke and digging in on the cramp roll. And she was loaded with anecdotal material—about Flo Ziegfeld, Ann Miller, Fred Astaire. It was a lot more interesting than Dr. Ruth and "Vhat form of birth control are you using?" Much more "Vell, you know who Cab Callovay really vas mad for? . . . Ach! Calista, no, no, dahlink. You're not breaking vith the knees."

At six-thirty Calista was sitting naked in the steam room of the Mount Auburn Club. Through the miasma of the humid clouds came the disembodied voices of two other women. One was special counsel to the governor of Massachusetts, and the other one was a vice-president of the Boston Stock Exchange. They were discussing something about the Governor's Commission on Affirmative Action. Heavy-duty group. The women's locker room was laced with talk like this. There was a preponderance of attorneys, computer software people, and therapists. They spent a lot of time helping other women achieve power and serving on governor's and mayor's commissions and panels. Calista had once served on a panel for the arts. But nothing got done, and she got a fancy certificate to commemorate the experience of serving on a panel that had accomplished absolutely nothing. Calista didn't listen that much when she went to the club. She looked at the naked bodies. There was an incredible range of form and size and coloring. She studied these bodies surreptitiously. It was part of her job. For beneath every clothed body that she drew was a moving, naked one. All plump bodies in children's books tended to look like jugs, roly-poly vessels with no movement or animation. But Calista had had a plump grandmother. She had died when Calista was very young, but she still had a vivid image of her whirling about a kitchen, lightly, full of grace and rhythm. She had of course never seen that grandmother undressed, never had the opportunity to study the anatomy of a plump, active woman. Here she did. Women trotted all over the huge locker room naked as jaybirds, their bodies pink and glistening from the steam room or the sauna. They lotioned themselves, sprayed themselves. The pleasant *thwack*ing sound of after-bath splash being slapped onto different kinds of flesh punctuated the air. There were all sorts of buttocks. It might surprise many people, Calista thought, to discover that fat women did not necessarily have fat fannies. Often their posteriors were surprisingly flat, and their cheeks drooped into flaccid little creases. And there were ways that breasts that had nursed infants sagged that Calista found beautiful, and there were stomachs that had folds across them that were as attractive as the trampoline-taut tummies that had been winched in by merciless numbers of sit-ups every day.

She found the peculiar, the irregular, as charming and sensual as the honed-to-perfection aerobicised body. This locker room was the best drawing class available. She even had a preview of her own body thirty, forty years hence. She had picked out her seventy-year-old counterpart. The tummy was flat but wrinkled as crepe paper. The skin gathered around the sunken navel like a drooping eyelid. The deflated breasts were slung like little pouches on either side of the sternum, which appeared almost concave with its bones exposed like the ribs in the hull of a finely built dory. The buttocks too had grown bonier, hollowing out on the sides, and the cleft was now just a shadow more than a neat little pleat between two rounded mounds. Where there was enough flesh, it had simply collapsed into very fine wrinkles and thin little folds. Where there was not enough flesh, it had drawn back tightly to reveal the scaffolding, the hinges, the levers, and the ropy musculature of the body. Such was the fate of thin women. It was not really a bad fate at all. The body looked used, worked in the best sense of the word. One could read those ridges, those valleys and hollows, like a geologist reading the stratigraphy of an outcrop. Erosion was beautiful. Erosion meant something had happened. Erosion meant history and, in that wonderful phrase of John McPhee, deep time. Calista found great beauty and mystery in this.

Calista herself was more circumspect in her naked peregrinations around the locker room. She always requested a locker near a vanity with a hairdryer so she would not have to walk too far. And she usually put on her underwear and often her stockings or tights before beginning to dry her hair and moisturize her face. Drying and moisturizing were the A to Z of Calista's beauty routine. However, if she were going to something fancy and felt she looked exceedingly pale, she would then put on rouge and some eye makeup.

At seven-fifteen she was sitting in one of the booths at Stellina's inhaling garlic and wondering where Charley was. Just at that moment he came through the door. She could tell by his slicked-back hair that he had actually showered before coming to dinner. Bravo, she thought. One small step for hygiene, one big step for mankind and maturity.

"Hi, sweetie. I ordered you that melted cheese thing on bread with tomatoes. Thought you'd like it."

"I'm famished. I'd eat it melted on a shoe." Charley slid onto the seat opposite her.

Stellina's was one step up from a diner in terms of its decor. The food was one step ahead of Lutèce, as far as Calista was concerned, and at a fraction of the price, needless to say. Most important, it represented a common ground, foodwise, upon which she and Charley could meet. Charley, to say the least, was rather pedestrian in his tastes, aside from his undying fondness and loyalty to squishy white nonnutritious bread, air bread.

The waitress came with the appetizers—crostados. The chopped tomatoes on top were sprinkled liberally with basil, olive oil, and garlic, and the smell was heaven. Calista believed firmly that if there was a God, heaven would smell like garlic, basil, and tomatoes.

"Umm, this is good," Charley said, taking his first bite. "What kind of cheese did you say this was?"

"Goat's milk. But don't let it prejudice you," she added quickly.

"No, no, not at all. Who'd ever think a goat could do anything as nice as this. No, this is almost as good as Velveeta."

"Charley!"

He laughed. He loved teasing his mom.

For their main course Charley had spaghetti with the plainest sauce they served, and Calista had òsso buco and risotto Milanese.

"What are you doing?" Charley asked as he watched her take her knife and poke at a bone.

"I'm poking out the marrow."

"You're what?" He looked aghast.

"Poking out the marrow," she repeated. "That's what you do. These are veal shanks. The marrow's in the holes. It's the best part."

Charley lowered his eyes and reached for his water glass. "I've got a marrow-eating mother," he muttered.

"Yes, and she tap-dances, too! What trials!"

He took several swallows of water and put down his glass. "You know I got a French test tomorrow, and I got to pass it or else."

"I don't understand why you're not doing better in French."

"Why! That's easy. Because Madame Morganstern yaps in French constantly. She never says a word in English. How does she expect us to learn anything? It was much better with Mr. O'Flaherty."

"Mr. O'Flaherty was the biggest oaf I ever met."

"He talked slow."

"He thought slow. You can't take a football coach and make him the French teacher."

"I disagree entirely. He said the words so we could understand them."

"He had the thickest Charlestown accent I ever heard."

"He wasn't from Charlestown. He's from Somerville."

"Well, it doesn't matter. You'll never hear a French *r* coming out of O'Flaherty's mouth."

"Nobody in the greater Boston area says *r* anyhow."

"But you're learning French, not Boston."

"It doesn't matter. And it's not the pronunciation that's going to flunk us. It's the grammar. O'Flaherty could explain the grammar real good."

"Really well, Charley, as long as we're speaking about grammar."

"Well, you know what I mean."

"Yeah, but I even had grave doubts on that score with O'Flaherty. On that one test last year it was quite apparent that he did not understand the subjunctive tense in the way he structured those questions."

"Subjunctive?" Charley said vaguely. "That's the would-be one, right?"

"The conditional tense, that's right."

"Well, you see, that explains it. O'Flaherty is a man of action, a coach. He operates in the here and now." Charley's eyes were twinkling. He loved arguing with his mother this way.

"Oh." Calista nodded. "Yes, that would explain why he should be on the football field rather than in the French class."

"No," Charley said emphatically. "Except for the subjunctive the guy was great. He explained all that stuff perfectly, in English. This lady, Morganstern, she's not even French and we've got to call her Madame. We never had to call him, you know . . ." He paused. "You know," he repeated. "The word for 'Mister.'"

Calista rolled her eyes. "'Monsieur,' Charley. Good heavens, you don't even know that word!"

"Just slipped my mind. Anyhow, we never had to call him 'Monsieur O'Flaherty.' She's just showing off, this

Morganstern lady. That's why she talks French all the time. She loves the sound of her own voice saying it. And she talks. God, does she talk! Mom, you never heard someone talk as much."

"So what about this test tomorrow? You going to pull it off or not?"

"I think I can actually do the irregular verbs part and the translation. The translation isn't going to be long. *Ne pas* long. But it's the dictation that's going to kill me. She says it so fast, and all of her words just mush together. And sometimes she spits. You should never sit in the front row in that class. Once Spider wore a raincoat."

"The Spider would. Anyway, what am I supposed to do to help you, aside from sending foul-weather gear?"

"Pray. Say a little prayer for me around ten thirty-five."

They left the restaurant with Calista humming "Say a Little Prayer for Me," one of her favorite Dionne Warwick songs.

"Mother!" Charley said, turning to her, his face as red as his hair. She resisted grabbing him in a headlock and kissing his head. He looked so dear when he blushed, but then again she didn't want to deal with a resuscitation on the premises due to embarrassment. On the pubescent angst meter this would make the bell ring.

47

7

There were no little prayers to be said for shaky French students in any of the books of hours Calista had thus encountered. Nor was there a liturgical hour of the day that addressed any such concerns. But Calista at ten-thirty looked up from her table in the reading room of the library toward a high round window and muttered a *broche,* or Hebrew benediction. Her Hebrew wasn't worth beans, but she figured that there was more chance of there being a *broche* for someone in Charley's situation than finding something in the books of hours. She had remembered her very ancient grandfather when she was a little girl coming to visit and whispering *broches* all day long. She had thought he was talking to himself because their housekeeper had explained to her that that was what very old people often did. But she couldn't believe that he would talk to himself in such a strange language. So she asked him. He wasn't talking to himself at all. He was praying to God.

"When I talk to myself I talk Yiddish," he had said. "When I pray to God I speak Hebrew." He had then told her that there were *broches,* or blessings, for all kinds of events. There were *broches* for the expected ones—for getting up in the morning and for going to bed at night. But then there were other wonderful ones that he told her about for unexpected and lovely things that might happen and mark a day. There were *broches* for seeing a new moon, *broches* for spotting a beautiful animal, *broches* uttered upon smelling a delightful fragrance. Her parents still had hanging in their living room a very early drawing of Calista's that showed an old man, his back bent but his head lifted as he watched an owl flying overhead. It was her grandfather, and he was saying a *broche* for seeing an owl. For Calista and he had seen an owl together one summer twilight when they had taken a walk before dinner.

So if any religion was going to have a blessing for a fragile French student who didn't quite believe in the subjunctive tense, it had to be Judaism. There was only one rule in saying a *broche,* really. It must include the words *Shem U' Malchus,* the name of God affirmed as king. So Calista muttered, *"Shem U' Malchus,* make Charley think, think clearly." That was it. She didn't feel it was cricket to pray for right answers to drop straight out of heaven. She just prayed that he would think and use his God-given gifts. It was possibly the first *broche* to be uttered in Houghton Library of Harvard University.

Houghton was the rare-books library of Harvard and possessed one of the greatest collections in the world of old manuscripts. Calista had come that morning early and had now spent more than an hour just going through the slide catalog of books of hours to figure out which manuscripts would serve her best in her search for the illusive color green that she needed to see. The color distortion on the slides, of course, was monumental. There were skies that appeared green and grass that appeared blue. But she had it narrowed down now and decided that her best bets lay in a 1471 Dutch *Book of Hours* called the *Getydebok,* and another one from northern Italy of the same period, nearly the same year.

She had been allowed to bring only her magnifying glass and a pencil into the reading room. She had checked her "guns" on the other side of the red leather door. Those were the rules. No pens, no pocket books or satchels of any kind. After saying the *broche* for Charley, she walked up to the desk and filled out a form requesting to see the two books incarnate rather than in Koda-chrome.

As she waited for the books she looked about her. There was a man down at the other end of the table who was doing something on e. e. cummings. He had a folder that looked like original correspondence. Calista's house was a stone's throw from the old cummings's house. Calista wondered if she should walk over and tell the cummings scholar this. The man was sort of attractive. Or maybe she should just walk up and say, "Hi, I'm one of those Cambridge ladies with the furnished souls. You know, the ones e. e. writes about who believe in Christ and Longfellow. Well, actually not exactly Christ. See, I'm Jewish, and I just said a *broche* for my son, but still you get the picture . . ."

The librarian interrupted this reverie. She brought two rather small books. One was in a lovely flat box containing the fragments that had been left from the Italian book. The other was a very small, very fat book measuring four by five inches and was a good three inches thick. When she opened it it took Calista's breath away. She forgot about cute cummings scholars and Charley's French test. She forgot about everything except the color green. It was as if she had seen the color for the first time ever. Maybe it was like a baby seeing snow for the first time. Her mind was surprised, her eyes seemed fresh and young, and the world new and full of charms.

In the manuscript there was a large S in gilt, and within the open curves of the S a man, a crusader, perhaps, knelt in prayer on the most beautiful green grass Calista had ever seen. His sword and his shield were cast aside. It was a luminous, pellucid green. Green was the hardest color of all. Green so often turned murky or worse yet bilious and phlegmy, and she felt her own green envy at the artist's ability.

She did not know how long she looked at the page and feasted on the color green. She had never in her life had such a visceral reaction to a color. It was sensual. She could almost smell it. Somewhere deep in her brain there was a part that responded to color the way perhaps gourmands responded to food and enologists to wine. Three-quarters of an hour had passed before she even turned to the other book, the one from Italy. The color couldn't compare. The characterization, however, was quite interesting. Especially when one considered how tiny the faces were. She took out her magnifying glass to study the faces more carefully. Leave it to the Italians to make St. Andrew a sexy devil rather than one of those somber, militant types the French and the north countries seemed to favor. There was a head floating in the border, a lady's head with a face just like Mrs. Fitchborne's, Calista's old piano teacher from her girlhood. The cherubs in the corners of the border were quite arresting, too. Babies with beer bellies. These bellies were not at all the poochy tummies of babies, but real beer guts hanging out there. Their wings were exquisitely rendered. Calista sketched quickly in pencil on some small index cards she had brought with her. She went back to the Dutch book and sketched the sword and the shield of the man in the gilt S. That weaponry would be roughly of the same period as *Marian's Tale*. The sheriff's thugs would be carrying swords and shields. Marian and the boys of Sherwood would just have bows. She was after details. There was no way, however, that she could sketch that color green. She looked at the green once more. This would be hard. Calista painted in acrylics—plastics. She had started painting in them when Charley was little because they were indestructible and there was no way a toddler or rambunctious kid could mess them up. The trade-off, however, for the indestructibility of the medium was that you had to work harder to make it subtle. This green that she wanted did not come from any bottle or tube. She knew what these old illuminators had done. She had read about it extensively. This particular green she would bet dollars to doughnuts came from the same stuff that the Limburgs' *vert de flambé* came from—wild irises and massicot, a yellow crystalline mineral form of lead monoxide. All she had was Aquatex number 63. That would not do at all. She would have to build the green up carefully layer by layer starting with yellows and blues and maybe a little of her Vermont red.

8

There was a note on the mail desk. *No calls. You need more floor wax. See you Thursday, Vicki.* She had been at the library longer than she had thought if she had entirely missed Vicki, her garrulous cleaning lady, whose cleaning days Calista looked forward to. The house indeed was immaculate. She had also missed lunch and was starving, so she went directly to the kitchen.

There wasn't much inspiring in the refrigerator. A jar of Vienna sausages in brine, the kind that looked like babies' fingers, another tribute to Charley's appalling palate. He loved them. There was also a can of opened pineapple rings. God forbid someone would offer Charley a genuine fresh pineapple. Oh, this was going to be disgusting! There must be something else. She peered deeper into the fridge, hoping. There were some ominous little packages wrapped in tinfoil and something in plastic wrap that had lurked there for too long. Just throw them out, Calista! she ordered herself. Don't look at them. They'll probably have fur. Just throw them out before they walk out on their own! And to think people were worried when they had begun to set up all those recombinant DNA labs in Cambridge. For heaven's sake, she probably had a host of mutant killers right in her own refrigerator. She reached in and grabbed a fistful of little packages and marched them to the trash can. These would not rate the garbage disposal because then she would have to unwrap them. Yuck. She really must become more organized about groceries and meal planning, but it was so hard when the only other person to cook for was Charley of the leaden palate. She went back to the refrigerator. The only decent candidate in the lunch department was one tiny chunk of Jarlsberg. She supposed she could stab it with a toothpick and then put a Vienna sausage on it and then stick part of a canned pineapple ring on that. *Zut alors!* Oh, well. There was no other choice.

East meets West, she thought as she washed down the dubious luncheon materials with a Kirin beer. God! This stuff did for bad food what ivy did for bad architecture. If she had a beer during the day, however, she needed coffee to keep her alert and full of nerve for her afternoon's work and the continuing onslaught to crack the code of green, the Rosetta stone of the painter's palette. The color green from the *Book of Hours* was still fresh in her head. She might as well try mixing it up out here while she waited for her coffee water to boil. She opened the fridge again and this time took out a small jar half-full with a dark rusty goo. Vermont red. It was actually some oxide she had skimmed off a Vermont stream where she sometimes fished. She got an egg, too. Then went to the basement for some linseed oil.

Five minutes later she took a sip of her coffee and looked at the mixture in her bowl. "You old wizard, you!" she exclaimed happily. Indeed the very color she had been searching for was beginning to come through. Give this five, ten more minutes to warm up, and the sharpness would leave it and she would have her *Book of Hours* green, or something pretty close.

She did. Ten minutes later she carried the precious color into her study.

There was something wrong. The minute she walked into the room she knew it. She felt it. The bowl began to quiver in her hands. Somebody had been there in her absence, and it was not Vicki. Vicki never came into her study, not even to clean. Something was different, not just different—wrong, out of order. There was a book on her drawing table. Right on it, leaning against her work. Nobody ever touched her work. Her work was covered.

So it probably was not harmed, but if any messages were to be left, any packages, they were left either on the mail desk or perhaps the flat part of her desk, but never the drawing board. This was tantamount to touching the eggs of a bird's nest that a mother had left unguarded. It was unnatural. It was a terrible invasion. Calista stood there and stared at the book. It was one of hers, *Nick in the Night.* She began to tremble more fiercely. Her mouth felt suddenly dry. She was frightened to touch it. Frightened of her own book. But she sensed then that somehow, some way, this would no longer be her book. It had become an alien thing to her. She willed herself to pick it up.

She grasped the pages between her thumb and other fingers and flipped them. The print and pictures blurred. No note dropped out. But one of the pages . . . what was that? There was a mark on a page, on many pages. She turned back. Nothing on the first five pages, but on the sixth . . . Calista felt a wave of nausea pass over her, and the rank taste of the Vienna sausage welled up in the back of her throat. There on the sixth page was little Nick flying through the night. But instead of that swift little nude body skimming across the clouds, he now wore diapers! Her eyes widened. She turned the page. On each of the succeeding pages until the very end of the book diapers had been drawn on the little boy's figure. Tears sprang to her eyes, more for the child, Nick, than herself, for he had been invaded as well. She sat down slowly on her stool and looked about.

There was something else wrong. There was something missing. "Where's Owl?" she whispered; staring at the wing chair. The stuffed animal from the Hedge and Owl series always sat there except when Charley sat there. Then he put it on the floor by the chair, but it was not there now. Hedge still resided on a high shelf that held the *Encyclopedia Britannica,* shoulder to shoulder with the last volume X–Z. "Where's Owl?" she whispered in a low, trembling voice. Then she ran up to Charley's room. Owl was not there. She went to the alcove on the third floor where she kept her sewing machine and where a second Hedge resided experiencing life as a pin cushion. But Owl was not there either. She went through every room in the house searching for the stuffed animal. Owl was gone and Hedge was without a buddy!

Calista was stunned by this defacement of the book and haunted by the loss of Owl. She went back through the book again. There was something indefinably grotesque about the way the diapers had been drawn, or was it simply the effect that was grotesque? In any case she felt her character had vanished. The original Nick was lost, abducted, and in some way his memory shamed.

She wanted to cry. She had created a lovely innocent child, a little boy of three or four years old, and they had destroyed him. The whole book leered at her now. Who could have done such a thing? And how? Vicki had been here. She must call Vicki.

She tried to keep the tremor out of her voice as she spoke to one of Vicki's daughters. No, Vicki wasn't home yet. She worked afternoons, after Calista's, at the Clarks. Calista thanked Vicki's daughter for the number.

"No, Cal. No, dear. Nobody delivered anything. No, nobody came. . . . Weird. I can't imagine. . . . No, I was there all morning. I had a cigarette on your front porch, but you know I was right there by the door and the back door was locked. No, I don't understand how anyone could have gotten in."

Neither did Calista. Just as she hung up the phone rang. She nearly jumped. The kettle was now whistling, too, as she had put on more coffee water. It was as if the whole world had begun to shriek at her. She raced from her study to the kitchen to turn off the water. She wanted to run out the door, run out the door, run out the door of her own house! She almost did not want to pick up the telephone. But she did.

"Calista!" The voice was raspy and tight.

"What?"

"Calista, it's me, Margaret. I just got the most awful thing."

"No!" Calista almost shouted the word.

"Yes." Margaret paused. "Yes, why did you say it that way?" It was suddenly dawning on Margaret McGowan that there was something odd about the alacrity and intensity of that "no" that had exploded out of the phone.

"Me too." Calista's voice dropped to a hoarse whisper.

"What?"

"What did you get?"

She heard Margaret suck in her breath sharply. "This horrible . . . horrible copy of my book *The Dark Knight of Kyre,* they've put a crown of thorns on Rothgar. You know the book only has a few illustrations. But in each one with Rothgar they've drawn in this crown of thorns, and—" Her voice broke. "Calista . . ."

"What?"

"It didn't come through the mail. I found it on my front hall carpet. Whoever it was just dropped it right through my mail slot."

Calista would refrain from telling Margaret that she herself did not even have a mail slot. That the person had come right through a door, or a window, that the person himself had entered into her own house. His foot had actually trod on her carpeting. He had breathed the same air. She realized Margaret seemed quite bad off and appeared to be hyperventilating.

"Margaret, are you okay? Margaret!"

"Yes, dear." She breathed deeply as one might to summon up courage. "But you know, it is the last illustration that is the worst."

"Yes?" Calista asked in a small voice, not really wanting to hear.

"There are these wounds?"

"Wounds?" Calista whispered.

"Yes, wounds. Those horrible kinds of wounds. You know, like those twisted northern European painters used to paint, I don't know, in the early Renaissance. Very precise little slits spurting blood."

"Oh, God!"

"Yes, 'Oh, God,'" Margaret said weakly. "It's absolutely revolting." She paused. "But worse than revolting, Calista, it's scary." Her voice was tremulous again.

"Yes." There was silence. They were both thinking of the loathsome little man at the conference and the murder of Norman Petrakis. Was this related? Could it be? "I think I better come right over and look at this. Maybe we should talk."

"Yes, yes. I'd feel better if you'd come over."

"Okay, give me a few minutes."

She dashed around the house not looking for Owl now but checking every window and door. Nothing seemed disturbed in any other part of the house. She returned to the kitchen and screwed the top on the Vermont red and put it back in the refrigerator. Damn! Damn! she thought as she placed the jar with its deep red contents on a shelf. I don't want to think about red! I want to think about green, green! But all she could think about was the scrawl on the wall in the Sheraton Hotel and now these gruesome little slits spurting blood. She sought refuge in Tom's study, where he had worked inventing the formulas that might pin down the hidden parts of the universe, where he had explored the nature of time, space-time in the cosmos, and that most alluring billionth of a second when the universe and time began.

It always calmed Calista to come into Tom's study. The desk was now covered with papers of Charley's for some report that was due soon. She sank down on the chair and absently, as if in a trance, began stacking index cards, putting some photocopied newspaper articles in the folder. The desktop didn't look all that different from when Tom had been alive and working at it. The clutter had a sameness, although the marks on the papers were different. There was still the sign—GRAVITY QUANTICIZED HERE—and the small box holding some of Tom's favorite flies, which she still used on occasion. This was her kind of sentimentality. She liked fishing with his old flies, ones that she had tied especially for him—old Marabou Streamers and Royal Wulffs and Humpies.

She opened the box now and picked up one of the flies, twirling it between her fingers. She wanted to calm herself down before going to Margaret's. She wanted to think clearly about these odd events. She did not want to be overwhelmed by their luridness. She had to think. But it was difficult. She stared out the window between the photos of Cygnus X-1 and the Crab Nebulae at the garden. The shoots of daffodils were poking up, the blossoms still sheathed in their tight green jackets. She had called this perennial garden, this view of it, Tom's black hole break, the pause that refreshed from thinking about singularities, infinite gravitational densities and imploding stars, and the inexorable events that would follow from such starry disasters. The Charioteer himself had now crashed.

And were the vile defacements of the books, were these the ripples spreading out from the event, from that starry crash, that implosion of life that splattered the night with blood?

"Hi, Mom."

This time there was no hiding it. She had not even heard the front door slam. He had probably gone upstairs first to check his E-mail, electronic mail, on the Mac in his bedroom, and now she had been caught in flagrante terrified!

"What in the world is wrong with you?" He had just bitten into an apple and was setting down his skateboard. He looked up with his luminous gray eyes into his mother's. "Mom, you look like you've seen a ghost or something."

"Charley, I received the most horrible little . . ." She paused, searching for a word. "Surprise today."

Three minutes later Charley closed the book of *Nick in the Night* and gave a shudder. "Yuck."

"Yuck is right," Calista said. "And also . . ."

"What else?" Charley said, looking up from the book.

"Owl has disappeared, the one that sits in the wing chair. You didn't take it anywhere, did you?"

"Me? No." Charley resumed looking at the book. "At least this isn't one of the books where the kid looks like me. That would really be creepy."

"Oh, Charley, don't say such a thing!" Oh, God, she thought, she simply could not endure another close call like the one she had had with Charley almost two years before.

"And you say Margaret McGowan got a book of hers messed up like this, too?"

"Yes, well, not exactly in the same way." She thought of the blood Margaret had described spurting from the precise little slit.

"So maybe we should go over and see Margaret's book?"

"Oh, you don't have to come, Charley."

He looked stunned. The luminosity of his eyes hardened into the same slate gray as the sky. There was no light, no hint of spring. It could have been a winter day outside and in. "Why shouldn't I come?" The voice was taut with a combination of disbelief and frustration. "If it has to do with Petrakis's murder, it . . ." But he let it go. He did not need to say any more. If it had to do with Petrakis, it could have to do with his mother. And especially if it had to do with books, it meant Mother to him, his mother, his only parent. She might be the world's most famous children's book illustrator, but she had failed utterly with her own son in terms of the proscription of the Dua Khety text from the Middle Kingdom.

9

There was a particular street in Cambridge, Foster Street, that was known for its especially small houses. Built in the early 1800s for the servants of the larger houses, and sometimes mansions, on Brattle Street a block north, these houses had come to be called the Cambridge dollhouses. Clapboard structures, they stood erect and unadorned, many even shutterless, but they possessed an elegance based entirely on proportion and minimal detail. Margaret McGowan's house was one of these, and it stood as prim and starched as a Quaker lady in its fresh coat of dove gray paint and cream-colored trim. Except today there was one thing out of place, totally wrong, and Calista noticed it immediately. A raw unpainted board had been crudely nailed over the mail slot, a terrible testimony to the offense that this particular household had just suffered. The effect of the board was not a particularly remedial one, not the natural scar of a wound that had healed with time or a neat bandage for a deep cut. It seemed like another wound itself on the immaculate exterior of the house.

Margaret's house at one time had been the home of a butler and his wife. The wife had been a cook for the Longfellow household at 105 Brattle Street, and the butler had worked next door at number 101, the Oliver Hastings house, a rather grand English Regency villa. Their son had been in the employ of Professor Eben Horsford, the noted chemist who lived round the corner on Craigie Street. All quite convenient.

"These houses are so small," Charley said as they rode up on their bikes. "How does anyone fit in?"

"Margaret is very small, and she lives alone."

They had opened the front gate. "I better chain my bike," Charley said. Charley had a bike lock that cost nearly as much as the bike but did guarantee the replacement of the bike if it were stolen. Calista had a junk bike. She had had the same junk bike for fifteen years and could leave it anywhere. Nobody ever dreamed of stealing it. She occasionally treated it to a new pair of tires.

They walked up the brick path and Calista heard the latch of the front door turn. She looked up and saw it open a crack. Margaret's tiny head peeped around. Calista felt a resurgence of the same anger she had experienced during the panel at the children's book conference. The anger caused by an old woman being frightened. It made no sense that this frail, elderly person should be afraid to open wide her door; that she must peer around its edge like a frightened, hunted animal. This was not just ridiculous. It was obscene. She grew madder and madder.

"Oh, Calista, I'm so glad you're here. Oh . . ." She looked startled. "You brought Charley."

Calista had a sinking feeling that Margaret thought it was somehow grossly inappropriate that she had brought along Charley. Well, it was too late, and there was very little she could do about it. When you lived alone with a child, when you were a single parent, there were very few buffers or blinds one could put up. Sooner or later, things, be they feelings or facts, spilled out.

They went into the little house. It might be a prim Quaker lady from the outside, but inside was a different story, more like a velvet-lined jewel box sparkling with old Oriental rugs the color of garnets and walls covered with a marble-green paper. The house swirled with a secret life of its own. A Tiffany lamp, or a darn good copy of one, glowed in shades of celadon and amber in a corner. Windows were lavishly swagged in chintz draperies that were tasseled and had dragon-head tie-back fixtures on the walls. There were stuffed dragons all over the place sent by Margaret's devoted fans of the Knights of Kyre chronicles, which featured dragons prominently throughout all ten volumes. The dragons sprawled across tables covered with fringed tapestries and crawled up the delicately curved legs of a Queen Anne walnut chair. One spread its wings over the top of her fold-out writing desk. Margaret was actually one of those writers who worked at a desk that looked like what an author should be writing on. The desk had the straight lines of a Sheraton piece, and the top that folded out was inset with leather. The back of the desk rose up into a nest of cubbyholes. A small herd of miniature dragons along with some papers peered out of these. There was no word processor in sight. She was the last of a breed of writers.

In addition to the dragons there were cats, real ones stalking about, two or three at least. Calista spotted a Manx and a long-haired something or other curled up on what looked to be a gigantic velvet mushroom with fringe. It was a settee, and Margaret now shooed off the cat so Charley would have a place to sit. "Off! Off, Clicquot." The cat opened one eye and gave her the how-dare-you look that seemed to Calista common to felines and certain maître d's. Margaret hustled over and plucked it off the couch. "We'll have none of that, Clicquot," she admonished in her best Scottish nanny voice.

"Clicquot, that's a funny name," Charley said.

"She's named for Veuve Clicquot because of her beautiful coat. That's a champagne, Charley—Veuve Clicquot, in case you didn't know. Named for a French-woman who was called the widow Clicquot."

"I think I've heard of it. Don't you have some of that, Mom?"

"Yes, it's my favorite champagne," Calista said.

Margaret now raised the cat high up for display and made gurgling noises at it. "Yes, you have what they call a champagne coat." She turned to Charley. "It's a common color to many of this breed. And you have a bubbly personality to match except when you're being sulky like now."

"Is she a widow, too?" It just slipped out. Calista hadn't meant to say it at all.

"Well, if she is, it hasn't slowed her down! Had to have her fixed. I couldn't face another litter."

Thankfully Margaret did not connect the widow reference to La Veuve Jacobs. How self-centered can you be? Calista thought. Why should people always think of her as some archetypal widow? In any case Clicquot the cat was doing better than Calista the human as a widow. One disastrous affair over a ten-day period in the last three and one-half years of widowhood was hardly grounds for getting herself fixed. There was little fear of more litters.

Charley's eyes seemed to be watering up, and it wasn't over her widowhood. Oh, Lord, she thought, he did have allergies, and long-haired cats could trigger them. He began to sneeze.

"Oh, dear! Charley, I bet you're allergic to Clicquot. Many are. Don't worry. Look, Calista, I'm going to take Clicquot into the back. In that pot over there is some Benadryl." She pointed to a chinoiserie cache pot on an urn stand. "I keep them handy for allergic friends. Let me get you a glass of water, and Calista, how 'bout something stronger for us."

"Yes. I think we need it."

When Margaret returned she was carrying a tray with a glass of water and two rather ornately cut crystal decanters. It suddenly struck Calista that with her potions and dragons, her tasseled velvet settees and luxurious cats, her old Orientals and chinoiserie, Margaret's home was not a house so much as a lair of some sort, a lair for a meeting, or would it be a mating . . . between who? Colette and Merlin seemed like the obvious pair. And yet here was Margaret as plain as a bun, so fragile and now so frightened. What a multifaceted person she really was— just like her books. At first glance, or just from the jacket copy, her books might appear to be simple adventures in the land of high fantasy where good is always pitted against evil. And at first glance this house seemed so constrained and correct and positively eighteenth-century New England, giving lie all the time to its interior. But here was Margaret now with her many facets all singularly transfixed into one aspect of fear. She walked stiffly toward Calista, holding out the book, open in her hands to the page. There was something oddly ceremonial about the way she held the book and even in the way she moved. Her lips seemed to tremble with unspoken words, and her eyes, pale blue eyes, faded with age, were wide and fearful. Again Calista felt the surge of anger. Charley got up from the velvet mushroom.

"Weird," he said as he and Calista looked down at the page. It was a full-color plate, and Rothgar was shown engulfed in the mist from the Lake of the Deathless. It was a beautiful painting done by Leo Krell, a marvelous artist who had been illustrating children's books for over forty years. He worked exclusively in oils, and Calista had nothing but admiration for his art. But now with a very fine-nibbed pen a crown of thorns had been drawn in on the head of Rothgar.

"Now look at this." Margaret's voice was low and dusty. She turned several pages to the next color plate. It was a picture of Rothgar on the Plain of Crystal Doom. He was not wearing his armor, but it lay in shards along with his sword, for that indeed was the fate of one who traversed the Plain of Crystal Doom. Things shattered, except for Rothgar. All his worldly possessions had shattered, but if he could repeat the incantation of the Good Wizard of Mor, there was a chance for his body. No chances here. The seven wounds of Christ had been meticulously drawn in. No ragged wounds, just neat little slits from which blood spurted, precise little teardrop-shaped spurts.

"Oh, how awful," whispered Calista. And then she looked to the immediate foreground of the picture. One of the crevices of the plain that Leo had so meticulously rendered had been painted in red so that it absolutely gushed with blood. Calista looked up at Margaret and tapped the crevice with her index finger. "Too much blood. Too much for those wounds."

"Like Norman!"

"Yes, like Norman!" Calista repeated.

10

"Yoo-hoo!" The cheerful greeting split the air and seemed to reverberate through the room with its warmth.

"Oh, goodness, it's Mammy. How comforting!" Margaret sighed.

"Mammy?" Charley wondered aloud.

"Oh, Calista, dear, do explain to Charley about Mammy, and now that she's here please both of you stay for dinner. She cooks so much better than I do." Margaret turned to go to the kitchen and then turned back. "Let me have the book a minute. I want to show Mammy this gruesome business. She might have some insights." She then scurried out to the kitchen.

What there was to explain about Mammy was that in liberal Cambridge Margaret McGowan had been blessed with a black housekeeper who had the unfortunate name of Mammy. It was not a name given to her by the descendants of some antebellum family from Peach Tree Street in Atlanta, Georgia. It was given to her by her own parents when she was born in Antigua and was a truncation of Mamita. Mammy was pushing eighty and had worked for over sixty years in Cambridge homes. Each family had tried unsuccessfully to change her name. But she was adamant. She preferred Mammy to Mamita. Some people nearly gagged saying Mammy. But she insisted. "Do I look like Aunt Jemima? Am I fat? Do I wear a kerchief and have those big shiny teeth? As Shakespeare said, what's in a name? I like Mammy. I hate Mamita. It sounds like some kind of fruit, and I don't mean one of your pansy boys. I mean a big, juicy, sweet fruit that grows on a tree, hanging there all ripe till it drops and rots. Nobody's going to call me Mamita!" She had to say all this to one old liberal, a retired editor of *The New Republic.* He stood there clenching his pipe between his teeth and rubbing the suede patches on his houndstooth jacket as he observed the stocky but trim figure that stood in front of him in the Pierre Cardin warm-up suit and New Balance running shoes. This was Mammy's work uniform. Now she worked exclusively for Margaret as a housekeeper–copy editor. She was Margaret's first reader. She told Margaret if it sounded right and when she had gone too far, and she got rid of the excess commas. Margaret was promiscuous in her use of commas. Mammy was also a better speller than Margaret. She couldn't type, though. She therefore kept the commas down to a minimum and kept the plush velvet cushions plumped up and the Jensen silver polished, or, as she put it, she "fussed with all that clutter" that Margaret kept around. When the dragons got dirty she washed them in Woolite or sent them to the cleaners. She mixed up her own potions of vinegar and baking soda to keep the Tiffany lamp sparkling and the woodwork gleaming. She even functioned as something of a secretary for Margaret, organizing her fan mail, although Margaret was careful to answer each one herself.

"Well, that beats all!" Mammy said, bustling into the living room. "Howdy, Calista. This your fine son?" She was wearing little golf socks and had apparently left her shoes in the kitchen.

"Yes, Mammy. Charley, this is Mammy. Mammy, this is Charley."

"You folks stay for dinner. I fixed a nice pot roast for Margy. There's plenty. You hit a good night to come. I'm cooking. None of that awful English food she likes to cook."

"Well, Mammy, I'm afraid there is a pudding, a milk custard, in the refrigerator for dessert." She looked at Charley rather dolefully. "It's hard being British."

"Well, we'll put some rum on it and jazz it up a little,"

Mammy said, and then paused. "Calista, you like rum, don't you? What are you doing drinking that Scotch for?"

"Oh, I'm sorry, Calista. I didn't even know we had any rum in the house," Margaret apologized.

"You don't know what you've got in this house, lady. Let me go fetch that gal some rum. You take it with soda, don't you, Calista?" Calista nodded.

The pot roast was good, and Mammy had joined them.

"Well, what do you think we should do about this?" Margaret said, gesturing at both books that rested on a nearby Welsh sideboard. "We should report it, don't you think?"

"Who to?" Charley asked.

"The Boston Police Department, those detectives we met. I guess," Calista said. "And I suppose we should tell Janet and the folks at Thayer."

"Yes. I suppose so." Margaret nodded.

"Charley," Calista said, looking at him. "You look doubtful of this strategy."

"I'm not doubtful, exactly. I'm just not that convinced about the Boston Police Department. I mean, you tried to call that cop, or detective, the other day, didn't you, Mom? To find out how the investigation was going, and he never called you back. You called a couple of times."

"Yes, but they were probably just really busy."

"Well," said Margaret. "They didn't appear, either one of those fellows, to be mental giants to me."

"The New York Police Department must be plenty smart. They tracked that Son of Sam killer through parking tickets and their computer," Mammy offered. "They must be plenty smart."

"They did?" Charley asked with sudden interest. "That's how they did it? Tracked him down through a computer?"

"They sure did, honey," Mammy answered.

"They were probably just working within their Unix if it was parking tickets. Probably didn't even have to download from a mainframe for that," Charley reflected.

The three women looked bewildered.

"What's he talking about?" Margaret asked.

"Uh . . ." Calista hesitated. Damn, why did Mammy have to mention the Son of Sam and the computer thing? That awful feeling was coming back to her, the same that had clutched at her gut two years before when she and Charley had first begun to have suspicions that Tom's death had not been an accident, but something more. They were those same feelings, instincts, really, that at that time had warned her this was not for children. That she should put a damper on it right away. But there was no way of dampening Charley in these instances. She had learned that. "Oh," she said, turning to Margaret and Mammy and trying to sound light. "Computer jargon, you know."

"Oh, well, then count me out," Margaret said. "I know nothing about the beasts."

"Me neither," Mammy added.

But not Charley, Calista thought. Count him in. She could tell by that strangely opaque look in his eyes—he was off and running, every brain cell and neuron firing. If things hadn't seemed to fit for Charley, they still might not, but now he saw a way of possibly making them fit or getting the missing pieces. And after all, computers could talk to one another when people didn't or refused to do so. If the Boston Police Department refused to return their calls, Charley had at his disposal other means of contacting them. The chips were never down! There was a whole world of electronic communication that could bypass such inconveniences as not having calls answered.

11

"How're you doing with the Benadryl?" Calista said as they wheeled their bikes down Margaret's path. "You think you can operate the heavy machinery of this bike?"

"No problem," Charley answered.

It had gotten cold, and a wet wind blew in from the northeast. "I don't believe this!" Calista called out as they were cutting across the Common on their bikes. A large wet snowflake had landed on her nose. "I mean, this really is awful, you know it!" The flakes were falling lazily through the Cambridge night.

By the time they got back to James Place it was snowing hard. They put their bikes in the garage and came up onto their front entry porch. Calista looked around nervously, half anticipating another book or little surprise. She felt a chill run down her spine that was not from the weather. She shook it off. Damn these people! They went in the house. She peered into her study cautiously.

"Is it all okay?" Charley's voice made her jump.

"Yeah, it's fine." God, she hated this. Why should he have to see her scared? This was all so wrong. She suddenly felt unbearably sorry for them both. They had been through so much, she and Charley. Why this now? Why did fear spread itself through their house, their little world, like some poison gas? She felt her anger welling up again.

Ten minutes later she climbed up the ladder of Charley's bunk bed to kiss him good night.

"Do me a favor, sweet pea."

"What's that?" he said, turning over on his side to face her and propping himself up on one elbow.

"Cool it on this business."

"Yeah, well, okay. But will you try to reach those cops again?"

"Sure."

She wasn't even sure what either of them meant by "cooling it." She looked at him again. The eyes were clear. He knew that she knew that he was hot. But she still wasn't exactly sure what she meant by "cooling it." Such was the state of being a parent. Uncertainty grew as knowledge grew. Rather like surface-to-volume ratios of one to three. The volume of what you didn't know was the cube of what you did know. Or what you didn't know expanded three times faster than what you did know. Differential scaling. She studied Charley's face. That gentle curve of his cheek was gone now, vanished into the new emerging face. It still had that sweet vulnerability, but there was something else there now, something a little less innocent. She had drawn that face so many times. It had crept into so much of her work when there were young children to portray. It didn't matter whether the characters were boys or girls. They could sometimes even be animals, but there was so often a Charley-ness about them, something so quintessentially Charley. The essence now had not changed, but the contours and the light in the eyes had changed in some infinitely subtle and elusive way. She couldn't use it for young children anymore. Will Scarlet, perhaps?

The telephone rang just as she was walking out of Charley's room. It was Vicki. "Cal, I figured out how that book got in your study."

"How?"

"Well, you know, it's been bothering me all day. I just couldn't make sense out of it." Calista wished that Vicki would get to the point, but this was Vicki. She always had to give you in addition to the facts a certain emotional content. She could make a narrative out of anything. Calista was patient as Vicki continued. "So I said to myself . . . something funny did happen today, but I'd been wrestling with that rotten discolored tile in the corner of the kitchen, and you know I think sometimes the fumes get to me."

"I told you, Vicki, forget that stain. I don't want you passing out over a bucket of Clorox."

"Well, in any case, the doorbell rang, and it was the man to read the gas meter. So I just let him in and pointed him toward the basement. And you know how that is, they just kind of waltz in and waltz out. I heard the door slam a couple of minutes later."

"So you think it was the gas man?"

"Well, this is it . . . I say to myself, Gee, that's funny—wasn't that gas man here just last week? Or was that over at the Benchleys? You know, you work all these houses, you get a little mixed up about these things, and I got the Mr. Clean fumes and the Clorox. But he had a uniform and all that."

"It's got to be the gas man."

"Actually, now that I think about it, he had some sort of parka on and then a billed cap that said Gas Company or whatever on it—just the cap, you know."

"That ought to be easy to get," Calista said.

"But I don't understand, Calista, why would anybody, a gas man or not, want to do this?"

"I don't know."

"Well, I just thought I should call and let you know."

"Oh, I'm glad you did. At least it wasn't a break-in exactly."

"No, you won't have to go and get all the locks changed."

"Right. Well, thanks for calling."

"Try and have a good night's sleep, dear. And I'll see you the day after tomorrow."

"Yes."

It was not a break-in, yet she had never felt so violated, and the fact that she didn't have to get the locks changed was of little solace to her. The person, whoever he was, had penetrated into the heart of her home and taken a swift, precise stab into the center of her imagination through this wanton attack on her work. It was totally unnerving. She was exhausted from it all, and now she was more than ready for bed and for sleep.

The night was not really black but seemed slightly bleached by the swirling snow. And she sensed that sleep, the nice, dark, comforting numbness of sleep, was going to escape her. Lethe and Nepenthe, those muses of the night, were not on call. She tried hot milk and then resorted to half of a Halcion tablet. It would not be the smooth black silk sleep that came without the pills. No, that sleep was only delivered unaided by those Greek muses that Calista fully believed resided somewhere in the brain, not perhaps the most primitive part, the limbic region up front, but still somewhere within a relatively old and venerable region. Calista tended to think of those early regions of the brain, the ones associated with primitive behavior, as venerable. Of course they were not as complex or beefed up as the other parts that dealt with rapid manipulations of great megabytes of information. Still, they did have their charms. One of these charms was the little miniature Greek muses she imagined floating about through the cortical chambers and convolutions of her midbrain. Forget that these so-called primitive brains didn't know Greeks from crocodiles. Forget the fact that this part of the brain structure evolved long before there were Greeks. There was the capacity somewhere midbrain, in the neocortex—which, when it was functioning up to snuff, did not need to be jogged by chemicals and would release the little muses quietly, no fuss, no muss—to spread the balm of sleep.

Not tonight. Calista's chemically induced sleep was fractured by fragments of dreams and images. She, indeed, felt as if she were stretched across the Plain of Crystal Doom. Nothing seemed quite whole but lay like shards of glass, ragged and sharp, in a penumbra of restless sleep, sleep that was not quite dark enough. She saw Rothgar with his crown of thorns slipped jauntily over one eye and the awful wounds spurting *vert de flambé!* The Limburgs' old color. But too much blood! Too much blood! The fissures of the plain roiled with the blood, and Charley was picking his way through the debris and wading through the bloody streams. She woke herself up. This was ridiculous. Wrestling with colors all day and all night long. She got up and washed her face.

She would fall back to sleep, she knew it. She always did after she had taken a Halcion. What a dumb name for a drug that did this to you. It was still snowing. Oh, Lord, it would probably be a snow day and school would be canceled. Only in Massachusetts did they cancel school in April. She didn't understand it. What the hell did they do in Alaska, for Christ's sake? There had to be something between mushing huskies and the antiquated snow removal systems they had in Boston and Cambridge. Last year they had gone over the snow removal budget. Run out of money for salt or some dumb thing. They never canceled school when she was a kid out in Indiana. There was no such thing as a snow emergency. Pshaw! Snow, that's nothing. The major emergency that they anticipated back in those days was a nuclear attack! You got under your desk and covered your ears. It was the era of bomb shelter parties. People went off gaily popping corks into the face of destruction. Spit in its eye! It was the last ragged mile of an old frontier and just before the beginning of Jack Kennedy's New Frontier. Not only were there no snow emergencies, for Christ's sake, there were not even wind chill factors. People were just plain cold, and the temperature figures were given straight. It was that time long ago when spaghetti was not yet pasta and who knew, or cared, how cold it was with the wind blowing. You just went out and froze your ass. Charley had refused to go skating one evening in January at the Cambridge Skating Club when he heard that the wind chill brought the temperature down to minus 35. What had happened? Strong midwestern-Russian-Jewish stock diluted! Chicken soup and Wheaties, the occasional Heath bar, that's all it used to take. None of this pasta crap and talking wind chill factors.

Her mind was in the full lather of internal dialogue. Getting back to sleep might not be so easy. The branches on the dogwood tree outside her bedroom window were laden with snow. The thing was supposed to bloom in another three weeks. It always bloomed the first week in May. All through April you could watch the buds swell up, like engorged nipples, the same color, too, a deep, dusky red. And then they opened. For the first eight days the blossoms were the color of new potatoes. They lightened each day until they were the most delicate shade of pink. People came and took pictures of the tree during the spring. It fanned out in all of its russet-and-pink glory and covered the entire front of the house. The house appeared like a pointillist's painting through the dogwood, for the blossoms hung like a screen of pink lace. Behind this screen the mass of the dark-brown-shingled house broke up into shadowy fragments. She knew those blossoms up close, too, from her bedroom window. She knew their shape, their complicated interiors, striated with even subtler colors. She was an intimate of the swift, tough beauty of their unfolding petals. But what would happen to them now in the middle of this northeaster, what would happen to dogwood time with the heavy wet snow? Branches might break. Calista yawned. The chemical Lethe and Nepenthe were beginning to ensnare her again. This was what was wrong, of course. She felt listless and heavy-limbed herself in the face of the snow-laden limbs of her dear tree. She tried to visualize the splay of the four petals of the blossom. They could be quite perfect in their symmetry and even demonstrate what physicists called spin, a property in which a subatomic particle either maintains or does not maintain its same appearance through a complete revolution. Calista remembered hearing how the blossoms were used in Easter services as metaphors for the crucifixion with their four nail holes, one at each tip. Oh, dear! She thought of those terrible wounds again, so meticulously drawn onto the color plates of Margaret's book. And who could those horrible people be, or person, to do such a thing, to wreck books and disfigure characters in such a way? She drifted off again.

She awoke with a start. It wasn't a bad dream, at least not one she could remember. And yet there was the same kind of feeling as after a nightmare. Then she remembered. It was not a dream at all. It was something about those tulips. Of course, the Little Red Riding Hood ones. They must be frozen stiff! How could she lie there and think about tulips expiring under the icy glaze of this storm? A rescue mission was called for.

But did she really want to go out into her backyard at two o'clock in the morning? What if? She stopped the thought. But it wouldn't stop, of course. Here she had been planning, before Vicki had called about the gas man coming to read the meter, to call the locksmith tomorrow to change all her locks and now she was contemplating walking out alone into her own backyard at two in the morning. Forget the fact that there was an icy northeaster blowing. It wasn't weather that was bothering her. Then she got mad and sat bolt upright. Shit! She would not let her life be ruled by fear. This was what she resented the most. She would not become a prisoner in her own house. She would not be scared to go into her own backyard. Anger was the best palliative for fear. She got up, pulled on her long underwear under her flannel nightgown. She headed downstairs and put on her heavy wool Red Riding Hood cape. It was the easiest thing to wear over a nightgown. She then pulled on the old Muk Luks that Tom had brought her from Alaska, grabbed a pair of scissors and a basket, and stomped out the back door.

It had stopped snowing and there was an unearthly stillness. Everything was sheathed in heavy snow. The very air seemed not so much bleached now as suffused with an almost spectral light. It was weird. Was she stupid or what coming out here in the middle of the night of the same day she had received that defaced book?

But suppose the sick person who had delivered these

books had wanted to enjoy Calista's shock and terror? Suppose he was out here in the bushes waiting for her to come out on this sleep-fractured night? She peered out from around the edge of her hood and began to tremble. Now hold it right there! she ordered herself. No person, no matter how sick or insane, would expect insomnia to drive someone out for a turn in his own backyard on a night like this. Her anger returned and like a vengeful catharsis swept every particle of fear from her. She was pissed! So pissed. Pissed for her sake and for Margaret's. That a decent law-abiding citizen like herself had to be scared out of her own yard! She stomped off in the direction of the tulips. The new bags of peat moss and mulch that she had just had delivered wore blankets of snow; the wheelbarrow lay turned on its side, under its wheels a glaze of ice, and Charley had not put the trash cans in the shed after taking out the garbage. She must get some of these yews pruned back, not to mention the hemlock hedge. She was making this mental list of yard chores as she rounded the bend and gasped.

Something was bleeding! That was her first thought. Like immense globules of blood the tulips swayed in the wind against the snow. The image exploded in front of her eyes. For one dreadful moment the engorged blossoms seemed to be spurting into the white night. She was breathing hard. This was crazy. She had to get these images of blood out of her head. She took out her scissors and began to cut. She could not help remembering the bloody scrawl on the hotel wall. She tried with every atom of her being to will herself to be calm, to concentrate. You cannot have your life hamstrung like this. You cannot allow these devastating inroads to cut into your psyche. You cannot! You cannot! The words puffed in her mind in a total inversion of the message of the little engine that could.

As she was bending over, intent on her work, she felt something. There in the garden, a presence. Within the shadow of her hood she turned her head slowly to the left, toward a large rock that marked the beginning of the stepping-stone path—the rock that looked like the sleeping cat—and now she covered her mouth in horror. The scream froze in her throat. Perched atop the sleeping rock cat was Owl, grinning luridly at her, his mouth a bright red gash. The scream wouldn't come. But something drew her toward him. She felt this inexorable pull. The horrible face frozen in a peculiar grimace beckoned her. Clutching the tulips she slowly walked across the small patch of icy grass, in a daze, mesmerized by the stuffed animal's disfigured face, drawn into its hideousness. The owl's terror hung like a shriek in the frozen night and the little button eyes gleamed so blackly, watching her so carefully.

She could smell a familiar smell. It was the smell of paint. For some reason this comforted her. She must touch it. There was no way she could not. But fear lay coiled in her stomach as she put the tulips in the basket on her arm and picked up the stuffed animal. His head had been slashed and some stuffing exploded from one side. Her hood fell back as she stared at it, transfixed by the little owl's suddenly ghoulish face.

Close up the face did not look so ghoulish as much as pathetically disfigured. She examined it with a mixture of horror and sympathy that one might experience when seeing a facially deformed or scarred child. She could feel the wet cold on her face. Who could have done this?

As the rest of the neighborhood slept through its own frozen, untroubled night, Calista stood in her backyard at two-thirty in the morning with the mauled stuffed animal in the crook of her left arm. There was something out here. It had already come into her house once. It had defaced her book, and now it had disfigured the little owl. It moved closer and closer, becoming less and less abstract with each advance. It was striking at her imaginary children now, but would it . . . She could not complete the thought. She raced into the house, up the stairs, and climbed the ladder to Charley's top bunk. He slept peacefully. She brushed the hair off his forehead and kissed him. He stirred slightly.

By the time she returned to her own bedroom the weird light of the night was beginning to dissolve into the thin, pale light of the dawn. The sky, which for days had looked like the marbled endpapers of a book, broke clear and fragile. She loved the frailty of this early dawn light. It washed into the bedroom.

Calista sat down now in a rocking chair near her bedroom window. The last stars still hung dimly in the dawn sky, which was now the color of eggshells. It was as if these last stars were shining through the eggshells from the far side. She watched them now wink out, one by one. She tried hard not to think about the mutilated stuffed animal. She was wondering how she would tell Charley about this latest development. There would certainly be no cooling it for him now. She should at least try to get in touch with the police before he woke up. She should give a semblance of being in control, being the director of things. After all, she was the parent in this twosome.

Toward six o'clock she called the snow link number for the Cambridge Public Schools. Sure enough, school was canceled. She went in to run a bath and turned on the switch so she could hear the start-up of Morning Pro Musica. The first five minutes of air time of the program were devoted to the sounds of birds tweeting. As Calista sank into the deep claw-footed tub, the tweets swirled around her. She poured in some bath salts and then rested her head on the bath pillow that was hooked onto the rim of the tub. She lolled in the tub, thinking with a washcloth draped over her face. She would have to call the cops this morning—while Charley was there. It did not thrill her to have to make the call with her son hanging right over her shoulder. But she had little choice. Damn the Cambridge Public Schools and their snow emergencies. And if she couldn't reach the cops? What then? How long would he cool it? What could he really do, though? He had a modem. She supposed he could use it to get into crime files or parking ticket files. The birds had finished, and the music of Francis Poulenc's piano concerto filled the steamy bathroom. Oh, God, if she could just spend all day in this warm tub listening to music. She sprinkled some more Vitiver in the tub, resoaked the washcloth, draped it over her face again, and tried to figure out how worried she should be about Charley. Was he vulnerable? Would he make himself more vulnerable by starting to poke around electronically?

There had been a time just after Tom had been murdered when Calista was really worried that Charley showed all the indications of becoming a classic nerd in the true MIT sense of the word. For what better way was there for a young kid who had just lost his father and who had trouble dealing with emotional issues than to lose himself in that strange, weird world of the computer? That world at its worst became an isolationist one conducive to setting up walls and erecting barriers between an individual, a hacker, and the rest of the real world. All the confrontations were controllable. There was logic and there was certainty and there was the pleasure of manipulating a powerful machine. Calista could see Charley being sucked deeper and deeper into the quicksand of this isolation in those months after Tom's death. It was terribly frightening to her. And although she had very little faith in psychiatrists, she had sought out one to figure out how to deal with it. The woman was helpful and gave Calista some good suggestions. Charley seemed to have gotten over the hump. His interest and prowess in skateboarding had perhaps helped as much as anything. He was not particularly good at team sports, but he had an undeniable skill and grace with the skateboard. And that was also why she was so pleased that he had enjoyed *City Step*. Not liking one's body, feeling physically inferior, was unfortunately part of the nerd syndrome. Only at MIT would they have something called the Ugliest Man on Campus Contest. But she was fairly sure that in Charley's case of incipient nerdhood, his low self-esteem in terms of body image had been a passing phase, a kind of window of vulnerability during a very stressful and vulnerable time in his life. Besides, he was, if nothing else, just too good-looking these days. He had grown rangy, and there was a hint of real muscle. His hair, once an impossibly curly, bordering on kinky, mop of red, had calmed down. He now used the blow dryer regularly and went through a can of mousse every two months. Any kid who used that much mousse was a pretty poor candidate for nerddom. Of this Calista was convinced.

For now, Charley mostly used his modem for sending E-mail through the network to his various user friends, or whatever they called these network pen pals. They gossiped. They played games. They bragged. Charley said that bragging was the downfall of crackers. Crackers were evil hackers. Charley was careful to make this distinction. Hacking was something you just did for fun. It wasn't illegal and didn't make the kind of trouble that caused big-buck problems like viruses that got into defense-system mainframes. But they all bragged— hackers and crackers alike. They bragged about writing programs that could solve the Towers of Hanoi puzzle, or they bragged about getting into the TRW computer that controls all credit references. Charley mostly logged in to the recreation groups that had to do with games and skateboarding. If you had questions, you could post them and receive answers through your E-mail mailing list program.

Just a few short years after Calista and Tom had had the birds-and-the-bees talk with Charley, they had to have the hacker or cracker talk. Charley had, when he was nine, engaged in his first, and as far as Calista knew last, computer criminal act. He had managed to put himself on the subscription list for a *Dungeons and Dragons* magazine, a magazine that his parents had thought was too expensive to buy. It was the electronic equivalent of the kind of shoplifting young children sometimes do when they just want to see what it feels like to steal. Tom and Calista had made him send back a note of apology and confess to having hacked into the subscription files. He was grounded, his allowance suspended for two months, and he was made to do extra chores around the house. But it wasn't anything as bloodless as computer crime that was now occupying her thoughts, and if Charley started poking around, how long would it be before that computer started spurting blood?

No, he just had to cool it. This was for her to handle through the proper channels. She flipped up the drain and felt the water sucking out around her toes.

She got dressed in her favorite cold-weather outfit, a Cal Tech sweat suit, and went downstairs to make breakfast. Charley slept like a log, and that would be her salvation. He never woke up on his own before nine. She always had to get him up on school mornings. If the Boston Police Department woke up before Charley, it would be nice. She called them at seven, but Lieutenant McCafferty was not in yet. She left her name and number. She called at seven forty-five. He'd been in but was out again. "Thanks for returning my call," she muttered. She didn't exactly know how to proceed. The thing with the stuffed animal and the book's defacement had happened in Cambridge, so theoretically she could call up the Cambridge cops. But what would they say to someone calling up and reporting a stuffed animal smeared with paint and diapers drawn on a boy in a book? And it wasn't the Cambridge Police Department's business. It was the Boston Cops' bailiwick because it was all related to the murder of Petrakis. Someone was trying to scare her and scare her good. But why? Why scare her and Margaret?

She turned on the "Today" show and made herself another cup of coffee. There was a most attractive man being interviewed by Jane Pauley. Gads, he was attractive! But what in the hell was he talking about—the Vatican as a dysfunctional family? Oh, dear! Jane was addressing him as "Father." Of course. Calista had seen his book in the window of the Harvard Coop. What was his name? Father something or other, a Dominican or Jesuit who had been silenced by the Vatican. Oh, maybe he'd get defrocked! One could always hope.

The next person on after Father Whoever was Betty Furness. Calista switched the channel. Oh, no! She knew what this was already. Somehow she just sensed it. It was a local show, and this morning they were calling in about sex. They seemed to do that topic at least once a week. What was the angle today? Sex fantasy. Great. The visiting expert was quoting something from Masters and Johnson about men wanting more, more sex, more than one woman at a time—that was one of their big fantasies. He quoted some statistic. They then took a commercial break. Was this planned or what? A voice came on singing, "You've got to give more! 'Cause you're a mom!" It showed a mom beaming as she served her child a sandwich. "You got to give one hundred percent 'cause you're a mom. So buy Twain's Bread."

"Oh, for heaven's sake!" muttered Calista. "A little guilt in the morning for Mommy, Mommy who hasn't made enough love for Daddy, that insatiable satyr! What kind of number are you doing on us?" Calista often talked to machines. Televisions, washing machines that didn't behave, hairdryers that overheated. She had once stood in a gas station and yelled at a talking Coke machine. Charley had said it was the most embarrassing moment of his life. "Dear me! Dear me!" she now muttered as the sex experts came back on. And to think that she had the simple fantasy of one man and she'd long ago given up on Charley eating whole-wheat bread. By God, she wasn't going to feel guilty about that! She picked up the phone to try the police department again.

"Lieutenant McCafferty, please . . . He's not in? That's what you tell me every time I call. Look, I would really like to talk to him. It's in regard to the Petrakis murder case. This is Calista Jacobs. Lieutenant McCafferty and the other man, yes, Detective Stevens, that was his name, interviewed me extensively after the murder. Now I have left numerous messages for them to call, and no one returns my calls, and . . ." She hesitated. She didn't want to tell all about the books and the stuffed animal on the phone to this secretary. "Well, there's been some new and unsettling, uh . . ." She searched for a word—"developments," that was it. That might excite them into thinking something was breaking. "Developments," she continued, "and I would really like to talk to them about it . . . No . . . no, I don't want to talk to you about it. No offense, but really I think it's most appropriate that I speak directly with Lieutenant McCafferty or Detective Stevens . . . Yes . . . yes . . . Okay. Goodbye."

"No dice, huh?"

Calista wheeled around. It was Charley, barefoot and yawning in his striped pajamas.

"Charley, how long have you been up?"

"Not long. I heard you when I was coming through the pantry. So you're not getting anyplace with the police department?"

"No, I guess you can say that." Calista sank down in her chair. She would have to tell him. "Charley . . ." She inhaled sharply.

"What?" The sleepiness had vanished instantly from his eyes.

"Something happened last night," she said. She tried to keep her voice steady.

"What?" He leaned forward across the table where he had just sat down. Calista got up and walked to a broom closet where she had put the plastic bag with the stuffed owl.

"I found Owl"—she paused—"on the cat rock in the garden," she said, taking out the stuffed figure. The paint smell rose from the bag. Owl didn't look quite as lurid in the morning light. The markings on his face seemed more like the scribbling of a child. But a shocked gray look crept across Charley's face.

"Owl was out there in the backyard."

"Yep."

Charley swallowed hard.

"I don't want you to get too frightened, Charley. I've thought about it, and I think people who do stuff like this, well, it's kind of like obscene telephone calls. This is the extent of their kicks. They don't act out any further. It's just sort of a perverse pleasure in scaring."

"But they have acted out further. They've murdered Petrakis."

"I bet it's not the same person." She said this so firmly

83

that it surprised even her. But she felt an acute edge of truth in this statement. She would bet that it was not the same person. Different strokes for this different folks. It might all be related, but one was a compulsive graffitist and the other was a murderer, both perhaps sides of the same coin, part of a currency she did not understand as yet.

"But what's really bugging me is that I can't get hold of the cops, those two detectives who interviewed Margaret and me downtown. It's hard to just call up and say, Hey, someone marked up my book and wrecked my stuffed animal. I got to get hold of those two guys. I just don't think they're paying much attention to this murder. You read about so many of these murders. They're on the front page for one day, and then what happens? Just another statistic."

"Petrakis didn't even make it to the front page."

"I know, and I just hate to think of him becoming another statistic, another unsolved crime on the roster." She sipped some of her coffee, which by now was lukewarm.

"You really feel that way, Mom?"

"Well, of course I do . . . but wait, Charley . . ." She started to hold up her hand in a cautionary gesture.

"Don't worry, Mom. Let me just try one thing, right here."

"What?" she asked cautiously.

"The police department must have a public relations office, right?"

"I suppose so. Public information or something like that."

"Okay, what's the number you've been calling?"

"Here." She pushed a piece of paper toward him. "What are you going to do?"

"It's nothing bad. It's nothing illegal."

"I should hope not."

"I just want to find out what kind of hardware they use."

"What do you mean, hardware? They use guns and nightsticks."

"Not that kind of hardware, Mom. What kind of computers. And what their operating system is."

"Well, okay. Let me get you a robe, though. You make me feel cold just to look at you, and what do you want for breakfast?"

"Uh . . . I don't know. You decide." He was already dialing. When she came downstairs again, he was just hanging up. "They gave me another number to call."

By the time Calista had sliced an orange for him, toasted him a bagel, and scrambled two eggs, he had called two more numbers and was in the middle of another call. "Well, I'm just a junior high student in Boston, and I'm supposed to do a report on computers in law enforcement, and all I want to know is the name of your computer and the operating system. Yeah, but if I write a letter and by the time that office gives clearance, it'll be beyond the deadline for my assignment, and couldn't you just please tell me . . ." He waited expectantly. "Okay," he said, and hung up the phone.

"No dice?" Calista asked.

"No dice." He did not seem all that disturbed. "You see how awful it is, Mom? I mean, here we are, two law-abiding citizens, just trying to get some information on a violent crime, the victim was our friend. Well, not exactly our friend, but certainly your friend, and they won't return your calls, and they won't tell me anything. And you and Margaret get these weird books, and they aren't even there to report it to."

He was working up to something. She could tell. "I think that's just the way it goes, Charley."

"What are you going to do about it?" He had a way of absolutely skewing her with the luminous gray light from his eyes when he was asking her one of his "no exit" questions. And this was definitely one of them.

"Well," she began cautiously, stalling like an ill-prepared student in a recitation. "I think we take this one step at a time." It even sounded like bullshit to her.

"What do you mean by that?"

"I suppose I should next call Janet Weiss or, better, Ethan Thayer, and see if he's had any feedback from the detectives, and I guess also tell him about this"—she hesitated—"latest development." At that moment the phone rang. Calista jumped for it. "Oh, hi, Matthew . . . Yes, isn't this nice, a snow day in April . . . Yes, just what every mother wants. Okay, here's Charley." She handed the phone to Charley. "Why don't you guys plan something for this morning, and then I'll take you both to lunch at Elsie's."

Charley took the phone. "Mom's bribing us. She said she'll take us both to lunch at Elsie's if we plan some wonderful educational activity for this morning that will make us better citizens of the world."

"I said no such thing, Charley!" Calista protested.

"She said no such thing. She just wants us out of her hair until lunch . . . Okay. Yeah, bring that program. See you." He hung up.

"He's coming here?"

"Yep."

"What's he bringing with him?"

"Oh, this cool modeling program."

"Modeling?"

"Yeah, didn't I tell you about our ideas for doing this thing for the Martin Institute?"

"Oh, my God, Charley!" Calista slapped her forehead. "I forgot that yesterday was your first day over there. I never even asked you about it with all the commotion over the books and going to Margaret's. Damn! This is what makes me so mad about all this! It's so disruptive to the real stuff, the good stuff of life and the things we should be focused on and attending to."

Charley didn't answer. He just looked at her calmly with the no-exit light in his gray eyes. "So is it neat over there?"

"You mean at the Martin Institute?"

"Yes. What did you do? Are you in a lab or what? I hope you're not in the AIDS lab."

"No, don't be silly, Mom. They're not going to put kids in the AIDS lab."

"Well, where are you? What are you doing?"

"I'm in a guy's lab named Leventhal."

"Leventhal, I've heard of him. He's a big honcho in cancer research."

"Yeah, I know. I think he's the biggest according to Matthew's dad. He might even get a Nobel Prize for his work with the oncogene—see, I learned a new word on my first day."

"It's the cancer gene, right?"

"Tumor-producing genes, altered genes. When they're normal they do things like make scabs."

"Oh, Charley, that's so good. Look how much you've learned already. I think this program is wonderful. What do you have to do?"

"Not much." He made a face. "Basically Matthew and I and this other kid, Louise, she's from another school, we just have to look at all these protein bases that make up the chains of amino acids."

"You mean you look at them through a microscope?"

"No. No, I don't even know how to look through one of those electron microscopes anyway. No, you look at them through computers."

"Through computers?" She was definitely confused, but she also felt something of a letdown. She had hoped that maybe Charley would get away just a little bit from computers at the Martin Institute. She had had visions of him bending over test tubes and Bunsen burners. "How in the hell do they look at DNA or whatever through computers?"

"They have these X-ray photographs of genetic materials called autoradiographs, and they can use nuclear trace stuff and do experiments so they can figure out what the protein bases are. And they get thousands, maybe millions of sequences, and they make up into one of twenty amino acids. I don't quite understand it all."

"Just *quite?*" Calista opened her eyes wide. "I couldn't understand any of it."

"Well, I understand the fact that there are these four very fundamental bases in DNA and RNA called uracil, cytosine, and two others I can't remember, and when they link up into three they are called codons. And that these make up the twenty amino acids, which are the bases of proteins."

"What do you have to actually do?"

"I told you. I just look at the data from the autoradiographs and the other ways that they've tried to blow apart these proteins, and I look at these long chains of amino acids called peptides and I try to find stuff that might make a pattern, you know, correlations. They got the data for fifty or sixty of what they are calling the solved proteins. So we're supposed to look at those and become familiar with their sequences and then go and look at this other stuff. It's kind of boring, but I guess I'm learning a lot about DNA and all that stuff."

"I'll say. I mean, you're way ahead of me in one day, and I had two semesters of biology in college."

"You did?" Charley looked surprised.

"Yes. Don't rub it in."

"Ah, don't worry. They probably hadn't discovered any of this stuff back then."

"Ah, yes, back then at the dawn of the Pleistocene."

"You're very sensitive about your age, ever since you turned forty, which you have been for over a year now. I thought you'd get used to it."

"Funny about that. I'll probably be fifty before I'm used to being forty."

"I'm used to thirteen. I'm ready for fourteen, even fifteen. Definitely sixteen!"

"Don't rush it. So what is the program that Matthew is bringing over?"

"It's a modeling program that his dad got hold of. It's for molecular modeling. See, Matthew and I think we can relieve the boredom of this job if we can talk them into letting us build some models on the computer of these protein base arrangements. And then we're going to figure out how to do some really sensational graphics of all the patterns we do find or the known ones. You know, three-D stuff in color. It is so boring looking at all these gray, white, and black pictures. The Martin Institute is not into splashy graphics at all."

"Well, that sounds terribly educational and will certainly make you better citizens of the world." Calista winked.

And Charley smiled. He resisted the strong urge to wink himself.

12

"Well, it's not really illegal in the same way that the subscription to *Dungeons and Dragons* magazine was. I mean, you're not really stealing in this case."

Charley winced as he remembered that rather shameful incident. "I mean, you're not ripping anyone off," Matthew continued.

"Of course I'm not ripping anybody off. I'm not stealing, I wouldn't be hurting anything or anybody. I'd just be eavesdropping. I wouldn't disturb the files at all. It's nothing like Murray Kaploff."

"Who's Murray Kaploff?"

"A son of some friends of my mom's and dad's, and he wrote a virus and it got into the NASA mainframe and cost the taxpayers ten million dollars."

"Well, this is nothing. At worst it could be considered a violation of confidentiality."

"These guys aren't doctors. They're the Boston Police Department, and if anybody's their patient, it's Mom and her old-lady friend Margaret McGowan, and they have a right to know if this book thing is connected with Petrakis's murder."

"That is so gross. I can't believe someone would murder that guy. I have every book he ever did on the planets and space. And then that stuff to your mom's books and Owl."

"Yeah, I have all the Petrakis books on making model airplanes," Charley said.

Matthew was silent for a moment and then looked up. "Well, Charley, I think they're treating you like crap—the police department."

"You do?" Charley said. There was a plangent, hopeful tone in his voice.

"Yeah."

"Does that mean you'll help me do it?"

Matthew scratched his head. He and Charley had been friends, best friends, since they were three years old and had met in nursery school. Matthew had been peripherally involved when Charley and Calista had discovered that Tom Jacobs had been murdered. Charley had turned to Matthew at that time, when he had discovered that the files, locked files in his dad's computer, had been tampered with. Charley had suspected von Sackler, the undercover CIA agent, but knew that his mother was becoming kind of romantically involved. There was no one to turn to except Matthew. They had trailed von Sackler on that night. It had been Halloween, and somehow they'd gotten into some stupid fight and Matthew had stomped off, let down his friend, and then Charley had . . . Matthew couldn't bear even now to think of it. Charley had nearly been killed. He definitely owed Charley one. They didn't have those stupid fights anymore. They had matured, and what they were doing wasn't dangerous, really, and it wasn't illegal. Well, at least no one would be hurt by it. But it would be going against a promise Matthew had made to his own parents: not to get involved with cracker bulletin boards. But they wouldn't really have to be that involved. They weren't going to do anything wrong, nothing that would hurt anybody or vandalize any systems. No viruses. He told himself that for the fiftieth time.

"Okay," Matthew said tersely, and pressed his lips together tightly as if he had just taken some particularly foul-tasting medicine. "But we got to do it from your house on your machine."

"Of course. I'll take all the responsibility."

"Did your mom make you promise not to use cracker boards?"

"My mom doesn't even know they exist."

Cracker bulletin boards were like other electronic bulletin boards except that they specialized in purveying stolen information. They were electronic hock shops in that sense, and in addition to this they provided, like all bulletin boards, a way for the crackers to communicate, except they often used stolen AT&T credit cards or MCI numbers to pay for the calls. All one needed was a personal computer and a modem. It was through these boards that crackers then reported a wealth of information that they had in their possession concerning other computer systems—phone numbers, passwords, user names as well as credit card information.

"So where do we start?"

"I don't know. What are the names of some of those boards—Captain Kidd's? Isn't that one?"

"A lot of pirate names."

"Stands to reason."

"So how do we find them? From the straight bulletin boards?" Matthew asked.

"Yeah, if you watch those, you'll see listings, phone numbers that just stay on for a few minutes before the systems operator chases them off."

"Sam's—that's one. Sam's Equipment Exchange. I was over at Jerry Kline's the other day and we were in his brother's room. His brother goes to MIT, and he was looking for something on Sam's board and a couple of numbers disappeared, like, you know, within fifteen or twenty minutes. He said the systems operator was deleting them."

"You got the number for Sam's?"

"No. But it's in almost every issue of the *Computer Digest*. I think it even came in a handout they gave us when we bought our modem—you know, some sort of listing of services and bulletin boards."

Charley got up and went over to a shelf where he kept a

precariously high stack of magazines. He got a few. They found the number for Sam's Equipment Exchange in the ad section of the first magazine they opened.

"Okay," said Charley. "Let me shut this down." There was a picture on the screen of nucleotides that looked like bubbles arranged in a three-dimensional pattern around a ring of nitrogen and carbon atoms. They faded from the screen. "So much for us finding the cure for cancer." Charley sighed and remembered his mother's high hopes.

They watched the board and studied the listings and messages.

"I know that sci-fi outfit. I got Software Wars from it," Matthew said, spotting one listing.

"Okay, look . . . There it is, Captain Kidd's!" Charley scribbled down a number.

"Look, Digital Pirate!"

They continued paging through the messages, pressing SPACE each time to scan the board to see how many choices there were. They then went back to write down the numbers of possible candidates. The fourth time they hit SPACE for an outfit just after Digital Pirate, the computer indicated that that particular number had been deleted.

"Wow!" they both exclaimed.

"Let's go back and see if Digital Pirate's still there," Charley said. They did. Again a message came up that the listing had been deleted. They had been printing out as they went along. They tried printing now, but the number was just not there. They tried once more to print. A message came up: "No pirates permitted to leave messages on this board."

"We got some numbers, didn't we?" Charley said, picking up the printout.

"Yeah, I think enough to get started."

"The sys op must really be riding the range," Charley said as he checked the printout. "Sys op" was the abbreviated form of systems operator, and the one at Sam's Equipment Exchange was obviously on line cleansing his board of the pirate influence, running a tight ship and making the crackers walk the electronic plank. But the boys had gotten enough numbers to begin, and less than a quarter of an hour after they had shut down their cancer research project, they entered the subterranean labyrinth of the world of electronic bandits. There was no one on-line at the first three of the cracker bulletin boards that they tried. They could not leave E-mail in this situation. That was rule number one. They had to be able to have someone on-line to "talk" with.

13

Calista was pleased with the green. The egg and linseed oil had worked, and she was able to thin it out to that first barely green that stained the trees in earliest spring, which was when the story opened. It had gone fast, faster than she had thought. She had used for the most part a sponge to apply the green—actually a fragment of a sponge that she had bought in Chinatown and then attached to a small stick. It worked beautifully for dabbing on the vernal stain of early spring. She was now ready to begin work on the arm of Marian. She looked at her watch. It was getting on toward lunch, but there had been no growls of hunger from above. The boys must be totally absorbed in their modeling of cancer genes, or whatever it was. It would be exciting if Charley really got hooked on this project—my son the doctor, my son the Nobel laureate! It had a more comforting ring to it than "my son the computer wizard." Lots of young computer wizards, at least in Cambridge these days, tended to go into AI—artificial intelligence, not steak sauce, as she had thought at first when she had come across the initials in a magazine article. The Tech Square-Kendall Square area was apparently the artificial intelligence center of the world. She had read a little bit more about it after that first encounter with the term. Tom had explained some of it to her. She found it weirder than any of the physics he had ever tried to explain to her, more confounding in its own way than general relativity. Hard-core AI people believed that they could build not just robots, but minds. She found the whole area very strange. Some critics thought of it as a kind of mumbo-jumbo alchemy that had nothing to do with "real intelligence"; but the devotees, the hard-core, looked upon it as the next step in human evolution. It could conceivably come up with formulas or algorithms for intuition!

At the moment her algorithms were down. She couldn't visualize what this arm of Marian's should look like. It had to look like a woman's arm, a young woman's arm, but be able to shoot like a man's! She had to convey that tensile strength of the musculature yet delicacy of bone structure. She could actually see the arm but not visualize the strength, the coiled energy, in it. Of course, that was the problem! She was coiling the energy, putting it into a potential state, whereas it had already been spent, the arrow had been shot, the energy transferred from muscle to the arrow's shaft. She needed to show a relaxed muscle. She went over to her bookshelf and got down a very worn copy of Gray's *Anatomy of the Human Body,* as well as a book of Leonardo da Vinci's drawings. For body work they were an unbeatable combination. She opened the books and immediately found the drawings that would help her. So much for intuition and artistic impulse. Sometimes you just simply had to know the sources to go to and look at things really hard. She felt her stomach growl. She'd stop now. It was always good to stop when you were on top, when you knew where to come back to and what precisely you had to do. No waiting around for inspiration. It wasted too much time.

* * *

Elsie's was on the corner of Mount Auburn and Holyoke streets in the heart of Harvard Square. One did not go to Elsie's for ambience. Elsie's was before ambience, definitely before pasta, before anybody had ever heard the word *upscale*, and there was no other term for a downscale eatery than greasy spoon. Elsie's made McDonald's look like Lutèce. It was Calista's theory that it was started by somebody who had gone bust in the wood veneer business, for there were at least ten different kinds of plastic wood in the place and the walls were covered with the three most rejected wallpapers in the Western Hemisphere. You didn't eat at tables but at high countertops, sitting on stools. You placed your order upon entering. There were a few quaint things about Elsie's— just a few, but present nonetheless. The windows were very nice, mullioned into lots of smaller frames in much the same style as the rest of Harvard's window architecture. The other quaint thing about Elsie's was that they eschewed the French fry. There was not a French fry on the premises. Instead they had knishes. And it was "instead." Ask for French fries and they said, "No, but we got knishes." A tad strange, but there was something rather charming about the presence of a knish on such a menu. Their hamburgers were wonderful. You could go around the corner to Bartley's Burger Cottage and get all sorts of fancy hamburgers with bacon and saga cheese and pineapple put on top, but nobody put on the grease like Elsie's. And that's what Calista liked. It wasn't simply that they were excessively greasy. It was rather the way they let the grease seep into the bun that made it all soggy and wonderfully juicy through and through. The boys liked the hamburgers, or Elsie Burgers, as the double-decker ones were called, and the video games. There was a room off the one where you gave your order devoted to video games. It was hell to go to Elsie's during reading period because all the Harvard students hogged the games. But reading period was still a few weeks away, and there would be plenty of space in the game room, as Calista pointed out to the boys. They had seemed somewhat reluctant to leave their molecular modeling project. They played the games while they waited for their orders, and then Calista came in and got them. They found a counter near the Holyoke Street window.

"So what's new in the world of oncogenes? You guys going to turn the Martin Institute on its ear?"

"Sure," said Charley. He hoped his mother wouldn't dwell on this. He probably should never have told her so much about it.

"What's Leventhal like?"

"How should we know?" Matthew asked. "We never saw him when we were there. I saw his picture, though. He looks kind of like a Buddha, his shape, at least."

"Mom, I think you're getting your hopes up too much. Do you really think Leventhal's going to sit down with two eighth-graders and say, 'Now tell me, fellows, where do you think I should look next for the cure for cancer'?"

"They don't even talk about cancer there. They just talk about cells. They just want to find out how cells work. If they stumble across the cure for cancer, so much the better," Matthew said.

"You're right. That guy, the one who's sort of our adviser there, he's this graduate student or something. When he was showing us what he did and talking about all the stuff that he is looking at, stuff about membranes and biochemical pathways of cells, he's just talking really about how cells work, not necessarily cancer. They're hacking cells is what they're doing over there."

"Yeah," said Matthew. "It's a hack."

"A hack?" Calista was bewildered. "You mean as in computer hacking?"

"Sort of. They're just trying to tunnel into a system."

"Oh," said Calista. She took a bite of her hamburger. Was she a romantic or what?

14

Charley had been adamant about not leaving any E-mail on a cracker board. So when they returned from lunch they tried two more calls to find an on-line sys op. Their second call was to a board called Pieces of Eight, and someone was home tending the shop. Charley had logged on using his user name CHAZ. He then typed CHAT, indicating his wish to "talk" directly to the sys op. The sys op then responded:

WHAT DO YOU NEED?

Charley typed: BOSTON POLICE DEPARTMENT.

Sys op: YOU NUTZ?

Chaz: NO, VERY IMPORTANT. NEED TO GET IN.

Sys op: NO WAY, JOSE. YOU'LL GET CAUGHT. NOT A GENERAL-ACCESS MODEM. ALL HARD WIRE RUNNING TO EACH PRECINCT. THEY GOT TAPS ON EVERYTHING. YOU'D HAVE TO ROUTE THE CALL THROUGH EUROPE. COME ON, I CAN FIX YOU UP WITH MCI NUMBERS. YOU WANT TO GET INTO THE TRW COMPUTER? YOU NAME IT, WE CAN DO IT. REPEAT: NUTZ TO TRY BPD.

Chaz: GOT TO. NO CHOICE. WHAT'S THEIR HARDWARE?

Sys op: IT'S YOUR ASS. FINEST. WHY WON'T NCIC DO?

Charley and Matthew looked at each other. "What's that?" Charley asked. Matthew shrugged.

Chaz: WHAT'S NCIC?

Sys op: NATIONAL CRIME INFORMATION CENTER.

"That's not going to help me," Charley said, shaking his head. He typed again: NO. NEED BPD. LOCAL THING. PLEEZE!

Sys op: OKAY. LET ME TRY SOMETHING. I'LL CALL BACK ONE HOUR. WHAT'S YOUR NUMBER?

Chaz: NO, I'LL CALL YOU BACK ONE HOUR.
Sys Op: OKAY.

Nothing is a pain to a cracker, only a challenge. Nobody'd ever asked this before. So why not? It wasn't his ass if the kid got caught. Although he had a notion that if he could find who he wanted to find, it wouldn't be that dangerous.

Charley called back in an hour, but the sys op didn't have the stuff. He told him to call back in three hours or leave his number. But Charley wouldn't. Shortly before dinner Charley got what he wanted. Hobbit. Hobbit had just quit his job writing programs for the Boston Police Department's computer FINEST. He didn't have a general access number. He had something that was better than a general access number—a private one. He had installed it just for himself, so he didn't have to go all the way into town to fix things. He had quit three months before, but he still had his modem, and a "back door" into the system was still available. At midnight of that evening while Calista slept, CHAZ talked with HOBBIT and convinced him that he meant to do no damage, that he only wanted to get into the homicide files because his mom's friend had been murdered. It took very little convincing. Hobbit had a big fat grudge against the BPD. He probably wouldn't have cared if CHAZ trashed the whole system. So he gave CHAZ the telephone number of a modem connected to FINEST. Charley dialed and was immediately prompted to log on:

Chaz: HELLO.
Finest: RESTART.

So Charley immediately was cued by the word RESTART that this was not the proper way to log on to the computer system. They must have changed a few things since HOBBIT had left. This left only one option for Charley's next step:

Chaz: HELP.
Finest: RESTART.
Chaz: RESTART.
Finest: FMKLOG092F USER ID MISSING OR INVALID.

The next step for Chaz was to determine a valid user name and password combination. But this was easy once he was logged on, for HOBBIT had given him a few that he felt would still work. So within twenty minutes Charley was neatly logged on to the police department's computer and into the homicide files. He had never used a system like FINEST before, but the HELP command continued to be helpful and explained the nitty-gritties of moving through this electronic precinct.

There had been two people named Petrakis involved in violent crimes in the greater Boston area in the past year. Only one was male and named Norman, however, and unfortunately that file was the shortest. "Zilch," muttered Charley to himself. "Friggin' zero." The report listed Norman Petrakis's address and Social Security number, a three-line description of the crime and the detectives who were investigating the crime. There were no suspects, no leads. There wasn't even anything about fingerprints. How could there be a crime and no mention of fingerprints; even absence of fingerprints—wouldn't they at least mention it? Charley wondered. There was a number by the coroner's report, but there was no coroner's report. He must have to go into another file for that. Why not try it? The former sys op had given Charley a user name and a password for FINEST. The same user name, HICKS, appeared to be valid for the coroner's file, but a different password was required. The old password didn't work. This was a flaw in the system, a stupid one that benefited Charley, for it had told him the difference between a valid user name and an invalid password pair. For the invalid password it had responded with NOT IN DIRECTORY: REINITIATE LOGON PROCEDURE. So now all Charley had to do, knowing that his user name was okay but that the password was not, was to try passwords until he found one that worked for the coroner's file with the pathologist's report. He tried to call up the old sys op for the password to the coroner's file, but the guy wasn't on-line. Charley then had to make a decision. He could try his own thirty-thousand-word dictionary of most common English words and have his computer try each one as a password. It would take about five seconds a word. Although it would be under fifteen hours, it was still too long. It could result in revealing his presence in the system and alert the current sys op. Alternatively, he could just play with inversions of the password he had already used. But he didn't see much choice. He might as well try ransacking his dictionary at least for a little while until the old sys op came back on-line.

It only took a few hundred tries. Within the hour Chaz was back in business. But for all it was worth, the coroner's report didn't yield much. Norman Petrakis in this report had become *Decedent # 70-10879. Death by asphyxiation, contusions around the throat.* There was something that referred to *blood anomalies,* followed by some numbers and letter sequences that must have referred to blood types. Charley copied it all down, including the blood anomalies H1, H2, H1-H2, K3, K4, K5. For his sixteen hours of efforts he had very little to show. He was dead tired, and there was no way his mom would let him stay home from school the next day. So much for Boston's FINEST!

15

A reasonable facsimile of spring actually did arrive. And on schedule, undeterred and unimpaired by the snowstorm, the dogwood outside Calista's window blossomed. It was still in its deep russet stage as Calista opened her eyes this early May morning. She was thinking not of the glories of spring, however, but of Norman Petrakis. The detectives had never called her back. She had informed Ethan Thayer and Janet Weiss of the defaced books and the mutilated stuffed animal. Ethan had reported this to the authorities, but nothing had happened. They were carefully screening all the mail that arrived at the publishers for both Calista and Margaret. Margaret had gone off to England to visit relatives. Calista envied her. The only places that she had relatives were Long Island, New York, and Indiana, neither of which appealed to her at the moment. Besides, would she really want to have missed the dogwood?

What she wished she could have avoided was the whole month of April. She and Charley would go to Dallas in June for the American Library Association meeting, where she would pick up her Caldecott Medal. Dallas in June could hardly be considered idyllic. Other than that, there were no big plans for travel. They had traveled quite a bit anyway in the past year—to Japan and to Italy, where Calista's work had been honored at conferences and exhibits. She had looked forward to spending most of the summer in Vermont, where they had a summer house and where Charley could help out at a nearby commercial apple orchard and make some money. She had told him that he could bring a friend, too, for the whole summer. But now those plans seemed in jeopardy, as Charley was finding his work at the Martin Institute more interesting and had been making noises about working there for the summer with Matthew and this girl Louise who apparently was very nice. It seemed that although the project of scanning the protein base sequences was very boring, figuring out snazzy graphics and presentations for molecular models on the computer was really fun. The computers they worked on were very powerful and some of the programs very exotic. So this part of the job for Charley was like being in the proverbial candy shop.

The kids had unlimited time and license to fuss with this stuff. Charley and Louise had even prepared a graphic model for the great Leventhal himself that he had used in a European conference. The people at the lab were quite pleased with the young "mentees" that they were supposed to be mentoring. She had credited Charley's growing interest with the Martin Institute in helping him to, if not forget, at least ease up on the still unsolved Petrakis case.

But she would not think of that on such a spectacular morning. She didn't have to start rousing Charley for another hour. She should hop outside quickly and see what was growing in her garden, especially since this was the day that she would start the garden illustration, a double-page spread, in *Marian's Tale*. She was planning a spectacular walled garden for the convent where Marian was holed up.

After her walk in the garden Calista went back inside and turned on the "Today" show, Jane had changed her hairstyle yet again! Wonderful to have such flexible hair. Calista had worn her hair the same way for over twenty years. The masses of chestnut brown were shot through with silvery gray and was always madly unkempt. She kept it pinned to the top of her head with a monster barrette. This morning as she had come in from the garden and caught a glimpse of herself in a mirror, her hair had looked like a satellite picture of a weather front, she thought.

Such was not the stuff TV hairdos were made of! But then again she could keep pencils in her hair. By noon she usually had at least two sticking out of her head. She had remembered that Archie Baldwin had laughed at that when he saw her do it. She wondered how he was doing. They had talked a few times on the phone, but they always seemed to miss each other when he came to Cambridge for whatever it was he did with Harvard and the Peabody Museum. Thank God they hadn't missed at the important time when he had saved Charley's life.

Therefore, it was with some surprise, having just been thinking about Archie, that she heard the name Baldwin emanating from the television set. She turned abruptly from the stove to the set. What an odd coincidence. But it was not Archie Baldwin the man was talking about. It was that wimpy Neddy Baldwin, former governor of Massachusetts. Must be the same family, Calista thought. There were Baldwins all over. But how different they were. Ned Baldwin had been the governor years ago, before Calista and Tom had ever moved to Cambridge. After the governorship and an unsuccessful attempt to gain the Republican presidential nomination, he had gone on to a series of high, and in many cases rather ceremonial, posts—ambassadorships, special envoy positions, numerous boards and commissions. Averill Harriman he was not. He was, rather, a very wealthy, weak-brained Brahmin. And "Holy shit!" Calista muttered, and set down her coffee. There he was at a prayer breakfast with that bizarre television preacher Lorne Thurston. Good Lord, he was more weak-brained than she thought. What could he possibly be doing with that guy?

"Hi, Mom."

"Ssshhh!" Calista held out her hand to hush him.

Charley crept into the kitchen and sat down at the table, where there was a glass of orange juice waiting for him.

"I think we have to look at this whole issue of what we have been told is human evolution."

Calista's jaw dropped. She walked toward the television spellbound. This was not Lorne Thurston talking. This was Ned Baldwin, scion of one of the oldest families of the commonwealth, son of Harvard—albeit it was only genealogy, a wing and a prayer that got him through his undergraduate years—haute Episcopalian (probably a little Unitarian thrown in there, too, as was the case with many of these Yankee families), but there he was saying—let's hear that again. Oh, no! Now he was just being so folksy, and all those hick-brained fundamentalists were looking positively gleeful as he told them: "I just don't think the final word is in on all this evolution stuff, and if that's the case and there does appear to be evidence for some scientific basis for creationism, and then Genesis is—" Cheers drowned him out. The audience went wild.

"What is this?" Charley asked, staring at the television.

"This is the bully pulpit, Charley, and you'll never guess who that is up there, the one on the left."

"Who?"

"Ned Baldwin, a relative of Archie Baldwin."

"Archie Baldwin—the guy who saved my life?"

"The one and only."

"How can he have an idiot like that for a relative?"

"I'm not sure. The blood must have really thinned out at a certain point." Calista sighed. "He was, however, once governor of this state, and he's held a lot of important posts. I don't think anyone ever did think of him as a mental giant, but they didn't think of him as this, either." She gestured at the television screen. The news clip was over, and the commentator was discussing the growing popularity of Lorne Thurston, the television minister, and the rumors of his seeking political office.

"Why would this Baldwin creep be there with him?" Charley asked.

"I don't know. It's perplexing. Baldwin isn't seeking any political office. I think he's beyond that now. He just gets very fancy ambassadorships and serves on lots of important boards and commissions. There's no need for him to do this kind of thing. Why would he stick his neck out on this evolution thing? It must be so embarrassing to his family."

"If they're anything like Archie, it would be." Charley had taken an immediate liking to Archie Baldwin that seemed based on something more than the fact that the man had saved his life. There was just something about the guy that Charley liked, felt good about being around him, and yet he had only been around him for a very brief time. Somehow he couldn't match Archie up with the turkey he had just seen on television.

"Mom, are you sure they're related?"

"They've got to be. All these old Boston families are intertwined."

"And who's the other guy? What'd you say his name was?"

"Lorne Thurston. You know, you've heard of him. He's one of these TV ministers with his 'heavenly megaphone' and WATS line to God. Gets all those old folks to send in their Social Security money. Got his own network, and he's even got some sort of Bible college he runs."

"You're kidding—a college, too? Where?"

"Down in Texas somewhere."

"Oh, great! Maybe I'll apply when we go to get your award in Dallas."

"You'd last about one second, Charley Jacobs."

And then out of the blue Charley turned to her. His gray eyes seemed especially limpid as Calista later recalled. "I bet," he said softly. "He must have hated Norman Petrakis."

Something cold stole through Calista. "Charley, I can't believe that he would do anything like that. I mean, these guys I should think for all their fundamentalist ways would at least begin with the fundamentals of all fundamentals, the Ten Commandments."

"Yeah, I guess you're right." He paused. "But you said that guy at the conference was really obnoxious."

"Obnoxious, but not murderous. I mean, it's really not worth murdering over—human evolution." Her words struck her as very odd, oxymoronic, to say the least.

"But it's not exactly evolution," Charley said.

"What do you mean?" Calista asked. She looked up.

"It's politics." Then he suddenly looked confused by his own words. "I think that's what I mean. I mean, it sure doesn't look like religion to me, not that I'm an expert."

Calista rolled her eyes and smiled in agreement. She and Tom had never been heavily into organized religion. They had occasionally gone to services at Sanders Theater, where Harvard held them during the Jewish holidays, and Charley had had a brief whirl with Hebrew school at Harvard Hillel. They did have a seder every year with friends, and they lit candles for Hannukah. Charley had a definite Jewish identity. They ate Jewish, they celebrated Jewish holidays, and if they believed in God, it was only one, and that was about it. Charley was right. He was no expert. But then again, to use a favorite expression of her father's, he sure could "tell shit from shinola," and when he said "politics" he was right. This wasn't religion. Nobody needed a cable network, radio stations, and a college to have a little word with God or pray. It could become very cumbersome to try to cram an entire broadcasting empire though the eye of a needle. Yes, indeed, the camels had much more of a straight shot at the pearly gates than Lorne Thurston with BBN, his Bible Broadcasting Network. It was politics. But could it be murder? No, no way, she told herself. They wouldn't risk it. It was stupid. But who says they're smart?

"No . . . no . . ." She shook her head. "I just can't believe they'd do something like this. I mean, if he were found out, it would be curtains for him, and he wouldn't be crying over his lost souls, Charley, or his flock no longer having their shepherd. He'd be crying over his private jet and his estates and, gee whiz, the guy lives like a billionaire because he is one. He just wouldn't risk all that. It's out of the question. I think that Petrakis's death was the result of one crazy person working alone." She could tell, though, that Charley did not entirely buy that. He was still hung up on the notion of Lorne Thurston and his Bible-belting vigilantes.

"But you called it a bully pulpit just a minute ago."

"Bullies, not murderers, Charley. I think there's a difference."

"Hmm." It was not the sigh of satisfaction or resolution. And as if to confirm this, Charley's eyes took on that opaque look that signaled one thing—thinking, heavy-duty thinking. Oh, shit, had she opened this whole thing up again? Just three weeks before she had been worried about him getting overanxious with the police department. Luckily he seemed to have cooled on that. But now this jerky Baldwin and God's mouthpiece had reared their ugly heads, and . . . Oh, God, she didn't even want to think about it. She began biting her lip again as she watched Charley's still face.

16

Archie Baldwin slipped the key into the front door of his Georgetown town house. He was back home after two months in the field in Mexico supervising a Mayan excavation. He had not planned to be gone for two months, but the unexpected had happened in the best sense, the most positive and serendipitous of events that can befall an archaeologist: an entire lost city had been found. What had started out as a very ordinary dig a year before, which promised to reveal some rather classic textbooky-type pre-Columbian stuff, had indeed turned into much more as the first walls of the city began to poke through the rubble. Archie's role, originally that of visiting Smithsonian scientist, a drop-in appearance by the grand old man of the field, had changed dramatically. Not that it was simply perfunctory or ceremonial before. He was after all the one who decided on funding and approved the budget for an undertaking like this, but his role in the field was peripheral. After all, he had five other digs that he was overseeing and an international traveling exhibit he was putting together for the Smithsonian. But when the "sub-Tecla" had been discovered under the Tecla in the Yucatán peninsula, everything else was put on hold.

It wasn't simply a matter of it being appropriate and fitting that the man, the dean of American archaeology, be on the premises so that an adequate interpretation could be made during excavation. He was needed in a different way in this situation. Young Willburton, the principal investigator on this site, was as smart as they came and had a very promising career in the making. It would have been most inappropriate for Archie to simply swoop down and take over. But the fact was that no one else knew how to properly excavate around the corbeled arches without them all crashing in on the rooms, thought to be temple rooms, below. They didn't teach these kids enough architecture or engineering now. It should have become a mandatory part of any archaeology curriculum. Willburton, therefore, welcomed Archie Baldwin's presence. And Archie, the grand man from the Smithsonian, had sweated like a pig and worked his ever-loving buns off for two months teaching the young graduate students how to take a roof off a three-thousand-year-old gem without shattering the whole business. There was a crew of Maya-speaking Mexicans, but they didn't know any more than the kids about taking off these kinds of roofs. The result was that all Willburton's knowledge about Petén and Yaxuná periods wasn't worth a hill of beans, especially if the hill collapsed and crushed all the beans, crushed all the beautiful stelae with the hieroglyphics. So Archie not only saved the day, so to speak, but gave Willburton something to write about that would possibly make the young man's reputation.

Archie came back tanned and as fit as he had ever been in his fifty-two years. He still had the grime under his nails from the dig. But he felt great. How often does a guy at this stage in his career really get to go out there and muck around anymore? Usually it was just pushing numbers, approving budgets, sitting on august boards with a bunch of old farts. Christ, for a year and a half he'd had to serve as acting department chairman at the Smithsonian until they'd found a new one. What a drag that had been. These last two months had been fun. Really fun. The kids had worked hard. They didn't exactly treat him like a contemporary. He wouldn't have liked or expected that. But they hadn't treated him like a father confessor or Father Time, either. There was no romance, no flirtations, but gee whiz, you couldn't have everything. A warm body, however, on a chilly Mexican night would have been nice.

He walked into his front hall. Everything seemed in order. There were several stacks of mail on the small hallway table. He could see that there was more on the dining room table and, he assumed, more at the office, but at least Ruth Goodfellow, his secretary, would have that taken care of. He took his bags upstairs and then came downstairs praying that there might be a beer in the fridge.

There was a six-pack in addition to eggs, bacon, juice, milk, bread, and even tomatoes for a proper English breakfast. Along with it all was a welcome-home note from Goodfellow. God! Did she ever fail? How British. None of this Wheaties, breakfast of champions, business. This was a breakfast fit for empire builders, or uncoverers, as the case might be. He suddenly was starved, even though he had had dinner on the plane. He took out some bacon and began frying it up. When the bacon was done he slid the tomatoes into the pan, chased them around with the spatula for the better part of a minute, removed them, and put in the eggs. When it was ready he took it to the kitchen table with his beer and flipped on the television set. The picture frizzled. There was a short blizzard of snow and then an unmistakable voice.

"Neddy!" Archie popped open the can of beer. The picture had resolved itself into a crisp image. Archie blinked and opened his eyes wider. "Neddy!" he exclaimed as he saw the tall lean figure of his cousin on a stage with Lorne Thurston, the television evangelist. "What the fu—"?

"I think we have to look at this whole issue of what we have been told is human evolution. I just don't think the final word is in on all this evolution stuff, and if . . ."

"Stuff!" Archie exclaimed. This was not Lorne Thurston talking. This was his own cousin. He was actually standing on a platform with the guy and mouthing this garbage. Neddy was no genius. Everyone in the family knew that, but there was a difference between being a dim-witted Republican and this! "This is, I think, a philosophy, this evolution stuff, more than a—"

"Oh, no!" groaned Archie. The film report ended two minutes later and the newscaster was talking about rumors that Lorne Thurston might be seeking national office and looking for endorsements from high-ranking conservative Republicans. "What are you doing, Neddy? You need this guy like a hole in the head!" Archie was fuming at the television set. "This has nothing to do with you. Didn't you give up running for office so you could serve better? You call this serving—getting this nut national exposure so he can run? What the fuck are you doing on the stand with these jerks?" He slammed down his can of beer, leaned forward, and flicked off the television. This was ridiculous, screaming at the television. He'd call up Neddy directly. He lived in Washington now, just a few blocks away. He had become used to the Washington area after serving for eight years as a cabinet officer and then as chief of protocol. So after his term as ambassador to the court of St. James had ended, he had returned to Washington. It was a good base to take off from for all of his board meetings and goodwill missions for chiefs of state. Of course, he still kept the old family place in Dover, Massachusetts, and another summer place in Maine. Where was he now? The home front would know. He dialed Ned Baldwin's D.C. number. It wasn't that late. Someone would be up. The phone rang twice.

"Lacey?"

"Big Lacey or Little Lacey?" a youthful female voice said.

"Oh, Lace, it's you. This is Archie."

"Oh, hi, Archie. What's up?"

"Trying to track down your dad."

"Oh, no problem. Hold on a second while I get the schedule." She was back within a minute. "Okay, let's see, tonight it's Thursday, so it must be Dallas, and it's the Hyatt Hotel." She then rattled off the hotel phone number and the area code.

"Hey, kiddo, you're fantastic. I think they ought to be putting you up for a cabinet post." There was a slight pause.

"Archie?" The voice had a plaintive note.

"Yes, dear?"

"Did you see Dad with that sleazeball preacher? Is that why you're calling?"

Archie sighed and spoke. "I did indeed."

"I was somehow hoping that this would escape most of our relatives—you of all people, too!" Lacey almost wailed.

"Don't worry about me."

"I know, worry about Dad."

"No, no. Don't worry about your dad. That's not your responsibility, Lacey."

"It's a little humiliating."

"It shouldn't be, sweetie. People, I really believe, are able to separate the children of public figures from those figures and treat them as individuals."

"Should be able to, but not necessarily *are* able to. It's still humiliating."

"That is exactly what it should not be—humiliating. Your dad has his humiliations, and you will I am sure in time have your own."

"Oh, goodie!" Lacey rejoined.

"No, it's the truth," Archie said firmly.

"You want to hear my most recent humiliating experience?"

"What's that?" Archie laughed.

"I'm thinking of not going to Harvard."

"Well, now that's not humiliating. I did the same thing. So are you thinking of following in my Dartmouth footsteps?"

"Nope."

"You got in, didn't you?"

"Yes. But that's the whole point. I am thinking of going where no other Baldwin feet have trod or left their mark."

"Yale?"

"No, Antioch."

"Antioch! Well, now that is an imaginative choice."

"Imaginative has sometimes been considered humiliating."

"Oh, come on now, Lacey. You're making us into caricatures. Do they have kayaking at Antioch?"

"I doubt it."

"Hmm." Archie hated to see a great pair of shoulders like Lacey's go for naught. She had Olympic potential, and he had been the one to introduce her to white-water kayaking. "What do your folks say?"

"What do you think?"

"Hmm."

"Yeah, you got the picture. Mom's not too upset. She's coming around."

"How is Big Lacey? She with your dad now?"

"No. She flew on to someplace else from Dallas, a step ahead of him, so to speak, in, let's see . . ." There was a pause. Archie could imagine her looking at a bulletin board with a map of the world and pins tracking the movements of public figure parents. "She is in Dayton, Ohio, receiving an award for her work with the Youth Literacy Program."

* * *

Big Lacey had always been a step or two ahead of Neddy. She was one of those large, slightly horsey-looking patrician women who were immediately identified as being not only suitable but quite desirable because of their extraordinary common sense. This recommended them highly as effective wives and helpmates for men like Neddy, who were not very bright but were exceptionally good looking and possessed great geniality and charm. These men, due to their old money and genealogy, could rise effortlessly despite incompetency, but they really did require smart and skillful wives at their sides. Lacey had done just that for Neddy, beginning with his first run for the state legislature. Where was she now when he was making a fool of himself mouthing off about evolution on the same platform with that idiot Lorne Thurston? Being given an award for her work with a literacy project. How ironic! Archie said good-bye to Little Lacey, giving her his blessing for Antioch, hung up, and dialed the number in Dallas.

"Archie!" The warm rich voice on the other end exploded with genuine delight. Oh, God, he felt rotten about this. "Still got the last ten days in August slated in, fella?"

Well, he might as well come right out with it.

"Neddy!" He sighed deeply. "What the fuck were you doing up there with that asshole Lorne Thurston?"

"Now, now, calm yourself, Arch, just calm down. First of all—"

"First of all you don't know a goddamn thing about evolution or any science, and you know that as well as I do because you flunked that biology-for-poets course they used to give at Harvard *twice* and only made it through the third time because I tutored you solidly for two weeks while we were sailing."

"But you know this evolution stuff is not necessarily science."

Archie rolled his eyes and chewed on his pipe. "Oh, yeah, oh, great. This is the argument that the creationists are all using these days. Spare me, Neddy. I know their line. They are saying that we are saying that we cannot prove evolution, therefore evolution is a philosophy, a faith, conjecture. I heard you tonight on the news. But the fact is that evolution is a fact. There've been experiments with everything from corn to fruit flies, and remember the black moths in England . . ."

"Black moths in England?" Ned said in a bewildered tone.

"Yes. It's a clear-cut case of genetic change in a natural environment. The environment was getting to look like hell, sooty, dark, awful because of the factories. The black moths prevailed in this sooty atmosphere. Why? Because they blended in with the scenery and could escape predation. The gene pool changed. The start-up of new species, new genera, is based on just this kind of thing. This is evolution. Proven in labs and in nature. It's no theory. What is theory is natural selection."

"But Archie, I'm going to tell you that these guys are coming up with evidence."

"Oh, no! Don't tell me they're doing the scientific creationist number on you."

"They're not doing any number on me, Archie, and look, believe me, I know that you know this stuff cold, but there is something to be said for some of the data that they're coming up with."

"Data!" Even hearing his cousin say the word in this context shocked Archie. "Neddy, this isn't polling results we're talking about here. Don't say that word *data* in conjunction with these people. May I remind you that the last data these people came up with—those nutty Paluxy footprints, trying to show that man and dinosaurs tiptoed through the tulips at the same time—was total bullshit, and I was one, along with Farlow, Glenn Kuban, and Steve Schafersman, to call their bluff. They were the most pathetic fakes I've ever seen."

"Okay! Okay!" There was not even a shadow of testiness in Neddy's voice. "I hear you, cousin. Now take it easy. It's not worth getting your blood pressure up. Don't worry, I am not a fundamentalist, and believe me, one can do a lot worse than stand on the same platform with Lorne Thurston and pretend to hate Darwin."

"This is bad," Archie said grimly. "You are dealing with a small, regional—"

But Neddy cut him off. "It is not that small or regional. Lorne Thurston has a broader appeal than you might believe from your—"

"Don't say it, Neddy."

"Ivory tower? I wasn't going to say that, Arch, I was just going to say that he is not as dumb or as redneck as you might think."

"I never had thought that he was, either. Anyone who can rake in the money he does through that prayer network of his is not dumb."

"What I am trying to say, Archie, is that he is not only smart, but a lot less rough around the edges than he projects, and they are indeed coming up with some interesting evidence in the field of scientific creationism."

"They are coming up with a legal strategy for getting religion in the schools and hobbling free inquiry and that is all. Nothing more."

"You're really being awfully stuffy about all this, Arch. You should come down here and see some of the work going on at Lorne Thurston's college. They've got some very convincing evidence."

"For what, that crazy Flood theory of theirs, where four billion years of strata are squashed into the Genesis time frame?"

"No, no, it has more to do with some human skull analysis."

"Oh, terrific. Listen, just pray I don't come down there. I seem to have a nose for fraud these days—Paluxy Creek in Glen Rose, Texas, with the dinosaur prints. Then need I joggle your memory about the recent Harvard fiasco at Rosestone with the seeding of that site?"

"I'm going to be in Cambridge tomorrow, as a matter of fact."

"Giving a lecture on scientific creationism?"

"Very funny. No, it's a WGBH fund-raiser wingding. Remember, I'm on the board."

"I can't keep your boards straight. I wish you'd get off Thurston's board or whatever you're doing with him."

"I'm not doing anything with him, nor am I on any such board. I just went to a simple prayer breakfast, that's all." He sounded weary with Archie.

"Well, I think you're going to need a prayer or two yourself if you keep this association up."

"Okay, okay. But I really do not think that you would find Lorne Thurston all that loathsome."

"How does Lacey find him?" There was dead silence on the other end of the phone. Then a sigh.

"Okay. Be careful." Archie refrained from saying the obvious—that Lacey was smart, and it behooved Neddy to follow his wife on this. Neddy knew that Lacey was much smarter than he was, but he did not have to be reminded of it constantly.

"Don't worry about me, pal," Neddy said warmly. "I'll see you August twentieth for sure, if not before."

"Okay, good luck, Neddy, and do take care."

"Same to you, Arch."

17

Blood anomalies? Charley had wondered about that at the time. He wondered how he could find out more and had spent a very brief time considering whether he should hack into the police department's computer to see if anything had been added to the pathologist's report. It hadn't taken him long to decide, about five seconds. Nothing new had been added to the report. Charley knew very little about blood other than that type O was the most common, and from the report it looked as if Norman Petrakis had had type O blood. And yet there were these other letters listed, a sequence of K's and H's. Were these the anomalies? He hadn't even known what the word *anomalies* meant until he'd looked it up in his dictionary. Now he was going to have to find out more about blood. He wasn't going to go to a dictionary this time, or his *World Book Encyclopedia.* Who needed books when there were people? At the Martin Institute there had to be someone who could tell him all he needed to know about blood.

Charley got off the subway at the Kendall Square stop, crossed the street, Main Street, and angled to his left. Behind him to the south was Massachusetts Institute of Technology. To the east was the Charles River and a mess of construction. To the north was a hive of new office buildings housing bioengineering and computer firms with names like Biogen and Symbolics. These were for the most part started by MIT folks who didn't want to move too far away. They were all of brick construction, which was the dominant material of the Cambridge-Boston area. The Martin Institute was just beyond these firms, enjoying a plaza of its own. Charley liked the fact that it was not a multistoried building like many of the new ones in the Kendall-Tech Square area. It had a low, chunky look somewhat similar to Boston City Hall. He headed for the main entrance. It was Saturday, and although Charley would not be expected to come in on a Saturday, he knew that the lab would hardly be empty. They worked around the clock at the Martin Institute. Saturday looked just about like any other day. Sure enough, Steven Gillespie, his "mentor" and the project coordinator for the Look Ahead program at Martin, was there at his bench. He was bent over, pipette in hand, sucking up something to put into the centrifuge machine. Lab workers were seldom without their pipettes, the daggerlike instruments similar to eyedroppers that sucked up solutions. They spent more time with pipettes in their hands than pencils.

"Charley Jacobs! What brings you here this morning?"

"Blood," Charley said simply, deciding not to beat around the bush.

"Blood . . . blood . . ." said Steve somewhat distractedly as he made his way to the centrifuge machine. He put something in and then switched it on. He turned toward Charley. "So what can I do for you?"

"I need to find out what these letters and numbers mean," Charley said, drawing out a piece of paper from his pants pocket.

Steve Gillespie looked at the paper and squinted. "I might be able to help you with that. Let me finish with this centrifuge stuff."

Half an hour later they were sitting in Mary Chung's, a Chinese restaurant just a few blocks away on Mass. Ave. in Central Square, eating spring rolls, dun dun noodles with shredded chicken, and moo shu pork and drinking Coke.

"It's the antigens that are the anomalies. That's what those letters are. They represent antigenic markers, and they're getting a weird protein profile here."

"What's weird about it?" Charley asked.

Steve looked up from the little pancake he was neatly wrapping around a bundle of moo shu pork. "It's not human," he said quietly.

"Not human?"

"Yeah, I know. Weird. Where did you say this guy was killed?"

"The Sheraton Hotel here in Boston."

"Not a place where you'd tangle with animals—at least not the kind these antigens might indicate."

"What kind of animal would it be?"

"I don't know. I'd have to go look it up."

"Will you?"

"Sure, no problem."

"Good." Charley settled back in his seat.

Steven was a nice-looking fellow, but he dressed horribly. He wore pale plaid short-sleeved shirts in thin materials and very stiff jeans that always appeared too new and too dark. His clothes looked like something his mother might have bought for him. He dressed like a nerd, a classic MIT nerd. He even carried a package of plastic pens in his shirt pocket, and if he had worn glasses, they would have been broken over the nose bridge and taped. But he was nice, and Charley hoped that he had girlfriends despite the way he dressed. Charley also hoped that when he grew up, if he had muscles like Steve's, he wouldn't even consider wearing those wimpy shirts that made your arms look awful no matter what.

As Steve told Charley about the sophisticated blood analyses they were able to do now, Charley grew sorrier and sorrier for him. Somebody should tell Steve how to dress. It was sad to have your mother as your only clothing consultant. And he was now sure that this was the case with Steve. But it would hardly do for him to give advice. After all, in Project Look Ahead Steve was supposed to be his mentor, not the reverse. Steve was the one who had coined the term *mentee* for Charley and Matthew and Louise. He used the word as a kind of nickname or form of address on occasion. "Hey, mentee, want to see how we do these gels?"

"So you say this dude was a friend of your mom's?" Steve asked as he opened another can of Coke.

"Yeah. Not real close. They knew each other through their work."

"Well, I'll look into this blood thing for you."

"Gee, I really appreciate it."

"Hey, it's the least I can do. I mean, you, Matthew, and Louise have really worked your buns off around here. Leventhal's very pleased."

"He is?" Charley said excitedly.

"Yeah, I know he seems so busy you think he doesn't notice you, but he took those graphics of yours to that talk in England, and he thinks it's really neat all those models you got that software generating. It really helps us look at structure. And now next week you're going to start working with those brain proteins. That's the big debate going on now. It's hot."

"What's hot?"

"Well, not exactly what you're doing." He didn't want Charley to get the wrong idea. "But in the last couple of years there's been all this stuff coming out about intellamine and intellicone."

"What are they?"

"Well, this was going to be Monday afternoon's lecture from the mentor to the mentees, but I guess you'll get a preview."

He would need more than a preview, Charley thought. It was complicated.

"Can you run that by me again?" They had ordered a round of Peking ravioli and more Coke. "You mean that there are two different—what do you call them . . . these intellamine and intellicone things?"

"Neurotransmitters, proteins found in the brain."

"Okay, and how did they discover them?"

"A couple of years ago a lab, I think it was in California, did an experiment. The researchers out there wanted to figure out how neurotransmitters in general might affect higher-level thinking. So they exposed the subjects to a gas containing methadrill, which basically shuts down all creative and speculative thought. They gave the subjects spinal taps before and after the exposure to the gas. One specific protein was found to be missing from the second spinal tap, and not only was it missing, but on further analysis when it was finally pinpointed in the first tap, it was found to actually be a totally new neurotransmitter . . . Ta-da!" Steve held up his hands and snapped his fingers. "They discovered intellamine! It wasn't exactly earth-shaking news, but still it caused a few ripples in some of the scientific backwaters. The first article was published in *Endocrinology Abstracts*. Not a cutting-edge publication by any means. Basically they just talked about how this intellamine was a simple protein with four hundred bases. A primary structure was described, but they didn't have the vaguest idea about what the tertiary structure was. . . . See, get it?" Steve looked directly into Charley's eyes. "It's just like the modeling you're doing now on the protein folding problems: first you get just a long chain of amino acids, peptides in the primary structure, and then you try and find if and when it sheets, or curls into helices, the kind of stuff I was showing you the other day with those Styrofoam models. And that's the secondary structure, and then you take all that and jumble it around and see what kind of complicated molecules you get that could go into a tertiary structure. Anyway, on with the intellamine saga. They're trying to figure out all this, and in the course of it a second research group at University of Pennsylvania, I think, finds a different neurotransmitter—"

"That's intellicone?" Charley asked.

"Right. See, you're getting this. It only has five bases that are different from the other one, intellamine, but they come up with a tertiary structure for it. See, they figure out how these proteins fold into big fat smart-acting molecules."

"So that's pretty good that they figured that out."

"Yeah, very good. They published their report in the *Journal of Brain Chemistry*. Part of your assignment this week is to read that article, or at least the abstract of it. It just came out a few months ago. Now this got the folks at Duke and University of Minnesota excited, and they decided to jump on the bandwagon. This isn't a big bandwagon, by the way. It's not considered nearly as sexy and glamorous as AIDS research, but anyway, they wanted to find out exactly where intellamine and intellicone are used in the brain, if anywhere."

"How do they do that?"

"Complicated. They have to schedule time at the Brookhaven National Laboratory's positron emission tomography scanner. It's called PET for short."

"How does it work?"

"You synthesize the protein you wish to study using radioactive oxygen-eighteen. Then you inject it into the patient. The PET scanner lets you actually watch where the protein is in the brain. Ideally, it only gathers in the parts of the brain where it's being used."

"Jeez, sounds terrible. Who would allow themselves to be a victim for that?"

"Rats . . ." Steve paused. "And prisoners. They can make money, get sentences lessened."

"I don't know whether it's such a deal," Charley said. "So what do they find out? Where are these things used in the brain?"

"They find out that intellamine isn't used in the brain anywhere interesting—not anywhere connected with logical thought processes—but intellicone is used in the upper cerebral cortex near what they call the planning centers of the brain, and they're going to get a paper published in *Cell*, very distinguished scientific journal, and that's very hot stuff. So then there's a conference on it, a small one, and this thing starts looking kind of racial."

"Racial? How do you mean?"

"Well, the conference itself was kind of boring. I went to it. It was down in New York, and they mostly just showed graphs indicating the occurrence of intellamine and intellicone in various individuals, correlations with IQ and with different drugs, including recreational drugs. But at lunch I'm sitting around and listening to these guys talk, and it becomes apparent that all of the researchers who found intellamine were working with prison inmates, and those working with intellicone were using people from psychiatric wards. So first they figure intellicone is in crazy people, but by the second day of the conference they are saying it's racial. It just happens, of course, that all the prisoners are black and all the folks in the psych wards are white. This in itself is an obvious bias, and it does happen all the time, I am sorry to say. It's easy to get prisoners to be subjects for testing, and in a lot of prisons there are more black people than white people. The same is not true of psychiatric hospitals, where you usually have to pay to get in. This isn't the first time that researchers in their zealousness have overlooked the obvious.

"But in any case, they hypothesize that intellamine is in black people and intellicone is in whites. That was a year ago. Now these researchers are getting letters published in the *New England Journal of Medicine,* and they're finding slightly different variants in every race."

"They are?"

"That's what the literature says. But the clincher just came in last week. There was an experiment done where they injected a black male with intellicone and claim to have raised his IQ by twenty points."

"No shit!"

"So they say. They claim that intellicone is directly related to higher-order thinking."

"What's higher-order thinking?"

Steve Gillespie smiled at Charley's question. That's what he liked about this kid. He had a wonderful, raunchy sort of skepticism. He was always asking these knock-your-socks-off questions. He took a swallow of his Coke. "I'm not sure," he answered. "But supposedly we white honkies have it, and they don't." He didn't smile. "With this latest test they seem to be saying that if you have another form of it, the intellamine, your brain isn't doing as well. It's as if other races were trying to synthesize this brain chemical and just never got there."

"Do you believe that?"

"I got to look at the data. But this should be interesting to you mentees."

"I don't quite see the connection."

"Look—all that modeling stuff you've been doing is really a kind of mapping exercise. I've asked you just to look at the primary structures of a whole mess of proteins, find the similarities and correlations and see how they map into tertiary structures. You guys, granted, don't know how it all happens because you haven't had the background biochemistry yet. But you sure as hell know what you are looking at. You are familiar with the patterns. Okay, admittedly it is not a high-priority project. It's one that no one else here really has the time for, but it is interesting and it still is important and it could apply to this intellamine and intellicone stuff."

"But what about this racial thing? You say that it's like they're trying to synthesize it, black people?"

"Well, no, not trying. That in itself is a very racist interpretation. Who knows? Their lack of it might be benefiting them in some hidden way. Remember, the gene that causes sickle-cell anemia also confers resistance to malaria. You know, it's like four million years ago or whenever it was that apes started evolving into hominids . . ." Steve took another swallow of Coke. "I want to say this very carefully because I don't want to draw any racist analogies here. I'm your basic skeptic in this whole thing. But look back then."

"Back when?" Charley asked.

"Back four million years ago. The forests were shrinking and the savanna was expanding. There was less room for chimps to be swinging from trees. Fewer branches available. So if survival, in the Darwinian sense, is survival of the fittest, who would be considered the fittest in the high-rent district of the jungle where available real estate is shrinking?"

"The guys who could keep the turf," Charley said.

"Exactly. The big strong apes who could cling and swing the best. It was the weak guys who didn't cling and swing so well who got pushed out onto the savanna and were forced to adapt and walk. You can look at the savanna as the evolutionary bottleneck that caused the walk genes to float to the top and helped to create hominids and eventually human beings."

"So you're saying this lack of intellicone might do the same thing?"

"Not exactly. You can't anticipate evolution. You can look back and say where species have come from, but you can't say with any certainty what they might evolve into. It's just that one group's loss might be another's gain. But it makes me real nervous when science starts looking at stuff like this."

It made Charley nervous, too, but for reasons less sophisticated than Steven Gillespie's. "You know that guy who got killed? Did I tell you about his book and the guy in the audience?"

"You mean the book on human evolution that he'd written?"

"Yeah, that's the one."

Steve nodded. "You told me about it. People get real upset about this evolution business."

"Yeah. Did I tell you what the words were that were scrawled on the wall in blood?" Charley asked.

"Nope."

"Monkey's Uncle."

"Phew!" Steve Gillespie leaned back and raised his arm to run his hand through his hair. There was a damp ring in the armpit of his shirt.

18

There was dinner for eight at Julia Child's house. There was a lost letter from Edgar Allan Poe's mother when the family had lived on Carver Street in Boston, now Charles Street. There was a poetry reading by Seamus Heany and Richard Wilbur to be performed in a private home in the greater Boston area. There was a chance to carry a spear, or whatever Sarah told you to carry, in a Sarah Caldwell opera, and there were also a pair of original works of art by Calista Jacobs from her Caldecott-winning book *Puss in Boots*. Fifteen hundred dollars was the floor at which all bidding opened, and the proceeds would go to WGBH, the Boston educational television channel that for over two decades had provided classics in public broadcasting. The event was billed as the annual WGBH Five Star auction in which five priceless items or experiences were put on the block. It was about as glitzy an event as Cambridge-Boston ever put on. If it had been in New York, it would have been held at the Metropolitan Museum in the Temple of Dendur, and one of the items would have been a cruise on Donald Trump's yacht or the like. But this was not New York. So it was held at the Charles Hotel, a kind of new wave Algonquin in Cambridge. It was forever hosting literary and artistic events.

Calista arrived just as the auction was about to commence. She had missed the cocktail party beforehand on purpose. Calista hated cocktail parties. She found it awkward to stand with a drink in your hand and try to carry on a conversation. But worse than that, she always had the feeling that whoever she was talking with was scanning the room to find someone more powerful or better-connected to talk to. She hated the formlessness of a cocktail party, the lack of structure. There could be no beginnings, middles, and ends to conversations or exchanges. No smooth transitions. It was very hard to know how to move on at a cocktail party. So she had avoided this one. She spotted her neighbors Herb and Ethel Goldman. They waved to her and indicated that there was an empty seat by them.

"Do you want to bid on the Julia Child dinner?" Ethel whispered. "We could go halvsies."

"What a great idea. Sure," Calista replied.

"You know"—Herb was leaning over—"if we had really gotten organized about this, we could have enlisted some other people."

"Oh, you're right, Herbie. Why didn't we think of it?" They dropped out of the bidding when it got to $2,400. The Poe letter brought in the most at $15,200. Calista's pair of drawings fetched $8,750.

"Not bad, Calista! Not bad!" Herb said as they got up to go out onto the terrace for the buffet supper.

"Oh, doesn't it look lovely!" Calista exclaimed as they came out the double doors onto the terrace. Ficus trees in box planters had been strung with tiny lights, and on the tables covered with pink cloths there were soft explosions of anemones in baskets made from dried vines woven through with moss. It was a black-tie event, and the women for the most part wore long, somewhat dated evening gowns. There was not one of those ridiculous confections called "poufs" that made women look like spun-sugar bonbons. None of that at the Charles. The women were dressed in gowns of chiffon and brocade or beaded sheaths. Some had been bought especially for the occasion, but very few were designer dresses. Most had been worn to other events—a wedding, a debut, an anniversary party, a Boston symphony event or a gala at the Wang Center. Shoulders showed, and there were discreet peeks of bosoms. The women looked nice.

They looked special, but they had not dressed for any photographers. They had dressed for themselves and their husbands. Calista recognized across the room old Mrs. Belmont. She and her husband, Montgomery, lived in a beautiful house on Brattle Street. She was a stalwart of the Cambridge Plant and Garden Club, had even written books on gardening. Monty had been a lawyer for Harvard since God knew when. They were in their seventies. Calista could imagine that when Sally Belmont had come down that lovely curving staircase of theirs this evening in her indigo blue chiffon, her ample bosom crushed into the jet beaded bodice, Monty had said something wonderful about how she looked. She had a little mink stole around her shoulders on this fair spring evening. Now where else would you see a mink stole except in Boston? Calista thought.

Calista herself had on the most expensive thing she had ever bought in Filene's basement. She was convinced that it got there by accident. It was a long gray cashmere dress by Armani. It had a wraparound bodice that was cut to the waist and was sprinkled with tiny chip rhinestones. It possessed that deceptively simple tailoring combined with the soft luxurious fabric that was Armani's hallmark. It was fluid. It was sensual, and it went with her hair. She looked rather a knockout in this outfit. She knew it even when she had tried it on over her jeans in the basement that day. The idea of the dress was to wear a minimum of underwear with it. She had no bra on and a string bikini.

She was standing now with Herb and Ethel. She hoped

they didn't think she was clinging to them like some lost child. But she supposed she was. They were her neighbors, and they had been so kind to her and Charley since Tom had died. There wasn't a month that went by when they didn't have her and Charley over for a Sunday dinner. If there was any Harvard event that they thought she would be interested in but might feel awkward going to as a single woman, they always called and invited her to join them. When Herb had been on sabbatical at Stanford last year, they had still called every few weeks. As she stood there talking to them now telling them about Charley's experience at the Martin Institute, she caught sight of a familiar face across the room and stopped midsentence. That face! Hadn't she just seen it somewhere? Where?

"What are you looking at, Calista?" Ethel asked.

"Isn't that what's-his-name? Uh, Ned Baldwin?"

The Goldmans looked in the direction she was looking.

"Oh, yes, Governor Baldwin, or former Governor Baldwin," Herb said. "Of course, he'd be here. He's on the board of GBH. Has been for years."

"He has a roving eye. . . . Look at him," Ethel said. This was a typical Ethel remark. She specialized in certain kinds of information—gossip about public figures. She seemed to know things about these people that the rest of the world didn't, but she was usually right.

"Yes," said Ethel, now looking over at the tanned patrician figure of Ned Baldwin. "I've heard about his chasing about for years. No names. At least none that I recognized." She sniffed as if to suggest that if one were not sleeping with a major novelist, a critic for *The Times Literary Supplement*, or Margaret Thatcher, what was the use of even discussing it.

"Well, he might have a roving eye, but he's got something else, too," Calista said.

"What's that?" Herb said.

"A brain the size of a pea! Did you see that news clip of him on the *Today* show the day before yesterday?"

"No. What did he do?" Ethel asked.

"It showed him at some deal down in Texas with that guy Lorne Thurston."

"Lorne Thurston?" Herb said, somewhat bewildered.

"Yeah, that TV preacher."

"What in the world was he doing with him?" Herb asked.

"Discussing evolution, or rather the lack of it."

"What?" the Goldmans replied.

"I'm not kidding. It was the most preposterous thing I ever saw. He's up there on this platform with the guy, and he's saying things like 'They haven't got any proof for this evolution stuff.' "

"What? I can't believe it!" Herb exclaimed. "I mean, the guy is no genius, but he can't be that dumb. Why would he say such a thing? I . . . I . . . I mean . . . how . . ." Herb began to sputter. "How can he be on the board of directors of WGBH and not believe in evolution?"

Calista and Ethel both burst out laughing at this. Herb ran his fingers through his curly gray hair and squinted through his thick glasses.

They went through the buffet line and sat down at one of the tables with two other couples they knew from Cambridge. As dessert was being served a band started playing and a few people began to dance. Ned Baldwin was standing with two other men near the table where they had been seated. One was another board member, and the other was a producer for GBH.

"Hal, I think we've lost Sid," Ned said to the board member.

"I'm sorry," Sid said. "But that woman dancing with that rather squat man . . ."

"Oh, my goodness," whispered Ned. "She is lovely."

"Isn't that the artist, the children's book illustrator whose pictures they auctioned off tonight?"

"Calista Jacobs, of course!" said Hal Marteau. "The one whose husband was killed, the famous astrophysicist, Tom Jacobs, and all that mess with the CIA, and oh . . ." He waved a hand as if to clear away the mess. It had been a mess. Hal Marteau knew too well. He was on the board of overseers of Harvard.

"My, she looks better than she photographs," Ned said. "You know, my cousin Arch Baldwin helped her out quite a bit in that situation."

"She's very stunning in an unusual way," Sid said.

The three men gazed at her appreciatively. She looked like a column of moonlight in her soft narrow gray dress as she moved across the dance floor. Her weather-front hair now looked like a silvery nimbus around her head. She had just finished dancing with Jensen Reed, whose head came up approximately to her sternum, which in the case of this particular dress was partially exposed. Jensen chattered away animatedly about his grandchildren and how much they enjoyed her books. She thought he might have stolen an occasional glance across the moraine of her bony breastplate in search of a breast, but she had wrapped the bodice so that there was only a suggestion and no bosom visible.

A younger man suddenly appeared and tapped Jensen on the shoulder. "Cutting in, are you, Sid?"

"Indeed, sir."

My goodness, thought Calista. She didn't know when was the last time she had been cut in on.

"I'm Sid."

"I'm Calista."

"I know. I couldn't afford your drawings."

"That makes two of us." He laughed at her remark. "What do you do, Sid?" she asked.

"I'm a producer for *Earth Stories*."

"Oh, that's a neat program. My son watches it all the time. Do you get to go to all those places—the Arctic and the Galápagos?"

"Not always. Sometimes. Mostly I sit at desks and in editing rooms."

Out of the corner of her eye she caught a glimpse of Baldwin dancing with none other than Julia Child, who was a good two inches taller than he was, and Baldwin was nearly six feet. It didn't last long, however. For she soon saw him guiding Julia toward her table, where he chatted briefly with the other people. Amazing, she thought, how fluidly he moved between these two worlds. He was so much a part of this one. It became all the more unbelievable those brief minutes—seconds, probably— that she had seen him on the television news screen.

She and Sid chatted on for a few more minutes, and then Calista felt it happening. She saw the figure threading through the dancing couples, and she knew, just knew, that he was coming toward her.

"Sorry, Sid, my turn."

"All right, Ned. I never argue with a board member, and remember my graciousness when I ask you for funding for *The Vanishing People* series."

"Good sport." Ned chuckled as he took Calista's right hand. She was appalled. She hadn't been prepared for this repartee when she had seen him coming toward her. All the light talk might be a joke, but still she was the butt of it. It was her femaleness that made it work. She had just been bartered for, plain and simple. It wasn't fair. Calista's rules about ethnic or minority jokes were that they were acceptable only if they were told by a person identified with that group. She hadn't told the joke. Nobody had asked her permission. It wasn't funny. It wasn't just small talk. It was rude. But she didn't know what to do. And now she felt his right hand on the small of her back, pressing her lightly into the rhythm of the music, and his left hand beginning to steer her on a course.

"I'm Neddy Baldwin." He smiled warmly, and the taut skin around his eyes crinkled.

"I know." Calista nodded stiffly.

He continued to smile. "I just took a whirl with Julia. I must say you're more my size."

Don't count on it! Calista thought. She was madly ransacking her brain for an idea of what to do, how to end this, but she felt her anger welling up dangerously. This stupid jerk had been on the same platform with Lorne Thurston, and now he was dancing with her!

"I always make a point of dancing with the female stars of the auction."

"Too bad the old lady's not here," Calista said.

"What?" he asked, slightly bewildered.

"Mrs. Poe—Edgar's mother."

"Oh, ho ho!" He threw back his elegant square chin and laughed while pulling her closer to him. "Oh, my! You're very clever. That's cute. I like that in a woman."

"You do." It wasn't a question, and there was something rather chilling, an unnerving light that emanated from the dark hooded eyes, that made Neddy Baldwin swallow and look at her again. Had he said something wrong? God, she was intriguing. The silver-shot hair swirled about her head like smoke. Archie, he had sensed, had been quite taken by her, but there was something funny going on here.

Just at that moment Calista, as if searching for what to say or do next, looked up at the sky. It was a clear night. The stars were brilliant in the spring night sky. *Follow the arc to Arcturus and speed on to Spica!* So went the exhortation of ancient navigators. She saw Arcturus burning bright in the constellation of Boötes and Spica below, lead star in the constellation of Virgo, but suddenly she realized the Charioteer was missing. Where was her starry Charioteer! Slipped out of the sky on its transit through the seasons? Why in heaven's name was she dancing with this idiot?

"Are you planning to do a program on *Nova* on scientific creationism?" she asked suddenly.

"Wh-what?" He cracked a grin. "Whatcha talking about?"

"You, Mr. Baldwin. I saw you on the news the other day with that Christian thug Lorne Thurston."

"Oh, thaaat!" He tossed the noble chin back again and laughed. "You know, you're in a position like me, you get around all over . . ."

"Precisely!" Calista had stopped dancing and dropped her hand out of his. This was a point that had never been covered in the proper dancing school that Neddy had attended some forty-five years before: what to do if the young lady simply stops cold in the middle of the foxtrot and drops her hands to her sides. He had never seen anyone as still and as coldly angry as this stunning woman who stood before him like some blazing column of moonlight. He tried to reconcile those breasts, lovely mounds quivering under the soft cashmere of her dress, with those dark hooded eyes and the anger. She had seemed so delectable just minutes before, but those breasts were actually quivering in fury.

Calista's heart was pounding. Her chest seized in a tachycardia. She had never made a scene before, but she felt she might now. He seemed mesmerized by her, and he still had this silly grin on his face. God save this man if he said she was beautiful when she was angry. She'd kick him right in the nuts. She lowered her voice, but the words came out in a ratchety noise. "I think Lorne Thurston and all of those television evangelists are bullies, and I'm sick of their screaming from their bully pulpits. You should be ashamed, Mr. Baldwin. You and your storm troopers for God!"

With that she turned on her heel and left. Left Neddy Baldwin with his firm, aristocratic jaw dropped into a profile that made him look a hair's breadth away from being declared a certifiable moron. But worse than that, she had left this handsome scion of patrician New England without a dance partner for the first time in his life.

19

"Rabbit's blood!" Charley repeated. Steven Gillespie had just called him.

"Yep . . . and that other sequence you gave me, the trace sequence, indicates monkey's blood. But you said that was only in very small amounts."

"Yeah, at least according to the police report." Charley paused. "How does a human being get murdered and spurt rabbit blood?"

"In a Sheraton Hotel, no less. Sounds a little weird to me. Did he keep any pets? Travel with them?"

"He wasn't a circus. He was a science writer, a children's book writer, to be exact."

"Bunnies!"

"What?" Charley was shocked. There was something in the way that Steve had said that soft, plump little word that was absolutely horrifying. Some macabre connection was fighting to the surface of his mind.

"Oh, I was just thinking," Steve began. "You know, all the books for little kids. . . ."

But Charley wasn't even hearing him. The shadow of a monstrous notion began to slide across his brain. There were so many oddities in this situation, so many unlikely events and contradictions, that it was hard to know where to begin to look for a pattern, and if one could even exist within this batch of illogical elements—bunny blood, monkey blood, strangulations, and the words *Monkey's Uncle,* scrawled in rabbit's blood by what? An irate creationist who thought someone was taking potshots at God? Charley could live with disorder, with chaos, with breaks in the pattern. He found them intriguing more than threatening. It was what made black holes, singularities, and the origins of the universe so exciting. It was what had compelled his father to devote his intellectual life to the study of such phenomena, and it compelled him to look at chaos and not see it as the absence of order, but rather as the presence of randomness and the unpredictable. Chaos in Charley's mind could be another kind of order, an order that followed different rules entirely. But right now a monster shadow spread its wings like a dark dragon. A dragon! He suddenly remembered those dragons at Margaret McGowan's house. Sweet velvet dragons with satin wings and some spitting tongues of satin flames. He had to see that book again. It was a wild hunch, but nonetheless . . . "You going to be at the lab late?"

"Sure. Why?"

"I might want to bring something in for you to look at. It's just a hunch, but . . ."

"No, fine, Charley. I'll be here."

It was just a hunch, but thank God the police department was so inefficient, Charley thought as he biked over to Foster Street and Margaret McGowan's house. When Calista had finally gotten a message through to the two detectives about the defaced books she and Margaret had received, the police were supposed to have sent over someone to collect the evidence. This had never happened. It had not surprised Calista or Charley. Calista had started to think of cops like appliance repairmen. They never returned calls. They never showed up, and if they did, who knows—they might charge you twenty-five bucks an hour for labor plus parts. So Charley was sure that the book would still be at Margaret's, although Margaret was in Scotland and not to return until the end of the month. Mammy, however, was house-sitting for her, and when Charley biked up she was out sweeping the walk in a bright rose-colored running suit and billed cap that said La Costa.

"Why, hello there, Charley. You playing hooky or what?"

"Naw. It's an early release day. Public schools get out quarter to one so teachers can have meetings."

"That's nice. What can I do for you?"

Charley was chaining his bike to the front-gate post. "You know that book that Margaret got, the one with the—"

Mammy scowled. "You don't have to tell me. I know the one. Disgusting. Depraved! Lord, what sewer minds some people have . . . and going on to do something like that to Margaret! I said to her I hope Leo never sees that."

"Leo?"

"Leo Krell, her illustrator on that book. Sweetest little man you ever met. But he's had two bypass operations, and I think he's got himself a pacemaker now, and seeing

135

that horrible, horrible thing might just short-circuit him!"

"Well, Mammy, I have a favor to ask."

"What's that, son?" She stopped sweeping and looked up.

"Could I borrow that book just for a short time? I really need it."

"What you need a book like that for? Gives me the willies just having it around, but Margaret says we got to keep it for the police, but the police never come."

"Well, I got this kind of loony hunch, and I just want to borrow it for a short time. I'll bring it right back."

"What kind of a hunch you got on?" Mammy said, clasping her hands over the top of the broom handle and resting her chin.

"Well, if you don't mind, I'd rather not say right now. If my hunch turns out right, you'll be the first to know. I promise."

He broke that promise.

"Rabbit's blood!" Calista exclaimed. "That's rabbit's blood, not paint." Calista's finger trembled as she pointed at the picture of Rothgar on the Plain of Crystal Doom and the seven meticulously drawn slits spurting the teardrops of blood. "Oh, God." She touched her hand to her cheek. "I would have thought it was Aquatext seventy-two."

"No way, José," Charley said.

"You're sure about this?"

"Absolutely. They ran it through the blood analyzer in the hematology lab at the institute."

"How do they run a book through a machine?"

"Easy. All I did was lift some of the dried blood off using Scotch tape. Then this girl, Inga, dissolved it in some solution and ran it through the Ultra centrifuge machine. Then it was ready for the blood analyzer. It can analyze for about eighteen jillion things at once—hemoglobin counts, platelets, antigens, you name it. It was the antigens that gave it away."

"Bugs Bunny, huh?" She bit her lower lip lightly as she contemplated this information.

"Yep." Charley sprawled on the winged chair in the study and looked at his mom, who had about three pencils sticking out of her hair and was clutching a paintbrush as if it were a weapon.

"This is really getting sick," she muttered, and thought how both Walt Disney and Beatrix Potter must be turning in their respective graves.

"Listen, I promised to get the book back to Mammy. As a matter of fact, I promised that I would tell her first if my hunch was right, and I came home and told you instead."

"How did you ever hunch this in the first place?"

"I told you that the blood on the wall was rabbit with a little bit of monkey's blood."

"Oh, yeah, yeah. And you got that from hacking into the police files. That really makes me nervous."

Charley wanted to say that that should be the least that made her nervous, but he didn't. "Look," he said, "people do it all the time. It's absolutely untraceable, and even if it were, I didn't do anything criminal."

"Hmm."

Charley couldn't tell if it was a sigh or a moan coming from his mother's clamped mouth. Whatever it was, it sounded slightly skeptical but not totally condemnatory. He suddenly noticed a VCR tape to the left of his mother's drawing board. "What's that?"

Calista slid her eyes to the left and this time did sigh. *"Eddie Murphy—Raw."*

"Mom!" Charley grinned. "Are you kidding?"

"You know I've always thought Eddie Murphy was funny."

"Yeah, but . . ." The words hung in the air, begging an explanation. How could she explain that after dancing with Ned Baldwin the previous evening, the best anti-dote she could think of was Eddie Murphy? She had been so furious at that party that she had stormed out, barely saying good-bye to the Goldmans and claiming to have a headache. What she had was a monumental case of fury. She had almost felt a sense of contamination after dancing with him and staring into that genial but vacuous face. "The banality of evil," that fantastic phrase of Hannah Arendt's, was all she could think of. With Ned Baldwin, of course, it wasn't precisely evil. It was more like the banality of ignorance. But it was a case where ignorance could very easily slip beyond the border and into evil. And Eddie Murphy was about as far away from Ned Baldwin as she could get. He was bawdy, scatological, savvy, and even though he was for all intents and purposes antifeminist, he was so extreme and funny that in the end he merely became a caricature of what was considered macho. So who cared if he bragged about his big dick and used the word *fuck* like a comma? He came off as essentially smart, good-hearted, and hysterically funny. She had laughed until she'd cried, something that Ned Baldwin had not made her do. And now that she was staring at bunny blood, she needed all the laughs she could get. But she wasn't sure how she could explain the Ned Baldwin part to Charley.

"Did I tell you that I met Ned Baldwin?"

"Ned Baldwin? You mean that creep on television the other day?"

"The very one. And Archie's cousin, although he bears no resemblance whatsoever."

"You're kidding. Where?"

"At that GBH party last night."

"What was he like?"

"Well, I thought loathsome. Although I'm sure he passes." Her voice dwindled off as she thought of him chatting so amicably with all the A-list people and profiling so nobly.

"What do you mean, 'passes'?" Charley asked.

"People like Neddy Baldwin always slip through until they slip up," she replied, and then added somewhat cryptically, "It comes with the territory." She paused. "Anyhow, getting back to this blood thing. Somehow it doesn't make sense at all. But how in the heck, Charley, did you ever even hunch that those . . . those . . ." She hesitated, searching for a word. "Drops on Margaret's book, Rothgar's wounds, were really blood? That's just astounding to me."

"I don't know. I was just looking for patterns, not logical patterns, really, just something beyond surfaces, like beyond event horizons."

Something very deep ached within Calista. He was so much like his father. "And you found it. You found a new pattern."

"I don't know whether it's a new pattern or a new puzzle." He paused, his eyes becoming opaque. Calista tried to think, think like Charley, think like Tom. They so easily traveled beyond the surface order of things, across the lines to where the rules stopped and chaos began. They were not afraid to contemplate new complexities. She should try.

"Maybe it's not a pattern—the rabbit's blood."

"What do you mean?"

"Maybe we're asking the wrong questions."

"I wasn't exactly asking any questions," Charley said.

"Well, I was, sort of. I was trying to figure out that if we assume that a God-fearing Christian creationist was so outraged by Norman Petrakis's view that he would scrawl in blood the words *Monkey's Uncle,* how could he kill a rabbit to do it?"

"You mean how could Christian love kill a cute little furry bunny even though the guy was mad enough to kill another human being?"

"Yes, in a sense. I guess I think they would use lamb's blood or goat's blood. It's sort of the symbolic sacrificial media of the Bible. It's more religious."

"I don't know. Look at the Easter Bunny."

"Well, I never have been able to figure that one out. Not that I'm doing so well on this. But somehow rabbit's blood in this case just doesn't fit—at least not with these fundamentalists or scientific creationists."

"I don't know. You said that guy at the conference was pretty mad."

"Not exactly mad—obsessed."

"Obsessed enough to kill a rabbit—that would be kind of small potatoes for someone getting ready to kill a man. A little hors d'oeuvres."

"Oh, Charley!"

20

Dear Sirs:

I am interested in applying for admission to the Lorne Thurston College of Christian Heritage. I have a feeling that it might be what I am seeking in furthering my education both spiritually and intellectually.

Charley held the paper and read in a small voice from the top bunk. Matthew in the bottom bunk was spending the night. It was a Saturday night, and Calista was still prowling around. He didn't want her to hear this.

"I think it's real weird—just the name of the college," Matthew whispered up. "To say that it's a college of Christian heritage and then use a guy's name right in the title, weird! I mean, if you were to start a college of Jewish heritage, would you call it the Charley Jacobs College of Jewish Heritage? It's like this guy Lorne Thurston owns it all, the philosophy, the religion, the works."

"I know. It's sort of like a franchise operation."

"McDonald's."

"Right. McDonald's."

"Well, there you go. It makes me think of hamburgers, not God," Matthew said.

"You got to understand that these people are into owning things and franchising religion. They got radio stations and TV networks and colleges."

"Okay, go ahead. This is the first letter, right?"

"Yeah, I got an answer."

"And your mother didn't see it?"

"No, luckily it came on a Saturday when I was home to intercept it, and the other one—"

"There's another one?"

"Yes, confirming the receipt of my application and my interview date."

"Interview date? You joking?"

"No. But I'll tell you about that later. Anyhow, I told Vicki, our cleaning lady, to try and intercept that one for me, if it came when I wasn't here."

"And she did?"

"Yeah."

"Okay. Read on."

I really want to learn more about God and the Bible, and for the next four years I would like to attend a Christian college for this purpose. I think this will help me grow in my walk with God.

"Whew-eeee!" Matthew exclaimed. "Walk with God! Charley, too much!"

"It's not too much for these people. Wait till I show you their brochure. Everybody's taking walks with God and talking about being in a closer relationship with Jesus and studying with Jesus by their side."

"Come on and dance with God, do the boog-a-loo," Matthew sang.

"No. They don't dance. It's against the rules of Christian Life Standards." He continued reading the letter aloud.

I would very much appreciate it if you would send an application form and a catalog describing more about your college and the courses you offer. Also my mother and I shall be visiting in Texas in June and would very much like to take the opportunity at this time to come out and visit the campus and arrange for an interview if that is possible.

I look forward to hearing from you in the near future.

Sincerely,
Charles Jacobs

"I was going to sign it 'Your Friend in Christ,' but I thought that might be overdoing it."

"I think going for an interview will be overdoing it, Charley."

"Look, Matthew, how am I going to find out about anything if I don't investigate this? I got a hunch about these guys, and I'm going to follow it."

"But you don't know that it's Lorne Thurston and his guys. There are hundreds of these televangelists. Why does it have to be him?"

"Because he's the richest and the most powerful, and it was people from his college, at least some of them, that were involved in the fake footprints of dinosaurs and men down in Texas at Paluxy Creek, and they are spearheading this whole scientific creationism thing and all the stuff with getting it into the schools."

"Yeah, but Charley, how the heck are you going to pass yourself off as a college applicant? I mean, you're only an eighth-grader."

"By June I will officially be a ninth-grader, and you know I can fudge a little."

"But you're too short. You don't shave. You don't have much in the way of secondary sex characteristics, as they call them in sex ed."

"I don't have to stand naked in front of these guys."

Matthew laughed, and Charley felt the frame of the bunk bed shake. He was laughing too at the idea of him being interviewed nude and taking a naked tour of the Lorne Thurston College of Christian Heritage. "And I have the height problem solved."

"How's that."

"I'm going to get elevator shoes."

"What?"

"Elevator shoes. They make you taller. Mammy, this lady who works for Margaret McGowan, is going to take me to get them. She knows where. It's someplace in Boston."

"Are you ever going to tell your mother?"

"Sure. I'll have to. She's got to go with me for the interview. I just don't want to tell her yet. She's not totally convinced about the creationists' part in Petrakis's murder. But I am."

"Okay, read the next letter."

"Okay. This is the one where they just sent me the application and brochure. It's short but here. . . ." He reached over the side of the bed and handed down a large envelope with some materials in it. "You got to look at the brochure and the course catalog to get the full flavor of this place."

Dear Charles:

Lorne Thurston College of Christian Heritage is a great place to live and learn. If you are a person who is wanting to grow in both mind and spirit and deepen your relationship with our Lord Jesus, this is the place for you.

Enclosed you will find the application for admission to Lorne Thurston College of Christian Heritage. When I myself filled out this application seven years ago I had no idea of the far-reaching effects it would have. I met teachers and students with whom I have come to have deep respect and close friendships. They have taught me many subjects and I have gained knowledge, but most important I have learned how all they have taught me is related directly to God's Word. I think that you, too, if you fill out the application form, could participate in a similar experience. I pray that if the Lord wants you at Lorne Thurston College of Christian Heritage, He will work out all the necessary details.

When you and your mother know the exact dates of your visit to Dallas, please inform us and we shall be happy to set up an appointment for an interview and a tour of our campus.

Sincerely,
Tommy Lee Clayton
Assistant Director of Admissions

Charley leaned over and looked down at Matthew, who was lolling his head over the side of the bunk and holding the course catalog. "Well, what do you think?" Charley asked.

"I never really thought of God as a detail man. I mean, from the Big Bang on he seems to have gotten it okay. So I guess that is a lot of details."

"My dad, by the way, said that the Big Bang theory doesn't exclude God at all. That's why they liked my dad at the Vatican so much. He gave a speech there when they had the conference on cosmology. Standing room only at the Vatican. That's what my mom said. Pretty good in a place like that where the pope is the only game in town."

"Something tells me the Vatican is way ahead of Lorne Thurston College of Christian Heritage."

"Yeah, they sorted all this out hundreds of years ago, according to my mom. She says they must look at all this stuff here going on in this country with scientific creationism as really weird. Like, where you guys been for the last two hundred years?"

"Did you read this catalog?"

"Of course I read it."

"Did you see some of these weird courses? Christian Anthropology—Searching for the Ark. It's only given in the fall semester. Sounds like an Indiana Jones–type course. And this one, Flood Geology. It's offered both semesters. I can't believe this. Listen to the course description. 'A close examination of the Noachian Flood as a cataclysmic model in which the general order from simple to complex organisms is confirmed in the geologic column. A hydraulic refutation of Darwinian notions of evolution.'" Matthew paused. "What in the world is a hydraulic refutation?"

"I'm not sure. I think it means that this ordering of fossils was predicted or determined just by the mechanics of the Flood, all at once, right after the land drained, and that the order had nothing to do with things evolving over a long period of time. The Flood drowned them and then redeposited them in the fossil order that geologists find them."

"Gee whiz. They really go on with this Flood thing. Here's a course that's about the greenhouse effect and the Flood."

"Yeah. You see, they're always trying to be scientific about all this, at least up to a point. I don't think they like to have their theories tested like real scientists."

"Did you read the rules for Christian Life Standards?"

"Yeah. They're a breeze. I don't smoke, drink. I don't fornicate. I'm not a homosexual."

"You say 'shit' and 'fuck.' "

"Well, I could give that up. I just wish regular college was so easy to get into."

"Yeah. So what is this other letter you got back?"

"Okay . . . here goes. Now, Matthew, just hang on when I get to one part. I'll explain it. Don't worry."

"What do you mean—don't worry?" He leaned farther out of the lower bunk and looked up at Charley.

"Just hang on."

Dear Charles:

We have received your application form and we would be most happy to have you and your mother come to our campus on Wednesday June 20 for a visit. If you plan to arrive here by ten o'clock that morning, there will be ample time for us to give you a tour of our campus and have a talk. We have enclosed a map for your convenience. It is only a thirty-minute drive from Dallas, and at that hour you should have no trouble with traffic. We shall be sending to you character reference forms, one of which should be given to your pastor, the Reverend Matthew McPhail.

"What?" screeched Matthew.

"Look, you had to list your religious affiliation, the home church, and your pastor's name. It's no big deal."

"No big deal! Charley, what are you talking about? I am an eighth-grader in a Cambridge public school. I am not a pastor of any church, and I am not called Reverend McPhail. Somebody calls up my house and asks for Reverend McPhail, my mother's not going to know what the heck's going on. She might think it's the obscene caller we had from last fall and that he's just changed his line."

"What obscene caller?"

"Some weird guy used to call up and pretend he was taking a survey. Then he'd ask my mom about her breasts or something."

"Oh, gross!"

"Yeah, well, let these folks from this college call up and ask for Pastor McPhail and she'll think it's him again."

"They're not going to call up, Matthew. So just cool it. I don't even have to send these character references in at all now. They're willing to interview me without them. They just say that when these forms are completed that the application is considered complete. So I don't see why you're upset."

"You'd be upset, too, Jacobs, if I'd done this to you."

"No, I wouldn't."

"Yes, you would."

"Let's not get into a fight, okay? I'll make it up to you. I'll pay for three rounds of games at Elsie's."

"And an Elsie Burger?"

"Yes, an Elsie Burger."

"A knish?"

"A knish for Pastor McPhail. Yeah, you got it."

146

21

Charley did not buy his mother a knish or a round of games or an Elsie Burger for a bribe. Instead he stood watching her doing the Buffalo shuffle, shifting to a ball change for two measures, then a toe, heel drop and culminating in a Maxiford break to top off the last of the sixty-four measures. It was not a laughing matter any longer. He tried not to look pained. He wondered if the other people in his mom's class were quite as bad as she was.

"Well, what do you think?" she asked eagerly.

He thought she should stick to illustrating. That's what he really thought. "Well, I think your tap dancing has really improved, Mom."

"Really? You do? Of course, you haven't seen me do it, really. I mean, I can't believe you asked to see me practice this morning."

"Oh, well, you know, I just thought . . . but anyway, yeah, you're a lot better. You're not as good as . . . who's that black guy?"

"Gregory Hines."

"Yeah, him."

"Well, no way. I mean, that's really black tap dancing what he does. A whole other thing. I mean, not that I'm going to be Ruby Keeler. But my teacher says I've really improved."

"Listen, Mom. I want to ask you something."

"Uh-oh!" She paused. "Is that why you were being so nice about my tap dancing?"

"No, Mom! No. I was really interested. I mean, I hear you tapping away in the bathroom and here in the kitchen, and your feet clicking under your drawing board. I was just interested." She didn't believe him.

"Okay. What is it?"

"Well, you know how I'm going with you to Dallas."

"Yes, dear. My moral support while I get the award. I'm much appreciative. True loyalty." And she meant it. A thirteen-year-old boy's idea of heaven was not being at a convention with forty thousand librarians and eating practically every meal with small groups of these librarians while the publisher introduced them to their favorite and most beloved children's book illustrator. But she in turn had promised to take Charley and two friends to a Grateful Dead concert in the fall. It was all negotiation. That's what parenting boiled down to.

"Okay. Now do you realize that Green Acre, Texas, is only a thirty-minute drive from downtown Dallas?"

"No, but why would I want to go to Green Acre? Is that like God's Green Acre?"

Charley rolled his eyes. "Guess so."

"Well, why would I want to go to Green Acre, Texas? Is there a Grateful Dead concert there?"

"No," Charley said quietly. "But the Lorne Thurston College of Christian Heritage is there, and we have an appointment for an interview on June twentieth at ten o'clock in the morning."

"Charley!" She stared at her son, her feet dead in her patent-leather tap shoes.

22

Charley was holding up his end admirably.
He had run relays taking glasses of wine to his mom,
Janet Weiss, and Ethan Thayer, chairman of J. T. Thayer
and Sons Publishing, as they stood accepting the congrat-
ulations for the Caldecott Award in an interminable
receiving line of librarians. The librarians loved Charley.
He was polite. He was cute. And he read. But most of all
his face was traceable in the scores of children's books
that his mother had illustrated that they bought in
multiple copies for their school and public libraries.
They could go back home and tell eager young readers
that they had met *The Selkie Boy* or *The Night Glider* or
Edward from *I'm the Boss* or Peter from *Monster Pie*.
And did they know that one of the boys in the *Wild
Swans* was Charley Jacobs, the illustrator's son, and the
rest of the brothers were his friends? Often they asked
Charley to pose for pictures holding a book in which his
face had appeared. Then when they returned home to
their local public libraries or school libraries, they would
put up Charley's picture on their bulletin boards in
Peoria or Dubuque or Great Bend or Tacoma or Bethes-
da or Omaha. Charley, of course, did not tell them that
he no longer read children's books or even Y.A., young
adult, books. He'd finished with all that a couple of years
before. The Y.A. books bored him silly. They were all
about teenagers with problems. Even Janet Weiss, who
edited them, had learned not to send any more to
Charley and was sometimes heard to refer to this genre
as the teenage-problem-of-the-month syndrome. My
mother's alcoholic, my dad's gay, and I'm on crack—this

seemed to be typical fare of the genre. Problem-solving novels, they called them. It wasn't that Charley didn't think these were worthwhile subjects for contemplation. He just thought there was something terribly mechanical about it all—the plots, the characters, the style. It was all, in one sense, too solvable. If a kid did the right thing, summoned the right kind of strength and gritted his or her teeth, he or she would make it. He preferred Robert Cormier or S. E. Hinton, who wrote very realistic novels in which the problems could not always be solved but offered characters who indeed probed a more monstrous world and explored the darker side of teenage life. These "problems" might not have anything to do with drugs, but rather hideous power struggles and bouts with megalomaniacal gang leaders and corrupt adults. Charley liked them the best of the Y.A. fiction. But in reality his favorite reading material of late was stuff that would never be recognized by these librarians or make its way onto the lists of Best Books for Young Adults. They were mass-market paperbacks often published by companies with names that did not have any familiar bookish ring but sounded more as if they had something to do with semiconductors or silicon chips or even toys. Companies like TSR, parent company of Steve Jackson Games, that produced books like *Green Circle Blues* and *Bimbos of the Death Sun*. These books sold millions of copies, but they weren't on the reading lists of many of the librarians at this convention.

"Charley Jacobs!" a deep voice rumbled. He swung around with the glass in his hand that he was en route with to Ethan Thayer. A large lady with frizzy hair and wearing a stiff emerald green dress loomed before him, not unlike the Emerald City in the *Wizard of Oz*. He read her name tag quickly: Elsa Dineen, Petaluma County Librarian, Petaluma, California. He remembered her vaguely, probably from when he had traveled with his mom last year to California on a book promotion tour.

"You've been working so hard," the woman continued, "I thought you might need something yourself. Looks like this line is going to go on for another twenty minutes." She held out toward him a plate of goodies—little petit fours and pastries.

"Oh, gosh, that looks great. Let me get this wine to Ethan." It wasn't really wine, but Charley and Ethan weren't telling anybody. Ethan had arranged for a waiter to serve him vodka on the rocks. There was no way he could get through being so unmitigatingly charming to this endless stream to whom he owed his fortune without something stronger than Chablis. He loved them all, every single librarian from Petaluma to St. Petersburg. And they loved him because he was one of the last independents in publishing. J. T. Thayer and Sons had not been swallowed up into some disgusting amalgam of fast-food chains and amusement parks. His late father and his two sons had, over the course of nearly seventy years, published the books that they wanted to publish. They were the best. They promoted and marketed them skillfully, and they felt no compulsion to have a block-buster every other list because they had a backlist that any other publisher would kill for.

They were Quality with a capital Q. And as the old man, Ethan Thayer, Sr., had once said before he died, "Any outfit like ours that thinks they're going to be bought, kept, and pampered like a nineteenth-century courtesan to a king is mistaken. They aren't. They're going to be treated like a hot call girl for a limited period of time and then be thrown out on the streets. It's pure fantasy to think that you are going to become the jewel in the crown of one of these conglomerates that makes hamburgers and runs porpoise shows." The old man saw it all coming before it really arrived. He saw this sala-cious union between books and food and knew, antici-pated, leveraged buyouts before they ever got into full frenzy as they did in the eighties.

Calista Jacobs had been one of the jewels in the Thayer crown for nearly twenty years. She had come into their offices in Gramercy Park fresh out of college or, more accurately, the spring before her commencement from Bryn Mawr, toting a portfolio. She had gotten an ap-pointment with the art director because her father, a midwesterner with a restaurant supply business, was also an expert poker player and trout fisherman and had written a book on both entitled *Bluffing*. It had turned out to be a best-seller, and it was through his connection that Calista got the appointment. But art directors and editors had hundreds of such appointments with aspiring artists and writers with a "connection" every year, and very rarely did they turn into anything. However, the minute Michael Ronay looked at her portfolio he knew he had a gem. It wasn't that she was flashy, and it wasn't even her line, deceptively simple yet endlessly manipulable in service to subject and style. She had first of all this intensity of vision, an undivided attention that resulted in distilled images of great power. Then she possessed an uncanny intercourse with the classical world and a nearly magical ability to make it serve her without hesitation or pretension. It was all quietly there. Dürer, Altdorfer, Brueghel, da Vinci, the Limburg brothers, Grünewald. She integrated it subtly, gracefully, without ever missing a step, and yet it was all somehow her own. No one ever mistook a Calista Jacobs illustration for anyone else's. Michael had thought of her, in this almost mysterious relation with the classical world of painters and print makers, as some kind of idiot savant, similar to the autistic people who could do computerlike calculations in their heads and be able to tell you that Valentine's Day in the year 2093 would fall on a Tuesday. But she was no idiot. She was charming, sexy in a funny, offbeat way, yet perfectly normal. She was also very tough and soon became knowledgeable when it came to negotiating contracts—although she was quickly plucked up by an agent, which was all to the good since she would never have had time to draw and deal with all the subsidiary rights and ancillary deals that began to pour in. Tonight was her second Caldecott Medal, an award that guaranteed handsome profits for the publishing company and herself.

Calista looked around now for Charley. He really was a sport. She supposed it wouldn't hurt to follow this hunch of his and go out to this stupid college tomorrow. All of their official obligations would be over by then and they would be taking an evening flight back to Boston. Charley was very insistent about how she should look, and one of his ideas was that she had to do something about her hair. The gray had to go. It just wouldn't look right. He was probably right. Judging from the good Christian women she had seen on the television evangelism shows, which they had taken to watching in preparation, nobody let anything go natural. Helmet-style hairdos or cascades of rigor mortis curls, all dyed chromium colors, were in abundance. Makeup was basically applied with backhoes. But she was loath to dye her hair. Low maintenance in gardens and cosmetics was the name of the game. That's why she had granite in her Cambridge yard and gray hair on her head. You start dyeing your hair, she had told Charley, and there's no end to it. You got to keep fussing with the color, and it never turns out the same way twice. But leave it to Charley! He had found a temporary rinse at the pharmacy. Guaranteed to wash out with one shampoo. So she had agreed to become something called a Rosy Dawn redhead the next morning. She had wondered when she bought the bottle if the name was intentionally a classical allusion to Homer's rosy-fingered dawn that seemed to greet Odysseus every morning when he broached the wind in his sailing vessel. The things she did for this kid! Right now, however, he seemed to be bearing up quite well. A large green librarian was plying him with goodies.

"Umm, these are good," Charley was saying as he bit into something with whipped cream. "You know something?" he said, pointing to another pastry on the plate identical to the one he was eating.

"What's that?" Elsa Dineen asked.

"They got a thing in this city about squirting everything out of tubes and making it fancy. Every meal I've had since I've been here, if they serve you something like mashed potatoes or even creamed spinach, they squirt it into these little decorations. You know, it looks kind of like corduroy all the time. Doesn't hurt the taste. Just wonder why they do that."

"Wouldn't know," Elsa said. "Tell me, what have you been reading lately?"

"You want an honest answer or the other?"

"Why, Charley, you mean you haven't been reading all the Newbery winners?"

"No, I try to avoid them if I can."

"So what's it been?"

"Bimbos of the Death Sun."

"What?" Calista had just walked up. The receiving line had finished for all intents and purposes.

"I was just telling Mrs. Dineen what I was reading."

"Great title. What's it about? And by the way, I'm not a Mrs. but a Ms. But you can call me Elsa."

Librarians were really the most tolerant people in the world. One had to be if one read at all, Calista thought. It was categorically impossible to be a bigot if one read widely.

But Charley was worried. If this lady liked being called Ms., she might not like some of the story of *Bimbos*. He took the plunge. "Well, it takes place at this sci-fi conference. Everybody there's a sci-fi writer, and there's this murder."

"Where does the bimbo part come in?"

"Oh . . ." He paused. How should he put this? "Well, one of the writers has written this story, and the idea of it is how women who work on computers are being affected by sunspots. . . . It's kind of complicated, but it's impairing their uh . . . brain . . . uh . . ."

"Hmm." That was Elsa's comment. She paused and then asked thoughtfully, "Is it corrupting you, Charley?"

"Naw, it's just fun reading."

"Well, you know we're in censorship territory down here. Home of the Gablers and all those people who want to edit textbooks."

"Oh, God!" Calista sighed.

"Yes sireee." Elsa Dineen nodded. "Powerful group, and don't you believe for one minute that the publishers with large educational divisions don't cater to them. If a text gets adopted by the Texas Board of Education for use in the public school system, well, that is fat city for the publishers. We're talking tens of millions of dollars in profits! Oh, they're very sneaky about it. Norma Gabler, who has really spearheaded the movement, talks about 'balanced treatment.' She talks about how it is 'liberal' to give both sides of an issue, that it is incumbent upon us as parents and teachers to present both sides, and then she goes on and asks for both sides in the field of biology to be presented. Why can't we teach creation theory along with atheism? She calls that academic freedom. You know, go ahead and let in every crackpot idea. Slippery, isn't it?"

Calista and Charley both nodded. Neither one of them could believe that they were having this conversation on the eve of their visit to Lorne Thurston College of Christian Heritage.

"It's a hard argument to counter, isn't it?" Calista said after a long pause. She knew what Charley was thinking. Don't even try and counter it tomorrow, Mom!

"Indeed it is," replied Elsa. "But really it has nothing to do with academic freedom. Have you ever heard what John Dewey said about the meaning of real intellectual tolerance?"

"No, what was that?" Calista asked.

"He said that being open-minded was like placing a welcome mat outside your front door and being willing to be hospitable to those who come knocking, but that it was not the same as throwing the door wide open and putting up a sign that says 'Come on in. Nobody's home.'"

"What a great analogy. Reminds me of something that Ray Bradbury once said," Calista replied.

"Oh, what's that?" Elsa asked.

"There're more ways to burn a book than striking a match."

23

There were rosy fingers all right at the dawn. Calista's.

"Oh, God!" she muttered as she gazed down at her rust-colored hands. She'd worry about taking it off after she had fixed her hair in a style that she hoped Charley would consider suitable for this weird trip. How could she let a thirteen-year-old run her life like this? But he had actually, for the first time since he was an infant, been up before she was. He was dressed in his elevator shoes and was busy in his adjoining room slicking down his hair with some concoction that he felt would make him look like a "Pentecostal nerd." At this point Charley knew more about this peculiar phenomena in America's religious history than Calista. One thing she had begun to understand was that it was far from a purely religious phenomena. It was a social one as well. Charley had explained that the Lorne Thurston College of Christian Heritage was a Pentecostalist one. All the fundamentalists were evangelical, but a minority called themselves Pentecostalists, or charismatics, which meant that they believed that the Holy Spirit could work directly through them and thus let them prophesy and heal. Lorne Thurston was in this tradition, a tradition he shared with some others such as Oral Roberts, Jimmy Swaggart, Jim Bakker. According to Charley, Jerry Falwell, Pat Robertson, and Billy Graham were just straight evangelicals. Billy Graham was looking better and better to Calista. Why couldn't they be going to the Billy Graham University of whatever?

"You ready, Mom? How does it look?"

"You mean the color?"

"Yeah."

"Well, not so bad on my hair, but my fingers, I don't know, they might give me away." She looked up. She didn't look bad as a redhead. It was a very deep auburn color. Nothing flaming. But she didn't really look any younger, either, she thought.

"Remember, you can't wear it in that hurricane style. That won't do," Charley called in.

"Yes, Kenneth."

"What?"

"Kenneth. He's a famous hairdresser in New York. Does Jackie Kennedy's hair. Or rather Jackie Onassis."

Calista started to go to work with a curling iron, a blow dryer, and a can of industrial-strength hairspray.

"Great!" Charley exclaimed when she walked out of the bathroom twenty minutes later.

"More Annette Funicello than Tammy Faye, I think."

"It looks so set. Can I touch it?"

"Sure. This is up to gale-force winds."

Calista had pinned up the back of her hair into a French twist. She had then teased the top into a mushroom-shaped dome that was as rigid as it was smooth. She had pulled down a little fringe of hair over her forehead and curled it under with the curling iron into what had once been known as Mamie Eisenhower bangs. "You look pretty weird yourself," she said.

Charley had actually let the barber cut off quite a bit of his hair before they came on the trip. He now had it slicked down and was wearing nonprescription glasses. He wore a print cotton shirt that he'd found at T. J. MAXX and a narrow tie. Calista at the same time had bought a striped shirtwaist dress. She had never in her entire life owned a shirtwaist dress. She was also carrying a flat white handbag, the kind one always saw Queen Elizabeth carrying when performing her royal chores, at least those that did not require her to wear the crown and ermine robes.

"I think I'm too nervous to eat," Charley said.

"You're too nervous! You're the one who thought up this harebrained idea."

"I'm the one who's applying for admission, remember."

"God forbid."

"And it's not harebrained, Mom. This is the college, of all these Bible ones, that is the most antievolutionary and pro–scientific creationism. You heard Janet say that she found out from Norman Petrakis's editor that they had put all of Norman's books on their banned list and that Thurston himself had spoken out against Petrakis."

"You didn't say anything to Janet about this little jaunt of ours, did you, Charley?" She raised her finger ready to scold.

"Of course not."

"She'd absolutely have a fit, and she'd probably tell Ethan, and Ethan would . . . God, I don't know what."

Both Ethan Thayer and Janet were taking early morning planes back to New York. Calista had made some excuse about visiting some old colleagues of Tom's in the Dallas area, and for that reason she was taking a later evening flight back east. She looked at Charley. She had one nagging question that he had not answered satisfactorily. She sighed. "Now tell me again. What do you really think we can accomplish by going out there and going through this whole charade?"

"Mom, I told you. You don't know what you're going to find until you find it. But you got to start somewhere. This is the logical starting point. It's not just that these are the most fanatical. They have the most money, the most power, the most satellite linkups for their religious TV programs."

"But by the same token they have the most to lose by getting involved with murder."

"I'm not saying they did it, Mom. But we might find out something. They're the ones who are pouring money into that whole Louisiana thing for balanced treatment of creation science. They also run the Committee for the Study of Natural Sciences and the Institute of the Deluge."

"Institute of the Deluge?" Calista asked.

"Yeah, I read about it. They study delugology."

"What in the hell is delugology?"

"It figures out theories about the Flood, you know the one in the Bible, and how the Flood can account for all the fossils in the rocks. They even have this water vapor theory to go with it. A kind of greenhouse effect that worked with the forty days and forty nights of rain. You got to understand, Mom, that of all these Christian colleges this one goes the farthest in trying to making the Bible into a science. They teach a Christian anthropology course, Christian physics courses, Christian biochemistry. This is the center of it. Real weird."

"I'll say."

"But it's a science according to them, and they offer two courses in the deluge, Flood Geology one and two. Then after you take those you can go on an archaeology expedition and look for the Ark."

"Sounds like fun. Where do they think it is—Disney World?"

"Ha! Ha! Very funny. Now look, Mom. You got to get all your jokes out of you before we go. All right?"

24

     All the jokes were gone as they drove due east out of Dallas on Route 20 in their rental car—an enormous boat of a thing that felt like an aircraft carrier to Calista. But then again, Charley said it was perfect. Charley might have a future as a caterer with his attention to detail for occasions, Calista thought. They were quiet, Calista rehearsing in her mind not so much what she would say, but what she would not say. She didn't think it would be hard holding her tongue, actually. She would share nothing with these people. She had agreed to say that she was churchgoing, but if anybody asked her about when she had received Christ or last spoken in tongues, she was not going to say anything—or at most say that it was such an intensely personal experience that she found it hard to articulate. She was going as a widow. Her late husband had been a doctor, and she herself worked as an artist. That was all that she would say. Charley apparently had his whole spiel worked out. He wanted to come to Lorne Thurston College because he was indeed interested in a Christian education and walking closer with God, but also because they offered the best and most extensive program in creation science, a subject that interested him and that he had not been able to pursue in his public school education to date. As they drove Charley went over all the rationality of the creationist science that he had read in the previous three weeks: nutty notions all designed to jam the earth's history into six thousand years; notions that debunked, without data or any evidence whatsoever, everything from radiocarbon dating to geological stratigraphy. They were, however, very big on the second law of thermodynamics, which said that closed systems tend to become more disordered. Adam and Eve's Fall, the Garden of Eden, and the fact that the queen bee murders her sisters were evidence of that, said one creationist theorist. In creationist theory, therefore, organized living systems, such as humans, could not have evolved from less organized matter without divine intervention. Hallelujah. Praise the Lord and the second law! It all fit. Yes, Charley was well prepared—so well prepared that he had completely neglected to do a last research paper for school and would have an incomplete or possibly a C if he didn't do something about it by the end of the month.

They had already seen several signs for the college and the town of Green Acre. Apparently the town came first.

"What in the heck is that?" Calista asked.

"What?" Charley asked.

"That." She pointed ahead toward one o'clock. On a

nearly barren horizon a silvery sphere loomed out of the parched earth. A sign soon appeared: Lorne Thurston College of Christian Heritage, One Mile, Exit 22a.

"They even get their own exit," Charley whispered. None of the others had *a*'s or *b*'s. There wasn't a 21a.

"Hmph," Calista growled. "I'd like to give them their own exit all right."

They turned off at 22a. Where the exit road joined another road there was a second sign for the college, this one with a picture of Lorne Thurston on it.

"Imagine Derek Bok putting up his picture as you crossed the Larz Anderson Bridge into Cambridge."

"Mom, be quiet!" Charley said sharply.

The parched land suddenly turned green as they drove through an entry gate. At a guardhouse they were directed to the Dale Thurston Administration Offices. They parked in the lot in front of a bleached-yellow brick building. Calista took a deep breath and closed her eyes briefly.

"You okay, Mom?" There was a plaintive note in his voice as if suddenly he might have regretted this whole thing. If Charley lost courage, God, what would she do? It was so hard lying, not being yourself. She should have probably taken a Valium. She had considered it but decided not to since she was driving. She should have taken a drink, is what she should have taken!

"No, I'm fine." She said the words tightly. "Let's go."

The heat was oppressive as they stepped out of the car. It was only ten o'clock in the morning, but Texas had started to bake hours before and the temperature was nearly one hundred degrees. As soon as they stepped into the lobby of the building Calista felt better. There was a crucifix on one side and a cool tinkling waterfall that spilled into a pool on the other side. Calista noticed pennies glittering through the water on the aquamarine tile. By the pool was a small sign: "It is possible to give away and become richer." Proverbs 11:24. She wondered if this was really how they collected for their alumni fund. Almost immediately a young girl with silky blond hair and a band of freckles across her nose came bouncing into the lobby.

"You must be Charles Jacobs and Mrs. Jacobs!" she said, extending her hand.

"Yes." They nodded.

"I'm Beth Ann Hennessey. I'm going to be your guide for today. Why don't you first come into our lounge. After that you can meet Tommy Lee Clayton, our assistant director of admissions, and talk with him for a while, and then we'll go on the tour."

Five minutes later they were sitting in a lovely lounge while Beth Ann chatted on about how Lorne Thurston College of Christian Heritage had changed her life. She was a junior, and she had qualified for a scholarship.

"Now if you have any financial needs, we have a wonderful financial aid program here, and there's just so many ways you can supplement that. Like I'm working as a guide this summer. And I also work in the television studio."

"Television studio?" Calista asked.

"Sure thing. Right here. Didn't you know that 'The Lorne Thurston Gospel Hour' is produced and broadcast from right here on campus? We got the satellite linkups. Didn't you see the big dishes when you came in—or did you come in from Route Twenty?"

"Yes, we did."

"Oh, well, all that's over on the other side of campus in what we call the southeast quadrant. You'll see it on our tour. You saw the pictures in the brochure, didn't you, Charley, of our studios? And you know we have a wonderful communications program here. You can major in television ministry work. But even if you're not a major—like me, I'm majoring in youth ministry—you can get jobs in the station. Some pay, some don't. It's really fun. You learn a lot about TV production. I work there six hours a week in the summer and about four during the school term."

"Oh, that'll be neat to see."

"Is that the broadcasting studio—that large silver ball that we saw from the highway?" Calista asked.

"No. That is the Sphere of Faith." Calista must have looked a little blank, for Beth Ann quickly added, "Where we have our chapel services. And behind it is an outdoor amphitheater so that in good weather in the evenings we can have services outdoors under the Texas stars. It's just beautiful. Will you be here this evening?"

"No," they both answered quickly.

"Oh, that's too bad. There'll be an outdoor service. And Lorne Thurston's wife, Clarella—we all call her Mom—is preaching. She's wonderful." Then she lowered her voice to a conspiratorial whisper. "I think she's better than the reverend myself." She paused a moment and continued. "Sometimes they do broadcast from the Sphere of Faith. It has all the equipment, but that's only on special occasions. Are you interested in communication, Charles?" She paused briefly. "Do you like being called Charles or Charley?"

There was something very warm and engaging about this young girl, Calista thought. She seemed lively and intelligent. It was hard to believe that she could be as limited as one might suppose such an environment would suggest. And if she were, Calista thought, she wondered how flexible or inflexible those limitations, those boundary lines, were.

"Well, most people call me Charley. Yeah, I guess I might be. I'm really interested, though, in your science program here—the scientific creation courses."

"Oh, you are? Well, as you probably know, we really have a wonderful department in that area. I'm not so good in science myself. So I haven't taken that much. But it is one of our most exciting departments. So I'm glad you told me because I'll take you over to the Creation Center, that's where most of the courses are taught and where the labs are."

"Labs?" said Calista, her eyes widening. She shouldn't have said it. She knew it as soon as the word was out, and she could feel Charley tense beside her on the couch.

"Yes, you know, the laboratories where they do their

experiments and all that stuff." Beth Ann spoke rather offhandedly, so maybe she hadn't noticed Calista's incredulity.

Tommy Lee Clayton was one of those persons who precluded wondering about. One would never entertain the slightest notion about his limitations other than that they were fixed and eternal. Beth Ann had ushered them into the assistant admissions director's office. Tommy Lee didn't look much older than Beth Ann. But he looked set from his plastic molded hair to his sharply cut powder blue suit.

"Well, I am so pleased to welcome you to the college. We don't often get visitors from Massachusetts here." Did she imagine it, or was there a funny note in his voice, a slight sneer as he said the word *Massachusetts?* The same sneer that came into the voices of certain conservative politicians and presidential candidates when they spoke of that liberal state as if it were some arrogant and eternally erring child.

"And as I understand it, Mrs. Jacobs, you are a widow?"

"Yes. Yes," she said tersely. "My husband was a doctor."

"And do you work?"

She was taken aback by the question. There was something definitely wrong here. College interviews never started off with questions to the parents. It was the kids they were supposed to be focused on.

"Uh . . . yes . . . uh, I'm an artist . . . a comm—" She had started to say "commercial." But something stuck, and she coughed slightly.

"Commercial." He filled in the word, and she nodded and regained her composure. When you sold as many books as Calista did, you could certainly call it being commercial even if it wasn't advertising. Finally he turned to Charley and began to ask him some questions.

"So you like to skateboard, and I see from your

application that you have worked through your church on starting a youth skateboarding group."

Holy moley! Calista thought. What was this? Skateboarding for God! What in the hell had Charley gone and written on that thing?

"Well, yes," Charley was saying modestly. "At a church fair we put on an exhibition and had a safety clinic for kids just starting out. You know, just about wearing pads and helmets. We actually raised fifty dollars."

"Well, good for you, son! I got a nine-year-old nephew who loves to skateboard. And I don't think you can stress the safety thing too much. 'Thrashers,' isn't that the slang word for skateboarders?"

"Yes, sir." Charley's face suddenly brightened. God, had her child really found something in common with this guy? That Charley! "You know what we call ourselves, Mr. Clayton?"

"What's that, son?" he asked eagerly.

"Gospel Thrashers." He beamed.

"Well, I'll be." Tommy Lee Clayton slapped his thigh. "That really has a ring to it. You ever think of going into communications, Charles? You know, we got a great department here. Real on-the-spot opportunities. See, the main transponder for 'The Lorne Thurston Gospel Hour' is right here."

"Yes." Calista nodded. "Beth Ann told us about it."

"Yeah . . . Well, as I was telling Beth Ann," Charley continued, "I'm really interested in your creation science program here."

"Oh, now you're talking." Clayton pointed his finger directly at Charley. "We're really blowing some of these other so-called scientists off the map. We got some outstanding research going on down here and some real new breakthroughs which you'll be reading about in the not-too-distant future. You be sure to have Beth Ann give you a complete tour of our William Jennings Bryan Creation Science Center. We've got some excellent new young professors on board."

"Yes." Charley nodded. "I've been reading about this man Ferneld."

"Ah, yes, Gerry Ferneld. He'll be coming to teach here next fall."

"Yes, I've been reading about his theory of the vapor canopy that shielded the lower atmosphere from cosmic radiation and why that means that radiocarbon dating isn't really accurate."

"Well, my goodness, son, you are up on things."

"Yes, sir. And I'm trying to plan an experiment for the Westinghouse Science Fair that, well . . . you know." Charley squirmed and gave a very good impression of bashfulness. "I mean, it can't prove conclusively . . ."

"Yes, son, yes!" Tommy Lee was leaning forward, his elbows on his desk, eagerly awaiting Charley's words.

"Well, I think that there's a way that you can prove the water shield theory and the specific reduction of radioactive carbon if you start using amber samples."

"Amber? Well, I'll be."

"Yeah, you see, amber really keeps all those precipitates intact that come from the atmosphere . . ." Charley was off and running with his theory of amber precipitates as an index of an antediluvian vapor canopy. It was total gobbledygook. He was talking iridium and zinc indices and atmospheric scrubbing particles that could be evidence of a great deluge four thousand years ago. It was a bizarre mixture of chemistry and particle physics and Scripture. Light on the Scripture. He apparently had only read the creation part.

"And what happens if it doesn't turn out right?"

"Right?" Charley looked bewildered. Calista felt totally disoriented. Had such a question really ever been asked in such a way about scientific inquiry? "You mean if the experiment I do for the Westinghouse thing shows that there couldn't be a vapor canopy that would interfere with radiocarbon dating?"

"Yeah." Clayton's voice was flat. This was a trap. Shit! Calista thought, Why did Charley have to go mouthing off about this? Why couldn't he have come in here like any other admissions candidate? When was the last time they had one in this office who had aspirations for a Westinghouse Science Award?

"Well . . ." Charley paused. "It will be the wrong experiment."

Suddenly Calista saw what Charley was doing. "Right," she said. "No need to throw out the baby with the bathwater—or the Flood waters." She smiled weakly. At this a huge grin cracked Tommy Lee's simple face. What a pair of phrasemakers they must appear to be, Calista thought. "Gospel Thrashers"—"baby with the Flood waters!"

"Yes," said Charley, picking up on his mother's line. "You don't throw out the Scriptures. I must just be misunderstanding them in some way, and so I'll have to come up with a new experiment."

Tommy Lee smiled again. Calista breathed a sigh of relief. They had played the game right. Any model of a biblical deluge can be falsified, but the truth of the fact of the Flood cannot be. Models and experiments can be shoved and nudged, but not Genesis. Wasn't this in direct contradiction to the philosopher Karl Popper's dictum that a theory be in principle falsifiable? Tom had explained that Popper's dictum meant that a good theory not only explained fully, but also could predict what conditions or observations could prove the theory wrong or false. This meant simply that a theory could be proved conclusively false, or at least one of its statements false, if an observational consequence were false. Not here, however. If the observational consequence of the vapor canopy proved false, the scriptural statements stood truer than ever! Tom had explained falsifiability as being a cornerstone to scientific procedure and inquiry. But it didn't count for much in Green Acre, Texas, obviously.

Tommy Lee got up and leaned forward to shake hands with Charley. "I think you're going to do very well here. I think we might even be able to arrange for advanced placement."

Over my dead body! Calista thought.

25

They were now following Beth Ann along a baking concrete walkway that led from the Student Union Center to the BCN, Bible Cable Network, the real nerve center of Lorne Thurston's television empire.

"Over there." Beth Ann was pointing to a low building that looked like a ranch-style house. "That's our computer center."

"Oh, wow!" Charley said.

"Oh, Charley'll want to see that." Calista laughed.

"Well, it's not usually on the tour, but I can certainly take you there," Beth Ann said.

"It's not on the tour? Why not?"

"It's the computer center for BCN. It's where they process all the donations, and it houses our direct-mail operation for BCN's giving programs."

"Oh, you mean it's not for the college," Charley said.

"Well, it is and it isn't. You saw Morton Hall. That's where the students go to work on computers and learn about programming. Well, this is where you can go once you've learned. Another summer internship that you can have here is working in the computer center. It is directly connected with the television studios. Come on, I'll show you."

They walked into the building, which was much larger than it appeared from the outside. In the spacious lobby there was an immense color photograph of Lorne Thurston that dominated the entire space. If Jim Bakker was said to look like Howdy Doody, Calista thought, Lorne Thurston was certainly a dead ringer for an aging

Buster Brown, the one who had lived in a shoe with his freckles, pug nose, saucer eyes, and red hair. He beamed down on them, and above the picture was the scriptural verse "Give, And It Shall Be Given Unto You"—Luke 6:38. On either side of this portrait was a glass wall behind which were banks of computers and telephones. They walked up to the wall.

"They call that the pit," Beth Ann said. There were at least thirty people manning phones and at computer terminals. "It can be really hard work during broadcasting hours. Those phones never stop ringing. This is the headquarters, of course, but we have seven other regional branches throughout the country." It was fairly state-of-the-art as far as Charley could tell. There was an electronic ticker tape flashing up-to-the-minute calculations.

"What are those signs—Sphere of Faith, Partners in the Kingdom?" Calista asked.

"Oh, those indicate the varying amounts that donors can give. If you give over a certain amount, you can become a Partner in the Kingdom, that means you get to go to an annual prayer dinner with Lorne Thurston. If you are a member of the Sphere of Faith, it means that for a certain amount your name will be inscribed on one of the window plates in the Sphere of Faith Chapel here on campus."

Calista understood immediately. It was an old selling tactic. She believed it had been called, by Madison Avenue, the unique selling proposition. In more ancient times it had been called buying papal indulgences. You bought prayer dinners or breakfasts with Thurston, or perhaps you bought bricks or glass in his campus and broadcasting empire, as Beth Ann was now telling them.

"Every letter accompanying a donation is individually read and prayed over."

"I don't see how there'd be enough hours in the day to do that," Calista said as she stood almost mesmerized by the ticker tape flashing the current tallies that looked as if they were indeed rising.

"Well, they say they do it," Beth Ann said ingenuously.

It was the word *say* that made Calista think that this was perhaps the first time Beth Ann had questioned anything since she had come to the college. The word functioned like a slight hesitation in the scriptural recording that had been implanted in her brain. A tiny glitch in the tape. But she resumed perkily. "Now, you see that green light over there by the huge clock?" she said, pointing to a large green globe. "When they are on the air, that green light is on and then you can see a lot of activity in this room. You really notice the difference. The ticker tape, for one thing, is flashing a lot more, numbers really going up. The various clubs work on a kind of mini–goal system so that when certain donor levels are reached in the course of a broadcast, other lights and bells go off. It's real exciting."

"Goodness," was all that Calista could say. She looked at the green globe. She thought of the green light at the end of the pier that Jay Gatsby used to stare across toward, and she thought of the elusive green color that she had tried to track down at Houghton Library in the books of hours. This was not it.

"We can go into the television studio now. There probably won't be much going on today because I don't think they're taping."

"Clarella will not wear that dress on the air. She calls that puke yellow, and it's something like Tammy Faye would wear. . . . Oh, dear!" The young woman clapped her hands over her mouth as she came round the corner and met up with Beth Ann leading her charges around.

"Don't worry, Sue. We didn't hear a thing." Beth Ann laughed. "And I don't blame her. Yellow does not televise well, especially with her coloring. Are you taping today?"

"No. Not till tomorrow."

"Oh, by the way, Sue. This is Charley Jacobs and his mother. I'm giving them a tour. Charley is going to apply here."

"Oh, do!" Sue's eyes became dreamy. "It's the most

wonderful experience you'll ever have. Next year's my last year, and I don't know how I'll ever leave. . . ." She sighed. "But, of course, that's the whole idea . . . sense of mission, that's what it's all about."

"What are you going to do after graduation?" Calista asked.

"Well, I'm hoping to get a job with one of our affiliates in California. I'm real interested in Christian broadcasting. And if that doesn't come through, I might go down to the park for a while."

"What park?"

"Oh, you know, the Bible theme park that the reverend runs in Virginia. Bible Times, it's called. It's really fun. I did a work-study program there last spring and helped them set up a day-care center, and there's talk of some children's programming that would originate from the park. You know, kind of like Sesame Street, only Christian."

"Oh," Calista said softly. Somehow she had never imagined Big Bird as an evangelist. And presumably Oscar the Grouch would be turned into Satan the Slouch or some such thing.

From the BCN building they moved on to the William Jennings Bryan Creation Science Center.

In the beginning God created the heaven and the earth. And the earth was without form and void; and darkness was upon the face of the deep. And the spirit of God moved upon the face of the waters. And God said, Let there be light: and there was light. And God saw the light and saw that it was good. And God divided the light from the darkness. And God called the light Day and the darkness he called Night and the evening and the morning were the first day. . . . And God said, Let the earth bring forth grass, the herb yielding seed, and the fruit tree yielding fruit after his kind, whose seed is in itself, upon the earth: and it was so. And the earth brought forth grass, and herb yielding seed after his kind, and the tree yielding fruit, whose seed was in itself, after his kind. And God saw that it was good.

These first verses of Genesis were engraved in limestone over the front entrance to the William Jennings Bryan Creation Science Center. Upon entering the lobby Calista and Charley found other verses from Genesis carved into stone slabs that were set into the pale yellow brick walls. Within the walls of this building there was no doubt and there would be no inquiry. That was for certain. The lobby seemed to function as a sort of lounge. There were tables and comfortable chairs, and Calista paused as she passed by a magazine rack to look at what was offered for light lobby reading. There was a selection of pamphlets from an outfit called Creation Life Publishers. She casually picked one up entitled *God's Plan for Air.* Next to it was *God's Plan for Insects* and another called *Unhappy Gays* and finally *I'm a Woman by God's Design.* There was also literature from a group called FLAG, which stood for "Family, Life, America, under God."

The whole thing was starting to become a strain for Calista. She hoped that Charley was getting what he needed because she was feeling increasingly uncomfortable in this environment. But they were presumably at the heart of the matter here in the William Jennings Bryan Creation Science Center. Charley was standing at another rack of reading materials and motioned her over while Beth Ann had gone to a water fountain to get a drink. "Look at this!" he said, picking up some sort of newsletter.

"Oh!" Calista gasped. There was a picture of Norman Petrakis. And above the picture was the headline SATAN'S SCHOLAR VICTIM OF VIOLENT ATTACK. They both read the article silently.

Norman Petrakis, a longtime children's book author of nonfiction works, was found dead in a Boston hotel room. Mr. Petrakis had written extensively on the subject of human evolution. He was an outspoken anti-Creationist, and those of us in the Christian Community had long deplored this man's depravity and influence on young minds. Once a member of the Socialist party and rumored to be a practicing homosexual, Mr. Petrakis was indeed the perfect embodiment of the degenerate mind fostered by modernistic ideas. We who have long believed that evolutionary thinking leads to degeneracy, depravity, and the general dissolution of society feel that, although we regret any man's death, the manner in which Mr. Petrakis died is again proof of evolutionistic thought as the root of atheism, amorality, libertinism, and all manner of anti-Christian systems of belief.

Both of their hands had begun to tremble as they held the paper. Just at that moment Beth Ann walked up. "Ready to begin?" she asked cheerfully. Calista was ready to throw up. But Charley rebounded gamely.

The tour began with the lecture halls and some classrooms. They then proceeded to pass by what looked like standard laboratories where chemistry or biology classes might be held. It was difficult to imagine what such classes would be like or how observational data might be regarded despite the rather conventional appearance of these labs. "Now this is the lab where I took a course last spring semester—Biblical Archaeology. It was really neat. And then, of course, the Flood studies. I only took the first semester of that. It was kind of hard. You really had to learn a lot about hydraulics, and I'm not very good in physics and that kind of science. Professor Stark is a hydraulic engineer, though, by training. A dear man. He gave me a B minus, and I really think I should have just gotten a C. I think he felt sorry for me." She smiled sweetly. "He even encouraged me to go on the field trip this summer to Mount Ararat in the Holy Land. He goes every year in search of Noah's Ark, and they've turned up some really promising artifacts. But I couldn't go. It's really expensive, the airfare, and I just couldn't swing it. I mean, I'm on scholarship already, and my grandma and grandpa send me spending money from their pensions. I really can't ask for anything else."

"Can we walk through here?" Charley asked, nodding his head toward the archaeology lab.

"Sure thing." They entered. "Now if we go through that door, we get into the anthro lab."

"Anthro?" Calista asked.

"Anthropology," Beth Ann said. "It's a cultural anthropology course, for the most part. It surveys the biblical foundations of Christian missions. It focuses on practical methods which relate to cultural or racial barriers in the field. It's a requirement for everyone in the missions program. I took it, however, even though I'm not in the program. Next semester I'll take arid lands biology, and I will have completed my science requirements. Praise the Lord!" she whispered. "I'm just awful in science, but the anthro course is really interesting. And now we got this new neat professor and he came from up north, but he's really discovered some wonderful things."

"What?" Charley asked.

"Well, do you know that last summer they combined the Mount Ararat expedition with an arid lands biology expedition? They're doing a lot of that now that Professor Tompkins has come here. He's the one who came from up north, Minnesota or someplace."

"A lot of what?" Calista asked.

"Combining the anthropology and the archaeology with biology. I guess he's a biologist by training, but he's doing a lot with anthropology down here. And so they had this joint expedition, people from both departments went, and somewhere along the way they discovered these fascinating skulls."

"What kind of skulls?" Calista asked.

"Human skulls—very ancient ones from probably long before the Flood."

Now how ancient could they get? Calista was thinking. Weren't these folks trying to crush it all into six thousand years? She supposed that in their geological scale anything over two thousand years was considered ancient. Thus these skulls, from before the time of Noah, perhaps just outside the garden gates of Eden, seemed to them ancient.

"And do you know what they are thinking that they're on the brink of proving?" Beth Ann continued.

"What?" Charley asked.

"That the races were formed separately." Beth Ann's eyes widened.

"What do you mean?" Calista and Charley both asked the same question at once.

"It means that the races—you know, blacks and whites—started off separately from the beginning. I mean, we always suspected it, but now we know."

"We do?" Calista asked vaguely.

"Yeah, Wayne Tompkins, he's the professor who found the proof, dug it up."

"You mean this skull?" Calista asked.

"Yep. He showed a cast of it in a seminar he gives. My roommate saw it."

Calista worded her next question carefully. "But isn't this like evolution?"

"We don't believe in that," Beth Ann said firmly. "This is just like the Bible says in Genesis, really. Just as it says God made the beasts of the earth according to their kinds, and every winged bird according to its kind. He created man in his own image and then created the kinds of man."

"But it never says that, does it, in the Bible? That he created kinds of men?"

"No. You're right. It doesn't get that detailed, but Wayne Tompkins says that this fossil will certainly prove that the Book of Genesis could have indeed gotten that detailed."

Calista was confused. Had a fundamentalist switched the rules on her, turned revisionist? Could there be such a thing as a revisionist fundamentalist?

"Could we see the skull?" Charley asked suddenly.

"Well, I suppose I can ask Wayne. He's around here someplace. I saw him when I was getting a drink at the fountain when we first came in. Let me go see. You wait here."

They waited until she was out of the room. Calista wheeled toward Charley. "This is getting too friggin' weird, Charley. I don't know whether I can keep pretenses up too much longer."

"Mom, it's getting interesting. Can you believe doing science like these guys do it? Come on, we got to look at this skull."

"Have you ever heard of Piltdown man, Charley?" Calista hissed.

"No. What's that?"

"It was about the biggest fake in science, and these guys aren't even that smart. Incidentally, Piltdown man was rumored to be pulled off by a man of the cloth— Teilhard de Chardin. What we're going to see here is a papier-mâché skull. You can bet on that! Everybody knows that racial differences have never even shown up in the fossil record of hominids because there friggin' weren't any until twenty thousand years ago!"

"Mom, don't even say friggin'! Remember where we are." He peered at her through his nonprescription glasses. She could smell the gunk he had put on his hair.

"How could I forget?"

Beth Ann returned in a few minutes. Her color was high, higher than it should have been for this air-conditioned building, and she was visibly agitated. "I'm afraid that the skulls are unavailable at the moment. They are undergoing some further testing in another laboratory, and I really should not have mentioned anything about them at this point."

"Oh, dear," Calista said. "I hope we didn't get you into any trouble."

"Oh, no! No! Don't worry about it. No trouble." But she looked as if she were on the brink of tears.

"No trouble at all," a voice suddenly said. "Hello, Mrs. Jacobs and Charles." It was a nice voice, a reasonable voice, full of intelligence. From the moment Calista heard Wayne Tompkins speak, she felt more at ease.

He was around thirty, with a friendly, open face that was very nice looking but not quite handsome. He was dressed in khaki pants and rolled-up shirtsleeves. He walked over and extended his hand. "I'm just afraid that Beth Ann was a little exuberant here. She's a very enthusiastic science student. But announcing the find is just a bit premature. See, after our next round of testing we are planning a formal colloquium, and that is when it shall be officially announced. I'm sure you can understand."

Calista could not reconcile him at all with these surroundings. She could not imagine him walking through that lobby with those slanderous, vile pamphlets. He was in marked contrast with Tommy Lee Clayton, that was for sure. And it wasn't just that he was from the north and did not have an accent. He just seemed eminently reasonable to her and logical with no axes, biblical or otherwise, to grind.

"Yes, yes, of course," Calista said quickly. She looked at her watch. "You know, we must be going, Charley. We do have a plane to catch."

"You're going out of Dallas-Fort Worth, right?"

"Yes."

"Well, you might want to take a shortcut back. You take Route Twenty back, but you get off one exit early before Dallas. Here, let me draw you a little sketch." He got a piece of paper and drew on it, then handed it to Calista. This will save you going through downtown Dallas."

"Oh, thanks, thanks so much."

"Sorry about the skull."

"Oh, no problem. Don't worry, we won't spill the beans."

Wayne Tompkins smiled. "I'm sure you won't."

26

Neither Calista nor Charley spoke a word until they had driven out of the gates of the college. Then Calista sank back against the almost broiling vinyl of the car seat. "Oy vay!" she growled deeply. "Charley, the things I do for you!"

"Mom, that's not fair. You didn't do it just for me."

She sighed. "You're right," she said, and thought of Norman Petrakis. "Could you believe that thing, that filthy rag they had about his death? God, these people are totally screwball."

"You see, they had a motive."

Calista thought for a moment. Until this day she would never have really thought they had a motive. She would have thought of them as just a bunch of religious fanatics, but there was such vitriol in that piece, such real hatred and paranoia. It was the Nazis all over again. The whole operation was a bunch of shit even if Beth Ann and Wayne Tompkins seemed nice and relatively normal.

"Look, there's that damn prayer ball or whatever they call it," she said, nodding at it in her rearview mirror. "It's like something out of a Mel Brooks movie."

"Sphere of Faith," Charley said.

"It is written, 'My house shall be called the house of prayer; but you have made it a den of thieves,'" Calista said in a low voice.

"Who said that?" Charley asked.

"The Bible. New Testament."

"I didn't know you knew the Bible that well."

"I don't. The phrase just came to me. Once upon a time I took a religion and literature course as an undergraduate." She paused. "So did you get anything out of this, Charley?"

"Well, you yourself agree with me that they had a motive."

"But there's no evidence. There is still absolutely nothing to go on. I mean, these guys might screw around with scientific data all they want, but we haven't got one shred of evidence. Just because they might be hateful people doesn't mean they murder. Could you believe that Beth Ann could murder?"

"She was nice."

"She was. I . . . I feel sorry for her. I really do."

"You do?" Charley sounded surprised.

"Yeah, I do. I have the feeling that there's a story there with Beth Ann, or at least we don't have the full one."

"What do you mean?"

"I don't know—intuition. I don't think that coming to Lorne Thurston College of Christian Heritage was a real choice in the true sense."

They were silent for a while. "Can you hand me that little piece of paper with the map the guy sketched? I think we're coming up on our exit, and I have to know what to look for."

They had been off the main highway on a smaller road for a few minutes when Calista noticed a car coming up rather fast in her rearview mirror.

"God, what's that guy doing? Is he going to pass me or what?" She looked nervously into the side mirror. "Talk about tailgating!"

"Mom, he's not just tailgating!" The car had cut out abruptly and was pulling up even with them while trying to press into their side.

"Jesus Christ, what's he doing? He's trying to run me off the road!" Calista honked the horn. But she sensed the futility of this gesture as a kind of awful knowledge flooded through her being. This is what they did to Karen Silkwood, she thought.

"Gun it, Mom! Gun it." There was a terrible hot screech as metal glanced off metal. The fucking boat had no power. The other car was riding them hard, edging them over, easily keeping pace with them. Tail wagging the dog. Tail wagging the dog! That was all Calista could think of. Time for the dog to stop wagging. She slammed on the brakes. The other car spun out in front of them. Calista swerved sharply into the other lane.

"Good God!" Charley was on his knees on the seat looking back. The car had rolled down an embankment but left a tire behind that wobbled crazily across the road. "They friggin' tried to kill us!" she screamed, and gunned the car. She could feel her heart pounding, the blood pulsing through her temples. "Are they gone? They're not coming after us, are they, Charley?"

"No, they're finished. No way. Skidded into that deep ditch, lost a wheel. Why would they do that?"

Calista eased up on the accelerator. She looked at Charley. "They must have had a motive."

"Do you think it's them? The college?"

"Whoever it was knew who we were. They weren't kidding around. They were out to get us."

"Why are you going so slow now?"

"I don't want to get arrested for speeding in the state of Texas, Charley. Something tells me that in these parts Lorne Thurston has things sewn up. We're going to get home as fast as we can, but we're going to be careful."

Careful meant not waiting for their four o'clock flight to Boston but taking the first flight they could heading east. Within twenty minutes of arriving at the airport they were settling into their seats on a Delta flight to Philadelphia. Calista would figure out how to get the rest of the way when they got to Philly. They were still trembling as the flight attendant directed their attention to the safety features of the plane. Calista pulled the pins out of her French twist and began vigorously brushing out her hair.

"Okay. We're going to figure this out. But I need a very stiff drink first."

She ordered a double vodka martini. She had splurged

and bought first-class tickets. The wider seats were kind to the disintegrating disk in her back. Whenever she was on a plane she spent the first couple of minutes doing some invisible back exercises that her orthopedic surgeon had advised her to do before a long flight and once or twice during the trip. She did them now with a fierce concentration. Charley dared not interrupt her. His mother's mood had changed from scared to angry. "Profound piss-dom," he called it. It was just like the time two years ago when it had all come out about the CIA and his dad's death. They had sent in that creepy guy to seduce her and then steal the Time Slicer. They had hoped to embarrass his mom. But she didn't embarrass or shut up. She got mad. Real mad and had turned around and sued the pants off the government. They'd settled out of court for a huge sum. The government had hoped that it would save them having to have their dirty linen washed in public. But it hadn't. Then she'd doubly humiliated them by giving away most of the money to their nemesis—the nuclear freeze movement! And to make matters worse, she'd won her most stunning endorsement from that old conservative warhorse of the American Right—Barry Goldwater. Called her a brave woman, a true American, and if anyone should be embarrassed, it should be the federal government, whom she'd caught with their pants down, said he!

Charley looked at his mother now out of the corner of his eye. She had finished the exercises and was sipping her drink. Could they have been recognized? She hadn't looked at all like her pictures with the red hair and the new hairdo. Her picture hadn't been in the paper that much. Only that morning for the first time was it in the Dallas papers for winning the Caldecott Award the previous night. That seemed so long ago now—his conversation with the big green librarian and running vodkas to Ethan. But maybe the same people who had disrupted the conference that she and Petrakis had been at in April had come to this one. Maybe they infiltrated all these book conferences. If they were that scared of books, as the green librarian had said they were, maybe they made a practice of sending in spies. They could have been looking at her and at him, studying their every move for the whole three days. Maybe they had been on to them from the time Charley had first sent in his application to Lorne Thurston College of Christian Heritage. How many people from Cambridge applied there? Maybe it was the same people who had put the diapers on *Nick in the Night* and the rabbit's blood on the pictures of Rothgar and messed up Owl. Holy shit, maybe they were just taking a long glide down the Plain of Crystal Doom and they would soon crash and shatter! Charley looked out the window. They were above a layer of neatly fragmented clouds that floated below them like sky biscuits, round and fluffy.

"Okay, Charley. I'm ready. . . . I think there are at least two separate questions here: Did they know who we really were? That's one question."

Charley looked up, surprised at this conjecture of his mother's. "You think they might not have guessed our identity?"

"I'm not sure, and even if they hadn't, they still might have done the same thing."

"Huh?"

"Look, Charley, supposing they didn't really know who we were—just supposing. Then they wouldn't have thought that we were there in connection at all with Petrakis's death. Think back: when did they really get upset? When did the whole tenor of the visit change?"

"In the Creation Center."

"Precisely—when Beth Ann came back to tell us that the skulls were unavailable. She had made, unwittingly, a major gaffe. They have something planned for those skulls, and it really threatened their plans when Beth Ann spilled the beans."

"Jeez, I hope she's going to be all right. She almost looked as if she were about to cry."

"I know. I'm worried about her, too. Somehow I just resist instinctually throwing her in with those jerks.

"In any case, it was the mention of the skulls that made them antsy." She thought back on Wayne Tompkins, all smooth and engaging and very offhand. And he had seemed exceedingly intelligent, a kind of oasis of intelligence in a desert of abysmal ignorance. She had felt at ease with him. But had that just been all for show? Was that some sort of glaze over the hatred that springs from ignorance? Calista thought hard. She remembered faces, and even if she hadn't been quite aware of it at the time, she had, on some subliminal level, tucked away several hundred k, as Charley would call it, on this man. The bits and bytes came back to her now, the smallest, subtlest nuances and contours and gestures of the face came back with a full intensity to the eye of a consummate portrait artist. She could see him now so clearly explaining about the further testing and the future colloquium at which a formal announcement would be made. There was a slight quiver in the left corner of his mouth, and with that fragment of an image came the cold sure knowledge: It was the liar's quiver, the palsy under the mask as one tried to lie and look casual, speak falsehoods yet come across as a real person. The quiver was the giveaway. It said, "Are you buying this?" And she, of course, was trying desperately to appear as if indeed she were buying this. So she was probably quivering, too. And then it burst upon her. "God, how stupid!" She put down her glass a little too emphatically, and some of the vodka slopped over the edge. She'd have to order another one. "He set us up!"

"Who?"

"Tompkins, that's who. He sketched that map for us. Got us onto that road. There was hardly another car on that road. How do we even know if it would have led us around Dallas and direct to the airport?" Indeed, they had been so frightened that they had gotten off it at the first opportunity and wound their way back onto the main highway as fast as they could. It was so obvious that Tompkins had set them up, and yet they had never really thought of it until that moment. In the sheer adrenaline of the moment, and the aftermath, they had totally forgotten about Tompkins's map and the route supposedly being a shortcut.

"Well, I guess that's evidence," Charley said.

"Sort of. I don't know whether it would stand up in court. Do you still have the map he drew?"

"Somewhere," he said, digging down into his pocket. "Do you think he was the one driving the car, Mom?"

"I doubt it," she said quickly.

Charley looked up. "How can you be so sure?"

"I just have this hunch that he's the kind to get others to do his dirty work for him. He probably has a string of stooges." For some reason she thought of the paint-splattered stuffed Owl figure ghastly in the moonlight of that frozen Cambridge night of two months before.

Charley brought out the small crumpled piece of paper. "Why are we going to have to stand up in court with this evidence?" he asked.

"Well, I don't know, to tell you the truth."

"We weren't exactly murdered."

"You can bet that you don't stand up in court if you're murdered. Attempted murder, maybe."

"But you haven't reported it to anyone," Charley said.

"I know. Somehow I just don't have the faith in cops that perhaps I should."

"We got to do something, Mom. Who do you have faith in?"

"Archie Baldwin," she said quietly.

27

Beth Ann Hennessey felt absolutely rotten all afternoon. She hadn't meant to "blab." What an awful word. It was too close to gossip, which, of course, was a sin. And Wayne Tompkins had accused her of this. She didn't even know him that well, but she would never have expected such an outburst. What had she done to deserve it? She of all people. She squeezed her eyes shut in the glare of the setting sun as she walked across campus. She had to set things right. She had never been in any kind of trouble in her life. She couldn't endure any kind of blemish on her record. It wasn't that she herself had sacrificed so much to come here, but others had so she could be here—Reverend and Mrs. Bottis, not to mention her dear grammy and grandpa. Grammy and Grandpa hadn't any money to spare for things like this, but they had backed her up all the way and were so proud of her. This would be a terrible betrayal of everyone's expectations. She couldn't imagine that this one incident after all her hard work and good grades could really do her in, but she had to have a flawless record and be able to get the best recommendations possible.

She would be a senior the following year, and she was already starting to worry about a job. There was a lot of competition out there for the good jobs—the ones at the counseling centers or the mission support bases and the youth ministry programs. She had never ever done anything wrong or anything to draw attention to herself. For Beth Ann the distinction between the two was not that clear. Well, she was going to settle it up right now.

She didn't want Dr. Tompkins going to Tommy Lee Clayton as he had muttered about doing. How was she to know that this stupid skull thing was top secret? No matter, she would go and tell Dr. Tompkins how truly sorry she was and that she would never ever say anything again.

She wasn't sure if she should specifically ask him not to say anything to Dean Clayton. Tommy Lee Clayton had always thought the world of her, and she was counting on him for a good recommendation in her job file. She just wasn't too sure how smart it was to let Dr. Tompkins know how much she was counting on the dean's recommendation. She had liked that mother and son so much, the Jacobses. They just seemed special somehow to her. The boy, Charley, was so friendly and real smart, and his mother . . . well, although she appeared kind of nervous, she also seemed very sweet and kind—real Christian kindness. You could just feel it in her. It must be so nice to have a young pretty mother like that. These were the thoughts that were swirling in her head as she entered the William Jennings Bryan Creation Science Center.

She turned down the long corridor and then through the door of the anthro lab. The place was deserted. She walked through the lab and out a back door that led into a corridor where Tompkins's office was. The door was slightly ajar. She could look in.

"Dr. Tompkins," she said softly.

There was a figure reclining on the couch. She soon realized from the sound of the breathing that whoever it was might be sleeping. She poked her head in a little farther. She certainly didn't want to wake him up if that was the case.

That was the case. But there was something strange. She froze in a posture of dismay. There was blood on his shirt and a big bruise on his cheek. "Dr. Tompkins," she gasped out loud, "are you okay?" He stirred, rolled over on his side, and opened one eye. He didn't seem to recognize her.

"Yeah?" he said roughly.

"Are you okay, Dr. Tompkins?"

There was an ugly little smile, as if he were enjoying some private joke. "Yeah, sure thing. Now why don't you git out an' leave me 'lone."

Beth Ann backed away in a daze. That voice just didn't seem like Dr. Tompkins at all—flat and nasal. But it was he. Even with his bruised cheek and the gash over his eye, it was certainly Dr. Tompkins. He must have had some sort of accident. Suddenly behind her she heard footsteps. They stopped abruptly. Then she heard running. She turned just in time to see the back of a man disappearing where the corridor made a right-angle turn. What in the world was going on here? Beth Ann thought to herself.

Things were made no more clear that evening. Beth Ann had just hung up the phone in her dorm room. "Well, I declare," she murmured.

"What's that?" Her roommate, Sandy, looked up from her white Bible with the gold gilt letters of her name embossed on the cover.

"That was Dean Clayton. I'm getting to go to Bible Times. They got a job for me in the park—at the child-care center."

"Oh, you lucky duck!" shrieked Sandy, and plopped her Bible shut.

"Strange are the ways . . ." Beth Ann didn't finish the thought.

"What are you talking about, strange—this is terrific! It's what everybody would love to do and always has to wait until senior year, usually."

Beth Ann thought a minute. She had been about to blab again. There was no reason for Sandy to know just how strange this really was. This was a blessing, that was all. She must receive it that way. Tommy Lee Clayton hadn't been angry at all when he had called her. In fact, quite the opposite. He was calling up to apologize for what he gathered had been Tompkins's unseemly and rude outburst. It wasn't her fault at all, he had assured her, but, you know, Dr. Tompkins was just one of these weird scientists and had overreacted. He didn't want any more tours given of the science center because of the sensitive nature of the work going on there. These people had to be humored, you know. But Tommy Lee Clayton was not going to humor them at the expense of a fine, hardworking student like Beth Ann. As an apology to her, he felt that they owed her something. So why not take this plum of a job down at Bible Times? A girl in the day-care center had to leave suddenly and there was an opening.

Beth Ann hardly had time to pack her bags and no time to write her grandparents before leaving. The very next day she was on a plane to Lorne Thurston's religious theme park, Bible Times.

28

"There is only one thing wrong with Harvard." The man's florid face pushed across the table toward Archie Baldwin, filling the tight space between them. Just his luck to be seated across from this bozo benefactor.

"What's that?" Archie asked politely.

"They give too many goddamn honorary degrees to women, Jews, and blacks."

Archie was stunned. The words came on a wave of boozy breath. Whoever said vodka didn't smell was wrong. This guy smelled as if he had been marinating in it for days.

"You agree?" the man asked. His name was Hugh Ethelredge. "You see what I mean?" he whispered as he leaned closer and nodded toward a tall black man at the end of the table.

"I think I see all too clearly what you mean," Archie

said, regaining his composure. "For your information, I was the one to suggest that Germain Beyers be appointed to the board of overseers for the Peabody Museum of Ethnography"—Baldwin emphasized the last word, then continued—"and Archaeology."

"You and your goddamn ethnics, Archie." Ethelredge chuckled. "Glad your cousin Neddy isn't that way. Wouldn't have gotten my vote when he was running for governor." And he wouldn't have gotten mine, either, Archie thought, but he refrained from saying anything. Of course, Hugh Ethelredge would never understand that Archie Baldwin and Neddy Baldwin would never vote for each other on anything, but that both cousins would always reserve the last ten days in August to go sailing down east together on the sleek old Hinckley yawl, *Rogue Moon,* as they had for the last thirty years.

Baldwin sighed. "It's not my goddamn ethics. It so happens that Germain Beyers is the best damn lawyer in nonprofits there is, and he's also raised more money for them than you ever dreamed of contributing."

Ethelredge's color rose. One eyebrow flicked and took on an antic life of its own. "I'll have you know, Archie," the man fumed, "that I've contributed over two million dollars to Harvard in the last—"

"I know. And how much did you contribute to *The Green Review,* Hugh?" Archie paused just briefly. "I was sent a copy of it this spring by the Anti-Defamation League as an example of the most vicious and ugly sort of journalism," Archie said, getting up just as the waitress slid a plate in front of him with a glazed petit four inscribed on the top with a crimson H. "Now, if you'll excuse me . . ." He walked away from the table, leaving Hugh Ethelredge fuming and turning as dark as the crimson H.

Archie Baldwin desperately needed some fresh air. He ducked out of the dining room and into the entrance hall of President's House. Every president of Harvard since Lowell until Bok had occupied the elegant Georgian structure at number 17 Quincy Street. Now it was used only for entertaining and special functions such as the one this evening, the semiannual dinner meeting of the board of overseers for the Peabody Museum. Baldwin, of course, was shocked by Ethelredge's remark, yet he had been recruited for this board precisely because the director had hinted that they were in desperate need of fresh blood. The curmudgeon index was becoming intolerably high. The director of the museum had used an excruciating mix of metaphors at the time, actually—fresh blood and deadwood. The metaphor had proved apt, however.

Baldwin had been asked to join the board. They had literally begged him after the Peter Gardiner disaster of eighteen months before. He had been instrumental, along with Calista Jacobs, the eminent book illustrator, and her son, Charley, in uncovering the biggest scam in archaeology ever, which had been operating directly out of the Peabody Museum.

Hugh Ethelredge was obviously part of the deadwood that the director had been referring to. But Baldwin had brought in the fresh blood. Along with Germain Beyers, he had convinced Steve Herbert, a curator from the American Museum of Natural History, to join the board. The director had been jubilant. There had to be a better way of keeping the museum solvent and vital than relying on people like Ethelredge. Baldwin had just not anticipated the remark. Good Lord, why would people like that ever want to sit on the board of a museum dedicated to celebrating the diversity of human culture?

Archie glanced at his watch. He had time for a quick turn around the block before the after-dinner remarks and the slide show. He bemoaned his hard luck of being seated directly across from Ethelredge. His own social life wasn't so great that he needed to waste evenings having dinners with such people. Well, tomorrow night there would be a definite improvement in dining companions.

Calista Jacobs. She had called him, frightened to death. Someone had tried to run her and Charley off a road down in Texas. It had something to do with a strange story of skulls and the death of a colleague of hers. She had sputtered on about visiting this weird college run by that nut Lorne Thurston, whom she also had seen on television with Neddy. It was a complicated tale that she'd said she would rather explain in person—if that were possible. It turned out that he was coming up the next day for the Harvard meeting. So they'd made plans for the following evening.

As he took a turn in the neighborhood, he realized that he was actually quite near her street. He had wanted to see her again. But it seemed as if they were always just missing each other. When he had come to Cambridge last year at the time of the annual meeting, she had been invited by the Rockefeller Institute in Bellagio to come there for a month, a month coveted by many scholars and artists, to pursue her work in the tranquil beauty of the Villa Sebolloni. Then she and her son had traveled extensively in Europe. She also seemed to spend a lot of time at her vacation home in Vermont. Last fall she had been invited to Japan, where her work was being honored. At Christmas, when Archie had come to visit his family in Boston, she had been in Indiana visiting hers.

But tomorrow night he would see her—see her for the first time since the awful time, that crystalline fall day when she had come very close to losing her only child after she had already lost her husband. He tried to picture her face now, but it kept slipping away from him as it had for the past eighteen months. It was, as he remembered, a lovely face, strikingly enigmatic. So at one point he had gone to a children's bookstore in Washington to find one of her books in hopes that there would be a picture of her on the back or inside the dust jacket. What caught his attention on a display table was not a photograph of the illustrator, but an illustration of an incredible swashbuckling cat from her new illustrated book *Puss in Boots*. The cat standing on its back feet in thigh-high boots, a cape flaring out behind, and a plumed hat looked for all the world, in terms of posture and bravado, to be a feline version of Errol Flynn, except for the eyes. The eyes were her eyes—slightly hooded, very dark, with fierce sparkles of light that seemed to suggest other universes, distant and unreachable ones. Had her husband, Tom Jacobs, the astrophysicist, found analogs within his own wife's eyes? When he'd died in the desert in Nevada, bleeding to death from the bite of the rattlesnake that had been placed in his sleeping bag, had he looked up into the black dome of the desert sky, pricked with the light of the stars, and thought of his wife's eyes?

Baldwin slipped into the living room of the President's House just as the first slide was coming on the screen. It was the photograph of an umiak, a skin boat, that would be included in a joint exhibition with Russia that was to highlight East and West's shared cultural heritage through the Arctic connection. Baldwin could feel Ethelredge squirming on his seat with this latest wrinkle in the *glasnost* lovefest.

An hour later Archie was sliding the key into his parents' town house on Louisburg Square. Will and Nan Baldwin had already gone to their summer home on the coast of Maine.

"Archie?" a thin, scratchy voice called out.

"Yeah, Heckie! I'm in, all safe and sound. No need to worry. Didn't wreck the car, no necking on the Common."

There was a sound of parched laughter and a door closing. Heckie, gardener, handyman, sometimes chauffeur when he was younger, and on occasion taskmaster and baby-sitter for various Baldwins in their youth, had stayed up out of habit, a habit of over fifty years. He was now nearing eighty. He had come with Will and Nan Baldwin when they were a young bridal couple and previous to that had been in the employ of Will Baldwin's father, Tut.

When Will Baldwin married, and life promised to become immediately more complicated, Heckie came along, not as a servant, but more as a co-manager with Will and Nan to help run a large house in the city and ride herd over the five children that started arriving almost immediately. Will Baldwin had always been considered slightly odd by the extensive Baldwin family, whose genealogical tendrils, through blood and marriage, had intertwined with Saltonstalls, Warrens, and Cabots over generations of Boston breeding and interbreeding. Will Baldwin not only acted like a Democrat, he actually voted the ticket fairly consistently and espoused a lot of "Bohemian" causes like nuclear disarmament, worker-managed firms, and environmental groups. He had also, in a distinct break with recent tradition, made several millions of dollars in his own ventures. These ventures had ranged from publishing a small chain of local newspapers to getting in at the start-up of some of the mushrooming computer companies out on Route 128 and beyond. "Wang!" Will's uncle had said to him three decades before. This was obviously the first Chinese that any Baldwin had dealt with since the China trade merchants of one hundred and thirty years before.

Archie, Will and Nan's second eldest, was considered as curious as his father. Passionate about his archaeology, he had become the boy wonder of the field thirty years before with his extraordinary work in the desert West and the Paleo-Indian cultures of that region and the nearby Great Basin. He was now considered the dean of American archaeology. Just grazing fifty with close-clipped gray hair and intense blue eyes, he was startlingly attractive but lacked the gregariousness of his father and seemed to present a granitic exterior that women just loved to think they could crack. They seldom did. And when they failed they always went away telling themselves that Archie Baldwin was shy, or that maybe he was gay. He was neither. He just had not found too many women that he felt he could go the distance with. But he had sprinted with several. Of late he was finding these sprints less satisfying.

Now, as he went to his father's study, he could not for the life of him remember Calista Jacobs's face. He should have brought the *Puss in Boots* book with him. It had her picture on the flap, and of course there was that wild cat on the cover and throughout the book with her eyes. He remembered that even the cat's fur looked like her hair. He had brought a beer up with him to his father's study and sat down on an easy chair and began browsing through a *New Yorker*.

It was a curious collision of events, he thought as he looked at the cartoons, his seeing Neddy on television and Calista seeing him. Well, it had been on the national news. But then her going down to that dingbat's college in Texas, and how did her murdered colleague fit into all this? And why was she so scared? Had someone really tried to run her off the road? And these skulls, what was that all about? Come to think of it, hadn't Neddy mentioned something to him about some skull analysis? Well, he guessed he'd find out tomorrow.

Just at that moment the telephone rang.

"Archie . . ." It was his father's sonorous voice. His mother was on the extension. They chatted for a few minutes about some mundane matters such as timing for summer visits and could he please try to make it this summer for a good spell before he went sailing with Neddy, his nieces and nephews so adored him. "By the way," Will said, "I've been meaning to ask you since you got back. Did you by any chance catch Neddy a few weeks ago on the national news with that disgusting Bible thumper?"

"Lorne Thurston? I did indeed."

"It was absolutely mortifying." His mother's voice came through clear and soft. It was always soft, even when she was angry. And he could tell she was now.

"I mean," continued his father, "we always knew Neddy wasn't too smart."

Nan Baldwin spoke crisply. "I—I was so angry about his stand on abortion, but this is even more irksome in an odd way."

"I don't know what we can do about it," Will Baldwin said.

"I don't either. I called him up at the time, though, and bawled him out."

"Good for you, Archie!" his mother trumpeted. "You are a man of action. Well, I think I'll do the same. The more pressure brought to bear the better. Poor Lacey. God, she puts up with a lot."

"Yes, and Little Lacey isn't so keen on the notion of her dad up there with this Bible-pounding jerk, either."

"Is she still thinking about Antioch?" Nan Baldwin asked.

"Yes."

"Terribly refreshing choice, I think," Will added.

"Oh, before I forget, Archie dear, I have a great favor to ask you."

"Anything, Mother."

"Well, your father's underwear is in absolute shreds. Would you mind going to Filene's—the basement, of course—and picking up a dozen boxer shorts for him and some undershirts? Size thirty-six waist on the shorts. Extra large on the shirts. And it probably wouldn't do any harm to replenish your own wardrobe. If you go to the second floor of the basement over on the far left in the men's section, they usually have some good buys on sports coats. I got Will a wonderful Harris tweed on a second markdown for seventy-five dollars."

"Okay. I'll look."

"Good, dear. Thank you so much."

29

Calista had been stripping in Filene's basement for years. It was an acquired skill, which, when honed by veterans of the basement, could be raised to a minor art form. Basically one pulled the skirt on over the skirt or the trousers one was wearing and then dropped the nether garment. If you had planned ahead and worn an undershirt, you had it made, for it meant that you could actually strip off your sweater or shirt and try on a new top quite easily without baring too much. But if you had not planned ahead and found yourself just popping into the basement for a quick tour, and indeed discovered something worth trying on, it required a bit more dexterity to put on a blouse or a sweater with a modicum of modesty. Only a modicum was really necessary, as the basement shoppers were so involved in their tasks that eyes were rarely lifted from the merchandise. Next to the marathon it was the most competitive noncollegiate, nonprofessional sport in Boston, and the watchword in any race was never waste time by stealing a glance at the competition.

Today Calista found herself unprepared in the basement but nonetheless trying on a designer top that was on its second markdown. She had not worn a T-shirt under her sweater, and she had not worn a bra. So it was a bit tricky. However, she was very good at this business despite the fact that she did not possess the optimum specs that go into the design of a really great basement shopper. Shortness counted for a lot in the basement because it was really easier to see the merchandise between people crowding around a table than over them. Also, it was easier to strip without being seen if one barely reached the shoulder level of an average shopper. Shortness and a definite stoutness were the ideal attributes for ambushing merchandise and conducting table raids. Once one saw what one wanted on a table, it was often necessary to pry an opening in the crowd. There were certain basement shoppers who could do this with all the efficiency of a cold chisel. This was leverage buying at its most basic.

Being on the tall side and quite lean were attributes that normally would not work to the advantage of a basement raider. But Calista had become so skillful that it didn't matter anymore. She considered herself the Larry Bird of the basement. He looked clumsy. He couldn't jump. He was a white man in a black man's game. But he was so smart that he could look one way and pass the ball the other way. That was what she was doing just then. She had taken off the top and was still holding her sweater to her bare chest when she spotted the silk corner emblazoned with the gold chain links. Knotted gold chains and heraldic stamps meant just one thing—Hermès. Hermès scarves were as rare in the basement, especially in this area of the basement, as orchids in a field of soybeans. Her sensors warned her that there were most likely half a dozen women in the immediate vicinity who would pounce on the scarf in an instant if they spotted it. She looked the opposite way and reached for the scarf. What could be wrong with it?

"Calista!"

Shit! She clutched the scarf to her breast along with her sweater.

"Archie!" She was nonplussed. What was he doing here now? They were both speechless. She felt him look at her bare shoulders with confusion. He didn't understand any of this. He was not a denizen of the basement. It was egregiously obvious.

"You're early." That was all she could think to say.

"I guess so." He laughed, and his fierce blue eyes blazed. Jesus, she hadn't remembered he was so handsome. "I'm kind of lost, actually. I was looking for the men's department."

"Oh . . . oh, really . . . Well, you're in the wrong section. You've got to go upstairs to the second floor."

"But I thought this was the second floor," Archie said, obviously confused.

"No! How could you think that? This is the first floor."

"But first I went to the . . ." He began to point up. His voice dwindled off. "I mean, wouldn't you consider this going to a second floor even if it's . . . Jesus Christ, this is complicated."

"Oh, I see what your problem is. Yeah, you thought . . . Oh, I get it. It's just a matter of perspective. It's actually quite easy if you think of it in terms of upper and lower level and not first and second floor." Calista's long fingers were jabbing up and down in the air as she explained the levels of the basement. Neither the scarf nor the sweater slipped an inch as she conducted what had to be the longest discourse ever held in Filene's basement. "You know, I'm really surprised at you, Archie, being an archaeologist and all. It's just the old classic stratigraphy. This floor we're on now is the lower level. See, the bottom stratum comes first, is the earliest; therefore, you call it the first floor. Then we move up through the layers of time, or merchandise, as the case is here, and you get to the second level. That's where the men's department is. Just apply your basic geological stratigraphy and you got it."

"Yes, I guess I just never thought of it that way," he said, looking around. "They sell wedding dresses here?"

"Yes, yes, everything. You name it. Listen, just wait a minute while I get dressed, and I'll show you where you need to go."

"Wait while you get dressed?" Again he looked slightly confused. "Should I turn my back?"

"Oh, you're not used to this at all, are you?" Calista laughed and shook her head. "Well, if it makes you more comfortable, sure. But I'm so good at this. I mean, it's like sleight of hand. There're naked ladies all over the place here. It's just that we dress and undress at light speed, so you never see us." And as she talked she pinned the Hermès scarf to her chest with one arm and slipped into her sweater. "Dressed!" she announced. "Oh, wait. I forgot to take off this skirt." Archie blinked as she stepped out of the skirt and stood in her well-tailored slacks. "Okay. Let me just quickly buy this scarf. It's on a third markdown, if you can believe it."

Archie looked baffled. "That's a scarf? It looks the size of a tablecloth."

"Yeah, I think I'm going to make something out of it."

Calista paid for the scarf and then led Archie to the upper stratum and the men's department. "Well, here you are," she said. "You think you can find your way out from here?"

"Yeah, I think so." He smiled. He wished she'd stay around a little bit. He would never forget running into her that way. It hadn't been her eyes that had caught his attention in the basement. It had been her shoulders. She had great shoulders, broad, with fabulously elegant bones. "So I'll see you tonight?"

"Yes, of course. What time will you be by?"

"What time's convenient?"

"Well, six-thirty, and we can have a drink first."

"Okay, see you then."

By her calculations Calista had exactly three and one-half hours after she got home to sew the scarf into something to wear for that evening. Queen Elizabeth might wear these scarves to batten down her tight little perms at the horse races, but, by God, Calista was going to turn this into something sensational. Originally the scarf had been at least three hundred dollars. By the time it hit the basement it had been one hundred and seventy-five dollars, and then by the time it was on a third markdown, when Calista got it, it was eighty bucks. Still too much for a head scarf, but quite reasonable for a skirt. She didn't want to do a miniskirt, as was now quite popular again. She loathed kneecaps, especially her own, out of context. But she wanted something mildly sexy.

Gads! She had not remembered Archie as being that attractive. Of course, at the time of their last meeting Charley had just been released from the hospital. No wonder she had not been in a state of mind to observe him more closely. But now she knew that he had a great face, a face that she would draw and that might eventually thread its way into her work. Robin Hood! She had yet to be pleased with the eyes. The face she had found on the subway that day a few months ago was fine for the contours and the structure, but the eyes had not measured up. Archie's eyes! They'd be perfect in that face. Because of the trip to Dallas and all the Caldecott hoopla, not to mention her and Charley's near demise on a Texas highway, her concentration had suffered and there had been scant time to really work on *Marian's Tale*. She planned to get back to it, if not today, tomorrow. A September deadline loomed.

That afternoon, however, found her not drawing faces,

but sketching a design for the scarf skirt. Ordinarily a sarong-type look would have seemed appropriate considering the fabric and the fact that this was a scarf with beautifully hand-rolled hems, the hallmark of Hermès superb craftsmanship. The design should interfere as little as possible with the true quality of the scarf. The less cutting and darting the better. But the heraldic print of the chains and shields and ensigns did not look good on the bias. She wrapped the scarf around her and studied her image in the mirror.

"Yuck!" she muttered. At that moment she heard the door slam downstairs. "Charley?"

"Yeah."

"You home?"

"No, actually, Mom, I'm still out. This is my aura."

"Very funny. How was the Martin Institute today?"

"Fine, but I did not find the cure for cancer." She heard him bounding up the steps.

"Oh, shucks." Calista laughed.

"Why are you standing there half-naked wrapped in chains, Mom?"

Calista blinked at her image in the mirror and that of her son's. He had grown, but had he grown up that much? Good Lord, Charley could put things in an odd way. He was not ignorant about sex anymore, or of his mother as a sexual being. But this was a little much. Was this elegant scarf really kinky under its hand-rolled hems? A soupçon of bondage! Is that what Charley was saying? She had never thought of it that way. What did Charley know about such things, anyway? She looked at him, the aureola of red hair, thick and flaming around his still delicate face. The clear gray eyes.

"Well, I'm trying to make it into a skirt to wear tonight."

"Where you going?"

"Remember, Archie Baldwin is coming over and taking me out to dinner."

"Oh, God! Baldwin, I forgot."

"How could you forget? I'm hoping he's going to shed some light on this skull thing, not to mention the other events." She paused and looked at him. "I'd really like you to come, too, or at least be here to help me explain it. I still don't quite understand why you can't," Calista said. She did wish he would accompany her. She had never really thought of it quite this way until now. It wasn't just because she needed Charley there to help explain what had happened down in Texas. She could do that fine. She just wished Charley could be there. She knew why. She had found Baldwin uncompromisingly attractive. She had felt something stir within her during that nutty encounter in Filene's basement. She would feel safer, less accessible to her own feelings, if Charley were there. It wasn't fair thinking about her son like this. She could not use him this way. She was ashamed of herself.

"Now what was it you said you were doing?"

"I told you, Matthew and Andrew and I have to go and observe Scott."

"Observe Scott?"

"Yes, he's having a date with Anna Fredkin."

"A date?"

"Yes, a first date."

"How romantic having you three there to observe."

"But you don't understand. Matthew was supposed to have a date, his first date, with Anna."

"So, Scott beat him to the punch."

"Not exactly. Scott knew Matthew was going to ask her, but . . ." He paused. "It . . . you know . . . it just takes a while to build up your nerve to do these things. So Scott should have waited. It was very unfair."

"So do you think it's fair that you three little shy guys go and 'observe' Scott and Anna now? How do you think Anna's going to feel about that? She might never accept a date with Matthew if she sees him doing this kind of stuff."

"We're going to be very casual about it. They're going to the movies and then the Harvard House of Pizza. It's all going to appear very natural. Only Scott is going to squirm."

"Ooh, *les liaisons dangereuse!*" Calista said as she laid

the scarf on the floor and began to mark it with her tailor's chalk.

"What's that?" asked Charley.

"Nothing. But why don't you come and observe me on my date with Baldwin?"

"That's not a date," Charley said.

"What do you mean it's not a date?" Calista said, looking up with pins sticking out of her mouth.

"I wish you wouldn't talk with pins in your mouth, Mom. It really makes me nervous. I'm scared you're going to swallow one and die. Then I'd really be an orphan."

Calista removed the pins and began putting them into the hedgehog pin cushion.

"Okay, now tell me why this isn't a date."

"Because you're just old friends."

"We're not such old friends. I've only met him once under very trying circumstances."

"Well, that's just it. It was just an accident."

"But now it's not an accident. When I called him he said he was coming up and that he would love to take me and you to dinner. Not just me."

"Well, see. It's not a boy-girl thing like a date."

"But it's a man-woman thing. I mean, what do you call going out to dinner?"

"Not a date," Charley said, getting up and tossing a little ball in the air.

God, kids could be dogmatic. Charley wandered into his room and dropped the ball into the miniature basketball net that he had on the back of his bedroom door. "Did I tell you I saw Bill Walton in Harvard Square, Mom?"

"No, you didn't. How did he look?"

"Old! Old! The guy had to be at least thirty-eight. I mean, he's almost your age. Matthew was going to go up and ask him when he was going to play again. But I said it wouldn't be nice. He's had so many operations. His knees must look like road maps."

"Charley, what about those incomplete assignments of yours, the geography thing and that other report that you neglected to tell me you hadn't done? If it's not in by the end of the week you get C's. Gee, and how will we ever send your transcript to Lorne Thurston College of Christian Heritage with two C's?"

"I've done the geography thing, and the history report is very easy. It's not even a full report, really just a very small, very, very, very minor report on Pliny the Elder. It's a breeze. He didn't do that much."

"I can hear him turning in his grave now. Charley, that's very insensitive of you. How about someday if you were famous, some kid a millennium from now was doing a report on you and referred to it as being a breeze, very small, very minor guy, that Charley Jacobs, didn't do that much. I mean, if you can be so sensitive about Bill Walton, why not Pliny the Elder?"

"Not the same. He's not a Celtic, for one thing."

"He's a Roman, my dear."

"Well, it wouldn't bother me if I spared some kid from having to write a long composition."

At six-twenty she stood before her bathroom mirror in the little navy blue grenadier's jacket she planned to wear with the skirt. It was an Yves St. Laurent jacket, another gem from the basement. She was applying some makeup, which mostly consisted of a variety of moisturizers and eye creams. Gone was her palette of iridescent eye shadows, bright lipsticks, rosy blushes, and even at one time false eyelashes. That had been the makeup of her twenties and early thirties, which she thought of as first-strike cosmetics. Now, over forty, she was into defensive stuff. These creams announced their intentions boldly with their lexicon of vaguely scientific-sounding words like "emulsion" and "hydration." There were references to "moisture traps" and even "antiaging systems," and there was one product with the rather homey but to-the-point subtitle of "dewrinkling, firming cream" for below the eyes. She had bought that last one simply because she was charmed by the sound of the word *dewrinkling,* which apart from its meaning seemed to have a music all of its own. None of it was first strike at all anymore. What it boiled down to was protective reinforcement reaction. She was on the defense, shoring up against the onslaught, the ravages, of time.

She slid into the skirt. It looked terrific. Straight, falling to her midcalf. There was a chic side slash to the knee with welt finishing. To soften the military effect of the jacket she wore nothing underneath except a fake diamond brooch slung on a strand of real pearls against the modest V of her chest. She eyed herself in the mirror. Was the effect too calculated? Of course it was. How could it be anything else? She had been calculating for the last four hours. She pinned up her mop of hair and pulled down a few of her brightest silver strands for bangs. She heard the doorbell ring.

"Charley, can you get that?"

"Okay."

She heard Baldwin downstairs greeting Charley warmly. She stood for the better part of a minute at the top of the staircase, where she could not be seen, and just listened. It sounded so good, their two voices in the front hall. She felt a storm of butterflies, bright monarchs, she imagined, beating their wings madly somewhere within her rib cage. She buttoned the next button up on the narrow little jacket, squared her shoulders, and proceeded down the stairs.

30

It was hard to find a restaurant to talk about murder in. Maybe the Michelin guide should adjust their symbols. Three stars, a fork, a knife, and a gun.

Calista had given a great deal of thought as to where they should go to dinner. She had an idea that Archie would not do well in one of those nouvelle cuisine outfits with plates of food that looked like Mondrian paintings delivered by waiters of dubious gender. The Harvest, which had the best food in Harvard Square, managed to serve it chicly without the nouvelle pretensions, but she felt the place was still too trendy for Archie. And then again the bar at the Harvest was very nearly a caricature of a singles bar with its own Cambridge twist on it. Muttonchops and pop tarts, that about summed up the denizens of the bar. There was always a mélange of aging Ph.D.'s with thick sideburns just out of stale marriages and concupiscent miniskirted young women in horn-rim glasses. It was okay now to show legs, to show boobs. That hard-line power dressing, well, let them do it downtown or in New York. There were also older women at the bar, the ones who knew they were beyond mini-skirts but were still on the prowl. Eight, ten years ago they would have been wearing Marimekko dresses, a style Calista particularly loathed with its stiff fabrics and bold primary-color designs. Now, however, Marimekko was out, and these women would be wearing fiber-arts stuff. Sweaters and dresses with collages of knitted and netted appliqué work. Lots of yarn with weird stuff woven in—corks, feathers, you name it. They called it art. To Calista it all came off looking like a trawler's net. In any case, she didn't want to take Archie to the Harvest or her other standby, Legal Seafood—too crowded, too noisy. So they wound up in one of her old haunts from the years when she and Tom had first come to Cambridge, Chez André, halfway between Harvard Square and Porter Square, just off Mass. Ave. on Shepard Street.

The walls of Chez André were painted with some rather poor murals, and the wall-to-wall carpeting was an unfortunate shade of red, but the place was cozy and had an indefinable charm. The tables were covered with fresh white linens, and there was a bud vase with one or two bright flowers on each table. The menu was decidedly French, and the helpings were not at all nouvelle. With the entrées a heap of vegetables came in large covered dishes. No artfully arranged stringbeans on a plate. It was all presided over by a woman whom Calista instinctively thought of as La Maitresse. But she was not the owner. She was the headwaitress and had been for years. She had a beaked nose, a tiny pointed chin, and small dark eyes. She was tall and wore her dyed black hair in a style that had not been seen since the forties. Parted on the side and clamped with a barrette, it came to just below her ears and then frizzed into a little fringe. She always wore a black skirt with a white top and pinned a white cloth around her for an apron. She looked exactly like something out of a French Resistance movie. One could imagine her being quite pretty in her day, seducing Nazi commandants at the Ritz in Paris. After making love, she would slink out of bed to roll up her gartered stockings. Then wiggling her slim but delectable ass in the direction of Herr Goering, she would quickly fit the silencer onto the gun, turn around, and plug him right between the eyes.

"Ah, Madame Jacobs," she said softly, and handed Calista a menu.

Calista took the menu. She didn't even know the woman's name. She hadn't known it for all the years she had lived in Cambridge. And that apparently was the way it was supposed to be. One just knew that instinctively. None of this "Hi, my name is Mirielle, and I'm your server tonight." No, that was not how it was done at Chez André. They ordered drinks first—Archie a beer, Calista a Dubonnet on the rocks. It was a drink she rarely ordered, but it went well with certain restaurants, old-fashioned French ones, the kind with murals on the walls or old posters.

"You like meat, Archie?"

"Yeah, I like meat."

"They've got really good meat here. I don't eat that much meat, but it's so good here."

"Want to go for the Chateaubriand for two?"

That was precisely what she wanted to go for, but she had felt it might be a little forward to actually suggest the Chateaubriand. There were several other meat entrées that one did not have to share, but this one was the best.

She nodded. "Yep." And then she paused. "I was kind of hoping you'd say that. It's the best one."

"Then why didn't you say so?" He looked over the top of his menu and smiled.

"I thought it would be forward . . . oh, Lord," she sputtered. "I didn't mean forward. That sounds so weird." Archie was grinning. "Forward about meat . . . oh, dear!" God, she needed a bullwhip for those butterflies that were now rampaging through her. Why couldn't she edit her speech a little bit more? Goddammit, Calista! she scolded herself. Just go ahead and utter any harebrained thing that trips across your alleged brain. She took a deep breath, swallowed, blushed furiously. "What I meant to say was I wanted to give you a choice and not force you into this"—she laughed softly— "meat partnership because they only serve it for two, but you know, the veal is great, and so is the filet mignon."

Archie put down his menu and inclined his head toward her just a bit. "I've already made my choice. I'm glad it's yours."

Holy shit, he was appealing! "Uh . . . me too." She uttered those 2.5 words after some thought. Okay, Calista, get your head together. This is ridiculous. You cannot go through the entire evening putting your foot in your mouth and gasping. As a sobering thought, she reminded herself that she and Charley, a mere three days ago, had nearly been killed, run off the road by some religious fanatic, most likely, and that a dear colleague of hers had been killed two months before. She would just be quiet for a minute, sip her Dubonnet, and collect her thoughts. Archie was giving the order. "What do you want to start with, Calista?" he was asking.

"Oysters," she said crisply.

"Just one order, Madame Jacobs?" Oh, Jesus Christ, how mortifying! How could La Maitresse do this to her? Calista loved oysters more than anything in the world, and she always ordered two plates automatically. But that was two when she had been with her husband or by herself or with Janet Weiss or Ethan Thayer. But this was a date, and Archie was going to think she was Miss Piggy!

"Bring her two," Archie said without batting an eyelash.

"Oh, no, Archie, I couldn't."

"Oh, I bet you could. If you can't, I'll help you out, and I won't feel forced." He smiled and ordered something with artichokes for himself.

He looked at her after the waitress had left. She could be very quiet and still, as quiet and still as she was antic and lively and blushing. She didn't exactly blush when she said some of these nutty, charming things. She flared. You could see these spikes of red cutting across her cheeks and even down her neck. She was perhaps the most vivid person he had ever met. Her eyes, her mind, her language, her silvery hair. But now she was very still.

"You want to talk about this thing, this strange thing that happened down in Texas?"

She raised her eyes toward him slowly. They were hooded and dark, and they looked a little bit frightened. God, he didn't want this woman to be frightened! Archie felt something deep within him turn, stir, something that had never stirred before in this way.

La Maitresse had just brought the dessert and poured the last of the bottle of wine into their glasses.

"So that brings us up to now," Calista was saying. "Do you think I should have done more in the way of notifying the police about getting run off the road in Texas?"

"The Boston police?"

"Yeah."

"You said you tried."

"I did. Kind of halfheartedly. One of the guys was on vacation, of the two detectives we had originally spoken to when Norman was killed, and the other was out. He never returned my call. They never do. It's unbelievable."

"Well, I think that's your answer. They really don't give a damn about this case."

"But I do. Look, I've been threatened, threatened three times, if you take what they did to my book and

poor old Owl as a threat. First that, then the car. Luckily
Margaret McGowan is in Scotland."

"Did she receive any more threats?"

"No, not that I know of. Mammy hasn't told me
anything."

"Mammy?" Archie's eyes opened wide.

"Mammy's her housekeeper."

"That her name? Mammy?"

"Yeah, but that's a whole other story." Calista waved
her hand. "No, as far as I know there's been nothing else
sent to her, no threats of any kind."

"Now, can you repeat to me the stuff they said about
the skull, or was it skulls?"

"Well, they referred to more than one, I'm pretty sure.
And they said, or rather this lovely girl, Beth Ann,
said—I know this sounds weird, my referring to her as
'this lovely girl,' but there was something so nice about
her and rather vulnerable." She paused. "I really . . ."
She stopped again. "I know it sounds nutty, but I really
am concerned for her. Anyway, about the skulls, Beth
Ann said that they had these skulls that could prove that
the races evolved separately."

"Did she say where they came from, where they had
found them or dug them up?"

"Not really. Beth Ann talked about some fieldwork
combined in a joint expedition for arid lands biology and
the search for the ark at Mount Ararat."

"Holy moley!"

"Precisely."

"You mean they actually go out and hunt for Noah's
Ark?"

"Apparently."

"So you think that's where they came across these
skulls?"

"Well, she implied that it happened during this joint
expedition, the one including the arid lands."

"That includes a lot! She didn't say which arid lands?"

"Nope." Calista shook her head.

Archie settled back in his seat and folded his arms
across his chest. Calista waited. After a minute or more

he began to speak. "I'm assuming," he began carefully, "that these skulls are fake, like the Paluxy footprints. Only this time they're moving more cautiously because they really got caught with their pants down on that one. They're not rushing to announce it for that reason, but there must be another reason, too. If these skulls were real, they would rush to announce it. It's hard for these finds to be kept under wraps for long—too much ego involvement. Paleoanthropology is a field that attracts massive egos. I'm not being critical here. It's just a natural consequence of the discipline—the study of human origins, what could be more fascinating to human beings than their own history? And yet, what could be more volatile in terms of interpretation? One of the best Ph.D. theses in paleoanthropology I ever read was one by a young woman at Yale. It was about the narrative aspects of the science of paleoanthropology. How anthropological accounts of human origins follow some of the basics of the storytelling tradition. Fascinating. She points out how we try to write our own story into these fossils and how the story has changed over the years with our own changing perception of ourselves."

"And this is the case here? These guys trying to write their own story, a racist story?"

"I think so—a racist story or a biblical one that puts it all in the Genesis time frame, or maybe one that combines both themes. Grind any ax they want to."

"But if you say everybody does this, then how do they differ?"

"The other guys use real data. They can't wait to tell the world about finding the oldest common ancestor. Look at the Leakey camps down in Olduvai and Koobi Fora in the Rift valley, or Don Johanson in Ethiopia. My God, every time you open the paper they've found a scrap of something older, a jaw fragment, fossil footprints, a skull. This is the sexiest, the most glamorous, of all the sciences. Louis Leakey made sure of that. Some of these people are better scientists than others, and the very best ones admit their biases and confess readily to the natural biases ingrained in the nature of their work.

But all of them still rush to share their finds with the world, because the fossils they find are real, not fake. It is absolute torture for any real scientist to sit on a discovery. They want to get on top of the highest peak and scream the news to the world. They call press conferences in the most godforsaken places imaginable. They practically have hot lines to the *National Geographic.* They can't wait to name the goddamn things they find—often indirectly after themselves, or the region they have become associated with through their work, or perhaps after a benefactor.

"No, this is all wrong in terms of the nature of the field. If these folks have a skull that is real, there is no reason they'd be sitting on it. Even if it wouldn't turn out to be all they hoped, they would still bring it out. Eugene Dubois back in the last century, the guy who discovered the critter that is now known as *Homo erectus,* thought he had discovered our oldest ancestor, an upright-walking ape. The missing link. But the scientific establishment said no. He was so furious he went and reburied the bones underneath the floor in his own house. He didn't agree with them at all, never would. But as a scientist he had rushed back with these bones from Java so that they might be examined, scrutinized, and, he had hoped, welcomed with great applause. Why? Because the bones were real. They were still real even after the rest of the scientific world decided they could not be called the missing link. It was a question of semantics, and it pissed Dubois off royally. But he only hid them away after he had subjected the bones to testing. This is science—formulating hypotheses, sometimes by intuition or analogy, then deducing conclusions that can be tested directly or indirectly by observation or experimentation."

"They do claim to be doing some further testing. That's why they said the skulls weren't available to look at."

"But why haven't we heard about the initial discovery? And if they're doing testing, I sure as hell haven't heard anything about it. I talk to the Berkeley folks almost weekly. The molecular guys out there work hand in glove with the paleoanthropologists now. They got all the hardware to run every kind of test. State-of-the-art stuff. I would have heard about this from them. Good Christ, Vincent Sarich figured out ten years ago how to biochemically determine when humans separated from apes. This would be small potatoes for him to figure out this racial thing. He would have been the first person they would have gone to. No, Calista. There have been plenty of bruised egos in this business when fossils haven't turned out to be as old as someone hoped, or a newly declared species turns out to be the same old thing. Mary Leakey and Don Johanson have been going at it hammer and tongs for over ten years as to whether Lucy, the little three-million-year-old gal from the Afars region, is a new species or not. Bones of contention, that's what this paleoanthropology business adds up to more often than not. But these skulls aren't bones of contention. They are bones of pretension." He paused. "And for some reason your presence down there made them very nervous."

"So what do we do?"

"Try to flush them out. They're looking for the right time to expose this skull, or skulls, as the case might be. We've got to throw off their timing."

31

There was no question of timing—or will she, or would he? It was prim, it was proper, and it was as tense as all get-out. They sat on their respective libidos in Calista's study and sipped brandy. There was no choice because there were three sprawling adolescents in the living room watching a Monty Python movie. They had finished observing Scott and Anna, and now Calista guessed it was her and Archie's turn. But as objects of observation they apparently were not as interesting as Scott and Anna or Monty Python. Charley had come in and talked with them for a while, and Calista had reviewed what Archie had said about the skulls, and then Archie had talked about some people he would call and a bit about how he hoped to flush these guys out. Then Charley went back to his friends, who were going to spend the night, and Calista and Archie were left alone in the study. So they sat there, taut and wary, wary not of each other, but of the situation, and there was nothing more they could say or talk about in reference to the skulls at this point. Archie asked about her work. She showed him some of the drawings from *Marian's Tale,* and there was this great gulf of unspoken things and unexpressed feelings that became almost unbearable. So he left, and when he left he gave her a kind of sideways embrace, wrapping his left arm around her shoulders, the way she had seen coaches embrace players, slightly injured players, in those crushing hugs of empathy. However, it didn't feel like empathy at all. It felt hungry and slightly desperate. But it looked like a coach's hug, so she resisted dropping her head against his shoulder and curling up against his chest forever and a day because after all there were these three boys sprawled in her living room—three skilled observers.

32

"Did you hear?" Louise said as Charley walked into the computer room at the Martin Institute.

"Hear what?"

"Steve is putting our names on that crystallography paper he's doing, and if it's accepted we'll all be famous."

"What? How can he do that?"

"They do it all the time," Matthew said, looking up from his terminal screen. "That's the way it's done."

"What's done?" Steve had just walked into the computer room.

Louise turned to him. "We just told Charley what you said about putting all our names on the crystallography paper that you're going to submit."

"But how can you do that? We didn't write a word of it."

"But your ideas and your work on the protein-folding problems helped me, furthered my thinking. Louise is right. That's the way it's done. The head of the Martin Institute will be named, too, at the very top above my name, and Leventhal, as head of our lab, will be on it, and Felicia and Nate. That is the protocol; everybody in the lab puts their name on the paper whether they've worked on it or not, and oftentimes they haven't even read it."

"Like us," Matthew said. "We haven't read it."

"You should at least read the parts that show the graphs based on the modeling you did. Nate has yet to read it. Felicia has. She helped me a lot with the editing. But don't be shocked, Charley. As I was explaining to Louise and Matthew, this is standard operating procedure in biology. Besides, the paper probably won't be accepted anyhow. I heard that this particular journal has published an awful lot on the topic recently." He walked over to the computer where Louise was working. "Meanwhile, back at the ranch here, what are my mentees coming up with? Have you solved the intellamine-intellicone problem?"

"Nope," Matthew said.

"Oh, by the way, Charley. How was Texas? What with the Fourth of July weekend and all, it feels like ages since I've seen you."

"Oh, it was fine. Interesting." But Charley's mind was suddenly skipping ahead—or actually back, he realized. When Steve had mentioned intellamine, something had clicked in his brain, and why hadn't it clicked down in Texas when they had stood in that lab with Beth Ann and heard that wacko tale of skulls and races? Why had he not thought of those elusive brain proteins, the neurotransmitters, then, and the experiments that seemed to be coming up with evidence that intellicone was apparently absent in black people?

"It was so hard reading those papers," Matthew complained. "They were beyond us."

"Look, I'm your mentor. What didn't you understand?"

"All of it," Louise moaned. "Or at least as far as I got."

Steve scratched his chin and looked at his charges. "Okay, you guys," he said thoughtfully, "I'll buy lunch today."

"Yeah!" they all cried.

"Hold it!" Steve said, lifting his finger. "It's not going to be at Mary Chung's."

"Oooh!" they all groaned.

"We'll order in if you want, but the deal is we get the west conference room and I lead you through these articles. But you got to try reading them first and write down your questions."

Five minutes later Steve had brought in the articles and tossed them on a table. "Well," said Charley, picking up one. "Let's see . . . one, two, three, four, five, six, seven, eight. Eight authors on this one. How many do you think actually read it or worked on the project?"

"Don't know," said Steve. "But they're from good places—Duke, University of Minnesota, University of Pennsylvania."

"What's this Coastal Research Institute?" Louise asked.

"It's an institute, kind of like Martin, not quite the same power or clout or money. But it's loosely connected with Stanford, the way the Martin is with MIT. The head of it is James Atwell, a biochemical engineer. He's done a lot of work in cryogenics. Okay, kids, start to work. See you in two hours."

"Wait a minute!" Louise said. "First things first. Who's going to order from Mary Chung's?"

"You can. But please don't spend the whole morning figuring out the order or I'll have to delete your names from the crystallography paper."

He started out the door.

"One more question!" Charley called after him. "Is Mary Chung's name on the paper?"

"Jacobs, what a wiseass you are." He waved and left.

"Not wiseass enough to figure this out," Matthew muttered.

"It's so boring," groaned Louise.

The three youngsters plugged away for the better part of an hour marking up the papers with highlighters and scribbling questions in the margin. "I don't understand a darn thing I'm reading," Matthew finally said. "I mean, I can kind of interpret these graphs, but there's nothing I know about in these papers."

Charley looked up suddenly. "You're right, Matthew. There's nothing we know about!" And he had been reading hard, trying to link up the hypotheses of these papers, all the stuff about neurotransmitters and the stuff he had heard about down in Texas. How could you link bones with molecules, fossils with proteins? he wanted to know. He knew a little bit about both, but one thing suddenly startled him. For over three months they had been working on models of protein structures, similarities in the primary structures of proteins and how they mapped to tertiary. It was sort of interesting work, but hardly earthshaking and definitely not a priority. Yet so far in these papers not one had addressed the subject of structure in regard to intellamine and intellicone.

"Have any of you guys come across the words *primary structure* or for that matter *tertiary structure* in these papers?"

"No, come to think of it," Louise said.

"Me neither." Matthew shook his head. "But I'm a slow reader, especially with this stuff."

Charley's face was lively. "Hey, guys, that's our question! That's the most interesting question around. How come there's nothing about structure in all these papers? Steve had said that in the very earliest papers there was something. But in these, nothing."

"But we're not sure," Louise said cautiously. She was a robust girl with a thick mass of curly black hair. "We'll have to read everything first. I mean, it still might crop up."

"Don't be ridiculous." Charley jumped up. "You want to die of boredom? We don't have to read all this stuff to find out."

"The scanner!" Matthew shouted.

"Right-o."

Along with its marvelous machines for splicing DNA and synthesizing peptides, the Martin Institute possessed another wonder that did neither of these but instead was a computer that could encode written text into binary symbols directly from paper into its memory and then scan it. For some peculiar reason the folks in the computer center had named it Susie Q. So while Susie Q did her work scanning for the key words of the question—*primary, tertiary, protein folding,* and *structure*—the children spent twenty minutes arguing over their order to call in to Mary Chung's. When they came back with the food, Charley, who had been left to monitor Susie Q, greeted Louise and Matthew with a single word: "Zilch."

If Steve was impressed with his mentees' question, he was even more impressed with their newfound zeal. First they had requested the earlier papers on intellamine and intellicone, where structure at least had been initially mentioned. Based on these, it looked to Steve as if they were going to try and do some mapping of their own. The kids were staying late and coming in early. They were doing boring stuff, or so it seemed to Steve, making long, laborious correlations of everything they had discovered to date. There was foot after foot of computer printout listing the regularities in all of the hundreds of proteins for which they had made structural models. When Steve saw how gung ho the kids were, he was not only pleased to let them run with it, but gave them all the help he could. More specifically, he requested that one of the hotshot programmers, Liam Phillips, come down and help them figure out a sorting and categorization program so they could organize and compare the regularities even more quickly. This sped up their work immensely.

Liam was an elfin-looking man of indeterminate age but probably closer to thirty than forty. He had black electric hair that stood out around his head in a full-voltage nimbus of darkness. He took a swallow of his Coke and sat back. "So now that you've got all this data so neatly cubbyholed and observable, what are you going to do with it?"

Both Louise and Matthew looked at Charley. It was his project, ever since he had told them of the strange events at Lorne Thurston College. So it was for him to speak.

"There are these new brain proteins, and we just want to see how their structures compare with all the proteins we've already got structures on."

"You're just mapping the structures of these babies, right?" Liam asked.

"Yeah. Why?" Charley asked.

"You running any energy tests on these new brain proteins?"

218

"Energy tests?" all three kids asked.

"Yeah. How much free energy there is running round in the molecules of them. Another guy and I wrote a program for calculating free energy in molecules of structure proteins."

"No shit!" Charley gasped. "That's great. Gives us another thing to look at beyond the structure."

"Before the structure. They can only have so much free energy to exist."

"No kidding. So you know the energy range on all these proteins we've already been working with?"

"Sure. You don't even have to run the test on them. I'll just bring a disk down with all the data, and you can feed it into what you already got. Then you can run the program on these new brain proteins and see how it compares."

They would work for four days nearly around the clock, going in at seven in the morning and coming back after midnight. The Martin Institute fed them and gave them cab money, or rather Steve got it out of petty cash. He didn't inquire too closely as to what the kids were doing, but he knew they were going and going hot. He figured they'd come to him when they wanted to. They did at eleven o'clock on the fourth night.

The three youngsters stood in front of him, looking wan and somewhat exhausted but excited nonetheless. Charley jammed his hands into the pockets of his jeans and took a deep breath. "Guess what?"

Steve looked up and blinked. "What?" he said quietly, but there was a funny little pulse jumping around in his temple.

"They blow up."

"You ran the energy program of Liam's?" The three kids nodded. Steve coughed slightly. "Both of them—intellamine and intellicone?"

"Yep," said Charley.

Louise shook her head. "They can't exist. There's so much free energy they simply cannot exist."

"Not stable, huh?" Steve said.

"They'd just blow themselves apart," Charley said.

"Not only that, Steve." Matthew spoke. He was holding a sheaf of computer printout. "You should see the other stuff besides the energy thing. They have none of the regularities found in any of the other proteins we've mapped."

Steve smiled quietly to himself. This was where drudgery paid off. What the kids had done was to begin to sequence or, as Steve liked to think of it, walk a peptide chain of the amino acids that made up proteins that were in turn governed by DNA, the genetic coding molecule. A protein could be as many as four thousand bases of these amino acids. They had looked at a few thousand of these proteins to see how they folded into primary and tertiary structures and now added their own twist to calculate how much free energy each protein could maintain without literally falling apart, or blowing apart, as they called it. There was a critical mass beyond which a protein could not maintain its internal structure before disintegrating. There was nothing elegant that they had to do. All that, the designing and cloning of the probes, the splicing and recombinant work of the DNA, which governed the synthesis of these structural proteins, had been done by others. Even the rough sequencing and mapping had been done. All the kids had to do was to look at the tiny stuff and just search for patterns. It wasn't that these patterns didn't matter. It was just that searching for them was not top- or even mid-level priority in cancer research work. It was an all-guts-no-glory job.

In physics they might call these small patterns and correlations that the kids were looking for the butterfly effect—a syndrome that suggests that the fibrillations in the air caused by the wings of a butterfly stirring in Melbourne, Australia, could affect weather changes the following month in London. The technical name for the phenomenon was "sensitive dependence on initial conditions." Steve preferred the more lyrical name of butterfly effect, and he began to think of his young charges standing before him not as mentees, but as butterflies. They had stirred their wings, but now it was up to Steve to reveal that the elusive brain proteins of intellamine and intellicone were not simply elusive but illusive and positively mythical.

First, however, Charley had to tell him the rest of the story—why and how he had been willing to stay up for four nights in a row doing the dreariest task imaginable and drag his two friends along with him as they tiptoed through the proteins. And when he had finished late that night, Steve Gillespie was very nearly mesmerized by the possible cascading results of this particular butterfly effect. After he had put the kids into a cab that evening, he headed down Main Street toward the Charles River. As he crossed the Longfellow Bridge he stopped at the midway point and looked down at the dark, placid waters passing underneath the bridge—billions upon billions of molecules flowing down the river to the locks and into the harbor of Boston. Beneath the recognizable patterns were events, phenomena that could be called random because they were unseeable, incalculable— chaotic. But perhaps not. He thought of his three butter- flies, three little butterflies flitting around within the structure of the Martin Institute amid the soaring of the eagles, the Nobel laureates who headed labs and brought in millions of dollars to support their research and wrote papers that these three butterflies could barely get through. He looked at the dark, still waters of the Charles and thought of the poem so often cited to illustrate the butterfly effect:

> *For want of a nail, the shoe was lost;*
> *For want of a shoe, the horse was lost;*
> *For want of a horse, the rider was lost;*
> *For want of a rider, the battle was lost;*
> *For want of a battle, the kingdom was lost!*

Now what precisely was the battle being fought here, and who were the riders? And the kingdom—what kind of a kingdom did these people who had faked the proteins envision? He shuddered, feeling a chill pass through him on this very hot July night, and continued walking quickly across the bridge toward Boston.

33

It had been the second night that Charley had worked late down at the Martin Institute. He had told his mother that he would be working well into the night along with Matthew and Louise for most of the week. Steven Gillespie had assured Calista, as well as Matthew's and Louise's parents, that he would see the youngsters home safely, either driving them himself or sending them in cabs. All the parents were pleased that their children were so zealous about their work, and although it was another three and a half years off, not one parent did not indulge himself or herself in projecting how nice this would all look on a college application.

Calista probably indulged herself less than the other parents, however, not because she was any more confident about her son's prospects, but because, goddammit, it was very hard to think when one's hormones were in such tumult. She had long ago passed beyond mere horniness. It was there all right, but in a somewhat fossilized form. She did not, however, think of Charley's long nights at the institute purely in terms of enhancing him as college material. No. These nights could be a window in the long night of celibacy. But Archie was gone. Gone to see his parents in Maine! That really bugged her. And gone to do some preliminary snooping before he began flushing out these latter-day Piltdowners. That was a name that she had come up with and that Archie had begun to use.

He had been gone now for three days. Calista never went to bed before Charley got home. She couldn't, because although she could sleep, it was not a real slumber, thick and soft. It was more like a thin, scratchy blanket pulled over her on a chilly night. She would only half sleep in a kind of prickly somnolence, awaiting the turn of Charley's key in the lock. So she had decided to work. She didn't need daylight or north light. She mixed her colors, trying to duplicate the effects of the old formulas by beefing up the acrylics with an odd assortment of stuff that ranged from egg yolks to crushed stamens of tiger lilies in her search for the fabulous colors she had found in the books of hours. She had gone back to Houghton Library twice more to pore over some of her favorites. In the narrative of *Marian's Tale,* Marian had just escaped the convent that Friar Tuck had helped her get into because of the persistence of Prince John, soon to be King John. She had to escape because of a crooked prioress. Not exactly crooked, but she certainly knew which side her nonsacramental bread was buttered on, and when she found out that the pimply prince was on the prowl for Marian, she was all too ready to turn her over before she got locked in as a bride of Christ. Heaven's loss, another kingdom's gain. Of course, Calista hadn't exactly written it so coarsely in the book. It all was done with great delicacy and followed the old narrative traditions of maidens in distress being pursued by ugly guys. The twist here was that this particular maiden went from relative passivity to activity. Tuck was an all right fellow, but he had gotten her into this pickle, and thank you very much, she would get herself out of it now.

It was a month later in the story than when the book had opened, so the green had to be greener, and of course Robin Hood was going to show up. Calista had figured out the face for Robin—it was the guy on the subway with Archie's eyes. But the resemblance ended there.

This Robin was dreamy, slightly disorganized, and unsure of himself, and he didn't shoot as well as Marian. Not great on people skills, either, and his band was not a merry band at all when Marian arrives. They were grumpy, fractious, and disorderly. The story, however, was not really about how she whipped them into shape, but of subtler things about her experiences alone in Sherwood Forest. Marian actually spent very little time with the band in Calista's version, and there was to be no love story. She took forays into Nottingham and surrounding villages, always disguised, rather like the Scarlet Pimpernel, and performed daring feats of service and espionage. The plot revolved around her rescue of a baby. Good old Marian! Calista thought as she painted the scene where she swam in the tumbling waters of a stream. "No pubic hair, please!" she whispered, and shuddered as she thought of the diapers painted on Nick. How obscene that had been. The rush of the foam, the curling of water, provided the natural camouflage necessary for a mature young woman appearing nude in a children's book. There was simply no way you could show tits and ass of any female over the age of ten in a picture book. This Calista knew and accepted.

The telephone rang.

"Charley?"

"Nope. Archie."

"Oh, goodness."

"You expecting Charley at this late hour?"

I certainly wasn't expecting you, she thought. "Well, he's been working really late over at the Martin Institute, and he usually calls around now to tell me what time he'll be heading home."

"Oh . . ." The word hung there in the air for just a fraction too long. Was she reading too much into it—that "oh" and then the little oval of silence that followed? "Well, I just happen to be in Harvard Square, and seeing as I'm not a street singer and don't find their songs particularly fetching tonight, I thought I might walk over."

"Oh!" Her "oh" this time, and another oval of silence.

She swallowed. "Yes. Oh, do! I'd love to see you. Oh, goodie!" She rolled her eyes at herself. God, why did she always say these stupid things? She had to be the only person over forty who still said "goodie"! If there was one thing that Calista was not, it was cool. She had no way of sounding detached or even moderately disinterested if she was otherwise. She was, in short, your basic bag of exclamation points, asterisks, and other emotional punctuation marks.

Ten minutes later there was a knock on the door. She opened it. He stood there for just a second on the other side of the screen door, his face still but smiling, and even in the night she could see the fierce blue of his eyes. She felt as if he were drinking her in for that sliver of time. Then he came in. No more coach's hugs. He wrapped her up. She felt his chest against her and she felt his heart beating and his face crushed down upon hers in one long deep kiss and she opened her mouth slightly and when he had finished he said, the words hitting her someplace between her nose and eyelid, "When does Charley come home?"

"Late."

Everything strained and ached within her. Everything seemed to be open and ready. They stumbled into the study because there was no way they could make it upstairs in time. She was wearing yellow nylon running shorts, high-top sneakers, and a tank top with no bra. Archie's hand was plunged down into her shorts, and she could feel him hard against her. His voice was hoarse. "We don't have to have any awkward conversations about anything. I bought enough condoms to last into the next millennium."

"What a gent! Please get your pants off," she whispered as they crumpled onto the Oriental rug.

He didn't get them all the way off. He didn't even get his shoes off. But she peeled off everything except her high-tops. He probed her with his hand and then took his hand away and pressed his pelvis against her, not yet entering her, while he tore open the condom. She didn't know how she could wait a second longer. "I'll help you." She took the opened package and withdrew the condom. He lifted himself into a push-up. "You're beautiful," she whispered, looking straight down at his erect penis. "All over."

"You're not exactly ugly yourself," he said.

She laughed low, from the back of her throat, and slid the condom onto him. If he felt this great in her hands, Jesus, she couldn't wait. He drove into her—slow and hard. And they fitted together perfectly—like a billowing sea and a clipper ship. They rocked and swelled. He plowed and she rose again. They did it once. They did it twice. They did it again. They went through all sorts of weather together, and sometimes for Calista, especially when he came, it felt as if it were raining silver inside her.

Charley called at two-thirty. He'd be home in thirty minutes. They hadn't exactly intended to do it again, but they had been standing nude at her drawing board and Archie sank onto the stool and looked down at his crotch. "I can't believe it," he muttered to his rising penis. He then gazed up at Calista, who looked so lean and tan and silvery. "Please!" And she climbed on him right there, laughing.

"I hope we don't mess up your painting."

"I paint in plastics."

He left minutes before the cab pulled up with Charley.

34

In that drowsy penumbra between night and dawn, she awoke. She watched the earliest, weakest pink from her bedroom window steal over the world, filling the sky with its early tint as if it were some enormous transparent rosy balloon. It hovered briefly, this dawn color, and then began to drift on to a new dawn in another world.

She had once seen a dorado fish caught by her father in the Florida keys go through spectacular transformations of color, colors that would shame a rainbow, and she was reminded of this as the pink of the dawn stole into her bedroom and turned the cool gray walls fuchsia for moments only.

But she was far from thoughts of dying. She basked in the memories of her splendid night of lovemaking with this most wonderful man. She looked over at two very small Georgia O'Keeffe charcoal drawings that she had bought with the great windfall of royalties from *Puss in Boots*. She remembered what O'Keeffe had once said about her work: that she arrested beauty to arrest people and stop them from the business of their busy lives. Calista had always liked that notion, and suddenly she realized that for the first time in a very long time she herself had been arrested—arrested by beauty and love and some deep, unnameable goodness that seemed to flow out of Archie. And it was not only deep, this kind of love she was feeling, but it was deepening. She felt it within her. She felt something melt and turn and flow; some kind of spiritual unlocking and tranquillity was upon her at last. As she stared at those austere, dreamlike images of O'Keeffe's, she thought of the painter's later works—the huge monumental flowers with their vivid, intense colors and complicated interiors revealed by unfoldings of soft petals. She had become one of those flowers last night under the touch and the press and the rhythms of Archie. She fell back to sleep. When she awoke again shards of bright sunlight crashed through the window and something shrill scratched the air. There was a flash of blue outside her window. Goddamn blue jays! They were always batting around the southeast corner of her house screeching and squawking—the yentas of the bird world!

The telephone rang. Jesus, what time was it? She fumbled for the phone and blinked at her clock. Nine o'clock! Charley must be gone already.

"Hello."

"Hi . . ."

"Archie!"

"Yeah. I love you."

"Oh, Archie!" And that was all she could say. She loved him, too. But the word couldn't even begin to encompass her feelings. She remembered Woody Allen struggling with the inadequacies, with the brevity, of the simple little word in *Annie Hall,* or was it *Manhattan*? "I am in lurve with you," he had said to Diane Keaton, trying to stretch out the word, making it an oozing proclamation of love—an avowal. But Archie did not use words promiscuously. So it had been hard enough for him to say the word *love,* but the *r* was implied—she knew it, and she knew that this was an avowal that even Racine wouldn't flinch at, and certainly not Calista. They talked some more. He planned to fly to Washington that day.

"I want to talk to my cousin Neddy about this face-to-face."

"Maybe you better not mention my name."

"Why not?"

"He might tell you about our face-to-face encounter."

"Yours?" he asked, bewildered. "Where did you and Neddy ever get together?"

"At a WGBH fund-raising benefit."

"Oh, that's right—he's on the board. He's on so many boards, I can't keep them all straight."

"Well, he asked me to dance."

"I can think of worse things he could have asked you to do." Archie chuckled. "Pardon me, I shouldn't say 'worse.' But what did he do? Step on your toes fox-trotting?"

"No, dear. I stepped on his in the redneck shuffle. It was just before I went to Texas. But I had caught his stellar performance with Lorne Thurston on the news."

"This might not be news to you, but my cousin Neddy is not that smart." Calista resisted saying, "Yeah, and the pope's Catholic."

"In any case, we're very close. There's a bond between us, and it really pains me to see him making a fool of himself. I want to go down there and talk to him directly about all of this. But, Calista, believe me, my main goal is not to salvage Neddy. I want to get to the bottom of this skull thing and see what the connection is with you and possibly the death of your friend. I told you that I had talked to Neddy after I had heard him on the news and he mentioned some kind of evidence that the people at Thurston's school had come up with, and it did involve skulls. I had thought at the time that it was some antievolutionary, procreationist stuff. From what you say, these skulls were supposed to prove separate evolutionary histories for the races. So that isn't precisely antievolutionary. But I suppose if they could come up with a racist-creationist scenario, that might let a few fossils into the game; a kind of revisionist version that excludes apes but allows for separate evolution of races. You know—have their cake and eat it, too, any port in a storm."

"Sounds kind of complicated to me," Calista said.

"Well, if it sounds complicated to you, I don't have to tell you how complicated it must sound to Neddy."

"Yeah." She laughed.

"Did you really step on his toes—or was that meta-phorically speaking?"

"I did worse." She paused. "I stopped dancing with him."

The image was vivid in Archie's mind. He could almost hear the music and see the other dancers, and he could envision Calista still as death in her cold rage and Neddy stunned as he had never been stunned before. It was an image that would stick with Archie for a long time.

35

It was too hot to be outside in Washington. So instead they sat in the winter garden room. It was a perfectly appointed room with a cool green-and-ocher tiled floor, dark wicker furniture, and giant Chinese floor vases erupting with soft explosions of Boston ferns. At one end of the room a tall mirror with a curved top and set-in trelliswork reflected the garden behind the Georgetown house that had been lovingly cultivated over the years by Lacey Baldwin. Lacey was not there. She was at their summer home in Maine. The kids were all away, and so apparently was the maid. A thin layer of dust covered the surface of the English and French antiques. Sofas and chairs in the living room were draped in white covers.

There were no fresh flowers, and Neddy Baldwin, like many a summer's husband, found this his perfect season. There were no restrictions. Long weekends were the norm. The exodus began on Thursday, sometimes as early as Wednesday afternoon. Men of power commuted to summer residences on Martha's Vineyard, the Cape, Nantucket, Northeast Harbor, Maine—often in private jets. But there was really no end to the weekends for some of these men. It seemed to continue in spite of the fact that they returned on Sunday nights. They returned to empty houses with draped furniture such as Neddy's and often a lovely woman waiting upstairs, if she were the kind of woman you could trust to let herself in discreetly. It was the best of all possible worlds. Thursday through Sunday you ate lobster, sailed with children and grandchildren, uncorked bottles of champagne, and made clever toasts to your wife's prize rose that had been recognized by the American Rose Society and bloomed as it had never bloomed before. You even played croquet with your eighty-five-year-old mother and let her cheat, and there was always good bridge. Then you came home and fucked your brains out for the rest of the week. Nice.

Archie had never seen his cousin looking better. He would refrain from saying that, however, because it might lead to a reference to Neddy's current fling, and that was always uncomfortable. For although they were the closest of cousins despite their many differences, and they could discuss almost anything, there was a code. And part of the code was that they could not or would not talk about Neddy's infidelities because that would be a way of doubly hurting Lacey. It was not a question of Archie's approving or disapproving of Neddy's sex life. It was a question of another kind of disloyalty to Lacey, one that would involve not merely Neddy, but Archie, too, if he had begun to discuss these girls of Neddy's. Archie cared for Lacey. Lacey knew, of course, that Neddy had had his flings. Perhaps there were more than she was aware of, but Lacey and Neddy had come to some kind of an understanding. It was, however, an understanding between Lacey and Neddy and not Lacey and Neddy and Archie.

"So, cousin, what brings you here?" Neddy said, settling into a wicker chair and opening his can of beer. "Isn't this wonderful, by the way?" he said, lifting his can.

"What, the beer?"

"No, drinking it from the can. You know I can't do that when Lacey's around—always glasses."

God, Neddy was simple. Now Neddy knew that Archie knew what was probably going on here, and it was more than drinking beer from a can, and remarks like this one just underscored it. "You know, it's just so much easier in the summer. I don't have the maid except once a week or so. Half the time I eat those TV dinners. Life is simpler. Really pared down."

"Sounds like you're ready for Outward Bound," Archie said.

Neddy threw back his head and laughed. "Not quite, fella! Hey, those dates in August still okay with you?"

"Yeah," he said tersely. The image of Calista absolutely still amid the dancers was incredibly vivid in his mind. What had Neddy done at the time? Had he said anything?

"What's troubling you, Archie? You seem a little out of sorts."

Archie looked up. How was he to begin? "Uhh . . . Neddy . . ."

"Oh good Lord, Archie, are you still upset about me and the preacher Thurston?"

"Yes."

"Now look, Archie, you and I both know that although I no longer hold elective office, and"—he raised his hand to emphasize his next point—"I have no intention of running for anything in the foreseeable future, the work I do—this ambassador-at-large stuff, all these presidential commissions and panels—it's politics. And don't let anybody fool you about that." He narrowed his eyes.

"You trying to tell me you're not a statesman?"

"You can't be a good statesman unless you're a politician, and I for one don't think 'politician' is a dirty word."

"You saying your neighbor over there two blocks away, Averill Harriman, was a politician?"

"The best. He only indulged himself in all that statesman crap when he got too old. Loved the guy. Wife's a pain in the ass. And he loved politics."

"I don't know. I remember that 'joy of politics' speech

Hubert Humphrey gave years ago. Somehow I don't think of being on the same platform with that kook Thurston as being a joyous experience in politics."

"It isn't. The guy's an asshole. Although not as bad as you might think."

"But why are you with him? What's the angle?"

"It's a constituency down there."

"Are you trying to tell me that the president is worried about them? He won a landslide victory."

A look of relief swept across Neddy's face. Archie noticed it immediately. Had Neddy been tense before that? He hadn't realized it at the time, but now his face seemed more relaxed. Was that really it? The president worried about these fundamentalists as a constituency? But Archie had the strange sensation that he had led Neddy to this conclusion—when he had asked what was the angle. Was this the real angle?

Neddy was off and flying. He was quoting statistics. "Do you realize that two point four million American households tune in daily to Lorne Thurston? And Jimmy Swaggart, Jim Bakker, and Oral Roberts are just behind him. Now, would you rather have one of them for president or keep the one we got, even though I know he's not your first choice? We're talking power here, Archie, my boy. And they don't want to see one of those ham-fisted louts from the White House down there. They want to think they're talking to a cabinet officer or better."

"They want to see a statesman."

"Precisely."

Had the president actually sent Neddy? Well, it really didn't matter because what Archie wanted to find out about were those skulls and if they were part of the evidence that Neddy had mentioned to him over the phone. Maybe the president had sent him to assure those guys about the Louisiana ruling that would be coming up. Maybe it had something to do with a Supreme Court appointment. In a few very tight Washington circles there were rumors about one justice and his prostate.

That was enough to send the world into a tizzy if it got out. But now he just wanted to find out about this so-called evidence.

"All right, Neddy. Look, here's what I really want to know. On the phone when I called you that night after I saw the broadcast, you mentioned some sort of new evidence that was going to prove something or other about evolution. I want to know what it was. Frankly, I don't give a shit what you do, with whom, or why."

But why had he said "why"? There was a little click in Archie's brain when he realized this. These guys had their hooks into Neddy, and it wasn't because any president had sent him down there to massage egos or make promises about Supreme Court appointments. This realization flooded his brain, and he barely heard what Neddy was talking about. The evidence that Neddy talked about was referring more or less to some loony-tune hypothesis about the Flood being the product of some greenhouse effect and blocking the lower atmosphere from cosmic radiation. He didn't mention the skulls. Archie had heard all this other stuff before. It was the standard line issued by some Center for Creation Studies out in California. Now Neddy was going on about some top scientists, "real Ph.D.'s coming down to Thurston's college."

"Real Ph.D.'s as opposed to fakes?"

"Archie!" Neddy sighed. "You know what I mean. They're getting guys down there that have more than a degree from a two-year Bible college. They're not just ordained ministers teaching biology courses."

"Well, there's nothing worse than an ordained biologist. I'll tell you that right now!" Archie said, looking Neddy straight in the eye.

36

"Does this bedroom remind you of Lady Jane Grey?" Calista asked, yawning. Archie had caught the seven o'clock shuttle back to Boston from D.C. He was in Cambridge by eight-thirty. And Calista and he were in bed by eight thirty-five. They had, in fact, made it to the bed this time.

"What?" Archie propped himself on his side and traced with his finger the hollows around Calista's neck and collarbone and then ran his finger down between her breasts. "You mean that English girl in the Tower of London?"

"Yeah, the one beheaded by Queen Mary."

"Well, no, actually not. I wouldn't say the bedroom reminded me of her at all."

"Me neither. But I did it over, painted it and all, a year or so ago, and my editor, when she saw it, she said that. She said it looked so austere and virginal. Although I guess Lady Jane wasn't really a virgin. They'd married her off to the duke of Suffolk or somebody like that."

"Well, it reminds me of you. And I don't think austere or virginal are two adjectives that immediately come to mind when I think of you."

"You getting hungry for dinner?"

"Possibly."

She had had all day to plan dinner. She hoped it wouldn't look too elaborate. But there was no denying that she had been so excited that she had felt all that day like a teenager preparing for prom night with a favorite beau. She had run over to a fish store on Huron Avenue and bought soft-shell crabs. And then she had sawed off a few ounces from her precious stock of frozen gravlax. Once every other month or so Calista made gravlax by smothering filets of Norwegian salmon in a mixture of kosher salt, sugar, and Lap Souchong tea leaves. She then weighted them with a brick for five days in a dish in the refrigerator. The stuff froze beautifully. She served it on thinly sliced bread that had been spread with ginger butter and a dab of what Charley called her weird mustard sauce, which meant that it wasn't made with French's and that it had "foreign matter" in it in the form of chopped dill weed. She had made a cold vegetable salad of dilled peas and cucumbers and had been toying with the idea of steamed potatoes. But they had decided to do it one more time, and that meant there wasn't really time to fuss with the steamed potatoes. Sex was vastly superior to potatoes. The thought struck her just as they had finished doing it and Calista, who had been on top, was sitting astraddle Archie. She looked down into his intense blue eyes. "Love's not a potato. You can't throw it out the window," she said softly.

"What?" Archie laughed. He was still inside her, and she could feel him laugh way, way up.

"It's an old Russian proverb."

"Whatever made you think of that—do I remind you of a potato?"

This time Calista laughed, and he could feel her. "Great! Lady Jane Grey and the potato. What a pair! No, you don't remind me of a potato. It's just that I decided not to make the potatoes when we made love again 'cause there wouldn't be time."

"Oh! Any more proverbs?"

"Oh, dear, I just thought of one, not a proverb, exactly."

"What is it?"

"You know what my mother told me when I got married, her advice to the bride?"

"No? What was that?"

"Never get on top after thirty-five."

They both started to laugh now. "Why the hell not?" he asked.

"Because, you know, everything starts to droop—droop down."

If blushing could ever be called violent and aggressive, this was it, Archie thought as he gazed up at her. Once more the red spikes raked across her jaws and down her neck. No slow suffusion of capillary action gently tinting the skin here.

"You're not so droopy," he said.

"Jeez, Archie, you sly, silver-tongued old fox, old honey lips. Last night, what was it—'You're not so ugly yourself'—and now 'You're not droopy.' Blow me away with all this romantic talk! I hope nobody's taping this conversation." They both laughed. "I think I better dismount here."

They took a shower together, and Archie marveled at how wonderful she looked wet. "You look great wet," he said, embracing her. "Most people look like drowned rats."

"Oh, my God. What a wordsmith!"

They dressed and went downstairs to the kitchen.

She had put the butter and the oil in the skillet for the soft-shell crabs and was letting it melt. "Want a glass of champagne? I got some chilling."

"Champagne?" Archie lifted an eyebrow and pulled down the corners of his mouth.

"Yeah. I'm big on celebrations."

"What are you celebrating?"

"Us, you fool!"

"Oh!" He was embarrassed. Gee, this was going to be fun with her. She was so ready for everything. "Sure, sure. Bring it on."

Calista kept her wine "cellar" in a pantry separated from the kitchen by a rood screen that had been salvaged from a sixteenth-century English church. She also kept her good crystal and bone china there. She went to get out two champagne glasses. The kitchen was rather spectacular with its gleaming two-inch, cream-color ceramic tiles and handsomely finished wood antiques. The ubiquitous blond butcher-block counters found in so many renovated kitchens gave way here to polished black granite. The general style could be considered Jacobean, for there were several dark walnut English pieces from that period in the seventeenth century. But there was also a slightly ecclesiastical motif running through the kitchen design exemplified not only by the rood screen wine cellar, but also by a prie-dieu used for a kitchen drawing table, where she often worked on the coldest days of winter, for it was warmer than her study. And instead of sitting on a stool she sat on a bishop's chair. All the pieces had come out of English and Scottish churches and been bought for the most part through an antiques dealer in Bath. Calista usually did entertain in the kitchen rather than the dining room if it was for less than six. A dark walnut gateleg table with four mid-eighteenth century armchairs upholstered in red constituted the dining area of the kitchen. The tile ceased there, and a parquet floor began.

She returned from the wine cellar with the two champagne glasses. She eschewed flutes. Although she'd heard that they made champagne taste better, she didn't like their test tube contours. It wasn't as much fun looking at the bubbles. She went to the refrigerator for the champagne and came back with the black curvaceous bottle.

"Veuve Clicquot!" Archie raised his eyebrows. "You don't mess around."

"I started drinking it before I was a widow, actually. Funny nobody noticed then. Now they all assume it's some sort of signature with me. This isn't just the widow, however." She set down the black bottle. "It's the grande dame." Darkly fetching, voluptuous, maybe the most beautiful bottle ever designed, and certainly containing the most wonderful-tasting liquid. Archie was about to ask if he could uncork the bottle for her, but she had already started and seemed to be doing it with an ease and elegance that he could not have equaled. The cork popped, the champagne frothed over the lip of the bottle. He was ready with both glasses. She poured. They looked into each other's eyes and recognized in those reflections new lovers but very old friends. They raised their glasses in a wordless toast to both.

She took her champagne over to the stove and started cooking the soft-shell crabs. She dusted them with flour, and when the oil was hot she dropped them in. Their claws curled up.

"Don't worry. They aren't alive. They cleaned them for me at the store. *Clean* is a euphemism for *kill* here. Once they made a mistake, though, and forgot to clean them."

"What happened?" Archie asked.

"Kind of gross. I mean, they looked absolutely dead when I put them in the skillet, but they started hopping all around." She paused and looked up at Archie and wrinkled her nose. "You know what they reminded me of?"

"Lady Jane Grey?"

"No." She laughed. "Cab Calloway."

"Cab Calloway?"

"Yeah, I'm kind of into tap dancing."

"Do you tap-dance?"

"Only in private. I promised Charley."

"I'd love to see you tap-dance."

"No, you wouldn't."

"You're very well coordinated." He took a sip of his champagne and his eyes crinkled at the corners, the deep sun marks disappearing.

"I'm better at that than tap dancing." Calista chuckled.

They sat at the gateleg table, pulling their chairs close to each other until their shoulders touched while they ate the crabs and the cold dilled pea salad. He tried to help her clear the plates, but she told him not to. She got the dessert.

"This is my own invention," she said, bringing the ramekins to the table.

"What is it?"

"Frozen crème brûlé. Kind of an oxymoronic dessert. You burn it, and then you freeze it."

Archie took the bottle of champagne from the cooler and poured them a final glass. He looked into the glass at the bubbles and then into those dark eyes that sparkled like twin galaxies. For all her jokes, for all her absolute candor, she was an infinitely mysterious woman. He wanted to say something. But, after all, he was no wordsmith. So he settled instead for just drinking the champagne and looking at her.

Calista shut her eyes tight as she savored the last swallows of the champagne. She was thinking of stars and remembering the old blind monk Dom Pérignon when, after years of experimentation, he had finally captured the sparkle of wine at just the right moment and had called to brother Pierre, "Come quickly, I am drinking the stars!" And for a brief sliver of a second Calista's perfect happiness was tinged with sadness as she remembered the starry Charioteer, and her own husband, Tom, who had died in the desert facing the limitless cosmos he had devoted his life to figuring out. They would get back to the Charioteer, but not now, not right now.

Charley came in at two that morning and Archie left at one fifty-three.

37

Calista dragged herself up the next morning early so she could catch Charley. It seemed as if she had hardly seen him for the past two days, and she was not at all sure if he was eating right, for he often was gone before breakfast. The entire Martin Institute seemed to subsist on Chinese food and Coca-Cola. But this morning she had gotten an egg down Charley, a bran muffin, cantaloupe, and milk. He was certainly not telling her much about what he was doing over there and what was commanding such gargantuan hunks of time. But she had a sense that it was in some way related to their trip to Texas and the skulls, although she couldn't imagine how the reputed skulls and cancer research could ever cross paths. She had just sat down with a second cup of coffee and was dreamily reliving every moment with Archie from the night before. She supposed that someday soon they would have to face the music and tell Charley something. She didn't know what or how. But Archie could not forever skulk out of her house in the dark shadow of moonless nights and hotfoot it back to his parents' house on Beacon Hill. Of course, one day he would have to go back to Washington and attend to business at the Smithsonian. But if this continued, he would come up presumably for visits. Would he still stay at his parents', and would they still arrange their love-making around Charley's schedule? The telephone rang. Calista answered it.

"Oh, Janet!"

"Yes, Janet! Haven't heard from you in ages. How goes it?"

"Oh, fine, fine."

"And how is the lovely Marian?" Janet asked delicately.

"Who?" There was a small gulf of silence.

"Calista, Maid Marian, as in Robin Hood!"

"Oh, that Marian!"

"Yes, that Marian! Remember, you are doing a book for us. And that you casually mentioned something about finishes just after Labor Day."

"Oh, yes, yes . . ." Calista laughed nervously. She had not planned to tell Janet about Archie. Oh, she had been dying to, all right, but she felt so bad about Janet's single state with no prospects in sight that she didn't feel it was particularly tactful to mention her own happiness at the time.

"What is it, Cal? Something's going on. I can tell. Is it Charley?" Her voice was gripped with tension. "Did something happen to Charley?"

"Oh, no! No! Don't you think I would have told you?"

"Oh, God, you didn't get another marked-up book, did you?"

"Oh, no, please, nothing of the sort." She had better tell Janet lest she jump to other dire conclusions. How to put it? She paused. "Janet, the person from Porlock came."

"What? What in the hell are you talking about?"

"Come on, you old English major. You remember the person from Porlock in Coleridge. He came just when old Coleridge was smack in the middle of an opium dream and composing the *Kubla Khan*. Interrupted him and that was the end of it all. Poor old Coleridge lost his train of thought, and great chunks of the greatest lyric poem ever right out the window, down the tubes, gone forever."

"And that's what happened to you? The man from Porlock came?"

"About eight times in one night!"

"Holy shit, Cal!" Janet shrieked. "Why didn't you tell me?" Calista was laughing very hard now. "Cal, you are absolutely cackling!" Janet said, laughing herself.

"I know. I must improve my laugh. Whenever I laugh—" And she had begun again and could hardly stop to speak. "Whenever I laugh about sex I cackle. It has something to do with being Jewish and midwestern and repressed." She had dissolved into another cacophonous fit of cackles.

"Hardly a sexual enhancement . . . You sound like Old Mother Thwackham!" Old Mother Thwackham was a hen that Calista had immortalized years before in a book called *Barnyard Fables*. Mrs. Thwackham had borne a distinct resemblance to Eleanor Roosevelt but had possessed a sky-shattering cackle.

Janet seemed pleased, however, despite her disapproval of the cackle. Calista should have known that Janet, her best friend and only editor, would have rejoiced for her.

"Well, I didn't lose my entire train of thought on Marian. But let's just say that she hasn't been uppermost in my mind in the last few days."

"Oh, forget *Marian's Tale*. This is real life!"

That evening Calista and Archie had just finished making love when the phone rang. Calista answered it. "Charley!" She pulled the sheet up in a gesture of instinctual modesty that Archie found charming. "Yeah? You'll be home in fifteen minutes." Archie now got out of bed immediately and reached for his shorts. "Tell Archie not to leave? . . . ." She looked at Archie, and her eyes opened wide. "You've seen him the last three nights walking down Kirkland Street just as your cab turns the corner? You have something to tell us . . . Oh, dear, is it serious? . . . Very? Okay, sweetie. We'll be here."

She hung up the phone. This time there were even streaks of red across her belly. "Oh, my God. He knows about us!"

"Now calm down, Calista. Did he say that?"

"Not exactly. He just said that he had to talk to us about something serious. But he does know that you've been here—late every night. I mean, I didn't try to hide the fact that you are in town and have been over for dinner. But he's seen you, Archie."

"Look, you're jumping to conclusions. The first conclusion is that just because he has to talk to us about something serious, it has to be us. There are other serious matters in the world and his life even aside from us."

"Pliny the Elder?"

"What?"

"Nothing—just a report that he was overdue with."

"Okay, now your second conclusion is that he'll be upset about us, and I don't really think that is the case. I think that Charley likes me."

"Oh, he does, Archie. I know he does."

"And that's not all. I don't just like Charley. I care for him very deeply, deeply in his own right, and also because he is part of you—of you and Tom. I see both of you in him. And I cherish that."

"Oh, Archie!" Calista's eyes filled with tears.

He held her close and rubbed his fingers through the thick silvery-chestnut hair. "Come on, Calista. He's not going to be upset about us sleeping together. I really don't think so. I mean, I don't think he was born yesterday. But we don't have to rub his nose in it. We'll take our cues from him."

She knew he was right.

When Charley came in they were both dressed and sitting at the dining table in the kitchen drinking a cup of tea and looking very nervous.

"You are not going to believe this!" he announced as he dropped a thick wad of photocopied papers on the table.

"What?" they both said. A flood of relief swept through Calista. She knew right then that she and Archie were definitely not the serious item on Charley's agenda, if indeed they were on it at all.

"Okay, you know the project I've been working on at Martin since April? Right? Protein folding, all that?"

"Yeah, but brief Archie on it."

He did. Then he briefed both of them on the intellamine-intellicone project. Archie was vaguely familiar with it. He had heard mention of it through one of his colleagues, but it had very little bearing on his interests.

"Okay," Charley said. "Now, if you'll recall when we were down in Texas at Lorne Thurston College of Christian Heritage, they let slip about some skulls which they felt indicated separate evolution of races."

"Recall—of course," Calista was saying. "That's why Archie's here." The color rose violently in her neck. Archie blinked.

"Yeah, well, anyhow . . ." Charley was brushing by

that easily enough, Calista noticed. "You get the correlation here? Racial differences showing up in fossil materials, racial differences showing up in brain proteins?"

"Yes." Both Calista and Archie nodded. Archie was actually feeling a horrible queasiness in the pit of his stomach.

"And Archie, you suspect those skulls are going to be fake if you ever get to see them—like the Paluxy footprints."

Again Archie nodded very slowly but deliberately. "I think they're going to hold out to the last minute, hoping not to have to show them at all. Waiting for something else—and . . ." It suddenly dawned on Archie. "You got the something else?"

"Damn right I do. But they're not going to like it, and it's not going to be worth waiting for. The intellamine and intellicone proteins are pure fiction. They blow apart. We figured it out this week. We've been working on this dumb-shit project for months that nobody is really the least interested in, this modeling stuff."

"But I thought you said that Leventhal liked it. Took your models to some conference with him."

"He liked our three-D diagrams. He liked the fact that we had mapped so many of these proteins. Nobody else has the time to do that kind of work around there. Made it handy for him. We were just like glorified file clerks. We just worked on ways to collate data and make it more observable. But we didn't discover anything, Matthew, Louise, and me." He paused. "Until this week. Nobody had ever mapped intellamine and intellicone. And it looked weird. It just didn't have any of the regularities that any of the other proteins had, as least not from the data given in these papers." He tapped his index finger on the stack of photocopies. "And then this guy Liam, he's this real hotshot programmer. I mean, the guy can write code like you can't believe. He wrote this computer program that calculates the free energy in proteins. Well, he comes in and shows us how it works, and we run it on intellamine and intellicone, and the things just blow up on us. Like there is no way this stuff can hang together."

"So they faked it," Archie said.

"They sure did!"

"So you've got something being faked presumably on two levels, the fossil and the genetic level. Very high-tech. I guess they've learned something since the Paluxy footprints debacle."

"Right."

"But I don't understand. You said that there are papers from major universities and that they went to Brookhaven to use the PET scanner," Calista said, looking at the abstract on the title page of one article.

"They didn't have to go anyplace, really. They just had to have a plant in one or two labs—to write up data. Or they could have gone to Brookhaven and played tiddly-winks and pretended to run the scanner."

"But how did they get all these people to sign on to these papers?" Calista asked.

"That's the way it goes—especially in biology." Archie sighed. He'd taken out his pipe and was digging at his tobacco. "It doesn't mean that all the people who signed on the paper as coauthors had bad intentions. They did not set out to subvert the truth. They probably didn't know. There was a famous case just a few years ago. A guy up in Toronto, a molecular biologist, was faking the most elegant experiments imaginable. His data made sense. His work appeared flawless until he was caught. You know how they caught him?"

"How?" both Charley and Calista asked at the same time.

"Conceptually there didn't seem to be anything wrong with his experiments. But when one postdoc started to figure out how many culture dishes it would take to do those experiments, it was an incredible amount. More than a person might use in ten years. They went back and checked the lab supply sheets. There was no abnormal number of petri dishes being used. The experiments had been a complete fabrication. The director of the lab had signed on to the paper—after all, it made sense—and so had the other people in the lab. They had all signed on."

"I still don't get it. How could they not know?"

"It's protocol," Archie said quietly. "They all work in the lab together. Any work that comes out of that lab has to have on it the names of the head of the lab and the director of the department or institute. My name goes on all the papers that come out of the Smithsonian's Department of Anthropology. And I do read them all. But it gets more complicated in biology. For one thing, you trust your colleagues. You might not have been hanging over every petri dish. But you trust the people at the bench working with you, and if what they write up hangs together, sure, you put your name on it. It's important, especially for young postdocs, to get their names out there associated with important projects. God knows they aren't getting paid adequately for their time."

"That's exactly what Steve said. And guess what, Mom? Even my name is going to be on a crystallography paper he's writing. My name and Louise's and Matthew's. Just because of the work we did this spring. They'll be at the bottom of the list. But they'll be there all the same."

"So whose names are on these papers—not that it apparently matters?" Calista said.

"Well, there's only one that really matters." Charley took a paper off the top of the stack. The article, which had been published in *Endocrinology Abstracts,* was dated three years earlier and was entitled "Effects of Methadrill on Neurotransmitters As Related to Higher Order Thought Processes." A name was circled.

"E. W. Tompkins," Calista whispered. "Tompkins!"

"Yes, Mom. Remember the William Jennings Bryan Creation Science Center—that guy in the lab?" Charley said.

"Wayne Tompkins—this says E. W. How can we be sure? Tompkins is a fairly common name."

"Remember Beth Ann said that he came from up north? Look where this article is out of."

"University of Minnesota—guess that's north all right."

"Is this what made you suspicious, seeing his name on this?"

"No. Not at all. I didn't even notice his name until about an hour ago, when we went into Steve's office to tell him what we had found out. Then we just started making a list of every lab and university and person that ever had anything to do with intellamine and intellicone. And that's when his name kind of popped out at me."

"Do you have the list with you?" Archie asked.

"Yep. You want to see it?"

"Sure do."

Charley handed him the list. Archie took out his half-glasses from his pocket and began to read.

"Know anybody?" Charley asked.

"Lots."

"Oooh!" Calista groaned.

"Don't worry." Archie patted her hand. They had completely forgotten about being embarrassed in front of Charley. "It's like Charley said. This is the way they work. These top guys aren't the bad guys. I know a lot of the heads of the departments and the labs at these universities—Duke, Penn, Minnesota—James Atwell. . . . Now why does that name ring a bell? I don't know him, but the name Coastal Research Institute . . . James Atwell." Archie scratched his head.

"Oh, God!" Calista jumped up. "James Atwell, of course! That loathsome man. You know, Archie—the Nobel sperm bank."

"Oh, good Christ!" Archie removed his glasses and looked very nearly white. "You're right."

"Of course I'm right. I saw him on 'Oprah Winfrey,' where else? But why does this say Coastal Research Institute?"

"It's all part of the same thing. The connection between the sperm bank and the Coastal Research Institute isn't all that public, but at one time the institute did have a loose connection with Stanford. The sperm bank is into

high-tech breeding—and guess what they call themselves?"

"What?" Charley and Calista both looked at Archie.

"Genesis!"

"Oy!" Calista said.

Charley looked at Archie. He wondered if Archie
understood any Yiddish. It was definitely an "oy" kind
of night.

"Well, I got some good ideas on pursuing this now. But
I better go home and sleep on it," Archie said, getting up.

"Why go home?" Charley said suddenly. And if anybody had asked him why he had said it, he would not
have been able to explain. It just seemed that Archie
belonged here, here with him and his mom. Archie and
Calista looked at each other. "You might as well stay
here. It's late. You can sleep in the guest room." Archie
and Calista exchanged another glance. This time it was
not lost on Charley. "Or, you know, in my room or
Mom's."

Then Calista said the boldest thing she had ever said to
her son. "I don't know if he'd do very well on the bottom
bunk, Charley." And she smiled softly at her son.

"Well, I guess it should be your room, then."

And it was. But they didn't make love again that night.
They crawled into bed, and Calista sank back against the
pillows. "I don't believe this—where will it all end—
murder, phony brain proteins, fake fossil skulls, sperm
banks named Genesis, and—oh God, Archie, I forgot
those vandalized books that Margaret and I both received, plus dear old Owl. Everything's at stake here—
science, the First Amendment . . ."

"The whole way and manner and principle of scientific
thought is under fire with these guys because in their
view nothing is ever open to skeptical inquiry. The
evolution debate is only the opening wedge in a battle.
You see, now they're proceeding on to a racist scenario.
And for them, education is not a quest that ever involves
uncertainty—only the right answers."

"Archie, how did you know all that stuff about the sperm bank?" His eyes crinkled into a smile. "No, Archie, don't tell me you gave! You're not a Nobel winner."

"They apparently let a few lesser folk in."

"No, you didn't!"

He put his arm around her. "No, darling lady, I didn't. I just remember when the letter came in. Goodfellow— you know, Ruth Goodfellow, my secretary—she and I had an awfully good laugh about it."

"Well, I hope you didn't laugh too hard with her—I mean, Archie . . . you didn't give at the office, did you?"

"With Goodfellow? No. She wouldn't have me, for one thing." He was laughing now. "No, dear, I only want to give at the house on James Place in Cambridge, Massachusetts."

Calista sighed. "Sperm and drang!" she muttered.

Archie laughed out loud.

As Charley drifted off to sleep that night, he could hear laughter coming from his mother's bedroom for the first time in nearly four years. It sounded good, like watery bubbles. And that made him think of dolphins. Dolphins with their built-in smiles. He had once heard that there was a place in Florida where you could swim with dolphins. And when he finally fell asleep he dreamed of swimming with these dolphins with Archie and his mom, and all around them were swirls of bubbles and laughter.

38

The next morning Archie called up Steve and asked him and Liam to come over to Calista's house for a meeting. Charley called up Louise and Matthew and asked them to come, too. Calista and Charley first explained the extraordinary possible ramifications of this fraud. Archie felt it was imperative that this fraud not be revealed prematurely, because if it was, it could become more dangerous than it already had been for Calista and Charley. He didn't want to scare anyone unduly, especially the kids. But he wanted to make sure that when they got ready to move they had all the pieces in place. Steve and Liam were more than agreeable. It was apparent that this was more than the usual run-of-the-mill fudging of scientific data. These guys weren't just looking for more research money. They were playing for bigger stakes. As Steve sat in the Jacobses's kitchen he realized the intellamine-intellicone fraud was just one skirmish of many battles fought for one rather frightening kingdom—a kingdom of skinheads and scientific creationists—an unholy alliance if there ever was one.

The first step was for Charley and Archie to go with Liam and Steve over to SIPB, the Student Information Processing Board, in Building 11 at MIT, and sit down in front of "Binkly." All the computers in this center, as in many centers, had names. The names at SIPB were taken from the characters in Bloom County, the comic strip. They used a finger program, which is a program for "fingering," or finding out, information about people. The only other person in the center was playing Towers of Hanoi, a favorite game of hackers, which involved stacking towers in a graduated order. There were about seven or eight terminals. On the walls were a few signs that would seem somewhat cryptic for those outside the computer world—"Happiness Is a Working Laser Writer," read one sign. Another said simply "rm is forever."

They "fingered" every single name that had signed on as coauthor on every single article. Fingering did not come up with the equivalent of an FBI file. It could not yield as much or that kind of information. For the most part you could just put together where someone had worked, if they had had computer accounts at these places, what their interests and their expertise were, and a few vital statistics like their user name, telephone number, and where they worked out of. The finger program, coupled with the directory access program of the Unix system, could yield information about which computers they had used and to a limited extent what information they had gone after. Every university and institution, including Brookhaven, had a Unix operating system. They searched the directories diligently for any signs of the authors. They were able to finger several of them, including Wayne Tompkins. If a person had a user account, they were listed. It was not possible, however, to track how they had used a system or what specific information they had sought.

"Most places don't clutter up the works with that kind of data," Liam said. "They might keep the last time a user logged on, but that's about it."

How had this scam jumped from the fossil scale to the genetic one? And what exactly were the implications of this in the Petrakis murder? She thought about it as she waited for the take-out order from Mary Chung's that she had promised to bring to the fellows in Building 11 for lunch.

MIT was a veritable maze. She had to ask four people before she found Building 11. Calista had walked down more blind paths, gone through more tunnels, than she could count carrying her bundles of Chinese food. She had finally gotten to Building 11 through Building 5—or was it 9? None of the buildings had names. It was all confounding, and as she wended her way through the maze she began to think of it as a metaphor for the tangled tale of murder and fraud and "religion," if you could call it that. If she had been a Christian, she would have found it profoundly insulting. Of course, that was the problem, wasn't it, with all of the fundamentalists and the scientific creationists, whom she supposed were a subset of fundamentalists. None of them had any capacity for metaphor. There was no symbolic level to their thought at all. They would certainly have laughed at her if she had told them what she really thought of Genesis —that to her the Adam and Eve story, the whole story of creation, had a more powerful truth, more eloquence and beauty, than could ever be weighed or proven by scientific procedure; that she believed in that story in her own way, which was independent of science and did not hinge, in terms of its moral veracity or compelling beauty, on demonstrability. It was an epic, and epics did have their truth and their value. But they could not be measured by the same methods as scientific hypotheses, for they were symbolic truths.

But these people had no inclination or affinity toward symbolization or disposition toward metaphor. How thin and paltry their lives must be. No wonder they were moral cripples. If you could not imagine beyond the here and now, how could you ever empathize with another's pain, or joy, or freedom of mind and thought? And if you could not do that, then you could kill quite easily. So she was back to Norman again! But where was it all leading, and where the hell was this subbasement tunnel leading?

A wan-looking girl with a backpack and running shorts jogged by her. "Pardon me, I think I'm lost," Calista said. The girl looked up at her. She was wan indeed and had a rabbity-looking face. Her eyes were rimmed with pink from lack of sleep or from endless hours of staring into a computer terminal. Good Lord, was this like the white rabbit in *Alice's Adventures in Wonderland*? Calista fully expected her to spout out, "I'm late, I'm late for a very important date," and rush off. But she didn't.

"What do you want?"

"Building Eleven."

"You're in a subbasement of Building Nine. Continue to the end of the corridor, turn left, go up two floors and down the corridor, the same way you're heading now, and it will take you right into Building Eleven."

"Oh, thanks." But the girl had already scurried off.

She did what the girl told her. But she could not get certain images out of her mind—rabbits and mazes and bunny blood!

When she arrived at SIPB she found Archie and Liam and Steve and Charley huddled over terminals. They looked up as she entered. She had a strange look on her face. She was thinking that if you could just pull one thread, the whole thing could unravel. "Charley, I saw this girl in the basement coming over here from Building Nine. She looked just like a rabbit, and it reminded me . . ."

"Bunny blood!" Charley blurted the words out.

"Bunny blood?" Archie and Liam looked bewildered.

"Oh, yeah—bunny blood!" Steve said. There was a slow dawning tone in his voice. "Those antigens I tracked down for you."

Calista turned to Archie. "The words written on the wall of Norman Petrakis's hotel room were in blood. It was rabbit's blood, and so were the drops of blood on Margaret's book, the ones that were supposed to be the wounds of Christ. See, these people have no capacity for metaphor. They have to use the real thing!"

But nobody seemed to follow the line of Calista's reasoning. They were with her for the most part, however, struggling with her as she tried to make this intuitive leap. It seemed to promise something. But it was not a leap. It was more like scaling up an immense peak. "Who uses rabbits?"

"Lots of places," Steve said.

"Not the Smithsonian," Archie said.

"No, you know, biological labs, biology departments at universities. . . ."

"Would places like the Martin Institute that do genetic research use animals?"

"Sure," Steve said. "We use mice, monkeys on occasion, rabbits, but we try not to advertise that too much. The animal rights advocates get very upset about rabbits."

Calista searched back in her memory to that conversation months before in the Japanese restaurant with Norman. She remembered him telling about all the different kinds of genetic research being done—the molecular time clock stuff, cancer research, the thing that he had called the human gene project, the twins research project in Minnesota.

"Would they have used it in that twins research project out at the University of Minnesota?" she asked.

"Possibly," Steve said.

"And what about the Coastal Research Institute—the place that showed up in one paper as one of the labs involved in the intellamine research? Remember, Charley, it was on that list that you brought home and showed to me and Archie, the place run by that guy Atwell."

"The sperm bank man?" Charley asked. "Oh, yuck!"

"Well, Archie said they were into high-tech breeding. Maybe they'd use animals for their research," Calista said.

"Yes, I suppose so," Archie replied with a kind of weary disgust at the whole notion.

"Let's call them up and the University of Minnesota, the twins research project."

"And say what?" Liam asked.

"Well," Calista began, "I tell them I'm from a biological supply house and I'm selling rabbits or rabbits' blood. I'll ask them what they're paying, and I'll promise that we can give them a better deal."

"And then what, Mom?"

She paused. "I'm not sure," she said honestly. "But maybe it's kind of like those petri dishes that Archie was telling us about. Only in this case if they don't use any, we can maybe absolve them from any connection with Norman's death. But if they do use some or inordinate amounts—like enough to write 'Monkey's Uncle' on a wall of a hotel room . . . well . . ." She didn't finish the thought.

It was not a bad idea. It was at least another starting point. The searching for authors in the computer networks had not yielded the kind of refined information they really needed. They could at least narrow down the labs that used rabbits' blood. It was decided that Steve should do the calling. Having worked in biology labs, he knew the ins and outs of biological supply businesses. He could talk fluently about the price of outbred rats, nude mice, inbred mice, miniswine, and, of course, rabbits, be they outbred, inbred, or whatever. He could talk about strain designations and user benefits such as VAFS (virus antibody free) animals and COBS (cesarean originated barrier sustained) animals. He offered a toll-free number, genetic monitoring reports, and the guarantee that all animals were free of *M. pulmonis.*

The lab where Wayne Tompkins had worked at the University of Minnesota didn't use any rabbits—too expensive. This was a blow. At Duke they used them occasionally and would consider using the Ballard Laboratories (that was what Steve was calling his outfit), but he should call back next week when Robert Pitkin, the manager for the bio labs, was back from vacation. The Coastal Research Institute also used some. Lorne Thurston College of Christian Heritage did not use any lab animals at all.

"Figures," Charley muttered as Steve hung up and reported this news.

"I think we're still stuck." Charley sighed.

"Well," said Steve, "mice really are the favorite animals of genetic research."

"No, we're not stuck. No, we're not," Calista persisted. "We just have to build a bridge between this rabbit's blood thing and . . . and . . ." Her mind was groping. "When you did those searches to see if the authors' names showed up—what do you call it when they use a computer?"

"User accounts," Liam said.

"Yes. Did you check to see if Norman Petrakis's name ever showed up?"

"No. Why?" Steve asked. "He wasn't an author. He was a victim."

Calista smiled. "But he was an author, of very fine children's books on subjects like human evolution, and he also wrote on DNA. I remember his telling me and Janet and Margaret about it in the restaurant the night he was murdered. That's why I thought it might be a good idea to call the University of Minnesota, not just that it had been mentioned in those papers on intellamine, but because of Norman's connection."

"Petrakis had a connection there?" Steve asked.

"Not a formal one, but he was in the process of doing some articles—'Designer Genes,' he was calling the series. He had mentioned the twins research project at University of Minnesota." She again tried to conjure up the memory of that conversation at dinner with Norman, hoping for some shred of information that could help them. Had he mentioned anything about sperm banks? She couldn't recall. It would seem like a natural place to go in terms of an article on genetics. But she felt like a blind person, lost in a forest on a moonless night. Bits of remembered conversation from that night swirled about her meaninglessly, giving no direction.

"Well, I would imagine that he would have gone out to Minnesota and checked into this twins stuff, and then there's the molecular time clock stuff. I think they've done a lot of that work out at Berkeley," Steve said.

"Yes, yes. He mentioned that." She paused. "Do you suppose that Norman Petrakis uncovered the intellamine fraud before you guys? Maybe he wasn't murdered for his book on human evolution at all. Maybe it was because what Norman found out was the same thing that Charley and Louise and Matthew found out." She bit her lower lip lightly.

It was a stunning intuitive leap, but it made more sense than anything so far.

"But what about the Monkey's Uncle?" Charley asked.

"Trying to pass the buck to the creationists," Calista answered.

"You mean the creationists are the good guys?" Charley asked.

"Well, let's just say they might not be murderers," Calista said, and then added, "I'm sure, as with all of us, there is room for improvement, particularly in the form of some real functioning brain proteins. But we know for sure that they don't use any animals in their labs. I'm not saying that this exonerates them entirely. But I think in this case we have to follow the . . ." She paused. "Blood tracks, as it were. That seems to be the only thing to go on. The monkey's blood and the computer network for the authors of these papers. Those are the trails. And we know that Norman was seeking out this genetic stuff and it led him to a lot of the places where research was being done."

While they had been talking Liam logged on again. "Got your man, here. Norman Petrakis. He had accounts all over the place, or more precisely the same places that all these authors had them. None in Texas, though."

"So," said Archie, "he might not have found out anything about the skulls through the computer, if he knew anything about them at all then. For him this was strictly on the genetic level. Or we have to assume that."

"I guess for now we do," Calista said. "It doesn't seem that he went anywhere near Texas for his research."

Liam had just dialed a number on the telephone between Binkly and Oliver. The screen on the terminal changed. "Holy shit!" He ran his hands through his bushy, electric hair, which now really looked as if it had a few volts running through it. "This guy, Petrakis, he had an account at LBL."

"LBL?" Calista asked.

"Lawrence Berkeley Labs." Liam looked up. "This is great! We're not going to have to assume anything. You give me two days. Another guy who's a computer security expert is out there. He's a good friend of mine. Between the two of us I think we can trace Petrakis's path.

Petrakis's murderers, whoever they might be, did not go to any trouble to clean out his accounts."

"But I don't understand. How can you do this, trace him?" Calista asked.

"Think of it like that powder they put in the bag with the money when a bank is robbed. It explodes and leaves stains all over the place. Only in this case it's electronic footprints. All I need is a little time and to keep it quiet. We don't want to tip them off. Because then they might go in and cover the tracks."

"Maybe we should decoy them," Archie said.

"How do you mean?" Liam asked.

"Look, I think Calista's hunch is right. Someone might have been trying to pass the buck off on the creationists about this murder. And yet there is evidence that something was going on with fossils as well as on a genetic level in order to put one over about this separate origins of races. In a sense we might be dealing with two separate but related frauds. One has to do with fossils and is, I think, strictly out of the creationists' camp. And the second fraud is the intellamine thing."

"You don't see that as being part of the creationists' fraud?"

"Not originally. I don't think they would have gotten into the genetics thing intentionally at the start. They simply don't have the wherewithal to even begin to pull it off. Creationist science doesn't get that high-tech—at least not as high-tech as genetic research requires."

"But you think they did cross at some point—these two separate frauds."

"Possibly—"

"And you see that point being Norman?" Calista said.

"I don't think he knew about the skulls. I don't think that was his interest."

"But the creationists did know about him," Calista said. "They hated him. Charley and I saw these pamphlets attacking Norman for his book on human evolution."

"But that book came out a while ago."

"Yes, but there was someone at the conference who stood up on behalf of the Christian nation to take issue with Norman's views of evolution."

"But was he really a creationist?"

"Are you trying to say he could have been a disaffected geneticist in disguise?" Calista asked.

"Calista, you're the one who set out the idea in the first place of the genetics folks, the ones who faked the intellamine research, trying to pass the buck to the creationists."

There was silence as Charley, Liam, Steve, and Calista mulled this over in their minds. Archie waited, then spoke carefully, for he himself was not sure if this was truly the case, but there did seem to be the possibility of a connection between the two frauds. Perhaps it had not started out intentionally, but somehow two paths had overlapped, and Norman Petrakis had wound up as dead as he would have if he had been caught in the cross hairs of a rifle's sights.

"I think it might be to our advantage," Archie began slowly, "to try and play along with the original scenario. You know, like we're going after the creationists and flush them out of the woods on the skull thing. Maybe the timing's right for them to make their little announcement to the world. It might take the heat off you while you follow Petrakis's tracks through the other labs."

"Not a bad idea," Steve said.

"Okay, I'll start," Liam replied.

39

They were not grasping at straws now. They were pulling at threads. Calista had pulled at the first thread when she thought again of the rabbit's blood, which had then, through some tangled way, led her to think of searching for Petrakis's name. When his name showed up, things promised to unravel quite nicely. Archie sat in Calista's kitchen. He had just begun to pull at another thread. He had made a score of calls to his own network of colleagues and media people and was now on the phone with Colin Mercer, his close friend and editor over at the *National Geographic*. Colin loved a challenge like this. "We'll get these guys by the balls!" Colin had chuckled.

"Oh, and by the way, Colin," Archie said, "for all intents and purposes, I have disappeared. Out of the country for the next few days. I don't want to just keep a low profile in this thing. In fact, I want no profile of me visible. After the Paluxy footprints they're immediately going to think of me. . . . Okay? . . . Yes, if you have to reach me, I'll be at this number in Vermont." He gave Mercer the number of Calista's vacation home in Vermont, where they planned to retreat for the next few days. He hung up the telephone and smiled at Calista.

"This is great. We're going to get two birds with one stone here. Hopefully find out who killed Petrakis and then put an end to this so-called science of the creationists." He got up and slapped the table. "And guess what, Cal? We're doing it by good old-fashioned science!" He patted the telephone.

Calista laughed. She knew exactly what he meant. People liked to think that science always was "conducted" in laboratories by people wearing white coats holding up beakers of fluids or peering through microscopes. But it wasn't. The year before he had died, her husband Tom had delivered a lecture on the role of gossip, innuendo, and scuttlebutt in science. Good scientists were great gossips. As a physicist Tom had logged as much time on a telephone as he ever had in a lab, at an observatory, or at a reactor. And so had Archie Baldwin spent more time on telephones and flying about the country and the world to conferences than he had spent in the field with a trowel digging up artifacts. For that was largely how science proceeded. As a procedure, gossip and scuttlebutt were neither scientific nor logical. But then again the scientist did not seek to prove hypotheses through talking about them. A scientist hears about some ideas coming out of somewhere. It could be an experiment or a hypothesis, and he or she is in turn challenged to pick up on that thread of thought. They compare it, or contrast it, with what they are doing. Use it with a slightly different twist on it or toss it out completely. If it works, an initial idea has not been plagiarized or copied, but refined. There are not perhaps that many original ideas per se in science, but rather original ways of looking at old problems. But you had to be plugged in to the network. You had to hear the scuttlebutt that was going on. You had to know what to do with all that scuttlebutt—how to filter it, look at it, and see where it fit in with what you were doing. The creationists resisted every other standard procedure of science that required that they examine and weigh data against existing data. Their only textbook they claimed in the science of creation was God's written word—despite the fact that biblical scholarship and archaeology had proven that Genesis was developed by Hebrews from older Chaldean and Babylonian myths and that there were four authors. Now Archie wondered how they would do with this, the least heralded of scientific procedures—gossip. It was out there now, blowing in the wind—the biggest fossil news of the century—separate origins for the races. How would they fare under the glare of this publicity? Archie was ready to sit back and enjoy it all.

40

Charley had not wanted to go to Vermont. He had wanted to remain in Cambridge, more or less glued to Liam Phillips's side while Liam and his California counterpart, the security expert, a certain Corey Feinberg, wended their way through the electronic maze of a vast computer network, tracking for the late Norman Petrakis. But Calista would not hear of it. He could come with her and Archie to Vermont. He could bring Matthew and Louise with him if he wanted, or he could go with Matthew down to the Cape as the McPhails had invited him to do. He elected to do the latter, which Calista had to admit was preferable to him and Matthew and Louise all being in Vermont. She supposed that these two days could be considered a little honeymoon for her and Archie, which was not an unpleasant thought. She hadn't been to her Vermont house all summer, and although her good neighbors and caretakers, the Potts, looked after the place, they would not have had time to tend the garden. By this point of the summer the garden might look like some Rousseau fantasy run amok.

So Calista and Charley headed off to their respective destinations that morning just after Archie had finished making the calls. Charley seemed more than reconciled to his trip to the Cape by this time, and Calista had given him a substantial advance on his allowance so he could purchase a surfboard that was comparable to Matthew's. She had even agreed to go halvsies on the price of it, which was a singularly indulgent act for Calista. Charley had always told her that allowancewise she was the cheapest mom in town. She had always assumed that this was a typical adolescent complaint—everyone gets more allowance than me. But then she'd found out it was true! She hated materially indulged children. She didn't care if Charley worked or not, but if he wanted money beyond the five bucks she gave him each week for doing practically nothing, he was going to have to work for it. She watched him go down the walk, skateboard under one arm, surfboard under the other. He wore acid green jams with hot pink stripes and a T-shirt with the most god-awful graphics and the words BAD TO THE BONE. She had made him take back the one that said BADASS MAMA. On his head he wore a Benjamin Moore painter's cap. This was a fad that Charley himself had started: painter's caps. All the kids in school were now collecting them and wearing them. His red hair stuck out around the edges. He did look cute walking down the path, and when he turned to wave good-bye to her and smiled that sweet crooked smile of his, she shook her head in amazement and thought, He starts fads and discovers fake proteins, but for all intents and purposes he looks like a surfer. All Cambridge kids had this hankering to come from Southern California—Malibu!

Norman Petrakis had been a proficient hacker. It had cost big money to track him originally. Corey Feinberg knew because he had been paid to do it. He didn't know who precisely had paid him. A call had just come in from the University of Pennsylvania. There was a suspicion that there was an intruder in the system. They were not even that concerned about it because there was no classified information, really. This was not a military or defense contractor. It was a university. University systems were notoriously lax. The joke was that the reason for this laxness was that the stakes were so low in academia. But people were becoming more security conscious now with the rumors of damaging viruses loose, and even though Penn didn't feel threatened directly, they were correct in reporting this suspected intrusion. Any hacker who got into a system could inadvertently or advertently do damage, and it was a gateway to other systems. Corey Feinberg was the best electronic sleuth in the business. He was thought of as an electronic Sherlock Holmes. And he was a good friend of Liam's. The Petrakis case was distinguished in Corey Feinberg's mind only by the time it had taken him to catch Petrakis. The guy hadn't done any damage. He hadn't stolen anything. Corey Feinberg was in fact shocked when he learned that Wiley—for that was Petrakis's user name—had been murdered. He had handled lots of sensitive cases before, where crackers were going after volatile information and could have gotten murdered, but this guy had just been snooping around. The pressure to catch him, though, had built. But the case was so uninteresting that he had all but forgotten about it. It was nothing like the West Germans, who had broken into Defense Department data base systems. When he found the message in his E-mail to quick contact Lip, which was Liam's user name, he could hardly remember the nitty-gritties of the case. He called him directly on the phone first.

"He basically got into the system through a public library in New Jersey," Corey was saying.

"New Jersey?"

"Yeah, he must have lived there. It was a home phone linkup. And through the public library linkup he got into Princeton's computer system and Dartmouth's."

"Dartmouth? God, I can understand Princeton if he lived in New Jersey, but Dartmouth hasn't shown up in any of this. No authors from Dartmouth or anything."

"He got into a lot of places—at least fifteen systems, as I recall. See, once he got into LBL, it was easy—Penn, Dartmouth, Minnesota, Brookhaven . . ."

"Aha, Brookhaven!"

"Yeah, that mean something to you?"

"I think so. Tell me, how did you finally catch him?"

"We let him keep tunneling for a while. I think I even tried to decoy him at one time with some false information, but he caught on. I mean, the guy was slippery. But the idea was if we let him walk around enough in the system, we could catch him. I started wearing a beeper and any access port, the minute he entered, my beeper would beep and we would record, at that port, every friggin' keystroke the guy made."

The access ports were the points at which any telephone linkup outside the main computer gained entry into the system. "Let me tell you, this guy wasn't just skillful, he was fucking brilliant."

"What kind of information was he going after?"

"All kinds. But if there was any theme, it was biological data—DNA, genetic stuff. I think he got into Martin Institute at one time. But I can't remember."

"What? He got into Martin, and I didn't know about it? Why the fuck didn't you tell me?"

"It was brief, believe me."

"Hell, Corey, this is like not reporting a hit-and-run."

"It wasn't a hit-and-run—no such thing. As I recall, it was probably my fault, part of the decoy strategy. But it didn't work. I had the feeling the guy was tracking on his own, meandering around looking for evidence of other hackers—at least when he went into the biology labs."

"Huh?" Liam scratched his head. "What other kinds of information did he go after, other than biological stuff?"

"Jeez, I can't even remember what he was doing when he got into Brookhaven. And then he got into the files of that jerk newspaper, *The Green Review*. He was looking for stuff over there."

"No kidding."

"You want to know the weirdest thing of all, the thing I was never able to figure out?"

"What's that?"

"He had no billing address, yet every hour of on-line time was paid for."

"By him?"

"I don't know if it was by him or not. But let's just say it was all neat and tidy. Nobody was ripped off in that sense." Corey paused. "I kind of grew to like the guy. Had a lot of admiration for him, really. So he was really murdered?"

"Yep."

"Gee, that makes me feel real bad."

"And you never found out who hired you to track him down?"

"Not really. For all intents and purposes it was the University of Pennsylvania. The initial request came from somebody there."

"Who wrote your paycheck?"

"Penn, for the first installment."

"Then after that?"

"Well, that was a little weird. They told me to send the bills to this P.O. Box at Penn, and they paid me with a postal money order."

"How much did it cost them?"

"It wasn't cheap, let me tell you. It took me over seven months. I think it all totaled up to about thirty thousand dollars."

Liam whistled low. "Somebody had big bucks."

"Yep."

41

All Archie had to do now was sit back and try to relax and watch the fun begin. Through his network of colleagues in archaeology and paleontology, including Colin Mercer at the *National Geographic,* word of the skulls had spread like wildfire. Lorne Thurston's college would have to make some announcement soon. And Archie was enjoying the thought of them being bombarded by calls. Colin Mercer was calling up the college and saying that the *National Geographic* wanted to fly photographers down to Green Acre, Texas, and also to the site where the skulls had been excavated. He assumed that the college must have a team still excavating over there, wherever it was. It would be out on the U.P. wire services by now. A *New York Times* science editor was toying with flying someone down there. The story would definitely be covered, in any case. Archie had even called Goodfellow and had her call the college on behalf of the Smithsonian. Within twelve hours the academic world was abuzz with this news.

Sitting back and relaxing was not too hard a thing to do in Vermont with Calista. In fact, he could do this forever, he thought, skulls or no skulls! He rolled over onto his back in the black water of the pond and looked up at the stars. Calista was floating on her back next to him, and he stretched out his hand for hers. This was Calista's own pond, a lovely one just down the grassy knoll from her house. Sedges and cattails grew in thick clumps around its banks. At one end, where an old bullfrog presided, there were some lily pads with pale pink blossoms. They had been swimming naked now for almost half an hour. There was never any need to wear clothes even during the daytime at this pond, and they had gone for a swim that afternoon just after arriving from the hot two-and-a-half-hour drive. But tonight it was magical. Chips of moonlight were scattered across the water, and above in the sky were garlands of stars.

Calista knew not only all the constellations but the mythology that went with them. She had just started to tell him one he had never heard, about Vega, the brightest star of the summer triangle. It was a strange tale of jealousy and music and the casting out of the purest sister, the one who could tell no lies but was doomed through the spell of an evil stepmother never to speak. She sought refuge in a cave on a magical island with an old mathematician.

"Where was the cave?" Archie asked.

"Samos."

"Isn't that where Pythagoras went?"

"Precisely," she answered. They had begun kicking on their backs toward shore. "She had fled there because there was this tyrant, Polycrates, who was the governor of the island and making life miserable for everyone. The stepmother was Polycrates' sister—out of the same mold."

"Okay, I follow you."

"Now, keep your eye on the star while I tell you the rest of the story."

Archie did. But for the life of him he couldn't remember a myth involving Pythagoras and a young girl. There had never, for that matter, been any mention of female companionship in the cave.

"So she lived in this cave with this little old guy on Samos. It was really a beautiful island swirled with salt air and forested with pines. But she couldn't speak. He didn't bug her about it. He taught her that there was harmony in nature and variety within sameness and unity. That all this had a language of its own, the language of numbers. See, he was on his way to discovering the Pythagorean theorem, or the proof. That was just down the pike. But before that he was finding something just as exciting—even more exciting. It was the basic relationship between mathematics and musical harmony. For Pythagoras taught Vega that she did not need words. And over the years she developed the purest and most beautiful language of all—music. It helped him refine his ideas about the mathematics of music. Vega was humming Bach fugues long before there ever was a Bach."

"What?" Archie slipped his arm around Calista's waist. They sat now in the silty mud, chest deep in the water.

"Anyhow, eventually she died."

"Before Pythagoras?"

"Yes. She just sort of faded away. It was as if she had lived steeped in this world of abstractions and symbols so thoroughly that she had somehow become that. There was no material substance to her. She didn't die, really. She just left her body behind and climbed this starry staircase into the sky, to become part of the harmony of the heavens. She became the brightest star, Vega, in heaven's harp—Lyra."

"I swear I never heard that myth." He drew her wet body closer to his.

"Well, of course you haven't heard it. I made it up."

"You made it up?"

"Yeah, for Charley, years ago."

"Did you ever make it into a picture book and illustrate it?"

"No. I can't give away all of our secrets. I hate those authors who use their families constantly. Believe me, plenty of the Jacobses get into my books. We have to save out something that's just for ourselves."

"So you're a secret mythmaker."

"Not so secret. Some I've thought up I've written for publication. But not this one. Not many of the starry ones."

"It's funny. Here Tom was an astrophysicist, and you make up astromyths."

"Not that funny." She paused. "So what if astronomers can measure the speed and temperatures of stars millions of miles away. Everything needs a story. There's the natural history story that explains the numbers, the physics. And then there needs to be the other kind of story—the one that deepens the mystery and makes more awesome the beauty." They lay back in each other's arms, their shoulders and heads resting against the thick soft grass of the bank, their torsos and legs extending into the silty mud. "I've even got one about quasars."

"Quasars?"

"You know."

"Yeah, I know. But I get them mixed up with pulsars. Pulsars give those radio waves in short bursts, right?"

"Yeah. They're basically fast-spinning neutron stars. But quasars are more mysterious. They're those faint little starlike objects. That's what the word stands for, quasi-stellar radio source. They were only detected, when? twenty, twenty-five years ago? They're ripe for mythmaking. Tom had written a lot about them. I mean, they're part of the black hole scenario."

"Why's that?"

"Well, they think they're related to the collapse of whole regions of a galaxy—see what a story that could be!"

Archie chuckled. He could see her eyes sparkling in her wet face. A scroll of hair inscribed her cheek. She looked sleek as a seal, and she swam like one, too.

"What are you laughing at? You think it's weird, don't you? My talking this way."

"I like it weird. I think it's amazing. I think your mind is amazing."

"You know, Archie, it's not that amazing. People have been doing this for years. Michelangelo looks at a hunk of marble and sees the David embedded in it waiting to be released. A geologist looks at a hunk of marble and sees the silicate structure or whatever you call it. Both are right. Both see stories in the marble. One narrative is called natural science, the other is called mythology or art. But each has its own truths. So there!"

"So there!" Archie grabbed her and rolled her over in the mud.

"Oh, God, I always dreamed of mud wrestling!" She laughed as he began to slide inside her. "What will the bullfrog think?"

"He'll wish he were a prince!" Archie sighed deeply.

There was one thing that had been troubling Archie all along. Where in this tangled web of fudged science and religious extremism did his cousin Neddy fit? That afternoon in Neddy's house he had come away convinced that things were not exactly as Neddy had presented them. No way did he swallow that the president of the United States had sent Neddy to Texas as a kind of high-level emissary to pay court to those jerks. No, he had come away convinced that Thurston had his hooks into Neddy some way. But he could not imagine that his cousin would be on the take financially. No recent administration had earned particularly high marks in the ethics department. Kickback schemes were rampant, and conflict-of-interest situations, especially those related to defense contractors, had become almost epidemic. But there was some other reason why Neddy was down there, and it could not be money. He was just too rich. He wouldn't take such a risk for money. Could it be something with a woman? It didn't seem likely. And if Neddy was involved with the creationists, was he in on this intellamine crap, too? No, there was definitely something fishy. It smelled bad, real bad. Sooner or later Archie was going to have to confront Neddy. He just didn't have enough of the cards in his hands yet. But he was getting them. This morning he was reading *The New York Times* article on the reputed skulls. Calista had driven down into the village and bought every newspaper—all three. *The New York Times,* the *Boston Globe,* and something called the *Upper Valley News.* The *Times* and the *Globe* had front-page articles on the fossil treasures of Lorne Thurston College of Christian Heritage. A spokesman for the college was playing it very tight-lipped, not denying or confirming anything but nodding soberly that yes, skulls had been found that raised new questions about different evolutionary tracks for the races. No, he had explained patiently, this was not a racist theory, and it in no way compromised their views on the creation story and the scientific veracity of Genesis.

"See," said Archie, snapping the paper and folding it over to read the bottom half, "this is what these guys always do. They say that species can undergo limited changes because the Creator endowed them each with somewhat of a repertoire of genetic variability. Just enough to make slight accommodations necessary to survive in nature. No, monkeys cannot evolve into people, mind you. Just a few changes in hair and coloring. Now listen to this, Cal." She looked up from the paper she was reading. "This guy quotes here Henry Morris. He's one of the head honchos of the creationist movement. Holds a Ph.D. in hydraulic engineering. What else can you say? Every good flood needs a hydraulic engineer." Calista laughed. "Listen to this. It's the college spokesman quoting Dr. Morris on this subject of genetic variability. Dr. Morris says, and I quote, 'Since the Creator has a purpose for each kind of organism created, He would institute a system which would not only assure its genetic integrity, but would also enable it to survive in nature. The genetic system would be such as to maintain its identity as a specific kind while, at the same time, allowing it to adjust its characteristics (within limits) to changes in environment.' End quote."

"So they think these skulls show that kind of small change that races might make?"

"Yeah. They think that, even though LeGros Clark, the great English anatomist and anthropologist, has said that there has never been a fossil that has shown any kind of racial traces. A few people have been hoping, trying for something like this for years. Carleton Coon, a racist anthropologist if there ever was one, wrote a whole book about it back in the early sixties in which he declared that Africa might have been the cradle of mankind, but it was only an 'indifferent kindergarten,' as he called it, and that Europe and Asia were the 'principle schools.'"

"Oh, no!" Calista wrinkled her nose. "How vile. Do

they say yet where they found these skulls and what exactly they are or show?"

"Not yet. But the pressure's going to build. Mark my words. That'll come out tomorrow. And I'll tell you precisely where they're going to say they got them from and what they are."

"How can you know, Archie?" Calista looked up from her paper.

"Because if I were going to fake a skull for the reasons they are doing it, here's what I would have to do—not that these people are concerned with facts, but it is a fact that *Homo erectus* was the first hominid to travel outside of Africa."

"Oh, now wait a minute," Calista said. "Refresh me. Which one is *Homo erectus?*"

"You know, tall, dark, and handsome, invented fire. Kind of the matinee idol of the hominid world, the first one you might have been able to have a meaningful relationship with." Archie's eyes twinkled.

"Oh, come off it, Archie!" She wadded up a paper napkin and tossed it at him. "Okay, so he left Africa," she said.

"Not all of them. It's not as if the whole kit and caboodle packed up and left. Some stayed behind, but some left. Traces have been found in Asia and places in Europe. *Homo erectus* is generally regarded as the root stock of *Homo sapiens.* There were two waves of emigration from Africa. Now what these guys, I bet, are going to say is in that second wave these separate clumps of *Homo erectus* evolved into separate colors of *Homo sapiens.*"

"But weren't there intermediary forms? I mean, are you saying they've got *Homo erectus* skulls?"

"Yes, there were intermediary forms, and no, they're not going to come up with *erectus* skulls. *Erectus* is just their ticket. They are going to say that modern African skulls more closely resemble, say, Neanderthal skulls— one of which could be thought of as an intermediary form. That these modern African skulls resemble Neanderthal more closely than Caucasians. One of these skulls that they claim to have found is going to be a very old

Homo sapiens one, found in Europe. And it will look very Caucasian. Then they can say we whites have evolved much farther than blacks. At least if I were going to try and pull off something like this, this is how I would work it."

"Well, if you were going to do it, you wouldn't have to fit it all into the Genesis time frame, so that might make it a little easier."

"True, but watch—they'll manipulate that time frame to make it still hold up and work for them."

"Will they have a black skull, then?"

"No. They're just going to make this 'white' one very old but definitely found in Europe and within their favorite time frame. Listen, they don't even need to fake the skull to stir up a hornet's nest. People see too often what they want to see in fossils—glorified visions of themselves. Look how they convinced themselves on the science of Genesis. This wouldn't be too hard. They look at a skull, doctored or not, and they can read in a whole racist, white supremicist doctrine. In the last century, which was a veritable heyday for craniology, folks did it all the time. Samuel George Moreton ranked cranial capacity according to race. He measured the volume with mustard seed. You can bet he really pushed down the mustard seeds to make room for more in the white skulls."

"Oh, God!"

"Oh, by the way, he didn't even bother measuring women's skulls."

"What a shame! So anyway you say that they'll just need this one very old *Homo sapiens* skull and they'll basically say that the *erectus* that were left behind didn't evolve or did so into a black variety of *Homo sapiens* and the ones that came to Europe became white."

"Yep." Archie nodded.

"But isn't that almost mathematically impossible?"

"Exactly! It's mathematically impossible for three of four separate clumps of one species to evolve simultaneously into as complex an organism as *Homo sapiens* with only racial differences. It's the equivalent of saying that a room full of chimps all at typewriters will come up with Hamlet's soliloquy and only punctuation differences."

It happened almost precisely as Archie had described. The skulls had yet to be revealed, but in articles in the next day's *Times* and *Globe,* more information, "official information," had been given. There was just one skull, and it was definitely modern but very old. "Oh, my God!" Archie said. "All these years they're going on saying they don't believe in radiometric dating—now when it suits them, they use it! Listen to this: 'Although we do not believe in the validity of any of the radiometric dating techniques, even using those methods we see that this skull is significantly older than any thus found of modern human beings.'"

"How can they have it both ways? If they don't believe in the method, why use it?"

"They're scrambling, Calista. We caught them with their pants down. Any port in a storm. They're hedging their bets. See, they're invoking now a little Flood theory for deposition. They go on here to say that what they believe is that the geological column and all of the fossil-bearing strata were—and I quote—'arranged and worked out by the Creator long before anyone ever heard or thought about radioactive carbon dating.' Their fossil was found in very deep sediments."

"Yeah, like someone's basement," Calista said.

"'We can no longer be accused,'" Archie continued reading, "'of not submitting evidence for scientific testing. We have. And there now seems to be proof that this is a very old Caucasian skull, predating any of the other ones ever found.' Nobody has ever found a Caucasian fossil skull, buddy!" Archie growled at the paper.

"Where did they say they found it? Minneapolis?"

"Uh . . . let's see here . . . northern Turkey."

"Oh, of course, near Mount Ararat, where Noah's Ark was supposed to have finally fetched up. All the smart would-be white people got on the boat. There was probably, what—a speciation event on the Ark—and when they got off they were white. Better than 'Love Boat'!"

Archie laughed. "They're running, Calista. They're running hard."

"But why? Why would they do such a thing?"

"Remember, the Creator is supposed to have a purpose for each kind of organism created, and presumably you can extend it to each race since He has a purpose for each kind of organism created."

"So what would they perceive as the Creator's purpose?"

"I couldn't even begin to imagine."

"It scares me."

"Me too," Archie said quietly.

And there was still this other thing nagging at him in the back of his mind. Why Neddy? Where did Neddy fit in? How did they get to him? These people had big plans. They controlled networks now. Often they controlled textbooks. No presidential candidate, except for Pat Robertson, had ever claimed to have God tell him to run. And there had now been rumors of Thurston feeling out the terrain, he too claiming divine inspiration—a heavenly PA system. They were rich. The old Gospel tent had given way to the satellite dish. Notions of parish had given way to those of constituencies, and notions of constituencies might be giving way to those of kingdoms and empires. When Pat Robertson had won an early Michigan primary, he had declared triumphantly, "The Christians have won. . . . What a breakthrough for the kingdom!" But as one astute journalist had pointed out in an article, when Jack Kennedy won the West Virginia primary he didn't declare, "The Catholics have won. . . . What a breakthrough for the Vatican!"

The telephone rang. Calista got up to answer it.

"Oh, hello, Colin. . . . Yes, Archie's here. Hiding out, as it were. Just a minute." Calista knew Colin Mercer from years before when the *National Geographic* had done an article on Tom and his work with the Time Slicer in magnetic dating using trace elements.

Archie picked up the phone. "Hello."

"I didn't realize, Archie, that you were keeping company with the widow Jacobs. I envy you. That mustn't be such a bad exile."

"I'm bearing up."

There was a low locker-room-type chuckle from Colin. Archie knew that Colin was not one of Calista's favorites. He was a classic chauvinist pig. She would not have liked this laugh. On her behalf Archie gave a short cough of disapproval and did not join in the chuckle. "So what are you calling about?"

"What country are you supposed to be in?"

"I don't know. I never got that specific. Just away."

"Well, I think you should be in Israel."

"Why's that?"

"You know that team we're covering working in the Qafzeh cave in lower Galilee?"

"Yeah, yeah, sure. They come up with something?"

"They sure did, and the timing couldn't be better."

"What?" Archie said. Calista looked up from her drawing board. She could hear the excitement in his voice.

"Okay, now," Colin was saying, "the Texas boys claim they got an old skull proving that whites evolved separately long, long ago, but in Europe, while black guys sat down in Africa and didn't evolve much."

"Yeah, that's the scenario. Come on, Colin, don't drag this out."

But he was dragging it out. "Curious, this sudden interest of theirs in radiometric dating, isn't it?"

"Yes. Now what have you got?"

"A ninety-two-thousand-year-old skull from a 'modern,' not an archaic, human being from a cave in Israel, which ain't all that far from Africa. Only this one's real, and it's going to blow their little Johnny Walker White right out of the water. This one—it ain't white. It ain't black. It's just a good old-fashioned fabulous specimen of an anatomically modern human being."

"Good Lord! This is timing, but beyond that you realize that this pushes back the date for modern humans by at least fifty thousand years. They always thought the first ones evolved, what, thirty-two to thirty-five thousand years ago? And it also firmly supports the hypothesis that they evolved in Africa." Calista had stopped inking in the figure of Maid Marian and was trying to follow the conversation. "You're right, the timing couldn't be better."

"These guys are going to shrivel up and die, be blown away in the wind. We'll probably never find out why they went to such lengths."

"Don't count on it."

"Okay, well, keep in touch. And give the widow Jacobs a kiss for me."

Archie coughed again and said good-bye.

"So did you hear that, Cal?" he said, turning to her.

"Part of it."

Archie related briefly what Colin had just called about. Calista's eyes opened in amazement as he finished. "Can you believe it?" he said. "I mean the implications, not just in terms of this fake skull down in Texas."

42

"I don't like it!" Lorne Thurston said angrily into the receiver. A secretary poked her head into the room, and Clarella motioned her out with a wave of the long peach-colored nails that she was filing. "I don't care whether it's a new game now. I don't care if it's hardball. You don't play hardball with my students. . . . This'll blow over. . . ." His eyebrows raised as he listened to the voice on the other end. "I am not deluding myself," he barked. "This is nothing compared to Jim and Tammy Faye." Clarella looked up and winked knowingly at her husband, blew on her nails, and then picked up a buffer and began buffing them. "This publicity might be a minor setback," Thurston continued, "but we can overcome it. We're getting the numbers right on the Supreme Court. The textbook folks are backing off. In Iowa, Oklahoma, and Illinois we're getting education officials to insist on inclusion of biblical creationist beliefs along with the Darwin stuff. We are getting ahead. Our guidelines are going through for textbooks. The National Association for Christian Educators and the good people over at CEE are doing a great job. No, there is absolutely no way I will permit this. She is not a threat, and even if she were . . ." He listened silently for a few more seconds. "You guys are going too far, and I don't think I should have to remind you where your funding comes from. You're acting like a bunch of paranoids. No—this is the end of it. Not another word. Good-bye." He slammed down the telephone and glared out the window. "You know, Clarella"—he sighed deeply—"it's hard to pray for people like that. But by gum I'm going to try!"

He walked over to a corner area of his office where the carpeting stopped and some blue flagstones had been set into the floor. There were two potted lily plants and a crucifix. It was his own private office chapel. He sank to his knees with a groan. Clarella put down her nail buffer, walked over, and got down on her knees. She felt a run shoot up her left nylon. "Dear Lord . . ." Thurston began to pray.

Beth Ann had never thought again about that flat, nasal voice she'd heard come out of Dr. Tompkins. Not once since coming to Bible Times, which to her had been a dream come true. She adored her work in the Little Shepherd Day Care Center. And because they were also shorthanded in the hospitality office, she had been working there doing everything from helping people with travel arrangements to working on the printed materials that showed the new luxury suites. It was a real education.

But it was the beginning of Beth Ann's third week at

Bible Times when the first leak sprung, and it was then that she recalled that strange nasal voice of Wayne Tompkins. She had just come into the hospitality office to stuff envelopes. Nobody was there. Everybody was in the office next door. She could see them all huddled around a table looking at something. She went in.

"I'll be . . . ," a voice said in slow wonderment.

"They're saying Lorne faked this stuff."

"Not Lorne . . . the scientists. . . ."

"This is a plot . . . this is a commie plot. . . ."

"Work of the devil. . . ."

"What's going on?" Beth Ann asked a young man she knew who was standing on the edge of the group.

Before the man could answer she heard another boy say, "Gee, my roommate went on that expedition when they discovered those skulls. It was right in the region where they're looking for the ark." Beth Ann's heart sank. She felt a funny prickly feeling all over. Her head seemed to swim. "Look what it says here in the *Post*. . . . Yeah, and this here *New York Times*, well, everyone knows what that rag is. . . . Yeah, but the Fredericksburg paper has . . ."

It seemed unbelievable. Her blabbing could not have come to this—could it have? She suddenly had an image of her mouth, her tongue, reflected in an infinity of mirrors.

"Beth Ann, is something wrong?" It was John, the young man she had first asked what was happening.

"No, no . . . I'll be all right," she said, touching the edge of a chair and then holding on to it more firmly.

"Beth Ann, you look terrible." He took her firmly by the arm. It was as if her feet weren't even on the floor, but she could feel his hand on her elbow. It was a welcome support.

They were sitting in the far corner of a juice bar in a replica of the old city of Jerusalem. "So," John was saying, "you think that maybe the college did have something to hide; that it might be true what the papers were saying, that they did do something funny."

"I don't know whether they did anything funny or not with the skulls, and I don't understand anything about this science, but I told you what happened when I took that nice lady through, how mad the professor got at me. I mean, wouldn't you say that that sounds like they had something to hide?"

"Well, yeah."

"And then I get instantly shipped off to here. I mean, John, kids are dying to get these jobs. How long have you been on a waiting list for your job here?"

"Five semesters, I think."

"Well, see? I'd just signed up, let's see . . . this past fall."

"That is quick. But Beth Ann, you yourself said that Dean Clayton said it was just sensitive material. That doesn't necessarily mean there's some kind of funny stuff going on."

"Oh, yes. I know. But still I shouldn't have said anything, and I did."

"I think you're being too hard on yourself, and besides, it wasn't you who really spilled the beans. I mean, you didn't call up the newspapers and the press."

"No, certainly not."

"See, it must have been that nice lady and her kid who did it."

"Oh, dear!" Beth Ann whispered softly, and touched her cheek. But she was filled with feelings not of anger, but of anxiety. Suddenly she remembered the bruised face of Wayne Tompkins, the blood on his shirt. The ugly little laugh. No, she wasn't worried about Wayne Tompkins. She was worried about Charley Jacobs and his nice mother. She didn't care right now whether they had called up the press or not. She liked them. She just plain liked them.

It took a little doing to get the Jacobses' number. She had to call the admissions office back at the college, and there was no number, but she finally reached him through his pastor's home—the Reverend Matthew McPhail.

* * *

Calista's house in Vermont was an old eighteenth-century farmhouse. Her gardens were furious, untrammeled explosions of color. In Cambridge she had had no choice. Not enough sun could filter through the immense trees to coax any color out of anything. So she had been confined to shade plants for the most part with the occasional splash of spring colors from spring bulbs that could grow before the leaves had unfurled, spreading their embroidery of shade. It was in Vermont that she made up for the lack of color in Cambridge.

Off the back of the house was a terrace made from salvaged old bricks that had faded to almost pink. In the summertime and the early fall days, Calista spent most of her time on this terrace sunning, cooking in the brick barbecue, reading, and looking down at the meadow that swooped below for a thousand feet or more. The meadow ended in a bog that in June was filled with lady's slippers and strange, tiny orchids. But beyond the bog the low New England mountains rose in shadows of gray and purple, sometimes swathed in cloud and mist. Always gentle under the sky, so unlike the Rockies, which reared and clawed at the clouds above them, these mountains reminded Calista of sleeping women.

The coals were hot enough now. Calista took the trout she had caught that afternoon, which she had wrapped carefully in long grass, and buried them in the embers. She had found a couple of tomatoes ready in her garden and began slicing them. Archie watched her as she padded around barefoot. She wore these funny little outfits that were sexy, but not blatantly so. At the moment she was wearing men's light cotton drawers, boxer shorts, over some kind of a lace-trimmed body suit. She had stuck some pink roses in her hair. She looked quite frankly daffy, but undeniably sexy, springing around on her lean, well-muscled legs as she wrapped up fish in grass, discussed the merits of sedges versus cattails as a wrap for baking the fish, popped a sliver of the gravlax into Archie's mouth. She was most remarkable, this woman, this spinner of tales, maker of myths, with her observation on life, which ranged from contemplations of Dom Pérignon to insights into the fundamentalist mind. You never stopped thinking when you were around her or, for him, the other less cerebral activity—screwing. So this would either keep him very young or the reverse: he might go from fifty-two to eighty-two within a month.

While the trout were baking Calista settled on a cushion by Archie's feet with her drink and a bottle of calamine lotion and some cotton. This in Calista's mind was the perfect summer evening—to sip Mount Gay rum very slowly and count mosquito bites, dabbing on calamine lotion. "You have very nice legs, Archie."

"So do you."

"They're nice and straight with just the right amount of hairiness."

"Yours, too."

She laughed. "Why do men have more body hair than women?"

Archie chuckled. "There was once an evolutionary theory that tried to explain body hair."

"No kidding," she said, intent on a huge bite on Archie's knee. "Some people will do anything for a Ph.D. thesis."

"Yeah. It was hypothesized that the reason humans lost their apish hair was because when men had to go hunting and run around on the savanna chasing sabertoothed tigers and all, they could not perspire efficiently."

"But what about the women? Why did they lose their hair? They weren't hunting, I presume."

"No, that's what was wrong with the theory. For one thing it presumed that only men hunted. So there was no explanation for women's hair loss. And then it was a theory hatched in the heyday of man-of-the-mighty-hunter concepts. Now they're starting to realize that man didn't hunt all that much."

"Huh?"

"Yeah. Didn't have the social organization back then. Food gathering was a lot more efficient and a lot less risky considering the net calorie gain. So it's more likely that the first food-related tool was not a spear or a hand ax, but a basket."

"Oooh, I like that! And then if this skull from the cave in Israel turns out to be a woman's, it will all make perfect evolutionary sense to me!" Calista took a sip of her rum and looked up at Archie. He ran his fingers through her hair, taking care not to disturb the roses.

43

"You see, there was this woman guest on 'You Bet Your Life.'" Calista was talking through the screen door as she swept the terrace early the next morning. She was still in her nightgown. Inside, Archie was minding the coffee. She had been up since five working on *Marian's Tale*. The door swung open, and Archie brought out a breakfast tray to put on the terrace table.

"Yeah?" he said.

"So this lady had had twenty-two children, and she was explaining somewhat sheepishly to Groucho that, well, she just loved her husband. And Groucho says to her, 'I love my cigar, too, but I take it out once in a while.'" Calista very nearly cackled, but she remembered just in time and suppressed the cackle that threatened to explode. The phone rang, and she went to get it.

"Oh, Liam. . . . Yes . . . well, we're here. You've found stuff out . . . oh, great. Wait, I'll get Archie, and I'll get on the other phone."

"What?" Archie said. "No shit . . . *The Green Review?* You mean that nutty reactionary publication? . . . Okay, yeah, let me get a pencil and paper."

By the end of the conversation, Calista had sketched a

diagram of the hacking path of Norman Petrakis. Archie gnawed a pencil and stared at the map of institutes and labs where Petrakis had intruded. They were all biology labs working on genetic research of one sort or another —cancer, species separation, twins research. The one place that made absolutely no sense was *The Green Review.*

The Green Review—how could that fit into all of this? Funding! Hadn't Liam Phillips told them on the phone that his Berkeley contact had said big money had been put up to snag this intruder? Something to the tune of thirty thousand dollars. Big money was behind *The Green Review.* It was a very right-wing newspaper that was funded by very reactionary rich Ivy League graduates. It was not associated with any one particular school but had drawn from them all—Harvard, Dartmouth, Yale, Princeton. The staff was young and virulent.

Big money would have to be behind this protein-fudging scam. And who knew, the same kind of mind attracted to funding a rag like *The Green Review* might be attracted to this. He was beginning to see exactly where the fossils and the genetics separated and where they touched. The creationists had their own sources for money—coffers filled by those satellite collection plates, but the biology labs had to scramble, always an uphill battle for funding. You couldn't exactly get on the air and pass the plate as a biological laboratory, and if you were not very well connected with a big university, it would be tough. The labs that would be the most vulnerable were those not well connected—like the Coastal Research Institute and its little Nobel Sperm Bank—Genesis.

"You see," Archie said, looking at Calista, "Petrakis was on to this for a long time. He probably had all his facts down about the scam, but he wanted to know how it got funded. Penn, Duke, and Minnesota were places with labs that all had plants—people willing to corroborate the information, pretend they were carrying out experiments and getting other people in the lab just to sign on, as protocol so often dictates in these situations. Probably only needed two or three to get the ball rolling. Where they ran short of cash was in trying to stop Petrakis. Universities would only allocate so much for something like that, but the perpetrators needed the guy caught and were willing to spend, well, at least thirty thousand dollars. Maybe they tried Lorne Thurston. Who knows. But it was money that first got these two schemes—the fossil one and the genetics one—together. And one connection could have been *The Green Review*, which is the greatest assemblage of fascists and crackpots under the sun and probably makes the Lorne Thurston College of Christian Heritage look mild by comparison. The backers of it are a bunch of mean old farts like . . ." Archie paused.

"Like who?"

"Like Hugh Ethelredge." Archie's face drained of color.

"Who's Hugh Ethelredge?" Calista asked.

"A very, very, very rich old man, for starters. He is on the advisory board of *The Green Review*, and—brace yourself—he is also, along with me, on the board of overseers at the Peabody Museum of Archaeology and Ethnography. He informed me recently that there was only one thing wrong with Harvard."

"What was that?" Calista asked weakly.

"They gave too many honorary degrees to women, blacks, and Jews."

"How lovely. Sounds like he might be able to get a design job at the sperm bank."

Archie blinked. "Let's check!"

Fifteen minutes later Ruth Goodfellow called Archie back.

"Archie, I couldn't find the old Genesis pamphlet. I can't believe I would have thrown away such a rare document," she said in her cool, clipped English accent. "But I did find the old letter where they asked for your contribution, my dear."

"Just as long as you don't have it framed."

"Yes, I thought I'd put it on the wall with all your

family pictures. Most fitting. You know, people can check out the whole Baldwin gene pool."

Archie laughed. "So what did you find?"

"Well, your little friend Hugh Ethelredge is a donor, although of money and not sperm, to Atwell's Project Genesis. That's the official name, by the way."

"No shit. He really is?"

"Yes, and this is confirmed."

"How in the hell did you do that?"

"Well, his name is on the stationery as being a member of the advisory board. And seeing as the letter was old, I just thought maybe I should check up to see if he was still on the board. And then they said—and I quote the lady I spoke to—'Oh, yes. Most certainly. He is one of our major supporters.' So I just said, 'I trust by supporter you mean of money, not sperm,' and she confirmed this. Although she added that she was not allowed to disclose who the actual sperm donors were over the phone, but that Mr. Ethelredge had given generously in terms of financial support. I suppose we should feel relieved that he did not give in the alternate method."

"Yes. I guess so. Well, thank you, Ruth. This is above and beyond."

"Nonsense, Archie. But I do think that Nobel or not, your contribution could not help but raise their standards."

"Please, Goodfellow! No more cracks!"

"Well, as we know, they never give Nobels in anthropology or archaeology anyhow. So don't feel bad."

"Goodfellow!"

"Cheerio, Archie."

It wasn't five minutes later that the phone rang again. This time it was Charley.

"Mom!" Charley blurted out. "You'll never guess what!"

"What?" Calista felt something clench in her stomach. She told herself to calm down. Nothing could be wrong. Here, after all, was Charley alive and well and blaring over the phone. "It's Beth Ann. She's real worried, and she even got into some kind of trouble herself."

"Beth Ann . . ." It took Calista a minute. "You mean Beth Ann from the college?"

"Yes, that Beth Ann!"

"Well, how do you know she's in trouble?"

"She called me."

"She called you at the McPhails' from Texas?"

"Not from Texas. From someplace in West Virginia or Virginia. It got confusing. Her grandparents live in West Virginia . . . someplace called Blue Holler, or something like that."

"But how did she ever find you at the McPhails'?"

"It's a long story."

"It must be. Do tell."

"Look, when I applied to that college you had to list your pastor, so I listed Reverend McPhail."

"Fred?"

"No. Matthew."

"Matthew?!" Calista nearly screamed. "Matthew is your pastor?"

"Motherrrr! Not really—what have you done, lost your marbles?"

"Well, I know not really, but—"

"Look, Mom, that's not the issue. She found me, that's all that counts, and she was scared to death. Really scared. They shipped her out of the college for spilling the beans about the skull thing, and now she's in that Bible Disney World of theirs. And she didn't know about us being run off the road, but she saw that Tompkins guy, and he was all bashed up like he'd been in some sort of accident. She's trying to get to West Virginia. I guess it's where her grandparents live."

"Oh, my God! Oh, that poor girl. We have to think of something to help her." Archie had come over, his face tense and grim as he pieced together the part of the conversation he was missing. "Yes . . . yes, Charley. Well, let me discuss this with Archie, then I'll call back. Is Joan around, or Fred? I'll want to talk to them. . . . Yes, dear. Don't worry. . . . No, I feel terribly sorry for her. . . . Yes. . . . Well, we'll try to figure out something. Good-bye. I'll talk to you soon, within the hour. . . . Yes." She hung up the phone and sank down on the chair.

44

So that explained the blood and Wayne Tompkins's bruises. Beth Ann Hennessey felt entirely washed out, devoid of any strength and almost numb as she thought about what Charley Jacobs had just told her. Her hand still rested on the phone as if to confirm what she had just heard, to make this horrible reality palpable, less abstract. But it seemed so unbelievable—Charley and his mother nearly run off the road, then the other car had spun out and pitched into a deep ditch. My word, she thought. What were they so fearful of? What terrible power did these skulls possess that they had threatened the lives of the woman and her son? This sounded like the Devil's business if there ever was any.

She must go pray. She must go this minute to the small students' chapel and pray. It was late at night, and she would be alone. That would be good. She could cry if she wanted to and not bother anybody. She needed to pray for strength, and she needed to pray for guidance. Wrong had been done, and the wrong was not her blabbing. This much she knew. It went deeper, and it was far worse than blabbing.

She entered the chapel. It was hot and stuffy, as the air-conditioning had been turned off at this late hour, but it didn't bother her. She went to the very front and lifted a prayer pad off the seat of the pew and sank to her knees. There was only one light on, and the gleam of the beautifully designed modern cross seemed especially lustrous in the fragile darkness of the chapel. She saw a shadow slide briefly over the gleaming surface of the cross, but she never heard the movement behind her. She just felt something cold smash against the base of her skull, and the light on the cross went out.

45

When Calista had drawn the diagram of Norman Petrakis's hacking route through various computer systems, it had started to look like a spiderweb to her. She and Archie had begun to explore it and now were on a flight to Washington, D.C., where they would then pick up a car and drive to Morash, Virginia, where Bible Times was located.

They were searching for Beth Ann Hennessey. Liam Phillips had busted into the college's files in Green Acre and found out all the pertinent information necessary about Beth Ann. Beth Ann had no living parents. Her next of kin had been listed as her grandparents, Ola and Milford Arnette of Blue Hollow, West Virginia. It had been Calista's decision to go after Beth Ann. That was what she felt was the number-one priority.

The papers were full of the controversial skull and the new find in Israel. This seemed to be a last straw for the scientific world, which was already fed up with the shenanigans of the fundamentalists' forays into science. Headlines like PALUXY SKULL and RACIST FOSSILS abounded. The tabloids were having a field day with it. There were longer, more in-depth articles addressing the subject in *The New York Times* and the *Christian Science Monitor*. Paleontologists from around the world decried in no uncertain terms the outrageous abuse of science. They reiterated that the themes of bigotry and superstition, so rampant in the battle against the teaching of evolution, were rearing their ugly heads here with simply a new twist. However, the world had not even heard yet of the fabrications of the bogus brain proteins of intellamine and intellicone that had been going on in the genetic labs for the past three years. Once the link between these labs and the Lorne Thurston College of Christian Heritage could be made and the full dimensions of the abuse known, it would reveal not only fraud, but murder. Archie and Calista were still fairly certain that the creationists had been set up to be the fall guys in Petrakis's murder, that it was most likely someone trying to pass the buck off on the creationists about this murder. Still, there was the gathering evidence that some sort of bizarre plot was going on with the fossils that linked up with the fraud on a genetic level. It was designed to put one over about separate origins of races. It appeared that the words *Monkey's Uncle* had been written to throw everyone off the scent of the genetic perpetrators and somehow link Petrakis's death to his book for children on human evolution. That would explain the defacement of *Nick in the Night* as well as Margaret McGowan's book. Calista had been thinking about all of this just when Archie interrupted her. It was as if he were reading her thoughts.

"Those people from the Coastal Research Institute and the sperm bank and all the other folks they must have had planted in various university labs probably didn't give a rat's ass about the Genesis story and whether or not creationism got to be taught along with evolution or not. They had their own agenda that had to do with genetic stuff. The Bible thumpers probably just provided them with a kind of modus operandi and very possibly funds. From what you tell me after your visit to Thurston's college, and what we read about these television ministries, these guys are rolling in dough."

"But you already said they could get money from rich backers like this Ethelredge person."

"Hugh's rich, but he doesn't have it coming in at the rate of these satellite collection plates."

"Well, if the intellamine folks got money from Thurston, what did Thurston get from them?"

"A patina of scientific thought. This guy Tompkins has a master's in biology as well as a degree in engineering. Didn't you tell me there was some other guy down there that they mentioned that had a degree in hydraulic engineering?"

"Yes, Beth Ann mentioned someone."

"Well, hydraulic engineering would come in handy if you're trying to prove Noah's Flood did it all. And Atwell, he's some sort of engineer. There're always engineers in this business. Even if they believe in evolution, they can't accept ultimately the randomness of it all. They equate randomness with life devoid of meaning or purpose. They can't live with that. That is where guys like James Atwell and Hugh Ethelredge have a great deal in common with Lorne Thurston. If you're an engineer, then you assume you can fiddle with the system, adjust it to your purposes or what you perceive to be God's purposes. Why do you think Atwell has this damn Nobel sperm bank? He cannot live with the notion that there is no design to the universe. He wants to impose his own. Thurston and the creationists want to do the same thing through a literal reading of Genesis. Thurston needs the imprimatur of 'real' science, and Atwell needs money. Tit for tat, and who gives a rat's ass if it has anything to do with truth? Everybody gets what they want and comes away happy."

"Except for Norman Petrakis."

"Right." Archie paused. "There was an eighteenth-century theologian, William Paley, who compared life to a watch. He said just as a watch is too complicated to have sprung into existence spontaneously, so must it be with all living things. Because life is so complex, it, like a watch, had to have a design and a designer. The fundamentalists cannot countenance the notion of a blind watchmaker, for it means a world without purpose or reason."

Calista looked down at the map she had drawn of Petrakis's tunnelings into the various computers. She had scratchy lines running between the sites. It was looking very much like a spiderweb now. Norman had been caught in it all right. But it had not been spun by Norman or blind designers. The web, however, was spreading. She traced over the lines with her fine-nibbed pen. The drag lines were extending from the far upper left-hand corner, California, where the Coastal Research Institute was located, to Green Acre, up again to Minneapolis, down to Philadelphia, and then to North Carolina and over to New Hampshire. Which were the major sites, however, where the spinnerets produced the silken threads of this design? Was it the lab in California with its fragile ties to Stanford? Or was it down in Green Acre? Or was it somewhere else that she and Archie had never imagined? Were these spinners too obvious, and was Norman to be the only victim? That sent a chill through Calista, and she thought of Beth Ann.

Calista knew a little bit about spiders. As a fourth-grader, Charley had had to write a report on them for school, and she had helped him with it. They had looked spiders up in the *Book of Knowledge,* and Charley had attempted to rewrite the information in his own words. The chunky, abrupt little sentences came back to her.

There are three main types of web weaver spiders. There are tangled-web weavers. There are sheet-web weavers, and there are orb weavers. The web of a tangled-web weaver is the simplest. It is shapeless and attaches to a support like the corner of a ceiling.

Calista looked at her drawing. This was not a tangled web of the classical order.

Orb weavers weave the most beautiful and complicated webs of all. The webs are round, and the silk threads run from the center of the web like spokes on a wheel. Some orb weavers lie in wait for their prey in the very center of the web. Some attach trap lines to the center of the web and the spider hides nearby in its nest. When an insect lands, the trap lines shake. That's the tip-off!

"What are you thinking about—spiderwebs?" Archie said, looking down at the paper.

"Yeah. I'm starting to think that this whole thing resembles a spiderweb—an orb weaver's, to be exact." She traced the bridge line that went from California to Hanover and then the perimeters.

"Hmm." Archie scratched his chin. "It's starting to look kind of like an old-boy network to me."

"Where do you think Neddy fits in, or do you?"

"I don't know. I don't know. I can't believe that his involvement has anything to do with the murder. I just wish I knew what it was."

"It disturbs you a lot, doesn't it?"

"It sure does. And do you realize in three weeks I'm supposed to go sailing with Neddy? Our annual down east cruise."

"Well, I guess a cruise on a sailboat will shake any skeletons or skulls out of the closet."

Archie sighed, almost painfully. "I guess so."

When they got off the plane in Washington, D.C., Calista could not help but think of trap lines. Were they crawling up one now? Had the vibrations already begun?

46

Calista and Archie were walking under a fiberglass sky down a painted cobblestone street. On either side were shops hawking religious items—framed prayers, pop-up books with Bible stories for children, other religious books and records. And everywhere there were posters and pictures of Lorne Thurston and his wife, Clarella. They seemed to favor a somewhat regal stance in their pictures evocative of those formal portraits of the queen of England and Prince Philip. Lorne stood erect in a dark suit behind Clarella, who sat on a settee with a voluminous aquamarine gown flouncing up around her like a turbulent sea. Her hands were primly folded over a white Bible. Under his arm a larger black Bible was pressed. The message seemed to be: We are not just bringing the Word. We *are* the Word!

There were dolls of Clarella displayed in all the shop windows and selling for upward of two hundred dollars. If Lorne was the undisputed king of the airwaves, Clarella was certainly the queen of this kingdom here in Virginia. Her plastic face was everywhere, and for some reason it seemed to serve as a macabre twist on an old nightmare Calista had had as a child where she would desperately be looking for her mother and encountering instead plastic facsimiles. It had been a very unnerving dream of her childhood, and she had not thought of it in years. But she was not looking for her mother here. She was looking for a child—not her own, but nonetheless a child in need. And what had that child Beth Ann Hennessey been looking for? That was the real question, Calista thought.

There were ice-cream shops and theaters showing Animatronic presentations of the most dramatic of the Bible stories, ranging from "Daniel and the Lions" to "Noah's Ark." They were heading for the day-care center in hopes of finding Beth Ann. They walked through some brightly painted gates and found themselves at a desk tended by two scrubbed young girls.

"Can we help you?" one asked. The sign above read "Little Shepherd Day Care Center." In bright, air-conditioned, sky-lighted rooms beyond, Calista and Archie could see the little lambs.

"We're relatives of Beth Ann Hennessey, and we're

just down for the day from Washington and wanted to stop by and say hello."

"Oh, Beth Ann," said the one girl, looking at the other. "Yes, she was working here. But then they switched her just temporarily." She paused. "Did they put her over in the water park, Mary?"

"Yeah, I think so—on the River Jordan ride, the kiddie part of it."

"The River Jordan?" Calista said softly.

"I think that's where they sent her," the girl named Mary said. "But come to think of it, I haven't seen her at supper for the last two nights."

"Beth Ann? Beth Ann Hennessey?" A young, athletic-looking man in a muscle shirt, bathing trunks, and a whistle around his neck was staring out as if trying to place her face. He was looking directly at a gigantic water slide. His face suddenly clenched, and he blew his whistle. "None of that, fellows! Too rough!" He was pointing at two teenaged boys who were horsing about at the top of the slide. "Now let's see. . . . Yeah. Beth Ann. I remember her. I think she had to go on home. Something about some ailing grandparent out in California."

"Her grandparents—in California?" Calista said, slightly confused.

"Yeah, I'm sure they said that she was going to California, and it was something to do with her grandparents. You can check with the office. It's over at the broadcasting center. They'll know."

The big question was, should they really check with the office? Would that tip off someone who could cause problems? Archie felt they should. None of the kids they had spoken to so far had been lying. He was sure of that. They genuinely did not know where Beth Ann had gone. She admittedly had not made much of an impression, but then again she presumably must not have spent much time there. It had barely been a month since Calista and Charley had left Beth Ann down in Green Acre in her job as campus guide.

Calista and Archie had cut through the replica village of Old Jerusalem to head for the administrative offices. Just as they exited the village they saw a long silver limousine pull up in front of the stucco offices.

"Look, it's him!" Archie said. A bright carrot-top head bobbed out of the car followed by a platinum one. Aides rushed out of the building, and some others got out of the car. Two young men ran around to the back of the limo and started unloading what looked to Calista like Vuitton luggage.

"No, honey, put that back in 'cause we're goin' to be goin' right over to the Manor," Clarella directed with a thin, jeweled hand.

"You really want to go in and ask for Beth Ann?" Calista said. "With the lion in his den?" She paused. "Archie, I think we better lay low. I got a hunch she's not here."

"But we know for a fact that her grandparents don't live in California. Liam found out they lived in West Virginia—Blue Hollow, West Virginia, which is definitely not California."

"There's only one thing in California as far as this mess is concerned." She looked at Archie levelly.

"The Coastal Research Institute," he replied.

She nodded.

"Do you think that there's any chance that she could be with her grandparents in Blue Hollow, or that they would know anything?" he asked.

"I don't know."

"And if she's not there, I guess we have to assume she's in California. Although why they would feel she constitutes so much of a threat that she would have to be removed to California, I don't know."

"Me neither. Unless they have other plans for her at that sperm bank. . . . Oh, God! It nauseates me just to think about it. I suppose it might be worth a try going to her grandparents' place in West Virginia. What did you say—that place they live in is only one hundred miles from here?"

"Less than that. It's just over the West Virginia border."

"I think we should get out of here before we're found out, or before anybody gets any ideas about running us off any roads."

"Okay. I'm with you."

47

"You see," Ola Arnette was saying. "I think we were just too old for her. She came to live with us when she was just four, and we were already almost seventy then." She spoke in a soft but husky voice that for some reason reminded Calista of morning mist or ground fog. It seemed to lie on the evening air like a gentle hush, muting things, blurring them just a bit. They were on the front porch of the Arnettes' log house deep in the hills of West Virginia. "This holler warn't no place for a young, growing thing. Oh, yeah, there were a few youngsters around, but they all had young parents and most of them moved down to Benton after a time." Ola paused as if to contemplate the migration of younger, stronger people. "We were old and poor when she came to us. We got our patch here and do fine by it. Mind you, we're not complaining."

"Not complaining," Milford echoed. He appeared to be totally absorbed in his whittling, but every now and then he would say something, usually repeating a phrase of his wife's. The low mountains turned blue in the dusky twilight.

"I think it was loneliness that drove her to the church," Ola said.

"That and the indoor plumbing," Milford said, running his thumb along the piece he was working.

"Milford!" Ola exclaimed. Archie and Calista looked at one another. "She was always ashamed that we never had indoor plumbing. We have a johnny house out back. But as more and more of her friends started moving down to Benton and then when she started goin' to the junior high down there, well, she took to some ideas."

"Plumbing and sidewalks—the church had both," Milford said.

"Milford, these folks're going to think we're all heathens. It's not as if we don't go to church, and when we think of church, we just don't think of them conveniences you mentioned. It wasn't all that with Beth Ann."

Ola put down her work. She was braiding a rug, and she had long hands. They were gnarled and callused, but they were beautiful in their strength and now in their absolute repose as they settled very peacefully in her lap. "It wasn't just those conveniences." She paused as if to reflect. "It was the convenience of friendship, of being young with youngsters and being . . ." She paused and rested her elbow on the arm of the rocking chair and then rested her head heavily on her hand. "It's hard to explain to you folks, but, you know, Beth Ann's father, well, he warn't no good. He was a drunk, ran off from home before she was born. And her mother, well, Eulie, though she was my own daughter, she was not a kind child."

"She warn't really mean, Ola."

"No, she warn't mean. But you don't have to be mean to be unkind. She just didn't know how to be kind. She was too busy with herself and her own plans and dreams. So that's why she brought Beth Ann to us. And we was so old at the time. Two seventy-year-olds—ain't no place for a four-year-old to be. Oh, we loved her the best we could. But it's not the same. She knew she'd been passed off to us. At first her mama used to visit and sometimes write letters. But then she just stopped. And it was about that time that Beth Ann started going to church."

"And we don't just mean Sundays," Milford said, shaving off a curl from the wood with his knife.

"No, every day she could get down to Benton to church, she was going. I said to Milford when Beth Ann was just eleven years old, 'We're going to lose her. We love her as much as the church does, but there's no way we can compete.'"

"Ola was right."

"Yep." Ola rocked back and forth now and tapped her foot briskly as if for emphasis. "She moved down there that spring. Stayed with the pastor's family all the way through junior high and high school and then got that scholarship to college."

"Does she ever come back?" Archie asked.

"Oh, sure. She's dear to us. Brings us presents and stays with us and all. She don't even complain now about the johnny house and the no sidewalks. She's a loving child. We just couldn't give her the kind of love she needed when she needed it."

Calista looked around and tried to imagine what it must have been like growing up in this shady mountain hollow of West Virginia with its blue smoky shadows and scent of pine, with no electricity and no plumbing, with these two gentle old people.

They were handsome people both with their snowy white hair and fair complexions. They looked almost as if they had been powdered. They must have taken great care to keep the sun off their faces. Calista could imagine them working their patch shaded by straw hats with deep brims. Their clothes were clean and neatly patched. They could neither read nor write, but Milford had built the house and made every stick of furniture in it. Several vegetable gardens surrounded the house all perfectly kept, and they had referred to a field. These people were warm and loving, but it might not have been enough, especially for a child who already knew she had been rejected. Wouldn't there always be this nagging doubt at the back of one's mind about being loved by "real" parents who were young and lived in houses with toilets on streets with sidewalks? Doubts like these might become compounded during those years of adolescent uncertainty and lead to a quest for a perfect and unconditional love. And could that not lead in turn to a confusion between plastic facsimiles, the kind of mechanical doll mothers that terrorized Calista's own dreams as a child, and the real thing? And the real thing in this case might seem at first to be old worn rag dolls made from flour sacks, worn threadbare from work but still loving the best way they knew how.

"So you think that our Beth Ann's in some sort of trouble?" Milford stopped whittling and looked directly at Archie.

"Well, we can't be sure, and we don't want to jump to conclusions. But Calista told you the long story about her and her son's visit to the college, and Calista's son, Charley, said that when she called she seemed . . . uh, quite upset."

"And you say that she said she was at that amusement park they run over there?" Ola asked. Archie nodded. "Seems funny that she wouldn't have written us 'bout it. That had been something that she'd talked about doing someday and it being so near to home . . . seems mighty funny. Dear me!"

"Now, don't get worried." Calista tried to soothe the old woman.

"Is this something we should talk to Buford about?" Ola seemed to be wondering aloud.

"Who's Buford?" Calista asked.

"He's the sheriff."

"Well, I don't think he could be of much help yet," Archie said.

Both Archie and Calista were trying desperately to sound concerned, but not overly so. They hadn't dared mention anything about Norman Petrakis's murder or that their next stop was the Coastal Research Institute. If the notion of indoor plumbing and sidewalks seemed exotic to the Arnettes, Archie and Calista could not even begin to imagine what they would think of a bank specializing in the harvesting of human sperm.

Before they left in the gathering shadows of the evening, Calista walked with Ola around the small farm. They kept one cow, some geese, chickens, and a sow. That was about it. The vegetable gardens were perfect, several with raised beds. It was unimaginable how they tended all of this, yet it was still very clearly a subsistence-level operation. They were now walking between two rows in one of the gardens. "There she is!" Ola exclaimed. "I declare, she's put on another pound overnight." A most immense pumpkin lolled on the rich dark soil.

"Goodness!" exclaimed Calista. "It's this big and the summer's just half over!"

"Here's what does it!" Ola said, lifting the pitcher of milk she was carrying. "Now watch how I do this." She bent over. Her plump figure in the faded blue dress looked like a sack of laundry tied in the middle. A thin stream of milk slopped into the tin bowl set by the pumpkin's vine. "You see, I got it wicked."

"Wicked?"

"Yeah, I cut a notch in the vine and just lead a wick right up to it. The milk soaks in and climbs right up there to the vine. Pumpkins love milk. Makes them grow twice as big. And their meat tastes so good that way."

The first stars were just winking out of the dusty purple of the sky. A bobwhite whistled. A breeze came, and now along with the pine scent Calista smelled the sweet fragrance of Ola—of talcum powder and fresh milk. This was real. Calista had to help Beth Ann find her way back to reality even if it was not this one. She just had to help her.

48

"What are you doing bursting in here at this hour? For chrissake, Archie!" Neddy Baldwin came downstairs looking totally disheveled. There were lipstick smears on his cheeks. They had driven directly back from the Arnettes in West Virginia to Ned Baldwin in Georgetown. It had taken less than three hours to bridge these two disparate worlds.

"Just be happy I'm not your wife," Archie said. Neddy scowled at Archie. The scowl said, No fair! He'd gone off limits, limits that had been carefully preserved over the years.

"Hi." Calista came up the walk.

"What in the world?!" Neddy was absolutely speechless. This seemed to be his usual response to Calista, if two meetings could constitute usual. She wondered if she should ask him to dance. But she wasn't feeling cute.

"Come on, Neddy. You got some talking to do." He took his cousin firmly by the arm and hustled him inside. From upstairs a female voice called down, "Ned! Ned! You all right, honey?"

Archie rolled his eyes. "Neddy, you got to train them better than that! How the hell does she know it's not one of your kids or something? Tell her you're fine and to go back to sleep."

They went into the winter garden room. "Okay, now I'm not going to waste any time, Ned. You got to tell us everything."

"What are you talking about?"

Archie walked over to the cupboard that served as a

bar and brought down a decanter of Scotch. He poured some into a glass with no ice and handed it to Ned.

"I'm talking about your association with Lorne Thurston. I'm not buying that crap about your going down as a special emissary for the president. How did they get their hooks into you?"

Neddy paled visibly. He swallowed. He was not groping for words, just a voice. The first sounds came out all croaky.

"Why does she have to be here?"

"Calista is not *she.*" Archie nearly spat out the words. He suddenly found himself sick to death of Neddy, Neddy and his dumb good looks and his dumb attitudes toward women. He thought of lovely Ola Arnette's assessment of her own daughter: "Not mean. Just unkind." What were her precise words? "You don't have to be mean to be unkind." And maybe there was a certain point when plain old dumbness just slid over into unkindness. You simply weren't smart enough to be sensitive. "Calista is here"—Archie was choosing his words carefully—"because a friend of hers, a man who had been harassed by creationists, was murdered."

"They didn't do it!" But it was too late. There was a stricken look on his face.

Archie sighed deeply. "Let's sit down and talk about this. It seems you have a familiarity with the case. Would you care to share your views?"

Neddy lowered himself unsteadily into an armchair and then crumpled forward; a great sob shook him. Calista looked away. She didn't want to be here seeing this. She knew what would come out in the next few minutes would be even worse—some scummy, awful thing. Archie walked over to Neddy and put a hand lightly on his shoulder. "Just start at the beginning, Neddy."

It was not a long or particularly complicated story at all. Not the kind that involved laundered funds and elaborate cover-ups. It was short and sordid—a tale of betrayal of public trust and private indulgence. But it had snowballed into something more. "Snowballed" had been Neddy's favorite word in describing the accretion of bad effects from his initial action. And now this snowball in Neddy's mind had acquired a kind of demonic speed and weight, a life of its own. "It's getting out of control," he whispered.

"Do you have prints?"

"Yeah. They're in my wall safe."

"Can we see them?"

"Why not?" Neddy said with resignation. He rose and opened the safe, then handed the pictures to Archie.

These were not pictures that would make people gasp, at least not immediately. They were not lewd in the obvious sense. Nobody was fornicating. There were scantily clad girls all right, and one seemed to have her tits stuck in the face of a dark, very thin man. It was a party, and the picture was taken at a table. In the background there was a couple who appeared, for all intents and purposes, to be snorting cocaine. But was that so unusual these days? No. What was unusual was that this particular party was occurring in Panama. And the man at the center of the table was Neddy Baldwin, and he was flanked on one side by an infamous Central American political leader known for his connections with the drug world and on the other by an equally notorious billionaire arms dealer. Bad company for anybody, let alone a man on a diplomatic mission.

"Jesus Christ, Neddy!" Archie remembered when Neddy had been sent down years before to Panama on that diplomatic mission. "So what happened after this?"

"I wasn't very smart, Archie." He got up and began to walk over to the ferns in a gigantic vase. "The pictures in and of themselves weren't enough to kill me, just enough to scare me . . . scare me into turning my head on the drug dealings and money laundering. That guy . . . ." He pointed to the face of the Panamanian. Feline eyes appeared behind a face that was thickened with cruelty. "He is absolutely evil, Archie, and the country, Panama —good Christ, it was like a Disneyland for gangsters!

Secret banking systems, corporation laws that allow principals to remain anonymous. Smack-dab in the middle of one of the greatest trade routes. It's got it all going for it. Narcotics, no problem, laundering money, no problem. A fucking Disneyland for the scumbags of the earth!"

"So what? It was just all too tempting? I still don't get it," Archie said.

"Archie, you're so naive. I didn't do it for money. I haven't made a cent. I got no need for more money. And you know I'd never touch drugs." He sighed. "Archie, what's the one thing I have?" But Archie said nothing. He knew. "I got this." And Ned Baldwin almost magically drew himself up into a posture of incredible dignity and authority. Despite his disheveled state, he looked positively ambassadorial. For over thirty years he had played the role consummately. This was his stock-in-trade, his sustenance, his aphrodisiac. He was born to it—so tailored to it by some mysterious makeup of breeding and culture that his lack of real intelligence did not seem even to matter.

"So they used you?" Archie said. Neddy nodded. "But I still don't understand. How did this thing snowball, as you keep saying? How did it get from them to Lorne Thurston?"

"All too easily." Neddy sighed and stared into his glass of Scotch. "The Panamanian ran dope. Well, he didn't run it himself. He was at the heart of it. 'The facilitator,' they called him. And I became the facilitator's facilitator, especially after I began to serve on the president's commission on drugs. I didn't have to do anything except look the other way and try to steer the commission away. Nothing I did could have implicated me, at least I don't think so. These were sins of omission rather than commission."

"Just like the pictures."

"Yes. There is nothing precisely criminal, at least that I'm doing. It's just being there. But still it wouldn't have looked good. And that was the opening wedge. That was the leverage. I should have just said to hell with it and let them do what they wanted with the pictures. But I was scared."

"And it kept getting scarier."

Neddy nodded. "I kept getting drawn in deeper. I was always afraid of the CIA seeing this stuff. Imagine my shock when instead of the CIA, Lorne Thurston shows up. Not Lorne himself, one of his henchmen. They were down there trying to open a teleministry in Panama. They were, at the time, trying to start up several abroad. In any case, they were having some trouble, and they got hold of those pictures and put the screws to me. I pulled some strings for them there. No big deal."

"And?"

"And they botched the thing."

"Who botched what?"

"Thurston. They had people sending money for these damn ministries down there, but the money just wasn't going down there. So then the FCC gets on their tail and . . ."

This time it was Archie's turn to sigh. "So they leaned on you again, and you helped them get around the FCC."

"Yep. And from that point on it never stopped. They knew after that that they had me by the balls. Two years ago they came to me with all this creationist business. If they couldn't cut Darwin out of the textbooks, they at least wanted equal representation. And textbooks were their primary target. California and Texas dominate the textbook market. They account for more than twenty percent of total national sales. Books written for use in these states are often sold without any changes or modification to the rest of the country. I sit on the board of directors of the largest textbook publisher in this country."

Archie and Calista both groaned, and despite the heat of the summer night a dark chill feeling stole through the room.

There was something so essentially pathetic about all of it. Calista felt as if she had just listened to stories about experiences that one simply did not discuss in polite company. If there was any irony in this situation at all, it was not that a man of such patrician quality had sunk so low, it was the irony of his perceptions of himself. He had lived his life totally, completely, as an image, nothing more and nothing less. And it was a photographic image that had destroyed him—needlessly destroyed him. For although that picture was embarrassing and perhaps compromising, it was not enough to deliver a coup de grace, at least not to someone who had life beyond that of an image.

But where it had all led! It stunned Calista. She dealt in images. She made images. Images were her business. She abstracted from life and with her tools made representations that became distillations of life. But she knew the difference between what was real and what was not; what was image and what was actual. And now, in some odd inversion, sitting across from her was an image that had disguised itself as a pile of protoplasm. Throw water on him and he might dissolve like the Wicked Witch in the *Wizard of Oz*. Images should never come to life, and life should never come to images, she thought.

"But you say they didn't kill Norman Petrakis?" Calista asked.

"No. That's definitely not their style."

"Somehow I'm not relieved," Calista said coldly.

"Whose style is it—James Atwell's?" Archie asked.

"You mean that sperm bank guy out in California?"

"Yeah." Archie's voice was flat, his eyes steady as they observed Neddy.

"The guy's a loony," Neddy replied.

"What do you call the rest of you?" Calista shot back.

Neddy ignored her and continued to speak. "I don't know why they got in with Atwell and that Coastal Research Institute and his damn sperm bank. For some reason they felt they needed more real scientists around."

"I can understand why," Archie said dryly.

"They were getting ready for this Supreme Court

showdown on the Louisiana law mandating equal time for the teaching of creation science in the public schools," Neddy continued.

"I suppose we should be thankful you weren't appointed a Supreme Court justice," Calista said. Neddy gave Archie a withering look as if to say, "Where'd this broad get that lip? You're going to have trouble with this one, Arch!"

But Archie did not respond. He merely continued to stare coldly at Neddy, and for the first time it occurred to Neddy that maybe Archie might not want to go sailing with him in August.

Neddy continued, "The guy's a Nazi."

"No wonder Hugh Ethelredge likes him," Archie said.

"Oh, yeah, Hugh. He always has been drawn to that sort of thing."

"So they gave Thurston some science, and what did he give them?"

"Money for their operations. Stanford cut them off. I mean, Atwell was a mechanical engineer out of Stanford and taught there for years, but they realized he was going off the deep end. I never did think it was a good move on the part of Thurston to get involved."

"Do you know about that research that Atwell was doing?"

"Naw, not really. He was getting into some of that genetic stuff."

"He was cooking it, was what he was doing," Archie said, not trying to disguise the disgust in his voice.

"What do you mean, cooking it?"

"Faking it. It's all going to come out. Same way this skull stuff is coming out."

"Yeah, I guess Thurston cooked his own goose on that one."

"They were trying to do the same thing on the genetic level that they were doing on the fossil level—this racist bit, separate evolution for the races."

"Oh, Jesus!" Neddy shook his head and sank back in the chair.

"Well," Archie said briskly, "no time for remorse now,

fella." He strode quickly across the tile floor and put a firm hand under Neddy's elbow. Neddy looked up, slightly bewildered.

"What?" he asked.

"You're coming with us, Neddy."

"But where?"

"To the Coastal Research Institute. We've still got an unsolved murder, remember? And there's another even more pressing problem concerning a young lady who seems to be missing."

"I don't know what you're talking about, and I certainly don't know how I can help you."

"With the one thing you still have—your image. It's going to get us in there. Then I'll do the heavy work."

"Archie, what are you doing? Taking me hostage?"

"You can call it what you want, Neddy. But you're really going to start working now."

49

There was always a point, Calista remembered thinking on the flight to California, during long summers when one became fatigued by the monotony of the perfect days, hot weather, and the prevailing lassitude of it all. There was that time when one looked ahead longingly to schedules and the crisp weather of fall. Calista was at that point now, and Neddy reminded her of one of those long feckless summers. She wanted to be back, back with Charley, and it would be very nice if Archie were there, too. But the last place she wanted to be was on this plane with Neddy Baldwin.

Neddy was amazing. He had regained his equanimity and seemed to be as affable as ever. They flew first-class, and several people recognized Neddy and a few even addressed him as Mr. Ambassador, for that indeed had been his last foreign assignment—ambassador to the court of St. James. He enjoyed their attentions.

Archie had relaxed, but he seemed morose to Calista. He hardly spoke a word during the entire flight. Occasionally he would look across the aisle at Neddy and just stare at him with a kind of disbelief. It was as if Archie were giving himself exercises in realization—realization that his cousin, his lifelong friend, was indeed a bastard. At one point Calista saw Archie's eyes fill with tears. It was then she realized that he was actually going through a kind of grieving process.

Archie did have a plan of sorts in mind. The first priority was to find Beth Ann. They had called Charley before leaving to see if Beth Ann had called again. She had not. Archie intended to use Neddy as his front for busting in there and making demands. He did not want Calista to go with them to the Coastal Research Institute. They were obviously on to her, and it would be best if she kept a low profile.

"Besides," Archie said after the flight attendant had set down their breakfast, "what's a woman going to do at a sperm bank?"

"Collect!"

Archie laughed, leaned over, and kissed her on the neck. It was the first time he had laughed during the flight. She supposed she should feel relieved. But she didn't. She didn't feel good at all. There was some uncontrollable element in all this. Just then Neddy leaned across the aisle.

"Calista," he said, "I never got to tell you how much our grandchildren love your books. Just crazy about them. What's that one you do with the two little animals?"

"Hedge and Owl," Calista said coldly. This guy was unbelievable!

"What are you working on now?"

"Something about Maid Marian."

"Maid Marian?"

"Yeah," said Archie. "You know, from Robin Hood. Kind of a feminist twist to it."

"Oh!" said Neddy. "That's very interesting."

"Yes," Calista said, leaning forward a bit. "I'm thinking of doing a whole series." She had never thought of doing a series at all. It was a lie.

"What on?" Neddy asked.

"Warrior women," she said quite distinctly. She heard Archie stifle a chuckle. "Yeah, you know, like Boadicea, the Celtic warrior queen with the blades in her chariot wheels," she continued. It wasn't a bad idea. Of course, how would one deal with the likes of a Tamara in a children's book? Tamara, the twelfth-century queen of the Caucasian empire of Georgia, had distinguished herself not just through her political clout, but through her sexual voraciousness as well. These appetites had been immortalized in Georgia folklore.

Thoughts of a horny medieval warrior queen from the Caucasus were only mildly distracting to Calista at this time. Were they flying into the dead center of the orb weaver's web, about to jiggle the trap line? And what about Archie? Was he too distracted over his own grief about Neddy to be totally alert? She felt deep in her gut that she should go with them to the institute. Relaxed and affable as Neddy was, as passive as he always seemed to be in his actions and morality, he was not her cousin, not her friend, and she didn't trust him for a minute. She knew that in Archie's mind Neddy was just weak-brained, cursed by moral lassitude and cowardice, not capable of sins of commission, just omission. But it didn't make her feel one bit better or more relaxed. People like that, through their abject passivity, were capable of great destruction. Their own laxness and ability to turn their heads the other way and not see had a kind of energy of its own that could spill out of control and leave in its wake victims. Their survival instincts were quite strong, and cowardice had its own kind of manic energy. She didn't trust this sucker for one minute.

50

But Archie had convinced her that she should not go with them. "Just don't tell me a sperm bank is no place for a woman," she said as he kissed her good-bye in their hotel room at the Mark Hopkins.

"No! I would never say that." He paused. "It's no place for a mother."

He got her there. She knew he was right. Charley was her first priority. "Don't you think you should notify the cops? Take someone with you?"

"I got Neddy. He's better than the cops. He's the feds!"

"You know what I mean."

"The cops aren't going to come with us now. It'll sound like a wild-goose chase to them. Look how great they did in Boston when this was supposed to be a priority."

"I guess you're right, but it just seems . . ." Her voice dwindled off.

"It's premature," he said. Calista's lips curled into a funny little smile. "What are you laughing about, Cal?"

"When you say premature and I think of you guys at a sperm bank—well . . ."

Archie laughed. "Yeah, I know. These places do lend themselves to a lot of puns. Listen, I better go." He gave her a kiss and squeezed her. "Don't worry."

"Okay. I could make a joke about getting caught in a crossfire of you know what. But I won't. Good luck."

Archie and Neddy had rented a car to drive out to the Coastal Research Institute and Project Genesis, which

314

was just outside the town of Inverness. Archie promised to call her as soon as he knew anything. Calista, in the meantime, decided to walk through Chinatown. Chinatowns everywhere were her favorite stomping grounds for art supplies. An artist could buy paper and exotic brushes there that could not be found anywhere else. She spent the better part of three hours wandering through the streets. She had to buy a string bag to carry her purchases. And she especially liked the way the clerks wrapped things in wonderfully thin, crackly brown paper. She spent $150 on brushes and special pens that had bamboo shafts with beautiful sharp stainless-steel nibs. They were the most perfectly balanced pens one could buy. She had one store send thirty pounds of her favorite vellum paper back to Cambridge.

She dropped her bundles in her hotel room, taking a few minutes just to unwrap some of the brushes and pens to admire them. She laid them out on a table and gazed at them in anticipation. She couldn't wait to use them. She then grabbed her pocketbook and left the hotel, heading for Gumps on Union Square.

She loved Gumps and went straight to the second floor where the Chinese antiques were. There was a beautiful eighteenth-century Chinese painted screen with a waterfall and cranes hanging in flight above the fall's mist like benign specters from another world. It was lovely. It would look perfect in her living room, where she had tried for an effect somewhat reminiscent of the *japonaise* style in some French impressionist painting, notably Berthe Morisot, who combined a definitely French feel with an Oriental line. The screen, however, was $20,000. One quarter's royalties from *Puss in Boots* and *The Seal Woman* would cover it easily, but Calista was not that much of an impulse buyer. She would have to think. Oh, well.

She went to look at the antique kimonos. This was where she knew she was most vulnerable. She owned one already that hung on the bedroom wall in Vermont. Now she saw another one, even more beautiful. It was stencil-dyed in rich blues, pinks, and yellows. It was a woman's winter kimono, and it cost $2,500. This was tempting: $2,500 didn't seem as big an impulse as $20,000. She could wear it and hang it on a wall for decoration, too! On second glance she noticed the lovely orangy center of one of the flowers. The color reminded her so much of Ola's giant pumpkin. She was weakening.

As she walked up the hill to the hotel, there was a bounce in her step. It was the bounce of the inveterate shopper back in her element. She clutched the stunning Gump's shopping bag in her hand. If one couldn't wrap a purchase in that lovely brown paper, she supposed it was best to go the other direction with a lacquered black bag emblazoned with huge red poppies. What was the saying that her dad always kidded her mom and herself with? When the going gets tough, the tough go shopping!

That was what she was thinking when she slid the key in the door of her hotel room, hoping also to find a message from Archie. She shut the door behind her and was busy putting her packages down on the chair, so she did not look up immediately. But then she saw it and raised her hand to her mouth in a long, silent scream. The scream would not come. It was frozen as she stood transfixed before the bloody wobble of letters scrawled on the wall, the words coming together slowly in her brain—*Monkey Bitch*.

51

"Ninety-six percent of our semen is frozen in these liquid nitrogen tanks." James Atwell gestured to a phalanx of chrome canisters the size of water coolers. A woman in a white uniform was opening a hatch on one of the tanks. "Sally, can we come over and have a peek?"

"Sure thing, Dr. Atwell."

Inside the canister the space was divided into compartments. "What you're looking at are straws containing ampules of frozen sperm." Sally drew out one of the color-coded ampules. "Close the lid, Sal. We don't want to thaw out anything that's not supposed to be. You got somebody coming in?"

"Yeah. She'll be here in about forty-five minutes. So we're going to get this started."

Archie presumed that they did not put it in the microwave that he saw in a lounge area near Atwell's office.

"A tank like that can accommodate up to five thousand vials of sperm. You might have noticed that they are coded by number as well as color. With the improved methods of freezing and storing semen, we can now send frozen sperm through the mail. United Parcel, to be more precise. And we now have satellite banks. We don't call them branch banks—this is not money we're dealing with, after all. This is a much more valuable currency. In any case we can send semen back and forth. This capability is crucial to our program."

"Why?" Archie asked.

Atwell's eyes narrowed just for a sliver of a second. "Well, we can discuss that more completely in my office, but as you know, we here at Project Genesis want to make the genes of extremely able and intelligent men available to as many women as possible."

"But what about your recipients? Do you screen them as carefully as the men?"

"No, of course not. We screen them, but we don't have any hard and fast rules about who can and cannot receive semen. That, in our eyes, would be discriminatory. Look at it this way. If a woman wants to have a baby and has the biomechanics to do it, well, she's darn well going to do it. So why not inseminate her with one of ours? Why go to K Mart when you got Neiman-Marcus?"

"If you can afford it," Archie added dryly.

"We have donor insemination assistance programs. We call them motherships rather than scholarships." He smiled at the cleverness of it all, then continued, "We firmly believe that the more high-powered fathering we do, the higher the level of intelligence in our society will be."

"But still, don't you need high-powered moms? You're only focused on half the genetic material," Archie continued.

"Hey!" Atwell paused in a corridor. There was a glass window that looked across a separate corridor into another room. A young woman sat reading a magazine. "Look at that. There is one of our recipients—master's from Stanford in clinical psychology, cellist, scuba diver. Can't beat that, can you?"

"Sounds like the mom we all dream of," Archie said quietly.

Atwell furrowed his brow as if he were not sure Archie was being serious or joking. "Well, my point is this, Dr. Baldwin, and believe me, we would welcome your donation . . ." Archie smiled tightly. "But my point is this . . ."

It was hard talking about points in a sperm bank. Calista was right; every word took on a double meaning.

"We, of course, like our recipients to be bright, but in truth, only a dozen or so truly superb, what the Napa Valley people might call 'grand cru,' specimens are required for our program to work." They had continued walking down the corridor. "This area off to the left here is our donor area. So I would like to emphasize right here that we do not limit ourselves to Nobel sperm. We want bright, successful men. Creative people who have demonstrated achievement. This means that there is an implicit lower age limit because after all it takes a while for a person to make their mark on the world. We have no medical students, who traditionally have been the heaviest contributors. You see, a single ejaculate from a young man can yield as many as sixty inseminations. But that's not what we're after—quantity. No. We're after quality.

We therefore have no upper age limits because although quantity and motility of sperm often decreases in older men, the quality remains unaltered. You see, quality in this case means just one thing—genes!"

Archie still could not help but wonder if all those old Nobel codgers could withstand the rigors of being frozen in liquid nitrogen. But he put the question more delicately.

"What's the survival rate with frozen sperm?" It couldn't compare with the on-the-hoof rate, he was sure—Nobel or not.

"Yes, of course, fresh sperm has a higher viability than frozen. But as you probably know, cryogenics is my field, and just in the last year and a half we've improved our thawing procedures to such an extent that we now have a thirty percent higher motility rate than ever before in thawed sperm."

Archie felt as if his balls were receding on the spot—instantaneous testicular collapse. This guy really nauseated him. "In our catalog we list whether the donor's sperm is frozen or not. By the way, Dr. Baldwin, in our catalog, if you were to become a donor, we would list you only by number and a color code. Your area of expertise, hobbies, interests, and ethnic heritage would then be listed. The young lady we just passed is waiting for number twenty-six. See, this lovely young woman already has a two-year-old fathered by number twenty-six. In this way they shall be full siblings."

"Oh."

Archie and Neddy followed Atwell through an outer office where an attractive middle-aged woman was spraying a large potted plant.

"Hello, Anne. I'd like to introduce you to Ambassador Baldwin and his cousin Dr. Baldwin. Anne is in charge of our donor recruitment program."

"So pleased to meet you." She extended her hand toward Neddy first. She looked at both of them, her eyes burning brightly, as if she were scrutinizing prize bulls. Neddy, Archie noticed, shook hands very vigorously.

Archie himself delivered the first dead-fish handshake of his life. The phone rang, and she went to her desk to pick it up.

"Really? No kidding?" she said. "What's his IQ?"

Archie and Neddy followed Atwell into his office. It was well appointed. One wall was plastered with degrees and honors. James Atwell had made his mark as a biological engineer in the area of cryogenics. The Coastal Research Institute's abbreviation CRI served as a handy acronym as well for what had really been the foundation of the operation. He had figured out how to freeze all sorts of things—from human sperm and ova to French white asparagus and lingonberries. There were citations and plaques from medical societies as well as agricultural associations and culinary institutes. On another wall that was covered with corkboard were blueprints for some new machines and compressors in the works that would help with his quest to freeze the most delicate and precious of the earth's resources.

Atwell sat at his large desk and made a sweeping gesture toward the window behind him. "Across the courtyard out there, in that other wing, is our genetic-engineering and research center. We have a few bungalows on the other side there where some of our staff lives."

Archie wondered if that was where they had stashed Beth Ann. So far there had been no sign of her.

"So, Dr. Baldwin, you're interested in our overall program?"

Archie nodded. He wasn't sure how long he was going to let this bastard run on, but he might as well hear the whole grisly thing.

"Well, it is our feeling—and I'm sure you would corroborate this from your position as a distinguished archaeologist—that societies, civilizations, have been declining at an alarming rate. It's all deceleration and degeneration. You see, Project Genesis has been badly maligned in the past and misrepresented. We don't think we're going to get a Nobel Laureate out of this. That is not the realistic vision of this program. But what we do think we can do is improve the general gene pool. It's a question really of drawing a slipping species up by its bootstraps. Now as I have said, we want quality. IQ is the most reliable predictor. That is why we seek high-IQ, high-achievement scientists, even if they are not Nobel Prize winners." He nodded directly at Archie as he said this.

"So you really believe in the predictive value of IQ entirely."

"Entirely and absolutely. I don't call myself a race-ologist like some scientists, but we are starting to see that blacks have inherited certain biochemical deficits in regard to intelligence that indeed makes the races 'color-coded,' in the words of William Shockley."

"What do you mean by biochemical deficits?" Archie asked.

"There is some very exciting research going on in our labs"—he nodded toward the wing across the courtyard —"that I am not at liberty to disclose right now. But you might have read about some of it in a few academic journals. This research is not going on just here, but at other universities as well, and we are coming up with some very interesting data concerning neurotransmitters."

The phone interrupted him. He picked it up. "Yeah. . . . no kidding. Can you beat that? What a loss. . . . Okay. . . . Well, sure. We don't have to freeze it. . . . Yeah, he's to be around here for a while. . . . Sure. Good idea. Put Topaz on the fresh list in the catalog. . . . Yeah, we're reprinting this week. So you got to move!" He hung up the phone and looked up. "That, gentlemen, was in reference to one of our younger donors—our first Olympic medalist."

"Didn't sound good, Jim," Neddy said.

God, thought Archie, how can Neddy already be calling this guy Jim? He had slipped into his old role again, so easily. Of course he shouldn't complain, that was what got them into the institute so quickly and even got Atwell out of a meeting.

"Not all bad. He flunked the freeze tolerance test. We do a freeze tolerance test on all of our donors. Can you imagine an Olympic medalist flunking it? In any case, we'll just offer his fresh. He's very interested in developing a real pool of Olympic talent in this country. You know, the Russians and East Europeans nurture these kids from the time they're infants. They spend much more money on it than we do. Not the sperm banking, but just the training. It's hard when an American athlete sees that kind of focus going on in another country and not his own. This is this boy's way of contributing."

Archie shifted on his seat. He had had enough of this. It sounded just like *Lebensborn* to him, the Nazi selective breeding program in which elite German troops were encouraged to impregnate Aryan women to produce racially pure children. "The gifts of the führer," Himmler had called them. It was time to get to the business at hand. He tried to catch Neddy's eye to alert him, but Neddy seemed to be staring off into space. Oh, well. He had it fairly organized in his own mind and felt that the order of business should be first Beth Ann, then the cooked data on this neurotransmitter shit, and then the biggie—Norman Petrakis.

Archie leaned forward. "Dr. Atwell . . ."

There was a change in the entire atmosphere. The air suddenly seemed as charged as in an electrical storm. Archie saw Atwell's fingers coil under his desk and Neddy came back from wherever he was. There was no denying it—Archie Baldwin, although lacking any shred of the ambassadorial trappings of a Neddy or the gaudy charismatics of an evangelical preacher, could be incredibly formidable. There was no pomp and circumstance, nor was there the bright work of medals and gold braid; no visage bathed in the unearthly luminescence of divine knowledge. Just Archie. He leaned forward—a granite face slashed with bright blue eyes.

"I want to set the record straight: I am not here as a potential donor. I think your program is an affront to humanity." There was a stunned silence. Archie felt Neddy shift in his chair.

"Now, now, Arch."

What the fuck was Neddy doing? He didn't take time to look.

"I am here at the specific request of Ola and Milford Arnette."

"Ola and Milford Arnette. I don't believe I know them."

"They are concerned about their granddaughter, Beth Ann Hennessey." There was a slight twitch near Atwell's left eye.

"I don't know anyone by that name. Is she one of our recipients?"

"I hope not. We have reason to believe that she is here."

"Well, she is not so." He had begun to get up. "I don't know how I can further help you gentlemen."

Archie leaned forward and smashed his fist down on the desk. Neddy and Atwell jumped. "Sit down!"

"I beg your pardon? Dr. Baldwin, I'm going to have to call security if you don't leave this instant."

"I think you'd better call your lawyer."

Atwell sat down and tried to look casual. "Why would I need a lawyer, Dr. Baldwin? If I may be so bold."

"Two counts. First, that research you're doing on intellamine and intellicone." This time Atwell looked up. His gray eyes had turned to stone.

"How do you know about that?"

"Read some of those journals you mentioned."

"So what about it?"

"It's shit. You faked it."

"I faked it? I'll have you know there were four other labs that had projects going on concerning these brain proteins. There was just a seminar two months ago on it in New York, very well attended, I might add."

"Yeah, I know. I know all about it. So does the Martin Institute."

"What does the Martin Institute have to do with this?"

"They've got the evidence. They ran the energy tests. You can read all about it tomorrow in *The New York Times.*"

"I don't know what you're talking about." He was visibly nervous now.

"The Martin Institute took up where Norman Petrakis left off. Do I make myself clear now, Dr. Atwell?"

"Perfectly." Atwell's hand went for the phone, but it came back with a gun.

52

"Howdy!" The voice, flat and nasal, sounded different.

"You!" Calista gasped as Wayne Tompkins stepped out from behind the window curtains in her hotel room. He held a length of narrow-gauge wire. Her hand was still at her mouth. She spoke through her fingers. "You . . . you killed Norman, you sent the books, you ran us off the road." He just smiled as if enjoying this litany of his deeds.

Calista's mind was racing. He was walking toward her slowly, carrying the wire casually in his hand. Was there anything she could use as a weapon? Why, why had she shut the door? She knew what he was going to do. He was going to garrote her as he had Norman. You can't talk when you're being strangled. She'd better start talking now. What would she say? . . . Anything . . . anything that would come into her mind that might throw him off.

"Where'd you get the nice red paint?" she said, glancing at the wall with the writing.

"It's not paint. It's blood." He smiled slowly. "Animal blood. Messes up the police to find it."

"Oh, how smart."

He seemed to brighten at this. "You think so?" he

asked with genuine interest. There was something very odd going on here. This was Wayne Tompkins, and yet his voice sounded different and his whole bearing was different.

"Of course I think so. It not only confuses the blood issue, but they're probably trying to track down cult-type murderers. It's very smart. Very clever."

Calista wasn't so sure how long she could keep the compliments coming. He had stepped closer. She had no weapon. She had no strength. You didn't build muscle tap dancing. "You could, of course, have used something else, too."

"What's that?"

"Why, these." She gestured slightly to the table by the door where her newly bought art supplies lay and backed toward it. He came very close to her and looked down. In that instant she grabbed the hollow bamboo pen shaft with the double-pronged stainless-steel tip in a swift upward stroke that caught him in the eye. There was a terrible scream.

She raced out the door. A maid stood stunned in the hallway. "Get security!" she cried at the maid. "A man just tried to kill me."

53

"I don't believe this, Neddy. How can you?"

"Sorry, Archie, but you and that dame basically took me hostage, brought me here against my will."

In an extraordinary forty-five seconds Neddy Baldwin had convinced James Atwell that indeed he was on his side. "As I was telling you, Dr. Atwell, I have long believed in your endeavors and felt that there has not been the political climate to support them in this country until recently. But in my discussions with Lorne Thurston, and in detecting a change in that climate, I do think that I can help you both; as you know, I am in a position to do so. There is no need whatsoever that this business with Petrakis has to come out. I spoke to Lorne. He was admittedly ruffled about, uh . . ." Neddy hesitated and coughed. "The fact that suspicions were raised in reference to his group, but I think you got some bartering chips here. And I definitely have some now—at last! But you can trust me. I think together Coastal Research Institute and Lorne Thurston's ministry can forge a good bond. I think we can see some of your dreams come true. This will be a new coalition."

"What in the fuck are you talking about, Neddy?" Archie shouted.

"Shut up, Archie! You know, sometimes you're just too honest for your own good."

They were both insane, and that was why this was working. After years of deluding himself, Neddy had bought it all. There was no There, there. He was like a vessel waiting to be filled up. If Archie had been holding the gun, he would have been making a coalition with him.

"Okay," Atwell said carefully. "You will just wait right there, Dr. Baldwin. I'm calling my security people to help escort you."

"Where?"

"You'll see soon enough."

At that moment the door opened and two rather burly-looking surfer types—donors themselves, no doubt, *cuvée* Malibu, Archie thought—came in.

"Did you boys clear the CRI lab?"

"Yes, sir," they both answered.

"Those big freezers on full blast?"

"Yes, sir."

Archie got a queasy feeling—big freezers were not necessary for freezing sperm. Big freezers were meat lockers. Terrific!

Another man entered the room. It was Wayne Tompkins. Atwell looked up.

"Any report yet on the Jacobs lady?"

"She should be taken care of by now," Tompkins replied.

"What?" Archie asked. "What did you do to Calista?"

"Sit down," Atwell barked. And Archie felt the heavy paw of one of the blond gorillas shove him down into the chair. He ignored Archie's question. "We are now going to walk to the CRI lab, Dr. Baldwin."

"I take it this is not for donor purposes. I doubt if I'd be able to perform under the circumstances," Archie said. Neddy started to giggle. Archie felt the hair stand out on the back of his neck. He felt himself fill with hate. He actually hated Neddy.

They had walked down the halls, which had all been cleared of personnel except for Anne, the donor recruitment director. "You the one who's going to jack me off?" Archie said, looking at her. Her eyes narrowed.

"You know," he continued as they entered the lab, "I hope this is an object lesson for all of you. You might just possibly get some first-class sperm here from me. I mean, look at Neddy and me, both of us descendants from the oldest of New England families. Our family tree's peppered with Cabots, Lowells, Adamses, and Saltonstalls."

"What's the object lesson?" Atwell gave a superior little smile.

"Well, these are genes that according to your standards are very desirable."

"One might say we're going to kill for them!"

The gorillas laughed.

"Well, you should be careful," Archie continued, "because despite my impeccable breeding and my degrees from Dartmouth and Harvard—who knows, I might have had a Nobel even, but they never seem to give them in archaeology—one of the soft sciences, you know. In any case . . ."

"Yes, do get to the point. What's the object of this lesson?" Atwell said.

"Well, isn't it obvious? It can all go wrong. Imagine if

my genes get out there. You'll not just have smart folks. You'll have all these people who see through shit like this and will rock your fucking little genetic dreamboat." Archie was shouting now. "They might have values that cannot be color-coded or predicted by IQ."

Just then there was a commotion in the hall, the sound of running footsteps.

"Okay, freeze!" Two cops burst in the door. Calista was behind them, looking distraught, disheveled, and wonderful to Archie.

"Boy, are we glad to see you," Neddy said loudly, and smiled. Archie's jaw dropped. But before he could say anything he heard Calista.

"Stand back, asshole!"

Atwell had dropped his gun, and Neddy had started to reach for it. But Calista slid across the floor and picked it up.

"I don't know what she's talking about, fellas." Neddy spoke with a slight quaver in his voice.

"Keep your hands up, Mr. Ambassador, until we can clear this up," one of the cops said.

As the hands slowly went up, Calista caught sight of Wayne Tompkins. Her mouth dropped open. He appeared completely normal. "That's the guy who . . . who was going to kill me!" She gasped, pointing at Wayne. "Wh—what's he doing here? There's not a mark on him! I'm confused."

A smug grin slashed his face.

"I think I can clear this up." It was the voice of Anne. "Everybody freeze."

They turned. She stood in another doorway holding a chrome canister in her hands. The word *Danger* was printed in blue letters. "I throw this and everything explodes. So why don't you just put down your guns, Officers. Make it quick!" she snapped. They dropped their guns. The gorillas scrambled for them.

"Thanks, Annie," Atwell said, taking back his gun.

Calista was standing now by a tank of liquid nitrogen. She had been staring at the label when it finally dawned on her what it contained. Next to it were a pair of tongs and rubber gloves. A lever on the side of the tank read "Push to Open." She did. The lid popped open.

"Put that back down," Atwell barked, and Anne's face solidified into a mask of horror. Calista thought quickly. She jumped behind the tank, shielding herself with it. They'd dare not shoot her now. She peered into the tank. "Mr. Right, I presume?" She looked up merrily. Archie almost laughed.

"Mrs. Jacobs," Atwell said in very even tones, "I suggest you move away from that tank."

"I think that I'll just stay right here," she said, wrapping her arms around the tank almost lovingly. This was her ticket, their ticket, out of here. The rubber gloves were hanging on a hook attached to the tank. She managed deftly to put them on while embracing the tank. Everyone seemed mesmerized as they watched her. "Now put down those guns or else I'm going to start showing you my juggling act with Nobel sperm. You know, most people do use balls, but . . ." She found another lever that automatically raised the basket out of the nitrogen bath.

"You must lower that, Mrs. Jacobs," Anne said quietly. "If they are exposed . . ."

"Oh, dear. Well, I don't hear any guns dropping, and I was actually thinking of microwaving a few of these in that little oven we passed that you folks use for your soup." She had now used the tongs to take out a slender straw with a light turquoise band on it. She raised it in the air like a maestro about to begin conducting. "Drop the guns now," she ordered, and with her foot gave the tank a shove. It rolled wildly across the room. The cops lunged at Atwell. Archie decanistered Anne and sat on her. Three more cops had just arrived and clipped the two gorillas as they tried to dive out a window.

It was quick, like a squall. And suddenly it was over. Anne, the gorillas, Atwell, and Neddy were handcuffed.

Calista was still standing there stunned with her baton of semen raised in the air waiting for the Philharmonic to stop tuning up and settle down. Archie came to her side and wrapped her in his arms.

"What the hell do I do with this?" she muttered in his ear.

"Drop it!" he whispered.

She did, and a thousand little splinters and icy crystals scattered across the floor.

54

"You don't think they did anything . . . " —Calista paused—"you know, weird, to Beth Ann, do you?"

"Well, we know they abducted her and drugged her, but if by weird you mean try to artificially inseminate her, no, I don't think so. When we found her she was still so drugged up, and look, she'd only been hauled off from Bible Times, what—thirty-six hours before? They just wanted her out of the way, possibly for good. So I don't think they were looking upon her as a vessel for their prize bulls."

"Oh, yuck! The whole idea just turns my stomach."

They were sitting in the bar of the Clift Hotel. It was one of the most beautiful bars in the world with its soaring walls of redwood and immense reproductions of Klimt's paintings of Oriental women glitteringly robed in golden embroidery. They were dazzling, bejeweled, and gilded—benign she-dragons. Calista sighed and took a sip of her champagne.

"The poor child seemed so traumatized. I'm glad we could get her a room here next to ours." She paused. "What do you think she'll want to do after all this?"

"Not go back to Lorne Thurston College of Christian Heritage—that's for certain," Archie said, taking a sip of his beer.

"You know, she has only two more years to go. I wonder how many of those credits would be transferable."

"I would imagine several of them, except maybe the science ones. She probably took a pretty standard undergraduate curriculum. Why?"

"Well, maybe she'd like to come to Boston. I feel so bad for her, Archie. She deserves a break of some sort."

"She deserves a chance to think without being frightened into dogma, is what she deserves."

"That's it, exactly." She took another sip of her champagne and smiled. "Charley was telling me that at MIT the brother of a friend of his who goes there said that in their dorm there's a de-nerdification zone."

"De-nerdification zone?"

"Yeah, isn't that a funny name?"

"What is it?"

"It's a lobby or corridor or something where there are no computers but, you know, chairs, and sofas, and coffee tables—furniture set up into congenial configurations to encourage socializing. It strikes me that Beth Ann needs to go to a de-dogmafication zone."

"I think that actually her dogma is falling away from her in great chunks," Archie said. "Just from talking to her during dinner I could see it."

"It'll be interesting to see what kind of person she really is—I'm sure she's a good one. I just had that feeling about her from the start."

Calista went in to check on Beth Ann when they went back up to their room. She appeared to be sleeping, but then rolled over. "Calista? That you?"

"Yes. How are you doing?"

"Oh, okay . . . I guess. . . ." Her voice quavered.

"That doesn't sound too good," Calista said, walking over to the bed and sitting on the edge. Beth Ann's face was blotchy from crying. Calista picked up one of her hands. "This is going to take a while, Beth Ann. You've had a lot taken away from you all at once."

"I want to have my faith," she said almost fiercely.

"You can still have your faith. It's just not a faith in one man's vision. Have faith in yourself. You have every reason to. If you have faith in yourself, you'll discover your own visions."

Beth Ann's brow furrowed. "Are you a Christian, Calista?"

"Nope. I'm Jewish."

"You are of the Jewish faith?"

Now it was Calista who furrowed her brow. "I was born a Jew. I practice it in my own way. But I am one of these people who has never been very comfortable with anything organized, especially religion." She paused. "I have never felt close to God in a building."

"So when do you feel close and feel His spirit?"

"I cannot discuss it," Calista said quietly. "It is such a deeply personal thing with me that I simply can never discuss it."

"Do you ever question?"

"Of course—constantly."

"But how can you, with your deeply personal faith?" There was no sarcasm in the question, only a tone of deep wonderment.

"It is because of it that I can." She looked at Beth Ann carefully. "I shall not be betraying my private feelings if I tell you that it is my most profound belief that God loves skeptics." She paused. "And some of the most religious people I have known are the greatest skeptics—my husband, for one," she said, thinking of Tom with his wily blend of skepticism and reverence in the face of the universe that he probed.

When she went back into the bedroom, Archie was just hanging up the telephone. "They caught him."

"They did?"

"Guess Wayne and Dane aren't identical twins anymore. Dane's missing an eye." Archie paused. "They were never that identical. Apparently Wayne had the brains. That's how he got hooked up with the genetics lab at University of Minnesota. He came in via the twins study along with his brother, Dane. He had been studying engineering. Dane, on the other hand, had been a born-again Christian, but then he had some falling-out with the church. Dane was only too happy to set them up for murder. Or at least that's how it looks now. Dane did the dirty work."

"You mean the books, the stuffed animal in my garden, and all that."

"Yep. And Wayne was the mastermind behind it all. But he was basically working for Atwell. Atwell needed money, and it was through Dane's connection with Thurston that they tapped into all that money."

So she had been right about Wayne getting stooges to do his dirty work. In this case it had been his own twin brother. This would be a new wrinkle in the classic Minnesota twins study.

Archie patted the bed where he was sitting. "Come on to bed. You've got a donor waiting here to do it the old-fashioned way."

55

"Oh, my God!" Charley said over and over. "Mom, I can't believe this! Jeez, Louise. You and Archie really killed a few birds with one stone here." Charley had newspapers spread out on the kitchen table. Calista was putting the finishing touches on Friar Tuck. In the mornings she always worked at her kitchen drawing table at this time of year. There was more available light, and what was available in late summer and early autumn had a special golden quality. "So it was Dane Tompkins who killed Petrakis and tried to do you in, too?"

"Yep. He was the connection. He was the one with the foot in both camps. He got his twin brother into Lorne Thurston's college as a professor. Wayne was not really a creationist per se. More or less a biological engineer with Nazi dreams along with Atwell. They needed the money for their dreams. Dane was only too happy to help them screw Thurston and the creationists out of money and lay the blame for murder on them. It wasn't supposed to come to murder, of course, until they figured out that Norman was on to them. Money had been the original intention. Norman must have got on to the intellamine thing, or at least to Wayne's role in it, when he was doing the research for those articles at University of Minnesota. He had mentioned genetic stuff up there in relation to the twins study."

"What about the skull stuff?" Charley asked.

"Well, it's like Archie said. The creationists down there were dying to have a patina of science. That was what Tompkins was supposed to provide in exchange for the big bucks for Atwell's lab. So he came up with this skull idea—a bizarre and clumsy attempt that would not exactly disprove evolution but add a nice racist twist to things. The creationists weren't so interested in the racist thing as in getting a scientific scenario for Genesis. Their number-one priority was the textbook thing. They wanted to get scientific creationism equal time in textbooks. To do this they needed, quote, 'real scientists,' and Neddy Baldwin, who served on the board of a very powerful textbook publisher. But Atwell and his guys didn't give a hoot about Genesis, at least not the biblical one. They were just your basic Nazis with notions of a super race and insuring that those genes got out there."

"In other words, they could do their racist bit on two levels—the genetic and the fossil bone."

"Right," Calista said. "I can just imagine in Tompkins's and Atwell's twisted minds how elegant it all seemed—fossils and genes—you know, a double whammy!"

"A real double whammy if you consider that the creationists hated Petrakis for his views on evolution as much as Atwell and Tompkins hated him for finding out their fraud."

"Yes, truly a case of killing one bird with two stones!" Calista said. "But it was really Atwell's camp that was responsible for the murder."

"It sounds like this cousin of Archie's had a foot in a few camps, too."

"Indeed!"

"When's Archie coming back?"

"I hope soon. He had a lot to do. Deliver Beth Ann down to her grandparents."

"But she might be coming up here to live, right?"

"Yes, maybe. I wanted to ask you how you'd feel about that."

"You mean we could give her the room in the back?"

"Well, just for a start. I'm going to go over to Lesley College and find out if she might start there. I think most of her credits would transfer, and it might be the right place for her—small women's school, specializing in education—she has a lot of early childhood courses. And it's so convenient. Just two blocks away. So near Harvard Law School. Maybe she could meet a nice lawyer." Calista laughed. "I don't think I could get her into a dorm at this late date."

"Naw, it's okay with me if she lives here."

"Well, we'll see."

"Who'd pay for it?"

"Archie and me." She bit the end of her brush. "We have faith in her," she said quietly. It had been Archie's idea, really, her going to Lesley and his paying for it. Archie, too, after all, had lost something. He needed to invest his faith in something else. Calista had insisted on paying half.

"So where's Archie now?"

"Dealing with Neddy's family."

"I wish he'd come back and deal with ours."
Calista looked up and smiled. "You like him?"
"Yeah."
"He'll be back."

56

He did come back. They sat on the faded brick terrace in Vermont. The long, low-angle golden light of autumn that Calista treasured bathed the terrace. They were caught in a blaze of autumnal refulgence as the last blast of the day's sun sprayed out over the mountains to the west, igniting the russet and bright yellows of the turning leaves. The scent of sweet potatoes baking in the coals of the grill mingled with the scent of the apples on a nearby tree. They were momentarily alone with their thoughts. But Archie scratched softly on Calista's back as she sat on a cushion by his chair sipping her bourbon on the rocks. The rum of summer had given way to bourbon, her fall and winter drink. "Here comes Charley up from the pond."

"Did he get any trout?"

"How could he miss in the pond? He's so lazy about certain things like that. Won't go down to the stream where it's a fair fight."

"He's a fair fighter, Cal, if I ever saw one."

She dropped her head on his hand and kissed it. He ran his fingers through her thick hair. She knew what he was thinking about. Neddy. Everyone else's fate had been conveniently sealed except for Neddy's. Thurston's empire was crumbling around him. In the aftershocks of the fraud of the skulls and the revelation of his connection with Atwell, all sorts of other scams had been revealed. They were not guilty of the murder of Petrakis, but of influence peddling, FCC violations, and tax evasion. Atwell was behind bars without bail for being an accessory to murder, attempted murder, mail fraud, and a host of other charges relating to the intellamine-intellicone scheme. Dane and Wayne Tompkins were both in jail—Dane charged with Petrakis's murder, the attempted murder of Calista, and the kidnapping of Beth Ann; Wayne charged as an accessory to murder. It turned out that it had been an old classmate of Dane's from the Lorne Thurston College of Christian Heritage who had disrupted the children's literature conference in Boston that spring. He had needed little or no persuasion to do so, as these fundamentalist groups had been regularly sending out their troops to heckle at such conferences. Dane knew he could count on Petrakis being heckled, which meant a readily available scapegoat for murder. They needed Petrakis out of the way. He was on to their intellamine scam, and it would be the end of Coastal Research Institute and all of their dreams. The fundamentalists were a scapegoat made to order. They had also outlived their usefulness. Thurston was getting pressure on other financial fronts, and the well for Coastal Research was running dry.

It was Neddy whose fate seemed peculiarly unresolved. Neddy Baldwin was in McClean's Hospital in Waltham, Massachusetts, a mental hospital specializing in the breakdowns of the rich and distinguished, recovering from a botched suicide attempt. And the indefatigable Lacey, after years of being the perfect helpmate and wife, seemed to have broken as well. She was drinking and taking large doses of Valium. Little Lacey had just called Archie to tell him that she and her older brother were taking their mother out to the Betty Ford Clinic.

"Here they are!" Charley said, holding up the fish. "Cleaned and ready."

"Thank you, dear boy, just put them there beside the grill. You look wet."

"That's the way you get when you go swimming."

"You went swimming?"

"Yep. It's nice."

"Not too cold?"

"Mom, this is the warmest month of the year to go swimming. The water still has all the summer heat."

"It's certainly been a long hot one," Calista said, getting up to poke the coals into new life.

Archie had never seen Calista look as beautiful as she did that night. They had gone swimming, just the two of them, very late. It was chilly, but as Charley had said, the water was warm. To walk back up to the house, she had wrapped herself in her beautiful newly purchased antique kimono. Her dark hair was wet and molded to her fine head. Thick strands of gray ran like quicksilver back from her brow. He slid his arms under the kimono.

"I know this is an antique . . ."

"I take it you're referring to the kimono and not me."

"And I know it's very chilly."

"But Charley might still be up. . . . Look," said Calista. "This thing has survived one hundred years, but I think I'll just . . ." She let it slide off her right there on the small beach.

The moonlight blazed all around her. And across the grassy meadow surrounding the pond the night dew crept, spreading its veil of gray gauze. Her dark eyes shone like small galaxies with their faint glitters and mysteries. She looked as bejeweled and exotic as one of the Klimt ladies. But she was absolutely naked with the kimono crumpled about her ankles. She was unique. He had never met anybody like her. Where others might be *September Morn,* not Calista Jacobs. She glinted like some odalisque of the autumn night. She tilted her head up now to look at the sky. "Look," she said, "there it is." And she pointed up.

"What?" asked Archie.

She imagined it now so vividly, with the starry tracers, driving across the sky in its autumnal transit.

"It's coming back," she whispered. "Auriga—the Charioteer."

"Another myth?"

"If it only had been!" she said quietly, and pressed Archie's hand to her mouth.

About the Author

KATHRYN LASKY KNIGHT is the author of many children's books. Her adult mystery debut, *Trace Elements,* was a featured Mystery Guild selection. She lives with her husband, Christopher Knight, and their two children in Cambridge, Massachusetts, where she is at work on her next Calista Jacobs mystery, *Mumbo Jumbo*.